Ghosted

Emily Barr worked as a journalist in London but always hankered after a quiet room and a book to write. She went travelling for a year, which gave her an idea for a novel set in the world of backpackers in Asia. This became *Backpack*, a thriller that won the WHSmith New Talent Award. Her first YA thriller, *The One Memory of Flora Banks*, has been published in twenty-seven countries and was shortlisted for the YA Book Prize. Emily's third YA thriller, *The Girl Who Came Out of the Woods*, was published in 2019 and nominated for the Carnegie Award. *Ghosted* is her fifth YA novel. Emily lives in Cornwall with her husband and their children.

Follow Emily Barr
on Twitter @emily_barr
and Instagram @emilybarr01
#Ghosted

Books by Emily Barr

THE ONE MEMORY OF FLORA BANKS

THE TRUTH AND LIES OF ELLA BLACK

THE GIRL WHO CAME OUT OF THE WOODS

THINGS TO DO BEFORE THE END OF THE WORLD

GHOSTED

Ghosted

EMILY BARR

PENGUIN BOOKS

PENGUIN BOOKS

UK | USA | Canada | Ireland | Australia
India | New Zealand | South Africa

Penguin Books is part of the Penguin Random House group of companies
whose addresses can be found at global.penguinrandomhouse.com.

www.penguin.co.uk
www.puffin.co.uk
www.ladybird.co.uk

First published 2022

001

Text copyright © Emily Barr, 2022

Cover illustration by Kim Ekdahl

The moral right of the author has been asserted

Set in 10.5/15.5pt Sabon LT Std
Typeset by Jouve (UK), Milton Keynes
Printed and bound in Great Britain by Clays Ltd, Elcograf S.p.A.

The authorized representative in the EEA is Penguin Random House Ireland,
Morrison Chambers, 32 Nassau Street, Dublin D02 YH68

A CIP catalogue record for this book is available from the British Library

ISBN: 978-0-241-48187-5

All correspondence to:
Penguin Books
Penguin Random House Children's
One Embassy Gardens, 8 Viaduct Gardens, London SW11 7BW

For Craig

PROLOGUE

11 March

Mia was in hospital for a routine operation on her knee, and everyone said it had gone well. On Thursday morning she was still woozy from the anaesthetic and found that she quite enjoyed the enforced bed rest. Hospital tea was surprisingly nice, and the toast was comforting. She had magazines to read. The ward was quiet. It was fine.

Her boyfriend missed her; they hadn't been living together long and it was still all honeymoon. She knew she'd be home tomorrow and that he'd help her around on her crutches for a week or two, and then everything would be back to normal.

Mia hadn't been in danger at all, right up until, all of a sudden, she fell asleep and never woke up. Nobody knew why. Her records showed she'd had the right amount of painkillers at the right times, and nothing had given any cause for alarm.

Her family refused an autopsy because the idea was too upsetting. The consultant produced some paperwork and told them that Mia had probably had a heart condition, that this would have happened at some point, and it was just by chance that it had tragically occurred when she was in hospital. It was nobody's fault: it was one of those things.

Life had to move on without her.

Mia couldn't move on, though. She wasn't ready.

1

12 February 2019

'Wake up.' He was shaking my shoulder. 'Get up and get dressed. Time to go. Fresh start.'

I blinked awake and tried to make sense of the words. It was weird for him to be in my room and it was pitch-dark, with just the glow of my clock shining green on his face – 4:52.

I'd been so deeply asleep. Was this a dream? It felt like a dream.

I could smell his cologne, toothpaste and the tea-tree shampoo he used. No, this was real: he really was up and ready to go. And it was 4:52 . . . 4:53.

My mind caught up. He wasn't doing this. He couldn't be.

'What?' I said, sitting up. 'Where?'

'Don't worry!' he said. 'Everything's arranged. We're going, Ariel. I'll tell you about it in the car.'

I reached for the bedside light, switched it on and looked at him. That manic glint was in his eye. I'd known it would be. He scared me when he was like this. There was no reasoning with him.

'What about Sasha?' I asked.

He was wearing a dark blue fleece and his horrible jeans, and there was a bag at his feet. He was serious about this.

'What about her?'

'We can't run away. We –' I stopped. I knew I wouldn't be able to say more without crying, and it was a mistake to cry when he was like this. It wound him up.

I'd always managed to avoid these confrontations because Sasha took the heat for me. I swallowed hard as I realized that I was going to have to do a thing I'd never done before. I was going to have to stand up to him.

'No,' he said. 'You've got it wrong. We're not running *away*. We're running *towards* something. A new life. Fresh start. I've been wanting to do this for years. You've been through enough over the past year, darling. Your sister's chosen her own path, and that's up to her. She said she didn't need us, and that was her call.'

She said she didn't need you.

I didn't say that.

She needs me. *She needs me very much. She doesn't have anyone else.*

I didn't say that either. I had never confronted him. That was why I was his favourite.

He saw my paralysis and spoke faster. 'You need me and I'd never leave you. Never. Sasha's an adult and she's made her decision. That has nothing to do with me now. As she said last night, she doesn't care about my approval and so I don't care what she does. I've got a place to go. A job. A house. A new school for you. We can start again and –'

'Dad!' My heart pounded so violently that I thought it was

4

going to knock the house down, but I didn't speak loudly enough to stop him.

'– build new lives for ourselves. We deserve to –'

I pulled the duvet up to my chin so he wouldn't see me trembling. I was so scared of this man. I wasn't going with him (it was unthinkable) and that meant I needed to do the bravest thing I'd ever done.

He was still speaking, so I summoned every bit of strength and interrupted with as much force as I could manage. 'Dad, I'm not going with you. Sasha needs me here.'

His eyes were glinting and I had to look away.

'No,' he said, trying to duck into my line of sight. When that didn't work, he took hold of my chin and tilted my head back so I could only look away from him with my eyes. His fingers dug into my skin. 'It's all arranged. You can have whatever you want. Clothes. Books. How about a MacBook? You wanted a MacBook, didn't you?'

Everything inside me longed to concede. This time, though, I couldn't.

'I can't,' I said, and I swivelled my eyes as far from him as they would go. I saw a spider walking up the wall, its shadow huge in the lamplight.

'You can.'

'I can't leave Sasha. I don't want to. I'm going to stay here.'

The silence hung there. I forced myself to wait it out. His hand dropped from my chin.

'Do you mean it?'

I nodded, watching the spider. I heard him exhale in a huge huff. I held my breath. This was where it got dangerous.

Sure enough, he pulled back his fist and punched my bed. Suppressed violence spread through the room. Menace hung static in the air. He could do anything, and we both knew it. He walked over to a wall and punched it hard. Then he strode to the door. He turned at the threshold.

'Last chance,' he said, spitting his words so I could almost see them flying towards me. Our eyes met for a few seconds and I looked away.

'No. I'm staying here,' I said to the wall, and he left.

I heard him moving around downstairs, and then the door clicked shut and something landed on the doormat with a thud.

I waited for ages for him to come back, but he didn't. Time stretched on and on, and nothing happened. After a while I put on my dressing gown and fluffy socks and crept downstairs.

He'd left an envelope propped against the kettle with Sasha's name on the front. There was a note for me next to it, scrawled on a piece of paper from a pad that had *To-do List* at the top of each page in a stupid font.

A, I expected better of you. You have broken my heart. Call me when you change your mind. If staying you need to call yr school and cancel the email I sent last night. Enjoy life in foster care!!!

The pen had gone through the paper on those last exclamation marks.

I stood at the bay window and pulled back the curtain, my

hand making the length of fabric tremble. It was pitch-black out there, with thick clouds covering the stars and the moon, but the street light showed an empty driveway.

He *had* left. His keys were on the mat, posted back through the letterbox. I pictured him parking round the corner and creeping back to kidnap me.

I turned and screamed.

'Sorry,' said my sister, standing blinking in her blue dressing gown, confused. She was holding the envelope that had *Sasha* written on the front in Dad's best handwriting (which was still bad, even when he was trying; he was a doctor after all). 'What's happening, Mermaid? Why has Dad written me a letter?' She shook her head. 'Actually I don't need to open it. He's telling me off again about my irresponsible behaviour. Reminding me that I'll never be a doctor. I'm going to put it straight in the bin.'

I hugged her as tightly as I could. She resisted for a moment and then gave in and hugged me back. I didn't cry. I didn't cry. She smelled of Sasha and sleep.

'What's up?' she said. 'What's he done?'

'He's gone,' I said into her hair (Sasha was four years older than me and maybe four inches shorter too). 'It might be one of his mind games, but he said he was leaving. He had a bag. The car's gone. He . . .' I didn't want to tell her this part, but I knew I had to. 'This next bit's awful, OK?'

'Tell me.'

Sasha followed me into the kitchen. I put the kettle on and got out two mugs.

'He woke me up about an hour ago. Maybe more? Before

7

five. He was all showered and ready. He said I had to get up and go with him.' My voice cracked, but I carried on.

'He said it was a fresh start and he'd buy me a MacBook. He said you didn't need us. When I told him I wasn't going, he went all cold and stormed off. And now I think he's actually gone. Look. He put his keys through the letterbox. He left me this.' I showed her the note. At this point the tears started coming. 'Am I going to have to go into foster care, Sasha? Am I?'

That part was just beginning to sink in. I couldn't do that. I couldn't.

'Fuck,' she said. 'Oh God, Ariel. No, you're not. Of course you're not. You're staying here with me. I'm sure they won't take you away.'

When she opened her letter, we found it was more coherent than the note he'd scrawled to me. Coherent but psychotic.

I've worked it out. You and I don't need to have any more contact. I'm disappointed in your life choices. You told me to my face that you wished I was dead. I'm not going to stick around in your life any more to be spoken to like that. Enough is enough, Sasha, and I've had enough of your bullying. Ariel doesn't see it, but I do, and that's why I need to get her away from you.

Stay in this house. The mortgage is paid off. I'll transfer some money each month for bills. I have no faith in you to look after yourself, let alone another human, and despite what you think of me no grandson of mine is going to live in poverty. That will be the extent of my involvement. Ariel and I will be starting afresh with no contact. This is best.

'It's like a divorce,' Sasha said, putting a peppermint tea bag in a mug. 'I literally feel like my dad is divorcing me. Paying me enough child support to keep me quiet.' She looked up and forced a smile. 'That makes you the record collection or whatever. He wanted to take you, but he couldn't get you in the car, so he had to leave you behind. He's right about one thing, though: I did tell him I wished he'd been the one to die. I knew he'd never forgive me, even while I was saying it, but I don't care. I meant it. I'd love it if he was dead and Mum was still here. So would you.'

I couldn't quite be as harsh as that, and I certainly didn't feel strong enough to talk about Mum right now, so I just said, 'Sure you don't want a coffee?'

'No.' She patted her stomach. 'No coffee until July. I'll have a herbal tea and a piece of toast. You have coffee.'

'I will.'

We were silent while I made the drinks and Sasha put as much bread into the toaster as it would take.

'You're not the bully,' I said because I knew she'd be thinking about that part of Dad's note. 'He is. He's only saying it to make himself feel better.'

'I know. Hey, Ariel? We can do this. Seriously. I'm not sure we even need to tell anyone that Dad's gone. Do we?'

We looked at each other. Sasha and I were still feeling our

9

way. Our relationship had changed so much lately, and now it was shifting again.

'If they found out,' I said, with only a vague idea of who I meant by *they*, 'would they make me go into foster care like Dad said? Or a children's home? Like Tracy Beaker?'

'No.' Her voice was more brave than certain. 'I'm old enough. And so are you. Sixteen-year-olds can live independently. It's not like you're a baby. Plus, there's going to be an actual baby. If I can have one of those, surely I can keep an eye on you while I'm at it.'

I felt my heart calming. It made sense.

'Though I don't trust Dad,' she added.

I handed her the peppermint tea. I didn't trust him either.

I brushed my hair and put it into a French plait to make myself appear as wholesome as I could, then sprayed it in place. I made sure my uniform was clean and correct. I didn't even put on a little bit of mascara like I usually did. When I thought I looked like the girl with the most straightforward home life possible, I went to school early and made myself do a 'no big deal' smile as I stopped at the reception desk to try and work out how to delete whatever the hell message my dad might have sent them in the night.

The entrance hall was quiet. There was still the faint smell of overnight cleaning. I knew it would soon be overlaid with Lynx and crisps and sweat. I focused. I had to play this right. I'd hoped to find the computer unattended and hackable, but no such luck.

'It's really nothing,' I said to the woman. 'My dad's been

struggling a bit this year and he sent something he regrets. We're absolutely fine, so please do delete the email. No need to read it.'

I watched her write a note on a piece of paper.

'I don't think anyone's been through the inbox this morning,' she said. 'What's your dad's name? I'll do a search.'

'Alex Brown.'

'Of course. You're Ariel.'

She looked at me in that way that adults always did since Mum.

'Yes,' I said. 'And we're doing fine. Honestly. Dad's finding it difficult at times, but Sasha and I are all right. And . . .' I paused. It might end up worse if I didn't flag this up. 'I think the email might suggest that I'm leaving this school, but I'm not. He didn't mean it. So please just delete and ignore. He was just a bit confused. Half sleepwalking, you know?'

'*Ooookayyyyy*,' she said in a tone that made me suspect it might not be completely OK. In fact, her *OK* told me that the very first thing she was going to do when I walked away was search the inbox for my dad's message, and then she'd probably tell someone else and they would call him.

I texted Izzy:

> Where are you? Everything's
> gone to shit AGAIN.

2

'Shut up!'

I reach for the alarm with my eyes closed. The beeping of that clock is the worst sound in the world, except for the sound of the silence after you've been murdered.

This is the thought that jolts me awake.

I open my eyes and stare at the ceiling. Damp patch. Bigger than it used to be? Maybe. The ceiling is real. Real, real, real.

I turn my head. Yes, this is my bedroom. Clothes on the floor. Books piled on the table. Morning light coming through the blue curtains. My stuff is everywhere. My feet poke out of the end of the bed. I'm at home and this is normal.

I touch my neck. It's smooth and a bit stubbly. That's as it should be. I run my fingers through my hair, look at my hands, front and back. Obviously everything's all right. I am here and alive.

Of course I am.

I'm such a twat.

'Joe!'

Dad is shouting from downstairs. I sit up and yawn. I poke a leg right out of bed. It's hairier than it used to be. No shit. Fifteen years old, six feet tall, terrified by a dream. I give myself a shake and try to focus.

'Joe!' he yells again. 'You awake?'

'Yeah!' I say, or something like it. I get up and, because I'm only wearing pants, I pull on my dressing gown. Dad insists on seeing us with his own eyes before he goes to work.

I yawn as I open my door, blink at the light and focus on my dad.

He's standing on the stairs, wearing his jeans and the polo shirt with the name of the nursery embroidered on his chest: BOUNCERS. Yes, he is a male nursery worker, at the age of forty-nine. He's been doing it for so long that he's in charge of the place, but really he just goes to work so he can play. I don't know how he does it, looking after snotty little kids all day, but the thing with Dad is that he's always happy.

Weirdo.

'Bye,' he says, coming up to the landing and patting my shoulder. 'Have a good day. I finish at five, so I'll be home at twenty past. I'll run you back up to school at sevenish and wave you off.'

'Shit!'

'Joseph!'

He goes down the stairs. I follow. Dad hates anything that could be seen as 'bad language', however mild. It's one of the rules. Gus and I aren't allowed to swear because if we did 'that would make it feel normal, and then I'd start doing it at work and I'd be fired, and we'd have to get our food out of bins'. It's a legitimate reason. All the same . . .

'*Shit* is hardly swearing,' I say, jumping down the last three stairs in one go. 'But sorry. I forgot about tonight. That's all.'

Gus laughs at me from the landing.

'You *forgot* about your French exchange?' He points a finger. 'Not credible! You've been obsessing about it for, like, a year. You can't have forgotten it now because you're going *today*.'

I point back. 'I just woke up! I had a weird dream and I forgot. So shoot me.'

He makes his fingers into a gun and fires it at me. I clutch my chest and pretend to die, but it feels all wrong. My dream echoes round the house. I fall to the floor and expire dramatically, more to distract myself than anything else.

'You two!' Dad is putting his shoes on and checking he has his lanyard. 'You're worse than the toddlers. Yet I seem to be trusting you to get yourselves to school. Bye, babies!'

Gus and I look at each other after the door clicks shut.

'Where's Mum?' I didn't plan to say that, but those seem to be the words that come out. *Where's Mum?* Jesus. I walk into the living room. Gus follows.

'Mum?' He laughs. 'Hello? Gone to learn how to be a yoga teacher? As you know perfectly well. Do you need your mummy?'

My mind is foggy. I knew that. I just haven't woken up properly.

'Fine. Well, you've got to help me not go on the French exchange.'

I pace round the room. I don't know why I feel like this. I pick up the little clown that Dad won, sixteen years ago, at some circus awards. I look at its creepy face, then put it down facing away from me. It can stare out of the window instead. Our house is full of weird shit like that.

'How?' says Gus. 'Hide you under my bed? Stay there a week and I'll pass you a Twix when I remember.'

'I'd take that,' I say. 'Right now I'd do it. A week under your bed with your stinky socks and whatever else. And a Twix.'

He smiles, and I force a smile back. I don't know why I'm feeling like this. I am not the sort of person who freaks out. I'm going away for less than a week and yet I seem to have lost the plot. I'm going to have to fake it to get through the day. Do an impression of myself.

'It'll be OK,' Gus says. 'The moment you leave, you'll be on a countdown to coming back. Once you get going, it'll go quickly. Also he might be cool. Your "pen pal".' He makes quote marks in the air to demonstrate how incredibly uncool this concept actually is. 'Enzo. You know he's probably dreading it as much as you are?'

'Yeah. He'll *hate* me coming to stay. Thanks, bro.'

Gus softens. 'He does sound nice in his letters, to be fair.'

'He likes going to the cinema and riding his bike. Same as me.'

'*J'aime faire des promenades à velo avec mon frère?*'

'*Sans mon frère,*' I say. Without my brother.

I head for the shower. Gus doesn't fight me for it because he's at sixth form and he seems to go to college whenever he fancies it. Gus never had to go on a stupid French exchange because he managed not to take a language for GCSE because he's dyslexic. Some people are so *lucky*.

I have Troy's house-football trophy in my schoolbag and when I remember it makes me hot with shame. What's wrong with me? It's a little metal football with a boot kicking it. He won it yesterday: I thought it was going to be me, and so did everybody else. I took it from his bag when he wasn't looking because I was jealous. What a knob.

I shake my head, shove the trophy to the bottom of the bag and dash out of the house. I'll give it back to him later and say sorry. I'm a shit friend.

Troy is late. Maybe he's not meeting me because of the trophy, because he realized it was missing and knew it was me. I stand on the corner and wait. The woman from the next street lets her dog do a poo in the middle of the pavement. She doesn't pick it up and pretends not to hear me saying, 'Gross!' as she speed-walks away, her head down.

Mr Armstrong, the sad man who lives next door, ambles past and says, 'Ah, hello, Joseph. Just getting my paper.'

I have to make an effort with him. Dad says that since his wife died it might be the only interaction he has all day.

'Hello, Mr Armstrong,' I say.

'Everything all right at your house?' he says.

'Yeah,' I say. 'I'm going away later. French exchange trip.'

'Are you? Oh gosh,' he says. 'I used to love France. Bernadette and I went every year. Are you taking the ferry?'

'We are, yeah. We're going on the coach, and then the night ferry to Roscoff, and then the coach all the way down France.' I shiver. 'I don't want to go,' I add. Might as well give Mr A the facts. I feel tears pricking at the back of my eyes. What the hell?

'You'll have a marvellous time!' he counters. 'Do you have any francs? I have a few coins somewhere. I could give them to you.'

'Don't worry, Mr Armstrong,' I say, smiling at the thought of his old holiday money. 'Cheers for the offer, though!'

I smile and wave goodbye as Troy turns up after all. It's easy to see him coming because he's much taller than everyone else and has bright red hair. I always grin at the sight of him. He said once that he knows he looks like an illustration of a cheeky boy from a children's book, and he does a bit, but that doesn't keep model-agency people from stopping him in the street. He's a quarter Dutch, and reckons that's why he's so tall.

'Wazzup?' he says. 'And what are you doing chatting to that old perv?' I'm so glad Troy isn't pissed off that I laugh a bit too hysterically.

'He is not a perv!' I manage to say. 'He's a nice old man. He was married for years. I bet he'd only perv at girls.'

'Yeah?'

'He wanted to give me his French money.'

'Old man offers teenager money on a street corner?'

I know I should give him back that trophy right now. I

17

want to do it, but maybe he hasn't even noticed it's gone, and then he starts talking French, so I go with that instead. Troy is brilliant at French. He'll be fine with his host family. He can't wait to go.

It takes about fifteen minutes to get to school. Troy makes me laugh all the way. We talk about France, and wonder whether we'll have to eat frogs' legs. I feel myself coming back.

'Remember when we caught that frog on the playing field?' he asks. 'At primary school?'

'We tried to use it to scare the girls,' I say, remembering. 'But they thought it was cute.'

'They made it a hat out of a leaf and called it Froggykins.'

We gather more hangers-on as we walk, like people in a musical, but without the part where we burst into song and dance. By the time we get to school our crowd has dissolved into the tide of teens going into the building.

Lucas comes over to me, as usual. He was new last year, and he tries so hard to be my friend that I can't help taking the piss. I'm tall, and Troy's taller, but Lucas is massive. There was a story a while ago about a thirty-year-old who went back to school, pretending to be sixteen, and got away with it for ages: that feels like Lucas to me. Troy and I are kind of skinny, but Lucas is built like a shed. He doesn't look like a teenager. He makes me feel uncomfortable.

'All right?' I say.

'Yeah.'

'Shame you're not coming on the French trip,' I say, laughing as I speak because he knows as well as I do that I don't think that.

'Yeah,' he says again. 'Too expensive. *Dommage.*'

I roll my eyes and walk off. Then I turn back and say, 'Thank fuck,' in a way that's just quiet enough for him to wonder whether he heard properly, and then I burrow into the crowd. Lucas isn't in any of my Thursday classes, so I probably won't see him again today, and that means I'll be spared his company until I come back from France.

3

We would have been able to keep Dad's departure secret for much longer if he hadn't written that email. As it was we didn't even make it through the first day. During my last lesson (physics) two students came in. One of them handed a piece of paper to Mr Dean and the other sat down and joined the lesson. I was trying really hard to concentrate on atomic structure. I was proving (to myself, to Sasha, to the world) that I would manage in a household of two teenagers and a foetus. I had to show them that I wouldn't, wouldn't, *wouldn't* be better off in care. Right now that meant mastering isotopes.

Someone left the room. I looked up to see a boy from Year Nine going out of the door. The other one, a girl I didn't know, was just sitting there reading a book. It was strange that Mr Dean hadn't spoken to her or introduced her as new to the class.

I turned back to the isotopes but it was hard to concentrate. My mind wandered. We had no parents left at home. Sasha was my anchor and I had to be hers. We both had the baby, but that felt like a lot of pressure to put on someone who was only half gestated; who was, we'd only just discovered, a tiny little boy.

I thought I could tether myself with mass numbers, but I kept thinking of Mum, and of how excited she would have been about her grandson, and how furious with Dad. I was wondering whether I could will her back to life with the power of my longing, because I needed her so much, when Mr Dean said, 'Ariel? Could you pop along to the office?' He checked the clock. 'You may as well take your things.'

He put the piece of paper down on his table and gave me a sympathetic look. Everyone knew that *Ariel has been through a hard time this year*.

I glanced at Izzy and she patted my leg. I stopped caring about electrons. I needed to speak to Sasha right now to check whether school had called her. We had to get our stories straight.

'Thanks,' I said, and Mr Dean started walking around talking about atoms while everyone except the new girl (who just carried on reading) watched me gathering my things together. There were fifteen minutes until the end of the lesson and I could sense a lot of people with no real problems wishing they were the ones leaving early. I wanted them to stop looking. My hands were shaking as I picked everything up. I almost kicked my chair over, but Izzy caught it and put it upright.

Mr Dean walked over to Aisha, and sat down next to her to look at something in her book. He had sat down where the new girl was and she suddenly wasn't there any more. I didn't know where she'd gone. Aisha turned to stare at me, ignoring

Mr Dean and her book, and I wanted to ask what had happened to the girl who'd been beside her, but I didn't.

What was going on? I refused to lose my mind as well as everything else.

I looked at the boys instead, silently begging one of them to do something stupid and take the attention away from me. I focused on Jack, with his messy dark hair and sharp cheekbones. *Go on*, I thought. *Do something. Do it for me. Drop your book. Throw something. Fight with someone.* I wasn't being sexist: it was almost always boys that arsed around in lessons and, although Jack and I broke up when Mum got ill, we'd never stopped being friends. He would have done it if he'd realized I needed it.

As it was, though, no one did anything. I made it to the door. Jack said, 'Bye, Ariel!' as I left, and when I looked round the whole class was waving stupidly at me, and Izzy was mouthing, 'Good luck.'

I'd always had friends, but everyone except Izzy had melted into the background since Mum got ill. I knew I'd changed, and everyone else had carried on without me, but Izzy had been there, at the end of a phone, or right next to me, throughout. She had her own stuff going on, but she'd always drop it when I needed her.

I'd needed her a lot.

I texted her as I walked slowly through the silent school: **You're literally the best person in the world.**

Then I called Sasha and slowed my pace still further.

'Mermaid!' said Sasha. She and Mum were the only people who were allowed to call me that. I hated it if anyone else tried. The baby could do it, though, if he wanted to. 'Thank God. So I had a call from school wanting to talk to Dad, and I told them he was at work. Have they spoken to you?'

'On my way. They just pulled me out of physics to go to the office.' I quickly hung up and shoved my phone away.

'Ariel,' said the woman I'd spoken to that morning at reception, and she walked me straight to the head's office and deposited me inside.

Mr Morrow was in his forties, and one of those teachers who thinks he's cool and everyone's best mate. He said, 'Ariel! Great to see you. Grab a pew. So, what's going on at home?'

He leaned forward and started the meaningful eye contact. I looked away first. No way could I stare him out right now.

'Well, my mum died,' I said, just to make him uncomfortable.

He nodded in that *I'm listening* way. 'And what's happened in the past few days?'

'Nothing,' I said. 'I know my dad sent a weird message, but he didn't mean anything by it. He's been upset lately. It's like, you'd be sad if your wife died, right?'

Mr Morrow didn't flinch. 'I would,' he said.

'And my sister, Sasha. She's nearly twenty. So, even if Dad finds things hard, I still have her. She's an adult.'

'I can't argue with that either,' said Mr Morrow. 'However, in light of the email your father sent, and in spite of both your and your sister's insistence that everything's fine, we decided to call him at work just to check in. And so we were surprised to learn that he's left his job and taken up a new one in Inverness. Which would explain why he wrote that he was

23

taking you out of school and moving away to start afresh. Ariel, you and Sasha need to begin telling us the truth. Has your father relocated to Scotland without you?'

Busted on day one.

'I guess,' I told the top of his desk.

Shit, shit, shit. I waited for a social worker to walk in and take me away. I held on to the edges of my seat. I wouldn't go. They couldn't make me. I'd stay here.

Nothing happened. I could feel Mr Morrow looking at me, but I carried on staring at his desk. It was very neat. There was nothing interesting on it: all the paperwork was piled to the side with a local newsletter on top of it and a paperweight. I couldn't read anything, which I was sure was the plan. He had a poster of someone rock climbing, but at least it didn't have an inspirational quote underneath.

Still nothing happened.

'You guess that your father has moved to Scotland?' he said, and finally I looked up.

'I didn't know it was Scotland,' I said, and I could hear how tight and scared my voice was. 'He asked me to go with him. He wanted me and him to go, but not Sasha. He hasn't been happy with her since she told him she was pregnant, and recently he's gone absolutely mental about it. He's been awful to her. I said I didn't want to go, so he just drove off and stuck his keys back through the letterbox. And that's the truth.'

'Now this time,' said Mr Morrow, 'I believe you.'

'So I'm going to be absolutely fine living with Sasha,' I finished, too loudly, adding stupidly, 'I was concentrating really hard in physics just now. We were doing atomic structure.'

Inverness?

I couldn't believe Dad had gone that far. Inverness was (I was quite hazy about this) maybe six hundred miles away? If he started driving at about six this morning, which he had, then he probably hadn't even got there yet. He might have crashed on the way. I was sure he hadn't slept last night, and his driving was shit and aggressive at the best of times.

He must have been planning this for ages if he had a job all sorted. He'd known about Sasha's baby for a couple of months. Had he started job-hunting the moment she told him? What the hell kind of parenting was that?

People were supposed to be pleased at becoming grandparents. Or shocked, but then come round to the idea. They weren't supposed to run away in the night and move to Scotland. I wondered what it was like in Inverness. What would my new school have been like, if I'd gone? Was there a school register somewhere up there with my name on it? Was a teacher I didn't know going to say, 'Ariel Brown?' tomorrow morning and wonder why no one was answering?

And then I started to imagine what life would be like without Dad. If he had really gone – if he wasn't going to come back – then it might be . . .

Lovely.

I tuned back in sharply at the words 'social services'.

'No,' I said. 'We don't need social services. We don't need anything like that. We're fine as we are.'

'You know, Ariel,' said Mr M, 'I actually believe that you're

25

probably right. That staying where you are, with Sasha, will be much the least disruptive path. That's my point really. We *do* have to contact social services, so they can check that both Sasha and you are all right. It's a positive thing. Not a scary one. Is Sasha's partner involved?'

'Jai?' I said. 'Kind of. It's complicated because they were never really in a relationship. They were friends.' I bit back the words *with benefits*. 'But he's going to be around for Sash and the baby. He's cool.'

'Good,' said Mr Morrow. 'Well, Ariel, I'd just like to say that we're all impressed with the way you've coped over the past couple of years. You've been through more than many of us adults have, and here you are, still standing. I know Ms Duke has been helping out. I've brought her up to speed today, and she's going to have a chat with you tomorrow and on a much more regular basis after that, if you're OK with the idea. Thank you for confiding in me.'

I wanted to say I hadn't confided one single bastard thing, that he'd cornered me and given me no choice. I managed, instead, to say, 'Sure, thanks, bye,' as I ran out of the door.

The school had emptied out and there were just a few stragglers around, and the sound of someone playing the trumpet badly in a distant music room. Izzy had messaged: **I've gone home but msg if you want to meet.**

I needed to get my head round the day. I called Sasha back and filled her in; told her that Dad was in Inverness and that I'd be home in a bit, and then walked down to the seafront.

It was a lacklustre day, with the odd sunbeam poking out

from between the clouds. I walked along the once-grand pathway through the municipal gardens towards the beach. The palm trees stood perfectly still, as there was no wind at all. The flower beds were filled with drooping purple flowers and litter. I could smell junk food and the sea.

I stopped and closed my eyes.

I live with my sister, I said in my head. It sounded OK.

I was heading for the beach, but there was a group from school there, from my year, with cider and chips. I swung towards the amusements instead, where I changed two pound coins into one hundred two-pence pieces and pushed them, one by one, into the machines. Watching the coins nearly tipping each other over the edge was hypnotic, and when they did cascade down it made me jump. I put them all back in again, and again, until there were none left.

Then I wandered upstairs, into the mall. It wasn't a mall like the ones in American movies. It was just some shops under the same roof. It was a shopping centre really, and not a cool one, and it was called Beachview even though it had no windows to the outside. The air was stale, and most of the people in here were on their way to or from the pub upstairs.

I mooched around. I looked in the window of H&M. I flicked through magazines in Smith's until the security guard glared at me.

Mum had died. Dad had left. Sasha and I were almost orphans.

I wandered down a little corridor around the back of Boots. It looked like a place for staff only, but there wasn't a sign and I had a vague memory of going down here once before, when

I was very little. I had a flashback to my younger self waiting in a room somewhere around here with Dad. I remembered him sitting with his head in his hands while I stared at one of those brightly coloured magazines people buy for their children to keep them quiet.

The corridor ended in exactly the tiny room that was in my head. There was a small, grimy window high up in the wall, letting in the only natural light I'd ever seen in Beachview. One side of the room had a bench along it, the sort you found in swimming-pool changing cubicles, and the other had a row of pegs with nothing hanging on them. The walls were dirty cream, with peeling paint on wooden panels.

I closed the door and sat on the bench.

Dad had always been horrible to Sasha. He sometimes ignored her, sometimes shouted, and one memorable time he'd pushed her against a wall and yelled right into her face until Mum pulled him away. Nothing Sasha did was ever good enough. Even when she was acing exams and applying to study medicine, the very thing he'd wanted both of us to do, he had found a way to be disappointed. If she got ninety per cent in a test he wanted to know what had gone wrong with the other ten, whereas if I got seventy per cent he'd give me five pounds. He wanted us to be doctors to make him look good. A family of doctors. That was his dream.

I'd never dared to tell him I didn't want to be a doctor and now I wouldn't have to.

I leaned back against the wall, trying to breathe deeply, the way Mum used to make me do when she was ill. She'd been dead for nearly a year and I had missed her for every single moment of it. Once, I'd lived my life on the basis that she was always going to be around. She'd taught me to talk, to cross the road, to use a knife and fork. She had taught me everything I'd needed to know, and now I was sixteen, and I knew those things, and I would just have to get on with them.

I kept thinking about Dad punching my bed and then the wall. He'd wanted to punch me. I knew he had. I'd faced him down for the first time ever, and it had worked. I shivered at the memory of the violence that had shimmered around him.

I took a Sharpie out of my bag and wrote on the wall:

I HATE YOU ALEXANDER BROWN

I looked at it. It was vandalism, and yet it lifted something away from me. I smiled at the words. Yes. You are Alexander Brown and I hate you. I wrote it again.

You've gone. I faced you down and I won.

4

The one time I want a school day to go slowly, it speeds up. Typical. I actually enjoy today because it's normal. I can't imagine where I'll be tomorrow. I mean, I'll wake up on a boat, and by night-time I'll be at Enzo's house in St Etienne, like the band. It's a good name for a city. I like the band. So does Enzo. One thing in common! Maybe we can talk about other bands we like. For a week?

Every single part of me wants to stay at home.

I sit in registration and look at the photo Enzo sent me, of him and his family. He has thick black hair and dark skin. His brother looks like him, but taller, and his sister is small, hanging off his arm in the picture. His mother is white, his dad black. *J'ai un frère et une soeur*, I say under my breath, even though I don't have a sister. They have a mother and a father like regular people. I'd better figure out how to say 'my mum doesn't live with us' because that's the kind of thing you have to get out of the way before it becomes too awkward.

I guess she must have been frustrated living a suburban life with a husband who was a circus performer when they met, but who has since channelled all that energy into looking after sticky toddlers. Dad can be annoying, and I guess Gus and I were too boring or irritating to keep her here.

I look at the photo of Enzo's house. It's big, and it has a garden with tall trees in it, and a tree house.

1.   Talk about music.
2.   Hang out in the tree house.

'Hey,' says Troy. 'Wake up.'

I look around, blinking. It's registration. You can tell at a glance who's going on the trip tonight and who isn't. The ones who aren't are looking relaxed. Everyone else is tense. Or maybe that's just me. Why am I jittery?

What's happening to me?

I don't feel like myself, so I try to be more me. What would Joe Simpson do?

I turn to Troy and flash a big stupid grin.

'It's school,' I say. 'How can I wake up when the whole point of it is that it's boring?'

That is the lamest thing, but Troy laughs anyway. Our tutor, Mrs Dupont, is also the French teacher, so all she can talk about is the trip. This is her third year leading the French exchange and she's raring to go. She isn't French, but she's married to a French guy and obviously knows how to speak it. She's given us all laminated cards to carry with us in France. They say '*Je suis perdu*' and have her mobile number on them. Lots of the guys say they're going to keep that number.

31

Once, after a meeting about the trip, I hung around while Dad asked her all his supplementary questions. No, we won't have to eat snails (I wanted to die). Yes, the coach driver is British, but he *will* remember to drive on the right. Then they moved on to chit-chat, and she told him she used to be a flight attendant, but had given up, partly because it was much harder work than you'd think, and also because air travel was bad for the environment.

Mrs Dupont, to be fair, looks like an air hostess. I can imagine her with her hair up and a lot of make-up on. I saw the way Dad was looking at her at that point and dragged him home. Dad was properly married to Mum back then! Mrs Dupont is married to the mysterious Monsieur Dupont! Jeez.

I shake my head. *Stop getting distracted!*

'Joe?' she says now, and I wonder how many times she's said it.

'Yep!' I give her a huge fake smile. 'How may I help you, Madame Dupont?'

She rolls her eyes.

'Joe. You look jittery. Have you been on the caffeine?'

'You know me, miss. Always with the Red Bull.'

'Well, calm down and don't worry. The French trip is always a fun experience.'

'I'm not worried!' Everyone laughs because it sounds like such a lie.

'I stay with a family too, you know!' she says. 'I stay with the English teacher.'

'Bet you crack open the wine, miss,' says Troy.

I raise an imaginary glass to her. '*Santé!*' I say. 'Cheers to Madame Dupont boozing with her English teacher friend.'

I look round the room. Everyone's holding up their imaginary glasses and toasting them.

'Absolutely not.' Mrs Dupont is laughing. 'Or, if we do, it's behind closed doors when we're off duty.'

'You're never off duty, though, are you?'

'Tell me about it, Joseph.'

The bell goes, and we scramble away to lessons.

'Coming?' says Troy. We're standing outside the front of the school.

If I go straight back I'll be home at ten to four. That will give me an hour and a half to sit on the bed being scared before Dad comes back, and then there'll be another hour and a half of him trying to jolly me along.

Nope. Unbearable.

'Nah,' I say, and I struggle to find something else I can do. 'I'm heading into town. Got to get a present for Enzo's family.'

'I'm going home because I haven't started packing.'

'See you later.'

'Joe?' he says.

'Yeah?'

'You haven't seen my trophy, have you?'

'Seen your . . .?'

'The house-football prize.'

'No,' I say before I can stop myself. 'Of course not.'

'Cool. Not sure where it's gone.'

He pats my back and walks off, leaving me guilty and confused. Why did I take it? And why did I just lie? I'm so strung out I can barely breathe. I can't go home. I want to keep moving. I should be hungry, but I'm not. I could get a Coke at Beachview, and hope the caffeine sharpens me up because, in spite of what I said to Mrs Dupont, I have not, in fact, had any caffeine today.

It's stopped raining and feels warm for March. I want to take my coat off, but then I'd have to carry it, so I don't. The pavements are shiny with rain. I add a swagger to my step and iron the weirdness from my face. Everything is normal. Everything is fine.

The Beachview Mall does not have a view of the beach: you might see the sea if you stood on the roof of the upstairs pub. It is secretly, however, one of my favourite places. It's all contained. This is a small, knowable universe where you can buy stuff. The shops are exactly as you'd expect them to be: there's a branch of every low-level high-street shop in there. There's Smith's, a tiny but handy H&M, a health-food shop. And so on. It is boring but nice. My favourite thing, though, is a secret room I found a while ago. You just go round a couple of corners behind Boots, and push a door and it opens. Then you're in a tiny room with a row of pegs and a bench in it, and no one else is ever there.

I go to a stall to buy a can of Coke and, as I turn round, I walk right into a man. He's tall and thin and I had no idea he was behind me.

34

'Oh,' I say. 'Sorry.' I step out of the way.

'Fuck's sake!' he says, moving sideways to block my path.

'Excuse me,' I say. The anger flows all the way through me. I'm a volcano. 'It was an accident. I didn't know you were standing behind me, did I?'

He glares as if he actually hates me.

'Fuck you,' he says, and I am pleased to find that I'm feeling something. This is better. I feel more alive now than I have all day. I decide to laugh at him like I do with Lucas.

'Fuck *you*,' I say, and I walk away, still laughing like (I hope) someone very cool who will make him feel stupid, rather than a pantomime baddy. I hear him shouting behind me so I go and sit in the little room where he won't find me, and attempt to talk some sense into myself.

Mum went to do a course to become a yoga teacher. I'm pretty sure she's in India now because she always said she needed to learn proper yoga over there. I think I've known for a while that her leaving has messed with my head in all sorts of ways. I can barely remember some things from before she went. I'm not even sure how long it's been. A month? A year? Maybe a year.

I have no problem with anyone doing a yoga course that lasts maybe a year, but my own mother could have waited until we'd left home. Three years from now she could have done whatever she wanted. Three years must be a really short time when you're fifty. It's a tiny fraction of your life, whereas for me it's a lot.

One day when things were going weird with Marco I left school through the back hedge at lunchtime and came into town to try to work out what the fuck was going on. I got a cheap hoodie at H&M so I didn't look like I was truanting and tried to find a place to sit where no one would see me. I was about to head to the beach when I thought I'd try a passage around the back of the mall, which I'd never noticed before. The passage went along for a little way, with pipes and a cleaning trolley, and then there was a door that was slightly open. I pushed it and there was my secret room. I sat inside for ages.

At that point it became my place to go whenever I secretly needed to think. I keep a blanket in there, a pink fluffy one that Mum used to use for yoga. It's a comfort blanket. No one can ever know.

I push the door now and it swings open again. I wrap myself in the blanket and lean back against the wall, and find that I'm gasping and sobbing. I wipe my eyes with my sleeve and shout: 'PULL YOURSELF TOGETHER!' I yell it at the top of my voice. It echoes round the tiny room. I try to hold on to my anger at that man, but it's already gone. I'm back to being numb to almost everything, and filled with unnecessary dread about the trip.

It's only a week in sodding France. I do my best to talk myself down. We live about an hour from Plymouth, so the first part of the journey will be fine. I'll sit with Troy, at the back of the coach. It'll be fun. I'll give him back his stupid trophy, straight away, so that won't be a worry any more.

Then we'll sleep on the ferry. Four of us are sharing a cabin, and I like everyone, so that'll be brilliant.

Tomorrow we'll drive through France. That's great too. I have no idea why I feel panicky about the whole thing. Every atom of my body is braced, tense, feeling dread. I want to run away, but I don't want to go anywhere. I want to run away from the trip so I can stay at home.

Lamest. Runaway. Ever.

I sip my Coke and work on breathing properly and talking sense into myself. It will be OK. The only way to get past it is to get on with it. This is a blip, a wobble. Things always come easily to me. There's no reason for me to struggle.

I'm having to work very hard to keep that image up right now.

I put on my headphones and try to make myself feel better with some music. I only have one album with me, but it's *Different Class* so that's OK. I press play and relax into 'Something Changed'.

After a while the door opens.

5

8 March

A girl and a boy were standing at the front of the classroom, wearing uniforms from a different school. They kept looking at each other and laughing. Flirting. I couldn't take my eyes off them.

The lesson went on, and they just stood there, giggling. No one else could see them. Not only that, but they didn't seem to see us either. Just like that girl I'd seen and didn't recognize the day Dad left.

I looked out of the window. The sky was pale blue. It was calm and clear and I tried to keep it in my head. I was not losing my mind. I was fine. This was just a . . . blip.

When I looked back at the girl and the boy with the blue of the sky in my head, I saw that they were blue too. It was shining around them, out of them, as if there was a blue light inside each one. I stopped thinking about blue, and it stopped being there. I thought of it, and it was back.

Oh shit! I was losing it on an epic scale.

Ms Duke was going on in French, and they were a metre away from her. I spent a while making them go from blue to

38

not-blue in my head, until they looked at each other, burst out laughing (silently) and ran out of the room.

This was happening all the time. It had started with the new girl in physics, who suddenly hadn't been there any more. I'd asked Izzy, when I remembered, and she'd looked confused and had no idea what I'd been talking about.

'There wasn't a new girl in physics,' she'd said, stroking my arm. 'But you were in a bad place, and Mira did have different hair, so maybe it was that.'

I'd nodded and pretended to agree, but now I saw new people most days. I hadn't mentioned them to Izzy again.

Mad wasn't a nice word to use, so even internally I tried to rephrase it. This had to be me *experiencing the onset of a mental-health crisis*. But you were allowed to say anything you wanted about yourself, so I could say *mad* since I was self-diagnosing. Calling myself bad names was probably part of the condition, so it was OK. I am *mad*, I thought. A madwoman. Mad, mad, mad, mad, mad. I stabbed my pen into my book over and over again, perversely enjoying it, until I realized people were looking at me.

'Sorry,' I said to Madame D. I felt myself turning deep red.

'*En français?*' she said with a big smile to show she didn't really mind.

'*Je suis désolée.*'

She gave me a look that signalled, *After the lesson?* Ms Duke had a counselling qualification, and that was why she'd been looking out for me over the past year. Now she was supposed to report back if she thought I needed to go to a children's home, so I really did have to remember to be less mad in her lessons.

'Hey, Ariel,' she said (in English, luckily). 'So, what's up?'

I'd spoken to her loads when Mum was ill, and it had actually helped.

All the same . . .

'Sorry. I'm fine.'

'You seemed to be miles away this afternoon, and at one point you looked very distressed.'

She must have been due for retirement, I thought. I hoped she had a nice plan lined up. I imagined her living on her own with a fluffy cat and maybe some geraniums.

'Sorry.' I tried for a reassuring smile. '*Je suis désolée, Madame.* I'm OK now, I promise.'

I checked the room. Everyone else – real and blue – had left. That meant I could relax a bit.

'I don't really know what happened,' I admitted, sitting on a desk and swinging my legs. 'It just got on top of me. It's a bit scary sometimes. But I'm basically fine.'

She sat on her desk too, and took out some Werther's Originals from her handbag. She always did that: it was adorable. I accepted one when she offered them and unwrapped it.

'You and Sasha are doing all right?'

'We're doing brilliantly,' I said, speaking round the sweet. 'I mean, we really are. And nothing's changed, truly. I was just having a bit of a blip.'

'I'm full of admiration. Just do depend on me as part of the support network. Elderly French teacher by day, listener and provider of sweets or whatever you need by . . . later in the day. Or earlier. Whatever. Is Sasha really fine?'

'Yes.' I smiled at that. Sasha had blossomed since Dad left. 'She really is. She works at the cafe in the park and she loves it there. Dad said she was an embarrassment to him doing that kind of job, but now he's not here and everything's better.'

'Good for her.'

I loved talking about how my sister was doing – I was so proud of her. Our relationship was entirely different now. We were everything to each other.

'She's doing an Open University course in forensic science, as well as growing a baby. She's going to stop the cafe in June and start again when they reopen next summer. We have Mum's life insurance. We really are fine.'

Ms Duke patted my shoulder and I knew I was free to leave.

I ran to catch up with Izzy and the others, and vaguely pretended I'd got into trouble for not concentrating in French, though I felt bad when it made everyone say what a bitch Ms Duke was. Izzy waited until we were on the way into lunch and stopped. She gave me a little hug. A faceful of wild hair, a blast of Victoria's Secret body spray.

I said to her, 'Actually she was just looking out for me.'

'I kind of knew she would be, or I'd have stayed with you.'

Izzy was small and curvy, and she had the loveliest face I'd ever seen. She was known to everyone but me as 'quiet' (and chewed bubblegum all the time because she thought it made her look hard, so people would leave her alone), but underneath it all she was funny and dark and biting, and I knew she was the best friend I could possibly have. She bleached her Afro white-blonde, which was contradictory for someone who hated attention, but I understood that she didn't care whether people looked at her or not. She just wanted to feel like herself. They could stare at her, but she would decide whether or not she was going to talk to them.

'Still,' she said, 'what *was* that? You were pretty much going at it, stabbing that book. Do you want to take some time out? I can call Sash.'

I shook my head. 'I missed too much school when Mum was sick. It took me ages to catch up so I can't miss any more now. I was just thinking about my dad. That's all. I forgot I was at school for a minute. Fucker. It's the fact that he thought he could take me away with him. It makes me feel guilty. Kind of complicit. I can't shake it.'

I could, in fact, shake it because the fact that I'd stood my ground made me feel brave and amazing. But my head was full of people who could turn blue if I thought about it. Next time I'd try another colour. I wondered whether to tell Izzy. I opened my mouth to do it, but she started talking.

'But you didn't go,' she said. 'You stood up to him. You stayed here.'

There was no arguing with that. I smiled. 'I did, didn't I?' I said. 'First time ever.'

I was officially allowed to live at home with Sasha now. When the people from social services visited, they'd found us in the cleanest, most well-organized house in the world, with my homework out on the table and Sasha (who couldn't cook) stirring a pot of vegetable soup that we'd decanted from a couple of cans, with some herbs thrown in to make it smell home-made.

It had been fine. They'd asked lots of questions and said I could stay.

Now I was terrified that my brain was stepping in to sabotage me with blue people. I was worried that if I told anyone I might end up in a psychiatric hospital, like the ones you saw in films. Maybe I did actually need some heavy-duty medication, though, because it just wasn't normal to see blue people around your school who weren't there. It had been a shit year, and stress did loads of things, but I was sure it didn't do that. Yet this had started on the day Dad left for Scotland, so of course it was connected. I'd told Sasha about it, but no one else.

I filled my lunch tray with a jacket potato and cheese plus a side salad, and a massive cookie. Sasha had made me promise to eat properly at lunchtime and I did like food. The cafeteria was clattery and full of people pushing and shoving, and I made my way through the middle, confident, at least, in my place here. I was in Year Eleven, the top year in the school, but even back in Year Seven I'd been fine socially. I was tall enough, clever enough, sporty enough and had enough friends.

I had always felt a bit enchanted: I didn't have acne, or awful periods, or any of the other things that tripped people

43

up when they hit twelve. I had a wonderful mother and had mostly managed to keep out of the way of an unpredictable father. I had a big sister who thought I was annoying. I'd been able to see my path: I would do well in exams, take four A levels and go to university to study history. After that I was going to do a law conversion course and become a human rights lawyer. I used to feel that my biggest problem would be summoning the courage to tell Dad that I didn't want to be a doctor, and then having to deal with the aftermath of his anger.

Then everything had gone to shit.

Mum got ill and, in spite of the positive thinking and the healthy eating – in spite of the fucking chemotherapy – she died. I'd watched her change, had seen what the treatments did to her body (ballooning with steroids, shrinking down to nothing). She lost her hair and tied a scarf round her head because she didn't have the energy for a wig. 'I don't care if people stare,' she'd said. 'So what? Let them. I don't need to make strangers feel better.'

She taught me how to be calm. She showed me breathing exercises and made a magical place for us in space. 'I need you to think,' she said, 'about Venus. The cloud tops of Venus. I looked it up and that's the best place in the solar system for people to live, apart from Earth. It sounds lovely. Close your eyes and imagine we're there. That's what I do when it gets too much. I go to Venus.'

Even the cloud tops of Venus didn't have enough magic: from the day she told us about it to her final day was less than three months. For fifteen years I had lived through

March the fourteenth without even knowing that it would be the day my mum died. Nearly a year later I was stabbing my book in a French lesson because I was seeing things that couldn't be there.

I missed my mum so much that I couldn't think about her. I couldn't bear to remember, so I forced myself to forget. I was angry with her for being ill and dying. I was furious in a way that made no sense because it hadn't been her fault that she got cancer. Shit happened, and that was shit. I felt terrible for being angry. When I'd briefly seen the counsellor Sasha had arranged for us, he'd given me ways out of that thought spiral. They had helped. Except now. They weren't working on the people I was seeing all over the school.

Izzy and I sat at our usual table. I checked the dining hall. Everyone seemed real.

'Hey, Ariel,' said Priya, sitting opposite us, putting down a tray that held a salad, a Diet Coke, a Twix, a Snickers and a Creme Egg. 'When's the baby due?'

I made a show of looking at my stomach in mock offence, which got the laugh I'd wanted. This was how I made it through school these days.

'July,' I said. 'After the exams.'

'Considerate,' said Izzy.

'Are you excited?' said Priya. 'About being an auntie?'

'Course I am!'

'It's amazing,' she said. 'The most grown-up thing I've ever heard. A new generation.'

'Yeah.'

I looked up, distracted by a movement off to my left. There

was another of them. Two more. Two people who I knew weren't really there. A girl and a boy walking together. I thought of the colour blue and there it was, bursting out of them. I thought of green, red, purple, yellow, but none of them worked. Only blue.

I tried to process it . . . They were in a different school uniform. They weren't Victorian or Elizabethan or anything like that, and they didn't wear white sheets. So they weren't ghosts because ghosts, by their very nature, were from the past. Were they from the future? Or from a different present? An alternative blue universe in which this school had a better uniform? Or was I just making it all up, pulling them from some corner of my weird brain?

I looked over my shoulder. They were behind me too. There was a whole group of them carrying lunch trays. They were walking towards me and, as they got closer, they slowed down until there were ghosts all round the table. The whole room shone bright blue. I stared in horror as they put their trays on the table. A boy sat down where Izzy was, and I could see both of them occupying the same space. Izzy was just eating her pizza and didn't notice at all. A girl sat on – in? – Priya. And then I felt a prickly cold going through me and, when I looked, a boy with ginger hair was lowering himself into my seat.

I pushed the chair back and ran out of the room.

6

I wake up, telling the alarm clock to fuck off. It's the worst sound in the world except for the sound of the blow to the head that hits in the very place that will kill you instantly.

I jerk wide awake. I had a nightmare. I can remember quite a lot of it and I don't want that in my head. I sit up. Clothes on the floor. Books on the table. Half-light coming through the curtains.

French exchange! I yawn and rub my eyes. It's the French trip today. I have to go to school, which is unfair, but this evening we'll get on the coach and go to Plymouth, and catch the night ferry to Roscoff, and then tomorrow we'll drive to St Etienne.

Like the band.

I'm going to stay with Enzo. I like Enzo, but I don't want to go on this trip.

'Joe!' That's Dad.

'Awake!'

'Good lad.'

I put on my dressing gown because I'm only wearing pants, and Dad always has to see us up and about before he goes to work. I decide to have breakfast first and then shower and dress. After that dream I need peanut-butter toast to give me the strength to do anything else. And a cup of tea with two sugars.

I'm not at all hungry. Still, the idea of those things makes me feel better.

Dad is dressed for work in his branded polo shirt. He laughs as I stumble downstairs, yawning.

'Sleeping Beauty!' he says.

'Next time I want a handsome prince,' I tell him, very grumpy. 'Not a nightmare.'

'Oh, mate,' he says. 'Nightmares suck. What was it about?'

I can't bear to tell him, so I say, 'Zombies.'

'Oh sorry, Joe,' says Gus, behind me. 'That wasn't a dream. I mean, look at you. You really were visited by a zombie in the night. It ate your brain.'

'I'll eat *your* brain.'

'Children!' says Dad. 'Come on. You're worse than the toddlers. No brain eating. Joe, I'll be home at five twenty, so I'll have plenty of time before we need to get you back to school for seven and wave you off.'

'OK.'

'French exchange!' says Gus, pointing at me and looking smug.

'I don't think I'll go,' I say.

'Yes, you will,' says Dad. He kisses the top of my head. 'Bye, babies.'

He leaves.

'Can I live under your bed for the week?' I say to Gus as soon as the door closes.

'Nope,' he says. 'You can go to Enzo's house and *parler français*.'

'Mean.'

'You'll be fine,' he says. 'I wish I could go.'

'You can pretend to be me.'

He puts his arms out in front of him and does a zombie walk. 'Hello,' he says in a monotone. 'My name is Joseph. *Je parle français tray byen. Je voudrais des brains, s'il vous plaît*.'

I roll my eyes. 'That's not even a zombie voice. You're doing a zombie walk with a robot voice. Want some toast?'

I should be hungry. I eat anyway.

I stand on the corner and wait for Troy, who should be mad at me. Mr Armstrong offers to give me his old francs, and then Troy and I walk to school and I don't find the words to tell him that I stole his trophy. He's excited about the trip. I should be too, but all I feel is horror. Troy is brilliant at French and I'm average, but it's not that.

'Wish we were going to Paris,' he says. 'Now, if it was Paris I would seriously just stay there. Eiffel Tower. Mona Lisa. The city of love.'

'Would you find a French girlfriend?'

'Easily. We'd live in an attic overlooking the river, and I'd probably discover I was an amazing artist and so I'd become the new Picasso or something.'

'Yeah,' I say. 'Shame we're not going to Paris then. We go past it on the bus, so you could jump out.'

He nods. 'Might do. Tell the driver to stop because I'm sick and then run off to my new life. So what's up with you?'

I shiver. I should pretend to be fine, but instead I say, 'No idea.'

'Oh, it'll be great,' he says. 'Enzo sounds cool, doesn't he?'

'Yes.'

'So don't worry. Do you think . . .' He pauses and looks at me nervously. 'I mean, it's a shame your mum's not home because she'd make you feel better, right?'

I sigh. 'It's so stupid.'

'It's not,' he says. 'It's just unlucky. Bad timing, right?'

'Right,' I say, but I'm not really sure what he means.

I sit in registration and take out the photo Enzo sent me when we started writing. He does look nice. I'm sure we'll be friends when we meet.

I read his letter again. The words swim before my eyes. They are saying the wrong things.

Dear Joseph,

I know you will not see this message. But I want to write to you to say I am so sad and worried for you. I hope you will be found soon.

Please come to visit us when you are safe again. You are always in my heart. I send you flowers.

Enzo

I blink. That is wrong.

I focus and look again. This time it says:

Dear Joseph,
   Thank you for your letter. I am very happy that
you are coming to visit with me . . .

It says, in fact, exactly the things that it should say.

I punch the side of my head in frustration, again and again, and when I see people looking at me I change it into a comedy 'd'oh' thing like Homer Simpson. Enzo is excited to meet me, and we're going to do all the fun things there are to do in St Etienne. Apparently there are some good museums. I have no idea why I thought it said anything else. My heart is pounding. It was so clear. The words were right there. They were in front of my eyes. I saw them, as real as anything else. More real than most things. But they weren't there at all.

By the end of school I'm a mess. I cannot overcome the feeling that something terrible is about to happen. I can't go home so I set off into town and go to the mall. I buy a Coke and walk into a man who swears at me. I swear back at him and run to the secret room so I can try to pull myself together.

I sit there, feeling like shit, and then the door opens and everything goes blank.

7

I marched along the corridor with my head down. All I wanted was to get out of school and home to Sasha. I never saw the blue people at home, but at school now they were in every corner, lurking, waiting for me. I wished they could see me. I wished I could talk to them and find out what was going on.

Tomorrow, I thought. Tomorrow I would try again. I'd find one of them, on their own, and look them in the eye and speak.

I often thought about taking a day off to have a break from them. But it was GCSE year, and I was only going to be at this school for a couple more months, so I forced myself to keep coming in.

Mr Morrow was at the other end of the corridor, so I pulled my stupid blazer on. Being caught without your blazer in the corridors, or with your skirt hitched up, or (most criminal of all) wearing the demonic 'branded trainers' was the outside world's equivalent of being caught with a bag of cocaine and cash, speeding the wrong way down the motorway in a stolen car.

'All right, Ariel?' he said as we passed, but thankfully he didn't stop.

'Fine, thanks,' I said. Izzy had disappeared to hockey. I stuck in my earphones and set off home.

I would once have been doing hockey too, but I stopped everything like that when Mum got ill because why would you chase a stupid ball round a pitch with a stick when your mum might be going to die? Then she did die, and of course I hadn't gone back because why would you chase a ball with a stick when your mum was dead? I had loved it, and that love was switched off like a bathroom light, with a ping.

There were three of them standing between me and the door, talking to each other. I tried not to look, but I did anyway. They were just regular teenagers in their school uniform. I thought *blue* and the blue light shone round them all. It was as if they each had a blue light inside them that was only activated when I thought of the word. I closed my eyes and walked fast, right through the middle of them. Was I imagining the shiver?

I knew I wasn't.

'Oh, sorry!' It was a girl, a real one, who must have been Year Seven because she was tiny. She was apologizing because I'd walked into her with my eyes closed.

'Oh God, no,' I said. 'I'm sorry. I wasn't looking where I was going.'

'S'OK.' She scurried away, waving to someone.

I pulled my backpack on properly, turned up the Idles on my phone, and walked home with the most confident strides I could manage because I knew that if I let myself stop I'd collapse.

*

Sasha was in the kitchen, looking from a cookery book to a pile of vegetables. She had always been a fan of junk food and famously hated cooking, and I laughed at the sight of her so far outside her comfort zone. It felt good to laugh.

'Healthy-food time,' she said. 'How hard can it be, right?'

'Right.' I'd always enjoyed food tech and, even though I gave it up in Year Nine, I felt I knew more than she did about this. I stood beside her and looked at the book. 'What are we making?'

She pushed it towards me. 'Veg chilli. Good for the baby.'

I bit my lip. Veg chilli had been one of Mum's dishes. She'd often made it, and although we'd moaned about the mushrooms and pepper, the lack of meat, we'd loved it. Mountains of cheddar cheese on top, melting into it. Sour cream and (if we were lucky) guacamole on the side. We used to have it at least once a week, when Mum was well.

I was annoyed with myself for wanting to cry again. I had cried absolutely loads about her, had sat in front of counsellors without being able to find any words, had talked endlessly with Sasha and even Ms Duke, and now we both knew we had to get on with it. I couldn't sit around crying any more.

Who was I kidding? Sasha put her arms round me and, even though she was so much shorter, I let her look after me, just for a moment. Then I patted her shoulder, patted the baby and managed to say, 'Yeah. Vegetable chilli. Good idea. Vitamins.' I pushed her gently aside, wiped my eyes with the back of my hand, and started chopping red onions, since I was crying already.

We hadn't talked about the anniversary. I didn't know how we were supposed to get through it.

Later, we sat side by side on the sofa, watching a cooking programme and eating bowls of chilli that wasn't as good as Mum's, but that was, nonetheless, acceptable. The cheese was melting. The peppers were a bit burnt, and there was no guacamole because of course we didn't have an avocado. However, it was the best thing we'd eaten for ages. Most nights we had variations of things on toast. Beans, usually, or peanut butter, and then a banana or apple to make it healthy.

'Do you think,' I said, watching men shovelling food into their mouths on the screen. 'Do you think I should make a doctor's appointment? I'm still seeing the . . .' I stopped. I didn't want to say *ghosts*. They weren't ghosts.

'The hallucinations?' said Sasha. 'Oh, poor Arry. Yeah, maybe you should see a doctor. Why not? I mean, they'll say it's stress, and it probably is, but I know that sounds patronizing. You didn't mention it when you were having the counselling?'

'It wasn't happening then. It only started when Dad left. Sasha, I'm scared. What if they say I'm mad and send me away to a –' I reached for the most dramatic thing I could to make my fears into a joke – 'a Victorian asylum? Where I'd be chained to a bed and fed gruel, and the ghosts there would be *really* bad. I mean, they'd be proper ghosts, right? Sheet ones.'

'That's a possibility,' she conceded, 'but it's just a chance you'll have to take.' She paused, serious again. 'If you don't want to do anything official you could always talk to your French teacher. Hey, feel this. Hang on.'

She put my hand on her bump and I waited. I could feel a hard little lump in there, a foot probably.

'Hey, baby,' I said. 'Hey, nephew.'

We were spending an inordinate amount of time working on the perfect name for him. Sasha liked the fancy names (her current favourites were Rafael and Gabriel). His middle name should have been the male version of Mum's name, Anna, except that as far as we could work out that would have been Alan or Andrew, and Sasha didn't fancy either of them. 'They don't sound anything like Mum,' she said, so I was allowed to choose the middle name, subject to Sasha's approval, as Jai was currently too freaked out to be allowed a say. I spent far longer thinking of boys' names than you'd expect, but I didn't currently have anything that was exactly right.

The baby kicked me and just for a moment all the bad feelings went away. I cuddled up to my sister. We never used to be friends. Now she was everything.

By Monday I was feeling strong, but as soon as I left the house I started to freak out again. I went and stood on the beach in the blustery sunshine, and looked out at the sea. I inhaled the salty, greasy air, and took deep breaths until I thought I was ready to face school. I felt so different sometimes. Different from everyone else, and different from myself.

By the time I arrived, late, the stragglers like me were heading to their tutor rooms. I walked slowly, doing my breathing exercises, playing Mum's voice in my head talking about the cloud tops of Venus. I'd had a domestic weekend with Sasha. I'd seen the sea. I could do this.

Mum's anniversary was in three days' time. I had been motherless for a year.

I pushed my fingers through my hair, walked round the corner and stopped.

The corridor was empty because everyone but me was in tutor. However, it wasn't empty. It was crowded.

The school was bustling with hallucinations, or ghosts, or whatever they were. They were in their other uniforms, ignoring me, all getting on with their lives. I tried not to think of the colour blue, but that made it fill my mind and they all started to shine.

I'd never seen so many at once before. I forced myself to look hard while I had the chance. I could see now that their sweatshirts were burgundy, and that they were allowed to wear trainers, even branded ones.

I watched two girls talking. They weren't floaty ghosts: once you filtered out the blue they were just girls. I saw two boys standing next to each other. One was searching through his bag for something. I saw a tall girl eating a bag of crisps on her own, leaning against the wall.

They didn't seem to be from the past. If they were from the future that meant that they weren't ghosts.

It meant that if anyone was a ghost here it was me.

Was I haunting these people? Could I be the ghost?

'Ariel?'

It was, of course, Ms Duke, standing behind me.

57

'Sorry,' I said. 'Running a bit late.'

'Everything OK?' She gave me a searching look. 'You don't look as happy as I've seen you, Ariel, if I may say so.'

'I'm all right. Honestly.'

I worked very hard on those words being true. I wanted to be all right. I couldn't bear to be stopped in my tracks by a bunch of blue people who weren't really here.

It would be worse, though, to discover that I was the one who wasn't really here. Could I be dead? I didn't think I could. If I was dead then I'd be with Mum. Or she'd be here with me.

Ms D was looking at me. I tried to imagine telling her. She might help. She was one of the few people I pretty much trusted. She was waiting for me to say something more.

I looked back at the ghosts. They were still there, walking around, chatting to each other, but I couldn't hear anything. They were more like people on telly than anything else, if the telly was on mute. It was as if I was watching a programme set in a school, on a TV whose colour had gone strange, playing out in 3D against the backdrop of my real school.

Ms Duke clearly wasn't seeing them.

'I'm all right,' I said with more enthusiasm this time. 'We ate healthy food all weekend and did some housework.'

'Oh, well done! I wish I could say the same,' said Ms D, who had long grey hair in a bun and was a bit, just the tiniest bit, like my mum might have been if she'd been able to grow old. Though, up close, I now noticed that she didn't even look that old. It was just that she'd let her hair go grey. According to school gossip, she'd been married five times, though I didn't actually believe that.

58

She patted my shoulder. I looked at the corridor. I had to walk down there to get to my tutor room, but I didn't think I could do it. How was I supposed to make my way through the middle of a collection of telly-ghosts from the future?

'Will you –?' I said and then stopped. I drew a breath. 'This sounds really lame, but could you come with me to tutor? In G6? Just as far as the door?'

'Of course! Don't worry about being late, though. Mr Patel won't mind.'

'I know, but still.'

I let her get a little bit ahead and kept my eyes on her back. Every time I walked through one of them, I felt a blast of cold. I stared at Ms Duke. She was wearing regular teacher clothes: a red jacket, a black skirt, a white blouse. Her shoes clopped on the floor. She was older than Mum would ever be.

It was shit having to be brave all the time.

She pushed the door open, ushered me in and shouted across the rowdy room: 'Sorry Ariel's late, Mr Patel! My fault!', then waved at me and clopped away.

I sloped across the room and sat next to Izzy.

'All right?' I said.

'You?' said Izzy.

'Yep.'

'OK with Ms D?'

'Sure. She was just being, you know, *Is everything all right? We're always here for you*.' I tried to adopt a mildly mocking tone, but my voice cracked. Izzy put an arm round me and pulled me in close for one of her hugs.

One year. A year without Mum.

All the talking stopped when the music started. Mr Patel's way of being a *cool guy* involved him blasting us with one of his favourite songs at full volume in the morning. Today, as so often, it was 'Smells Like Teen Spirit', which got extreme approval from most of the class, and a lot of air guitar and drums. It lasted four minutes, and I lost myself in it for a while, and it felt good. Izzy and I both ended up singing along. It was impossible to talk while the music was that loud. It reset me.

After registration Izzy and I set off to history. The corridor was so full of real children that it was unremarkable. The day slipped back into being normal, or as normal as a day can be when you're particularly aware of the fact that pretty much everyone else has a mother and you don't, and you'd give anything to have her back. And that she's been gone very nearly a full year and you will never see her again.

I thought I might go to the Garden of Remembrance after school to talk to her about the hallucinations. The problem was that I hated it. This was a conundrum I often faced: there was a plaque in the garden with ANNA BROWN on it, and her dates, and it was the only place that felt like 'going to see Mum'.

But it was right next to the crematorium and there was always, always a funeral on. People would be standing around, wearing black, and it reminded me that everyone died, and that it happened all the time.

All the other places, though, had been overwritten by

things that had happened since. Nowhere else was so uncontaminatedly 'Mum'.

When I was leaving at the end of the day, I saw a boy out in the paved part of the playground. A tall boy with messy ginger hair was mooching around by himself. He looked distraught, and something about the way he was moving, his jerky walk, his spasms of grief, spoke to something in me. I was beginning to think that once you'd known actual sadness, real loss, you could recognize it in other people and I saw it in this boy.

I didn't recognize him from my year group, but it was a big school and I didn't know everyone. He could have been in Year Ten.

As I headed towards him I saw him pick up a piece of stone from the ground. There were often pebbles around that were a bit chalky, or that left a trail if you wrote with them. They were mainly used by boys to draw cocks on the tarmac. I watched him write on the wall. He was attacking it, and I walked faster, wanting to see what he was doing.

When I got there, though, I saw that he wasn't wearing our school uniform. He was wearing a burgundy sweatshirt. He was one of them. I shivered, and the boy was gone, like a TV switching off.

I looked at the words on the wall, still there even though he'd gone from my vision. They just said:

HELP ME

8

I wake after a nightmare. Someone smashed me on the head until I was dead.

I'm going on the French exchange today. I don't want to. I get through the day, feeling worse every minute, but trying to act like I don't give a shit, and then instead of going home I head to the mall.

I buy a carton of strawberry milk and a man swears at me for getting in his way. I find myself yelling at him. I go into my secret room and drop the act and let myself collapse.

I don't know what's happening, but I feel sure that there's something incredibly wrong. I've been dreading the French exchange for too long. I dread and dread and dread it, but it never happens: surely I should be on it by now? But that makes no sense.

I'm cold. I wrap myself in the pink blanket and hug my knees. I try not to cry: I have nothing to cry about, not really. Dad is brilliant, and I have Gus. Mum's one of those people who is obsessed with yoga and apparently she can't do it here, so she has to live far away for now. I can be cool with that. She didn't leave because she hated me. Did she?

I lean my head back on the wall and wish I knew how to make things better.

The door opens. I gasp and jerk my head up.

It's a girl. She has thick dark hair and she's tall and fit. We look at each other. I'm not meant to be here. She probably is: it's clearly a place for the shopworkers and I'd guess she's from H&M.

She looks scared. Scared of me? I guess no girl wants to walk into a small hidden space and find a strange mad-looking guy.

'Oh God,' she says. 'Sorry. I'm probably not allowed to be in here. I just thought . . .'

'That's OK. I don't think I'm meant to be here actually.'

'Oh! Don't you work in one of the shops?'

'Nope. I just come here to get away from everything.'

'Same.'

We look at each other and everything is marginally better. I nod at her to stay, to sit down. There's something about her. I want to talk to her.

'I'm Joe,' I say. I gesture round the room. 'Welcome to the palace.'

'I'm Ariel.'

'Like the little mermaid?'

'Yeah,' she says with a sigh. 'Like that, if you must.'

'Sorry. At least I didn't say washing powder, I guess.'

She gives me a half-smile. 'No one ever really says washing powder. I did notice it in the supermarket once and it gave me a bit of a shock. Just seeing your name on some washing-machine liquid. Like if you saw one that was called Joe.'

'Yeah,' I say. 'I'd probably buy it.'

She grins and sits at the other end of the little bench. We're close together, but far enough away that we're not in any danger of touching. She strokes the wall beside her with a fingertip.

'I wrote this,' she said. 'My first-ever vandalism.'

I can't see what she wrote, but I pretend I can and smile.

'It's about my dad,' she adds. 'I hate my dad. I wrote this so he'd know, even though he's hundreds of miles away. I thought he might feel it, through the atmosphere. I think I came here with him once or twice when I was little.'

'I hope he did feel it,' I say. Whatever he's done, if she hates him then I'm happy to hate him too.

'Why are you here?' she says.

I sigh. 'I'm going on a school trip to France tonight. I'm nervous. Staying with a French family? Weird shit. I came here to pull myself together, I guess.'

She smiles at that. 'France, though? Cool.'

'Yeah. I'm sure. I'm just a bit . . .' I don't know what to say. I used to know that kind of thing.

'My mum died almost exactly a year ago,' she says, surprising me. 'I came here today to talk to her. I don't like it at the Garden of Remembrance because of other people's funerals. I ran out of places where I felt like I could just talk to Mum in peace. So I came back here.'

'Oh shit,' I say. 'Sorry. I'll leave you.' I start to stand up. She waves me back down. She almost, but not quite, touches me. We look at each other. I shouldn't be thinking about how fit she is when she's talking about her dead mother.

'No,' she says. 'Don't worry. It's nice to meet someone new. I mean, I know I'm not really going to have a conversation with my mum because she is actually dead. I just wanted to get away from everything. I'm happy to get away from it with you.'

That makes my stomach loop. She wants to be here with me. 'I'm really sorry,' I say. 'My mum went away to do a yoga course. She always wanted to live in India. She's been gone for ages and I don't think she's coming back. I miss her. But that's, like, a million times better. I'm not comparing.'

Shut up, Joe. I *really* don't need to make this girl's tragedy about me.

She looks up. Her eyes are big and very dark brown. Again, we hold some kind of weird eye contact for a really long time. Something in me wakes up a bit.

'That's OK,' she says. 'No wonder you're feeling shit. Like, the only thing I've got on my side is this: Mum didn't want to leave us. And she never would have chosen to go. Never. So I guess that makes it better in a way. Do you have a dad?'

I grin. 'Yeah. He's great. He used to be a clown, among other things. Now he runs a nursery. He entertains the kids with all his juggling and that.'

'That's awesome!' she says. 'What nursery? I'm going to need to know about that kind of thing soon.' She catches my expression. 'I'm not pregnant,' she says with a laugh. 'My sister is.'

I tell her about Bouncers, and we talk about her sister's baby for a while and then there's a ping from her pocket, and she checks something and says, 'Oh, I have to go. I'm glad you were here. This has cheered me right up.'

'Me too,' I say. 'See you in here again maybe?'

She gives me a little wave. 'I hope so,' she says. 'Have fun in France!'

I want to call her back. I want to talk to her more. She's the only person who's made me feel real for a long time. I open my mouth to ask for her number, but she's gone. I walk over to the wall, to see what she wrote there about her dad, but there's just a picture of a smiley face, which makes no sense, unless there's some kind of deeper meaning that I'm not getting.

I trace it with my fingertip anyway. It's just two eyes and a mouth, but Ariel drew them, and she's the only other person I've ever met in here and I really, really want to see her again.

9

I walked away with a spring in my step, smiling at everyone. I'd met a boy and I liked him. That hadn't happened since before Mum got ill. I met a boy. I liked him. Had he liked me? I hadn't felt that he *didn't* like me. That was a start. I wasn't great at boy stuff and I didn't really have a clue.

Still, I was spontaneously smiling for the first time in over a year. *Was that OK?* I asked Mum in my head. *Is it all right if I feel happy for a bit?*

I smiled even more, imagining Mum's delight.

I met a boy, Mum, I whispered as I stepped out of the shopping centre into the sharp wind that was blowing off the sea. I stood still and waited. Although her voice didn't answer (try as I might, I couldn't summon her), I felt her glow through the biting wind. I tried to imagine bringing Joe home, if things had been different.

'Mum, this is Joe,' I would have said. 'My boyfriend.' (Yes, I was getting ahead of myself.)

'Wonderful to meet you, Joe!' said imaginary Mum. Joe would have talked about his week in France while Mum asked the right questions. 'It's a shame you didn't get a chance to do something like that, Ariel,' she'd have said. 'What an adventure!'

Mum would have loved that I'd met Joe. I knew that much.

I walked faster. I didn't even know him. We'd sat at opposite ends of a bench, but it was a small bench and we were close together, and I was sure there'd been something between us. He was objectively gorgeous.

I tried to recalibrate the scene I'd just imagined, but with Sasha in Mum's place. That could work, and this time, crucially, it could actually happen.

I was envious of his trip to France. I didn't know which school he went to: he was wearing a blue hoodie over his uniform and I hadn't thought to ask, but ours didn't run a French exchange.

I should have got his number. Was I going to have to keep hanging around in the room in the shopping centre, after his French trip, in the hope of bumping into him again? The idea made me smile.

Sasha was sitting on the floor, her feet stretched out in front of her, leaning back on the sofa and watching a Netflix documentary about street food in Bangkok. Her hair was a tangle of dark blonde around her face.

'Here you go.' I put the shopping down.

She'd texted me to pick up some Pot Noodles on the way home, and against my better judgement I'd done it, imagining myself putting one in the basket for Joe too. I liked a Pot Noodle, and we hardly ever had them because of the wasteful packaging, lack of nutrition, and so on. Mum had hated them.

'Oh, Sasha!' I said, suddenly understanding. 'Did the amazing Thai food on telly make you want a Pot Noodle? That's a tiny bit tragic, you know.'

She looked up. 'It's not. It's a brilliant short cut. The closest thing I could think of that involved no effort whatsoever. Near enough, right?'

'I'd have bought real noodles. And some things to cook with them. We could have made it like that.' I pointed to the screen, where a woman was stir-frying noodles on a grill in a Bangkok street.

'It's fine,' said Sasha. 'Stick the kettle on.'

I shrugged and flicked the switch. However, I decided that I was going to be a better sister and aunt than this. While the kettle was boiling, I sat at the table and wrote the days of the week on the back of a council tax envelope. Then I tried to think of seven different dinners, which was surprisingly difficult.

Proper noodles
Pasta
Pizza
Chilli

I stared at the page.

'Can you think of three things that people eat?' I said. 'Things that aren't noodles, pasta, pizza or chilli?'

Sasha didn't look away from the screen, but shook her head. 'I don't think people eat anything else,' she said. 'That's all there is.' Then, after a few seconds, she said, 'Curry.'

'Oh yeah.' I added: *Curry*.

'Chips?'

'Nope. I'm doing a healthy-meal plan here.'

'Salad? Lasagne?'

'Salad's not a whole dinner. Lasagne comes under pasta.'

'OK, Miss Picky.'

After a stupid amount of googling, I filled the empty slots with sausage and mash and some kind of fish, which would be particularly good for the baby. I was pleased with myself. It had taken so long that I had to reboil the kettle for the Pot Noodles. I stuck the list on the fridge with a Modern Toss magnet, and while the noodles were reassembling themselves, or whatever it was they did, I made a shopping list.

Meeting Joe had given me something. He made me want to be my best self. I'd been trudging along, believing Sasha when she said my only job was to get through my exams, but in fact I needed to do more than that. She looked after me, and I was going to look after her – properly – too.

Tomorrow, even though Joe would be in France, I'd go to the secret room and write something nicer on the wall for him to see when he came back. I knew I couldn't write my phone number, but I'd think of something good. Maybe I'd write it in French. That would be exceptionally flirtatious, and not like usual-me at all.

Then we might meet there again one day. I hoped so.

10

I wake up in the middle of a dream, and for some reason I urgently need to remember it. It feels like it's the most important thing in the world. There's a schoolbook next to the bed so I scrabble around for my pencil case and write on the back cover of the book. When I come to properly, with my pen in my hand and my eyes still half sealed with sleep, I look at what I've written:

Hurt head. French exchange? Girl in cupboard.

Ooookayyyyyy. Even more random than expected. Yeah, this is the day of the French exchange, and I'm dreading it, but if my dream was a mash-up of hurting my head, not wanting to go on the French exchange and some girl being in a cupboard, I don't think it's quite as life-changing as it felt a moment ago.

I touch my head, just to be sure. It doesn't hurt at all.

What kind of wanker writes his dream on his actual maths book? That's stupid. My blue curtains are half closed, so I fling them open and then check my cupboard just in case there is a girl in there. Obviously there isn't. I don't have a girl in my life. Or a boy. I used to have all the offers. I fancied Jemima with every atom of my being, but she thought I was an idiot, plus she was in the year above and didn't want to date down.

And there was Marco. I shake my head and send him out of it.

I'm downstairs before Dad and, for the first time ever, decide to make him a cup of tea and some toast. He beams when he sees it, then winces when he takes a sip. He knocks it back anyway, then makes himself a second cup and drinks it with evident relief as he eats the toast. At least I got that part right.

'Have some yourself,' he says, pushing a jammy half-slice towards me. I'm not at all hungry. I eat it anyway.

'Love you, Dad,' I say before he leaves for work. I didn't mean to say it: the words jumped out before I could stop them. I'm not sure I've ever actually said anything like that to him before. I would have thought it babyish and lame. Today the words just spoke themselves.

Dad looks surprised. I see him waiting for me to say '. . . not', but even I'm not that much of a twat. He doubles back to hug me.

'Thank you, Jojo,' he says, patting my back. 'I love you too. Very much. So does your mother. So, in his way, does Angus. We don't say that enough, do we?'

'Thanks, Dad,' I say, and a flood of warmth sweeps through me. It's like wetting yourself, but in a good way. 'Have a good day at work.'

He smiles. 'Don't worry, Joseph. Your trip will be fine, I promise. You'll have a whale of a time. We toured France once, back when I was in the little circus. We didn't exactly play the . . . the . . . the Paris Aerodrome.' I snort at his made-up venue. 'We were in towns and villages around the south, doing shows outside village halls. It was magical. The French are fabulous people. You'll have a . . . a *très bien* time too. Damn, wish I could think of the French for absolutely brilliant.'

He looks at me.

'*Génial?*' I hazard.

'Yeah. France is *génial*. Anyway. I'd best go and wrangle some little demons. But I'll be back to drive you up to school, OK?'

I nod. 'See you later.'

I watch him leave. I'll never see him again.

I shake myself. Of course I'll see him again. What was that? He just said he'll be back after work. There's no need for me to feel devastated. It was a dream. A girl in a cupboard. A head injury. A dream.

I walk with Troy. He's nice to me, even though I stole his football trophy, because he doesn't know it was me. He makes me laugh all the way to school. I'll try to put it back into his bag and then we won't ever have to talk about it. I try to avoid Lucas. I see Jemima from a distance and, though I know I had a huge crush on her, I feel disconnected, still living in the aftermath of my nightmare. I think I glimpse the back of Marco's head in a corridor, and remember the friendship that became so secret, so intense, that we couldn't even look at each other any more. Again, it doesn't feel like something that happened to me.

I try to ground myself. I want to remember yesterday, but can't make it come into focus. What the fuck has happened to my brain? I feel like I might have got paralytically drunk. Did I? Was there beer? Vodka? What else could have done this to me? Drugs?

I hide it, overcompensate by being loud.

After school I go to the secret room at Beachview. I don't know why. My legs just walk me there. I buy a drink that I don't want. I walk into a man who swears. I swear back at him and walk off. He shouts, but I don't listen.

I'm wrapped in Mum's pink blanket when the door opens and a girl comes in. She looks half familiar, but not. She's fit. I fancy her at once, then congratulate myself for feeling something so straightforward. Things shift and become a little bit better.

I stand up.

'Sorry,' I say, producing my most charming smile. 'I don't think I'm meant to be in here. I'll leave.'

She frowns and then gives me a massive smile.

'Joe!' she says. 'Hey! How come you're not in France?'

'I'm off in a few hours,' I tell her. 'How did you know?' She knows my name. I should know her. She's tall and fit. I'm sure I'd remember her.

'You told me,' she says. 'I thought you were going last night. You told me you were going last night, in fact. You did.' She seems to think about it for a while, then shrugs. 'Anyway, whatever. This is nice. How was your day today?'

Girl in cupboard. This is kind of a cupboard. It's definitely a girl.

'I think I might have seen you in my dream,' I say.

'Did you? That's cool.' She carries on talking as if we were the best of friends. She's saying how she's going to make a vegetable chilli for her sister once a week and that it makes them emotional when they have it because of their mum. I don't really listen to the words because I'm too busy looking at her. She is so alive. She's talking just to me. I know I'm gazing at her like an idiot, but she doesn't seem to mind.

I pretend to know about her family because I can tell that I'm meant to, and soon enough I've caught up. Her mother died nearly a year ago; her sister's pregnant and her dad left. She hates him, which seems reasonable.

We chat for a bit, about my family and hers, and then she says, 'Shit, I have to go.' She starts to say something, then stops, then starts again, then stops.

'What is it?' I say.

'It's just,' she says, 'do you want to swap numbers? I'd like to hear about your French trip when you're back. Maybe we could meet somewhere else. Take it out of the room, you know?'

I know I'm beaming.

'Yes,' I say. 'Yes. That would be great.' I tell her our number and she types it into some sort of PalmPilot thing. She asks for my mobile number too, looking a bit amused, and I give her that, pleased I can remember it.

She says, 'Brilliant. Have an amazing trip. Can't wait to hear all about it!'

For a second she looks as if she wants to hug me, but the moment passes and she gives me a little wave, and is gone.

She pops back in.

'I meant to ask – which school do you go to?' she says. 'I forgot.'

I say, 'Beachview.'

'Like this mall?'

'Yeah.'

She blows me a kiss and is gone.

She blows me a kiss.

A kiss.

And she's gone.

11

The vegetable chilli was perfect this time. We ate it sitting on the sofa because no one could stop us. In fact, the table had just become a place where we put random things: the sofa was our dining table now. The chilli was emotional because of it being Mum's thing, but I'd decided to conquer it, to push past the sadness of taking it over from her, so that it could become a family heirloom.

'A family heirloom!' Sasha was laughing. 'Oh, Mermaid. Explain.'

'It's for the baby,' I said. 'When he's big enough for proper food, I'll make it for him and tell him it was Granny Anna's dish, and that means that, in a weird way, Mum's cooking it for her grandson, and I'm a kind of medium, but not in a creepy way.'

'You're weird,' said Sasha. 'But yeah. I like it. We can do that, hey, beanie?' She rubbed her stomach. 'Can you make this at least twice a week, do you think? It feels so good for me.'

'Can it be consecutive days so I just make it once, but massive?'

'Sure.'

'Done.'

Izzy came over after dinner. We left Sasha doing some forensic-science reading and went to my room. It was a small bedroom, always quite messy, but I was pleased all over again, every time I walked in there, that they hadn't made me move somewhere else when Dad left, and that he hadn't forced me to go to Inverness.

I sometimes wondered what my life would be like if he had. He could have done it easily. He was a doctor: he could have drugged me and put me in the car while I was asleep, and by the time I came round I would have been halfway to Scotland. The fact that he'd woken me up and asked me to go had to mean that he didn't really care whether I said yes or no. If he'd *really* wanted me with him I knew I'd be there.

I tried to imagine myself in Scotland, starting all over again with only Dad as my family. I pictured Sasha alone in this big house eating Pot Noodles. It made me shudder.

I wondered whether we'd ever see him again. Although I would have given absolutely anything to have had Mum back, I didn't want to see Dad at all, though a stupid part of me still half hoped to see his name when I looked at my emails. It would be nice if he cared about us a tiny bit.

'What's in your parents' room?' Izzy said, looking at the closed door across the landing.

'Their furniture,' I said. 'But we're going to make it into a nursery. I think Sasha's getting a charity to pick up the bed and stuff at some point, and then we'll paint the walls, like, bright green or something for the baby, and we'll make it into the best kid's room ever.'

'Yay,' said Izzy. 'I'll help.'

'Thanks.'

I offered her a Penguin biscuit and opened one myself.

'So, what's going on with you?' she said. 'Something's happening, right?'

I finished my mouthful and grinned.

'Something is happening,' I said. 'Yes. I met a boy. I mean, I hardly know him. I've met him twice. We just happened to be in the same place at the same time. I keep thinking about him, though. I really like him. I think . . . I think I like a boy, Izzy! It's been ages. I haven't fancied anyone since Jack Lockett. And definitely not since Mum. You know.'

'Oh my God!' She bounced on my bed, genuinely excited, and I realized that Izzy hadn't had any love interest for just as long as me. Longer. 'Tell me everything. Where? What's his name? Everything.'

'I met him at Beachview,' I said. 'Remember I said that on the day my dad left I went and found a little room there, that I kind of remembered? And I wrote on the wall that I hated him?' She nodded. 'Well, I went in again yesterday, and then today, and both times there was someone already there. A boy. Joe. He's going on a school trip to France, leaving about now, but he's back next week and I've got his number.'

'Amazing. What's he like?'

'Really good-looking. He looks a bit like . . . like.' I scrambled around for a comparison. 'I don't know. He doesn't look like anyone except himself.'

'Who'd play him in the biopic?'

I thought about it, unexpectedly thrown. 'Robert Pattinson,' I said in the end. 'As Cedric Diggory. But that's very, *very* approximate.' I frowned. 'He doesn't look like that, but that would be the Hollywood version, I think. His mum's doing a yoga course in India. He lives with his dad and his brother. He's a bit weird, but I kind of like that.'

'How old?'

'Our age,' I said, then adjusted it to the actual truth. 'Bit younger actually. He's fifteen.'

'Which school?'

'He said it's called Beachview. Like the mall.'

'Is it a posh school?'

I thought about that. A few things fell into place. There were loads of little private schools around the area. It made sense. That would be why I didn't recognize him.

'I guess,' I said.

'Fancy!'

'I know.'

'A rich boyfriend! A toy boy!' cooed Izzy. 'And a good-looking one at that.'

'He's not my boyfriend. I won't see him for over a week.'

'Text him! Tell him you want to see him when he's back. Go on. Do it. He'll get it. It's France: you can text people there.'

'No.' I looked at her. 'Shall I?' She nodded. 'What shall I say?'

We crafted the perfect casual message. I looked for him on WhatsApp, but he wasn't there. I couldn't find him on anything else without knowing his surname. I copied our message and sent it as a text, then stared at the phone and waited.

A moment later I got a 'delivery failure' notification.

12

I go to school. I go to the mall. I buy a Mars milkshake just for the hell of it and walk into an angry man. I don't want to go to France.

I wrap myself in the blanket. The door opens. A girl is there. I've met her before, but I don't know who she is.

'Oh, for fuck's sake,' she says, and she looks super pissed off.

'Sorry.' I jump up. 'I guess I'm not meant to be in here. I'll leave.'

'Joe!' She knows my name and she's angry.

'Sorry,' I say again. I need to get away from her: there's a storm behind her eyes. 'I'm going, honestly.'

'Has anything you told me been true?' she demands. 'One single thing? You're supposed to be in France, for a start, and –'

'No.' I interrupt her. 'No, I'm going tonight. Tonight we set off on the French exchange.' It feels like a mantra.

'No.' She stands in the doorway, blocking my exit, her hands on her hips. 'Yesterday you said you were going to

France. The day before that you said you were going to France. The phone number you gave me doesn't work. The school you go to doesn't exist. It's just the old name for my school. I looked it all up. Everything you told me was a crock of shit.'

I am too confused to say anything for quite a long time. She just stands and waits, and in the end I say: 'I'm sorry. Have we met before?'

'You're a fucking psycho!' she shouts. 'Yeah, we've met twice before, as you very well know. The past two days. I thought we were friends. You've been lying the whole time. I'm going now and you'll never see me again.'

She's still standing in the doorway, so I can't leave because I really don't want to have to push past her. I do recognize her, but I don't know who she is. I don't remember speaking to her before. I have no idea what she's talking about, which one of us is mad here.

'Sorry,' I say. The last thing I need right now is some strange girl telling me how crap I am.

'What's going on, though? Who are you? Why do you lie all the time?'

I feel my eyes pricking with tears and try to blink them away. I want to punch the wall. I have no idea what's going on. Who is this girl and why does she hate me? Why does she think I lie all the time? I don't. I don't think I do, anyway.

'I don't know what you're talking about.' I turn away and – why not? – I do it. I punch the wall. I hit it hard, but my hand doesn't hurt. It should hurt. I want to cry.

'Do you have, like, amnesia or something?' Her voice is softer.

'I don't think so! I don't know. Maybe I do. Everything feels strange. I think it has for ages.'

'You literally don't remember that you met me yesterday and the day before?'

I shake my head. I think it's probably best if I run away. I take a step towards her, but she still doesn't move from the doorway. I take another and she steps away, just a bit, and now I'm in the middle of some kind of full breakdown, so I just try to push past her so I can run home and probably forget this ever happened, but it doesn't work. I try to nudge her out of the way in the least aggressive way I can, but it doesn't work because my hand goes right through her.

It's as if she's not there at all.

13

Joe and I went back into the room and sat down. I was trembling. I met a boy and got excited, only to discover first of all that he was ghosting me, and then that he was *ghosting* me. Or was I ghosting him?

I tried to think of any time when I might have died without noticing it, but I couldn't pinpoint one. I supposed, though, that all it took was one road crossing gone wrong.

But if I was dead where was Mum?

I thought of the figures I saw at school. I'd seen hundreds of them. No one else, as far as I knew, had set eyes on a single one. This was the next step. Now I'd actually had two conversations with someone who wasn't really there. I was completely losing the plot. That was what was happening. Ariel Brown needed psychiatric help.

I looked at him. I filled my head with the colour blue and there it was, a blue light shining out of him, all around him.

'What year is it?' said Joe, once we were sitting next to each other.

'I've been seeing ghosts all over the place,' I said. 'Not ghosts. Future people maybe. Hallucinations.' Then I added, 'It's 2019.'

When I looked up, I saw he was staring into my face. He was stricken.

'Are you serious?' he said.

This was it. He was going to be from 2050 or something. I was about to find out something unthinkable about myself. I grabbed the wall to keep myself upright. My voice was quiet. 'What year is it for you?'

'It's 1999,' he said. 'And I thought *that* was modern.'

For some reason we both burst out laughing. We laughed until we cried. It felt good to lose control for a while. I didn't care that I was crying with laughter in front of a boy I liked, now that I knew. I grabbed at him to steady myself, but my hand went right through his arm. I couldn't believe I'd forgotten already.

I wasn't the ghost. It wasn't me.

'OK,' I said. 'OK. This is weird. You're not the only . . . person like you. That I see. I hate it when I see the other ones. They don't see me. They don't notice me at all. They walk right through me. I don't hate seeing you.'

'Thanks,' he said. 'I'll take that.'

'I mean, you can hear me and you seem like a . . . like a real boy.'

'Like Pinocchio,' he said. 'Are you serious, though? *2019*?'

I watched his face. Now that we'd stopped laughing, he was looking very confused indeed.

*

86

Meeting Joe changed everything. It gave me hope. It made me see that, in this strange universe, I might be able to see Mum again one day. It went through me like lightning. Everything changed. Perhaps I would talk to her like I was talking to him. This was everything in the world that I wanted becoming possible.

Anna Brown, I said in my head as I watched Joe working out what being from the past actually implied. *Anna Brown, come to me. Mum. Please. Mum. I need you.* I thought of Mum, and the colour blue, as hard as I could.

'I can't be a ghost,' he said. 'I'm not dead. I'd know if I was dead, wouldn't I?'

Joe and I went to the same school. Sometime before Sasha started there, Beachview Secondary had become the South East Devon Learning Academy, known to everyone as Sedla, which was widely agreed to be a stupid name for a school.

We talked about details, but the magic of it all pulsed through me. It *was* magic. Ghosts were real. Even if Joe was alive somewhere in 2019, I was talking to his past self right now, and so it was possible to communicate with someone from the past and that meant I could talk to Mum again.

I didn't want to leave this room. I had found Joe, a link to 1999, and I never wanted to stop talking to him. I wanted him to tell me everything about what it was like to be him, and whether he knew other ghosts, but I knew he wasn't ready to do that, so we talked about easier things at first.

In Joe's world it was 1999, and he was about to go on a French exchange trip. In my world it was 2019 and Mum had been dead for a year tomorrow. In his world she was alive, but I was nearly four years away from being born. Sasha was in his world as a baby. She could have been one of the kids Joe's dad looked after. Had she gone to a nursery called Bouncers? I would find out.

'What happens next year?' Joe said. 'Do the computers stop working in the year 2000? Because that's what they're saying.'

I laughed. 'The millennium bug! Y2K! I've heard of that. No. Either it was never going to happen anyway, or they fixed it in time. It was a total non-event.'

'Oh. Cool. So what's been happening instead?'

I gave him highlights of the past twenty years as best I could. It wasn't great. There was 9/11, the Iraq War, and every bad thing that had come about after that, and then there was climate change, Brexit and Trump. It was an avalanche of crap. I told him that, by contrast, the nineties seemed really cool and that I envied him for living in them.

'Oh shit,' he said. Then he took a deep breath and said the thing I hadn't wanted to speak out loud. 'I guess,' he said, 'that I might not be alive in your world. If I was, then I'd be, like, thirty-five. And that would be weird. To be here now, talking to you, and also to be out there somewhere being thirty-five. But I'd rather that than the alternative.'

'Yes,' I said. I looked at him and knew that I didn't have a single reassuring thing to say. 'I have no idea. I mean, am I hallucinating this? Are we both imagining it in our different years? We might be. We're probably both alive. I'll see what I can find out, if you want. Right now.'

'No! Don't go.'

I smiled. 'Don't worry. I'm not going. I'll look you up on my phone.'

'What?'

'Online.' I held up my phone. 'On here.' I saw him frowning and slowed down. 'On the browser. I can search your name and location. And it will give me information from the internet.'

'On your phone?'

'Yes.'

We held each other's gaze for a while, each baffled. He was only from twenty years ago, but this was alien to him. It hung between us, making no sense. He really didn't get what I was saying.

'Go on then,' he said in the end.

I nodded and turned my attention to the screen.

'Joe . . . What's your surname?'

'Simpson. Literally the dullest name ever.'

'Joe Simpson. That's nice, not dull. Like the Simpsons. I'll put in Devon too, and 1999.' I typed it all into the search bar. 'Joe. Simpson. Devon. 1999. Oh.'

I looked at the screen. I looked at him. The boy in the old news articles matched the boy in front of me. They had the same messy light brown hair. They had the same eyes, the same sculpted cheekbones. That was him. Joe Simpson. Robert Pattinson, Cedric Diggory, Joe Simpson.

Joe Simpson was the star of such news articles as 'Local boy vanishes on eve of French trip'. The subject of: 'Joe's dad: please let my boy come back to us', 'Joe on CCTV at Beachview,' and then: 'We may never know what happened to Joe, say cops.'

The internet had barely existed in those days, but there were enough old articles uploaded to make it clear what had happened, and he was name-checked in more recent pieces over the years, almost always on a list of unsolved disappearances.

I passed him my phone, and he tried to take it, but either his hand went right through it, or it went right through his hand. He pulled his fingers back and I held the phone up in front of him so he could read the screen, and scrolled when he nodded.

Joe Simpson, fifteen, had gone missing the night before his school trip to France. Today, for him. His friend Troy had said goodbye to him outside school, as Joe was going into town and Troy was going home to pack. That was twenty years and two days ago, and Joe had never been seen again, except for an appearance on CCTV at the shopping mall. The general feeling was that he'd 'done something stupid'. That was code for killing yourself. Yet he was right in front of me and he had no idea what had happened, no intentions in that direction at all.

Also, they hadn't found his body.

I was looking at a boy who had vanished from his own life twenty years ago, yet who, somehow, was here with me. A boy who had said goodbye to his family one day and never gone home. A boy who was missing, and very much presumed dead.

I might have been the only person who had seen him since 1999. My thoughts pinballed around. Should I tell the police? His parents? Who could I talk to? What could I do?

I reached out again, just to check. My hand went through him.

I looked into Joe's face and saw my own horror and confusion a thousand times over. It was weird for me, but this was everything for him. He was shaking, trembling all over as if there was something trying to get out from inside his skin. I couldn't comfort him because I couldn't touch him. Blue light filled the room.

'Today,' he whispered. 'Now. That happened *now*. I know you saw me yesterday too, but I don't remember. Though it kind of echoes, when I think about it.'

'We'll work it out,' I said. 'I mean, I'll do everything I can to help. We'll find out what's going on. Do you want me to see if I can find –'

I stopped talking as his head jerked up and he looked at the door. I looked too, but it was still closed. My heart thumped. If someone came in, would they be able to see Joe or me? What if they were from Joe's time and I was their ghost? Could I actually be in 1999 now? You could have ghosts from the future: there was one in *A Christmas Carol*, for a start. Maybe it was my job to stop whatever was about to happen to Joe.

I looked at Joe, but he'd gone. I looked at the door, and it was still closed.

I ran out into the mall, searching for anything that anchored me to 2019. The shops looked different. Had Smith's been there twenty years ago? Yes, of course it had. I looked at the people. It was hard to tell anything. I ran up to a woman with a pushchair, thinking for one mad second that it was Mum with Sasha, but as I got close enough for her to glance up, to see who was hurtling towards her, I saw that it wasn't Mum and swerved away. I turned back, thinking I could ask her what year it was, but then I thought I couldn't.

My head was spinning so much that it took me infinite panicky minutes to realize that Smith's was a shop that sold newspapers, and newspapers had dates on them. I ran in and found a display, and there, at the top of the *Guardian*, was the date: Wednesday, 13 March 2019. I felt my heart slowing as I walked away from the shop. It was 2019 and normal again. It was the right day. I was in my own time.

A part of me was disappointed. If I had time-travelled back twenty years I would have tried to save Joe, and then I'd have gone to find Mum.

14

That was one weird dream, and it echoes through me in waves. I'll be free of it soon. I tell myself that it wasn't real, and this *is* real. There was a girl from the future – a future in which I was dead – in the cupboard at Beachview. She looked me up on a futuristic computer from her pocket and told me I'd vanish on the night of the French exchange and no one would ever see me again.

I shiver. That was awful. My worst nightmare. I feel my heart pounding. I think I'm sweating, but when I touch my forehead I feel normal. Quite cold actually.

I'm in my bed and I'm definitely alive. I pinch myself, like they do in stories, to see if it hurts. It doesn't really, but I feel it. I am alive.

I stand on my bed and throw myself forward on to the floor. That doesn't hurt either (it wasn't very far and I put my hands out to make it better without meaning to), but I hear Dad's voice from downstairs saying, 'Joseph? What are you up to in there?' and that brings me back to myself.

Of course I'm alive. I'm here, at home, and my dad is downstairs. I'm a massive idiot.

'I'm fine!' I shout. Then I add, 'Fell out of bed!' to make him laugh, which he does, loudly.

The bedroom door opens and Gus is there, looking at me lying on the floor.

'Fell out of bed?' he says. 'You massive idiot.'

'I know!' I stand up. 'I'm a massive idiot because I take after my brother.'

It's a lame thing to say, but I don't care because I'm happy. I am so happy that I want to sing. I have my dad and my brother right here. I'm not quite sure where Mum is, but I know she's alive, and she loves me. I am here and I'm alive.

'Ready to go and play at Enzo's house?' says Gus.

Enzo. I had forgotten.

After school I find that, just as in my dream, there's a girl sitting in the cupboard at Beachview. She's right next to the pink blanket I keep there, but she doesn't know it's there because that blanket is probably in landfill in 2019.

She is from 2019. I am dead. It wasn't a dream.

If I'm not dead then I'm very, very missing. I've been missing for twenty years, and that means that I'm dead.

I must be.

'Are you Ariel?' I say, remembering her name only as it comes out of my mouth. She nods. 'From the future?'

'Yeah,' she says, and for a moment I'm pleased with myself. I remembered! I got it right.

But then – 'I'm dead,' I say, and it falls on me like an apartment block in an earthquake. It's so enormous, so impossible that it crushes me, smothers me, stops me entirely. I'm dead. You don't go anywhere from there. It's final. It's the last thing that happens.

And yet here I am.

'We don't know you're dead,' she says.

'I thought it was a dream. I wanted it to be a dream.'

I pinch myself and again it doesn't hurt. She shifts along so I can sit down, but when she puts out a hand it goes through me. I suppose we could sit right on top of one another because we're ghosts in each other's worlds, but that would be weird, and the last thing we need now is more weird.

'What day is it for you?' she says.

'Thursday. March the eleventh. Still 1999.' I try to breathe deeply, even though it probably doesn't matter whether I breathe or not. In fact, this can't even be breathing. It must be something else, something that copies breathing. 'What day is it for you?'

'Thursday too!' We grin at each other, and some kind of hope flickers, but then she adds, 'March the fourteenth . . . 2019. It's four fifteen. I came after school. It was Thursday for you yesterday too, wasn't it? And Wednesday for me.'

'Was I going on the French exchange yesterday?'

'Yes. Last night.'

'But it's tonight. It's meant to be tonight.' I'm not quite ready to take this properly on board. 'I went to school and then I came here. I . . . I guess that's what I do.'

We look at each other and I can see her deciding not to say the thing I'm thinking.

I'm not ready for it.

'So it's quarter past four for both of us?' Her voice is too bright. 'That's something, right? I mean, we have different years and different days, but we do seem to live in the same *time* of day.'

'I guess.' I hold out my wrist with my watch on it, and she shows me her phone. Both of them say 16:17.

I am desperate not to confront any of the things that are in my head, and so I say, 'Are you *completely* sure that's a phone? Where are the numbers? How do you dial?'

She laughs, and we relax, focusing on a detail.

'Yes,' she says. 'It's an iPhone. It's made by Apple. I can get the numbers up by doing this.' She taps the screen and there's a keypad.

'Apple like the computers?' I wish I could take it and play with it.

'Yes! What's your phone like?'

'Nothing like that,' I say. 'I only just got it and I thought it was quite cool, but I never remember to use it. And, when I do, it's almost always to phone people. Or to send texts. There's a snake game.'

'Let's have a look.'

'I don't have it with me. We're not allowed them at school.'

There's silence. I don't want to talk about the thing, but I know I have to. I am beginning to face the fact that I live this Thursday every day and I can't bear it. I have no idea

96

how long it's been going on. I sense it as a bottomless abyss of horror and I try to look away, to go back to the time when I didn't really know. It doesn't work.

'Do you think . . .' I pick my words carefully and try to keep my voice steady. 'Do you think that I might have been living this day, every day, for . . .' I can't quite say the number. '. . . a long time?' I finish lamely. 'Am I trapped in this day? Do I do the same things every time without realizing?'

I can see from her face that Ariel thinks I do. Her eyes meet mine and she looks away, then back again.

'Maybe,' she says. 'That might be happening. Yeah. I don't think it makes sense, but none of this makes sense. It might be that . . . that it's because no one knows what happened to you, so there was never any kind of closure. So you couldn't go and do – well, whatever the next thing is.' Her eyes fill with tears, and I remember that her mum died.

'Mmm.' I'm aiming for something profound, but *mmm* is what comes out.

Ariel forces a smile. I feel my stomach clenching, and even that makes no sense because I don't have a stomach. It's a ghost stomach, fake clenching.

I wasn't normal today. I didn't go to the loo. Did I eat? I made Dad toast without eating any myself. I probably had lunch at school because everyone did, but I don't think it tasted of anything. I might have drunk some water. I might not. It's hard to remember.

'Shall we see what we can do?' Ariel's voice pulls me back to reality, or to whatever this is.

I nod. 'What, though?'

She takes a deep breath and blows it all out at once. Her hair bounces up in front of her face.

'I don't know,' she says. 'I mean, I'll do everything I can. I guess I need to find out what happened to you? I'm not sure where to start. But I'll try, Joe. I'll try. And maybe you could look for . . . Actually don't worry. First of all, tell me everything you remember.'

'Yeah.' I can't remember anything.

'You couldn't remember me before and now you can. So more things might come back. When I've been here with you before, you look up as if someone's in the doorway, but they're not and, when I look back at you, you've gone.' She stares at me with a question on her face, but I shake my head. I've got nothing.

'I'll try and concentrate on that bit today.'

'Yes. Do. And maybe you can tell me everything you remember about your day, and anything from the days before it. The old news reports talk about Beachview because everyone knows you came here, but there's nothing about this room. So already we know something they don't. We know you came here.'

I nod. 'And we know I looked at someone in the doorway.'

'Yeah. And then you weren't there. I went out. I was scared. I thought I might be in 1999, but I wasn't. Then I wished I had been.'

I lean back on the wall. 'I don't remember anyone at the door. Sorry.'

I feel the tears hot in my eyes and try to blink them away out of some stupid idea that you shouldn't cry in front of a girl. Then I remember how very much it doesn't matter and let them fall. I reach out to her and she reaches back towards me. We lean on each other and just keep going. I try to laugh, but it's not funny. I'd give anything in the world to be able to hug her.

I would give anything in the world, but I'm not in the world and I don't have anything.

Ariel is crying too. I think, again, about her mother.

'She died a year ago today,' she says, reading my mind. 'It's the anniversary.'

'Oh shit. I'm really sorry.'

'It's fine. Weirdly, this helps. Keep talking to me.'

'OK.' I can't think of anything to say, so in the end I crassly come up with: 'What was your best memory with your mum?' I hope she doesn't mind.

She sniffs and wipes her eyes and nose on her sleeve. 'Sorry,' she says. 'Not very ladylike. But it's different with you.'

'Go right ahead,' I say. 'No rules in here. Not even the basic rules. The ones about time and space. Life and death. Breathing.'

'My very earliest memory,' she says, 'is of Mum. I was sitting on her lap, looking at a book. I remember the feel of her. She was under me, around me, and her hair was falling on my head. I remember that feeling of security. I knew I'd always be all right because I had her to look after me.'

Her face is red and wet. She wipes her nose on the sleeve

of her blazer again, and gulps and gasps. I long to be able to hold her. I reach out to her once more. She reaches for me too, but we can't touch. I watch her crying, and I cry for myself, and we're two separate people. We both just sit there and wail, and, just when I am thinking I should pull myself together and talk to her properly, the door swings open, and I look up, and everything goes blank.

15

Suddenly he wasn't there. I was sitting in the little room, on my own, and I felt oddly better. I had cried and cried and cried. I'd cried for Mum, and Joe had cried for – well, for everything. It had to be shit to discover that you'd been dead for twenty years. We hadn't been able to touch, but the fact that we'd both wanted to meant a lot. I often hugged Izzy and Sasha; it was a very long time since I'd wanted to get close to anyone else.

Crying felt good. I had tried so hard to stop doing it, but now I thought maybe I should let it happen a bit more. Catharsis. That was the word, wasn't it? It meant when something big and emotional happened, and you felt better afterwards, even if it was horrible at the time. I'd met someone who understood me, and I loved Joe for that. I was the only person in all of space and time who could even see him properly: he needed my help.

I ran home, letting the sea air dry my face. I slowed down a bit to reply to text messages, trying to sound normal. At home I went straight to the list on the fridge, feeling more positive than I had for ages, though the absence of Mum hit me, as it always did, the moment I opened the front door.

'Hey, Mum,' I said to the empty air. I imagined her saying hello to me, kissing my cheek. I imagined her reaching out to touch me, and our arms passing through each other. I hoped she was there. She'd been gone for a year.

I checked the list. Today I was supposed to be cooking pasta. How hard could that be? It was literally the next easiest thing to getting a takeaway. I put the kettle on and checked the cupboard. There was a bag of twirly pasta. Perfect.

I got out a pan and thought about Joe. No one knew what had happened to him. I googled again until I had the names of his parents, Jasper and Claire Simpson, and then I turned my attention to them.

Were they still in town? That was the main thing. Was his dad here? Had his mum come back from India? Had she even been there in the first place? He seemed confused about his mother, but he knew she wasn't living with them. I tried not to judge her for leaving, but . . . who was I kidding? If Joe's mum had done the same as our dad, then I judged her exactly as harshly as I judged him, which was *very harshly indeed*.

Whatever had happened, though, she'd paid the ultimate price. I failed to track her to the present day because there were so very, very many people called Claire Simpson in the world, and before I could start to narrow it down I heard a key in the door. I tensed for a second, as I always did just in case it was Dad, even though he'd left his key behind, and then ran at my sister. I hugged her and put my face right down to the bump. 'Hello, little baby!' I said. 'It's Auntie Ariel!'

Sasha laughed. 'You're full of beans! Are you OK? I was worried about you today.'

I'd never kept a secret from Sasha before. Not a proper one. And so I started to tell her. I'd told her about the other ghosts, after all, and she didn't think I was horrifically mad.

'I went to Beachview after school,' I said. 'You know I said I found that weird little room at the back? On the day Dad left? I went there again and I thought about Mum, considering what day it is, and I cried for ages. *Ages*, Sash. More than I have since she died.'

'I thought your face looked a bit puffy,' she said, touching my cheek. 'And yeah, today's the day for it. Me too. But you seem happier.'

'Yeah. I met . . .' I looked at her and stopped. Blue ghosts were one thing. A dead or missing boy, who was living in 1999, but who talked to me here in 2019, was another.

We'd made it through this year, and Sasha had enough going on.

She was looking at me, waiting. 'You met . . .?'

'Well, I didn't meet anyone.' I paused. 'I met some kind of turning point. The end of a shit year. Something changed, you know? I met the point where I just had to confront things, and so I let it all out and, for the first time, it made things seem a bit better. And now I feel, like, isn't it actually amazing to be alive? To be here, in real life, living in the world? I know there's loads that's shit.' Sasha frowned and put her hand on her bump. 'I won't say "shit" once he's born, don't worry. But I've got you, and we've got the baby, and we have this house to live in and enough money. We made it through a year. We're lucky. We're on Earth for such a short time. Let's make the most of it, yeah? That's what Mum would want.'

'Well.' She laughed. 'Wow. Let me harness that energy, babes. I could do with a bit of that.'

I took her hand and tried to zing positivity into her. She pretended she'd had an electric shock.

I couldn't tell her about Joe because she wouldn't be able to believe it. It was our secret, mine and Joe's. It belonged to me and a boy from 1999 who had vanished this afternoon at quarter past five. Who vanished every afternoon at quarter past five. That had to be when it had happened, at quarter past five, on Thursday 11 March, twenty years ago.

What was it, though? What had happened?

'Right,' I said. 'Sit down and watch the telly, and that's an order. Dinner's nearly ready. It's pasta, but I'll make a tomato sauce, and maybe a salad? That would be good, wouldn't it? Lots of your five a day. And we can toast Mum again and be incredibly positive and brave.'

I opened cupboards, looking through the tins, hoping to find tomatoes. There was tomato soup. That would do. 'I'll buy fresh vegetables tomorrow.'

Mum had always made sure we knew we had to eat fruit and vegetables as part of every meal and we always did: even when things had been at their worst, we'd totted up the gherkin from the burger, the tomato on the pizza.

Mum had been an anaesthetist and the cleverest person I had ever known. Dad was a doctor too, and I hoped the people of Inverness were appreciating his skills, if nothing else. I bet he had a new girlfriend by now.

I didn't miss Dad, but it was weird having him just vanishing from our lives. I had no idea why Mum had stayed with him. He was horrible. He had been horrible to her, and to Sasha, and nice to me, mainly, I now suspected, as a way of being meaner to them rather than because he actually liked me. When Mum got ill he didn't get nicer. He just vanished into himself, and ignored Sasha and me until Sasha told him she was pregnant, at which point he had exploded, punched several walls, and gone out driving dangerously around town for hours.

I put the pasta into the pan and typed out an email on my phone before I had time to decide not to:

Dear Dad,

I wanted to write because it's been a year since Mum died and I know you've been missing her too. I hope you're doing OK in Scotland. Let us know. We're doing fine. It would be really great if you'd check in with Sasha at some point as I think she'd really appreciate it. So would I.

Ariel xx

I sent it and instantly regretted it.

I left the pasta cooking and the soup warming up, and went to sit with Sasha. My eyes were drawn to the photo on the wall. It was our favourite picture, the one we'd taken out of the album and had enlarged and framed. We were approximately three and seven years old, and Mum had us squeezed on to her lap, her special Mum-arms somehow long enough to contain us both. I was staring at the camera, pudding-faced and wild-haired, and Sasha (blonde and adorable) was looking at me and laughing, while Mum was clearly the happiest woman in the world. Although I looked stupid in it, I absolutely loved it. I knew that Dad had taken it, but apart from that I loved everything about it.

I wondered whether he'd reply to my message. Surely he would.

'You know when you were little,' I said, looking at our young selves.

'Yeah?'

'Did you go to nursery?'

'I went to Bouncers,' she said, smiling. 'It was lovely. I'd love to send this little bean there except it closed years ago. It had shut before your time. You went to that hippy place, didn't you?'

I remembered the hippy place. I remembered singing and dancing and playing with water and playdough. Mostly, though, I remembered crying because I missed Mum. Some things didn't change.

'Was there a man in charge there?' I said. 'At Bouncers?'

Sasha screwed up her face. 'There was a guy who used to come in with a guitar. But all the workers I remember were women. Why?'

I tried to speak casually, though my blood was pounding in my ears and my breathing had gone wrong. 'I was reading a thing online. About a boy who went missing. Years ago, before I was born, but he went to our school. His dad worked at Bouncers. That was all. I stumbled across it and thought it was weird. That a teenager from our school vanished from this town. From the shopping mall. And he was never found. I wondered if his dad used to look after you at nursery. That was all.'

'Oh, you mean Joe Simpson? Everyone knows about him. So are you saying it was his dad who did it? I don't remember that at all. But it's usually the parents, isn't it?'

I shook my head. 'Oh God, no. I don't think it was his dad. I mean, maybe? Who knows? I just saw where his dad worked and I thought you went there. Nothing more than that.'

'I guess he would have left that job after his son disappeared. Before my time. Joe Simpson probably ran away, you know? That's what boys do. I'm pretty sure it's what they decided in the end.'

Her hand went to her bump. We would make sure this boy never had any reason to run away.

'Maybe,' I said, because I couldn't add any more than that. I couldn't tell her that I knew he hadn't.

It turned out that tinned tomato soup didn't make good pasta sauce.

When Sasha went to bed, I looked up Gus Simpson, Joe's brother, who was surprisingly easy to find. He lived in our town, and when I saw his photo I gasped. It was so bizarre to see someone who looked a lot like Joe, but who was nearly forty. If he wasn't so old he would have been quite fit. Not as much as Joe, but almost. The whole thing made me feel extremely strange.

And then I saw his family. Gus had two daughters.

I needed to meet him, but I wasn't sure how to go about it. I could hardly send him a message explaining that I'd met his brother's ghost and needed to talk. I read everything I could on his Facebook, but he didn't say much (or if he did his settings stopped me seeing it): he put up pictures of his family and tagged his workplace, a legal firm in town. Maybe that would work. Could Sasha and I need a lawyer?

I clicked on his partner's profile. She was called Abby Fielding, and she looked nice. Friendly. The children were maybe about eight and five.

I thought about it for ages, and then made a flyer advertising my brand-new, just-invented services. It said:

Hi! I'm Ariel (like the mermaid). I'm sixteen and I'm an experienced, reliable babysitter. If you need any babysitting or childminding I'd be happy to help at evenings and weekends. Ages two and up, reasonable rates. References available. I love kids and love hanging out with them.

It sounded crap (and contained lies), but, from what I'd read in Abby's profile, she might go for that kind of thing. Mums probably loved friendly girls who'd play with their kids and had Disney names. I would print it at school tomorrow, just one copy, and then I'd find their address and put it through their letterbox.

*

On Saturday morning I woke late and scrolled further and further back through Abby's Insta until I found that, back when Mum was still alive, she had posted a photograph with the caption: I'll never take this view for granted ❤.

The picture looked as if it had been taken from an upstairs window. There was a distant sea horizon, a leafy tree in the garden, and between the two, I was almost sure, was the park with the cricket pitch. The whole thing was framed by pink curtains.

I was looking at the view from Gus and Abby's window.

Game on. If they still lived in that house I was coming for them. My visit to Joe was a fluster of plans and possibilities, and I promised to report straight back on Sunday.

Early on Sunday morning I crept out of the house, leaving a note to say I'd gone for a walk to clear my head. I narrowed it down to five houses by walking along the road next to the cricket pitch twice. Then I sat on a bench across the field, wrapped in my warmest coat and scarf, and pretended to play on my phone until I saw actual Gus coming out of number five and setting off for a run.

I tried to get my head round the fact that this man was two years older than Joe, who was a year younger than me, but that at the same time he was approximately twenty-one years older than I was. He was middle-aged. He had lived without his brother for twenty years, which was five years longer than he'd lived with him. I was older now than Joe had ever been, would ever be, and I was moving away from him every second.

Joe should have been thirty-five. The reality hit me properly for the first time. The boy I liked, the boy who was in Year Ten, was thirty-five. That was all kinds of icky.

I rearranged my hair and made a pouty face, while holding up my phone and taking a photo of Gus. It wasn't a good picture, but it was recognizable.

As soon as he was out of sight I pulled together all my brave atoms and walked up the garden path to number five. I saw one of those red-and-yellow plastic cars that little kids play in, on its side in the gravelly front garden. It looked old. Maybe it had once been Joe's.

I looked up and saw pink curtains at the upstairs window.

I pushed the flyer through the blue door and walked away fast, trembling. I went home via the supermarket, bought lots of fresh vegetables and cooked a huge soup for Sasha and the baby and me.

Then I realized that I couldn't meet Joe today, even though I'd promised I would. It was Sunday, and the mall closed at four. I hated knowing that I couldn't chat to him. I missed him. I hated, most of all, the fact that he would be waiting for me, that the only person he could really talk to wasn't going to show up.

I sent him silent apologies, and hoped he wouldn't think I'd abandoned him forever.

16

I wake up in the usual way. I write down everything while I'm still half in the dream, and stare at the words.

I'm dead. It is 2019. Every day is this day. Ariel from the future in cupboard at B/view. Meet after school.

YOU ARE NOT SCARED OF THE FRENCH EXCHANGE.

YOU ARE SCARED BECAUSE YOU'RE GOING TO DIE TODAY.

The French exchange! That's why I'm scared. My heart is pounding so hard I feel like it's going to knock the house down around me, and somehow I don't think it would matter if it did. I really, *really* don't want to go to France. Why, though? And why did I write that note saying I'm not scared of it when I am?

Why did I say I'm going to die? I shudder. Stupid dreams.

I check myself out in the mirror. I seem normal. I think I do. My hair is tangled, sticking up all over the place. But it's me, for sure. Joe Simpson, reporting for duty.

'Pull yourself together,' I say out loud, then see Gus in the doorway looking at me pityingly.

In the middle of morning registration I look round at everyone and realize that I'm never going to go on the French exchange, but I don't know why I think that. It must be an echo of my dream: if I was dead then I couldn't go to France. I shake my head, try to send those thoughts away. I take the piss out of Lucas, which makes me feel a bit better for a moment, and hang out with Troy, who's a bit annoyed with me because he thinks I stole his trophy, but I pretend I didn't.

I run into town after school, and buy a can of Tab. I walk into a man and he's angry. I tell him to fuck off under my breath and he calls me a little tosser.

As soon as I touch the door of the secret room I know I'm going to see Ariel and then I remember all of it.

I see Ariel every day.

I go into the room and wait. I close my eyes and feel myself disappearing into the horror of my existence. The horror is that I don't exist, yet here I am. The horror is the fact that I live the same day every day. That nothing I thought about myself today was true. I fight, as if I had any kind of power to reject it. Ariel is the only one who understands.

I wait. The walls seem to be closer together than usual, and moving inwards so slowly that you can't see it, but you can feel it.

I wonder if it matters that I forget everything about myself from one day to the next. It's probably better to forget than it would be to remember. I'm not sure how I'd get through a day if I knew what that day actually was.

I sigh. It's better not to know, but I need to try to remember. I should be trying to work out what happened to me. I'm supposed to be telling Ariel every detail of my last day, but it's already fading. It's slightly different every time. It must be.

I could write things down. I could try to leave myself a clue, but I have no idea how to do it, beyond sleeping with a pen and paper beside the bed and scrawling it all down the moment I wake up, and I seem to be doing that already with my maths book.

I think about that detail because it's easier than the other stuff. It's everywhere, though. The words are on every wall of this room. They are lit up, neon. YOU ARE GOING TO DIE, they say. TODAY. RIGHT NOW. I see them everywhere I look. If I don't die then I'll vanish for twenty years. There seems to be some kind of life after death, but it has taken me twenty years even to notice that I'm living the same day over and over again. I think my afterlife involves me going to school every day forever, around seven thousand three hundred times so far, and if I'd lived all those days properly I'd be thirty-five, but in fact I'm still fifteen.

Maybe I've gone to hell. This could be my personal, specially tailored purgatory: I am sitting in a little room on my own, knowing that I'll always be fifteen, waiting for my only friend, who should be here by now but isn't, and for the other thing. The bad one. Meanwhile the millennium bug won't happen, but climate change is worse than we expect, and the world's politics have gone unthinkably weird, and I will never be a part of the world in which those things happen.

Ariel told me Gus has children. That comes back in a flash.

She had nearly found his address. She was going to go there today.

I stare at the door and feel myself spiralling out of control. I wait and wait for Ariel, but she doesn't arrive, and after a while I realize that it's five o'clock, and she's not going to come.

She's all I have. What if she's ill? What if she has died too? Maybe she's decided to stop coming to see me. She might have thought that she imagined me and that it was time to pull herself together for her sister's baby.

I tremble. I stand up on the little bench and jump off. It doesn't hurt. I throw myself down, making an effort not to put my hands out, and land face first. It still doesn't hurt. I bite my arm. Nothing. I punch my nose until it should bleed, but no blood comes out. I headbutt the wall again and again and again. It hurts in the end. Thank God.

I imagine Gus waiting for me to come home tonight. I wonder when he'll stop being annoyed and start to get worried. I wonder when Dad will call the police, when Mum will come back from India, whether Dad is still a nursery manager or whether your own child vanishing stops you being able to look after other people's kids. My thoughts leap around from now (can you pinpoint the moment when you stop being annoyed someone is late home and start to worry about them?) to the future (I hope Ariel is OK).

I wonder whether Mum and Dad are even still alive.

Gus has kids. I'll never meet them. Unless Ariel could bring them here? Perhaps they'd see me too. Perhaps Gus would.

I know I have to focus, to concentrate as hard as I possibly can, as I'm going to look at the door soon and someone (I suppose) will come in. If I can remember who it is, when I wake up tomorrow morning, that would really help.

I might be able to do that. I'm remembering more. I take a pen from my schoolbag and write it on my ghostly arm: REMEMBER EVERYTHING TODAY. It won't be there when I wake up.

For what feels like a few minutes, I let go. I slide down to the floor and revert so fully to babyhood that I basically have a tantrum. I kick the floor. I punch it with my fists. Nothing hurts. I'm still sobbing when the door opens. I look up, but it isn't Ariel. It is . . .

Everything goes blank.

17

Monday was an OK day at school. Izzy and I laughed about stupid things, caught up on our homework, and for once I didn't have to blink back tears at any point, which was kind of momentous. I sat with Izzy at lunchtime, overcooked jacket potatoes in front of us both.

'I guess he's back from France,' she said. 'That boy who gave you the fake number? You're not going to see him, right?'

'Oh, that,' I said. I longed with every atom to tell her about Joe, to bring her into my new world. But I knew she'd think it was all in my head. I'd think that, if I was her.

I couldn't tell her any more than I'd been able to tell Sasha.

'I am most certainly not,' I said with exaggerated dignity. 'Nothing is as off-putting as a fake phone number. He ghosted me so he's dead to me.' I shivered. I hadn't meant to say either of those things.

'Bastard.' Izzy shook her head. That ended the subject.

We made a list of potential middle names for Sasha's baby instead. We spent the whole afternoon running a World Cup of boys' names, canvassing opinions from whoever was nearby, eliminating some and sending others into the next round, and by three thirty the results were in: the baby's middle name was Camembert (pronounced phonetically: Bert for short). That cheered me up immensely and I texted Sasha to inform her that her son's middle name was Camembert.

Fuck off, she replied. **Though I do quite like Bertie. Hmm, thx, I guess.**

I saw the telly-ghosts around the place whether I thought about blue or not, but I wasn't scared of them any more. I thought I was seeing parts of Joe's last day at school, since I was in the building where it had happened, just as I overlapped with him in the Beachview room. I didn't know if I was right, but that was what I'd decided to believe.

I looked each of them in the face, in turn, hoping to find Joe here too and wondering whether we'd be able to speak to each other if we met away from our usual space. I had no idea why I could see him. Partly, I supposed, it had to be because of Mum, but I was also starting to think that perhaps I was supposed to find out what had happened to him. Would that help him move on? It might.

In the afternoon I found myself in the loos with a cluster of ghost girls, and no one from 2019.

'Hey,' I said. 'Excuse me. Do you know Joe Simpson?' I waved both arms. 'Hello? Can you hear me?'

They ignored me. They couldn't see or hear me at all, and then a toilet flushed and a real girl I didn't know came out of the end cubicle, smirking.

I was less freaked by the kids from 1999 now that I had an idea about who they were. This wasn't my story: it was me helping Joe with his, and that took the pressure off. They weren't a symptom of me losing my mind in the way I'd thought, and that made me want to hug them. They were connected to Joe (they had to be: they wore his uniform and looked like nineties kids). That meant they could be a part of him reaching out to me for help, and I tried my best to embrace their presence, though my favourite times were very much the rare days when I didn't see them.

I often found myself wishing that Mum had had any reason at all to be at our school in 1999. If she had I might have been able to see her. But she didn't, and so I couldn't.

I ran to Beachview.

'Ariel!' he shouted, jumping up. He kind of hugged through me, and I shivered at the strange chill as his body vanished into mine. It was a bit like cold, and a bit like fizziness, a concentrated version of what happened when I walked down the corridors at school when they were filled with his people.

'God, Joe,' I said. 'Yesterday, right? I'm so sorry. I just didn't think.'

'What happened?' He was bouncing up and down. 'I was so worried. I ended up . . . Well. Don't laugh. I ended up lying on the floor, completely losing it. I thought something awful had happened to you. I thought you were ill, or you didn't want to do this any more, or you'd decided it was all in your head. And then I realized that, without you, I'll never be able to do anything except live this day over and over and over again, for all time. And it was the worst. Just the actual worst thing. The abyss, you know?'

I put my hand through his shoulder. I had to find out what had happened to him. Even if it didn't change anything, at least then he would know.

'I'm so sorry,' I said again. 'It wasn't any of that. It's just that it was Sunday, Joe. The mall closed at four. That was all. I didn't think of it on Saturday, which was stupid because if I'd given it a moment's thought I would have realized and then you wouldn't have had to worry. I'll never be able to see you on Sundays, but now we know that we can be prepared.'

I hesitated and then decided to carry on. 'Joe, I missed you. It hasn't been long, but I can't imagine not being able to see you every day. Nearly every day. I'm kind of obsessed with working out what happened to you.' I looked at him, slightly nervous of how exposed that made me feel, but Joe was laughing and crying at the same time, every bit as intense as me. 'So I'll never decide I don't want to see you any more,' I added, 'because you kind of feel like my best friend.'

'Ariel,' he said. 'You're amazing, but I don't want this to be too much pressure. Yesterday made me realize that, even though I've only just met you, I'm completely dependent on you. Like when someone's sheltering someone in a war. Like Anne Frank. Or something.'

'Hey,' I said. 'I'm not going anywhere, right? Friends?'

We were looking at each other in a way that made me feel magical. This wasn't really *friends*. Izzy was my best friend. Joe made me feel that I was opening up, transforming into someone new. It was like staring into the sun. He lit me up and scared me. He was more than a human, more than a

119

ghost. He was all the mysteries of the universe, the unknowability of life after death, a rip in the fabric of reality. But I was going to call it *friends*.

'Best friends,' he said. We stared into each other's eyes and then I pulled myself together. He was at the same time a rip in the fabric of reality and an extremely good-looking boy.

'Right,' I said, trying to be brisk. 'Updates time. I found Gus's house. It's one of those nice ones by the cricket pitch, like we thought. I waited outside yesterday morning. Sitting on a bench, pretending to play with my phone. And then he came out and went for a run.'

'You saw Gus?' Joe was stricken. 'Was he . . . was he thirty-seven?'

'Yes. It was so bizarre. I felt like a stalker, but I did this for you. When he was quite near, I pretended I was taking a selfie, and I took a picture of him instead.'

'You pretended you were what?'

I picked up my phone and demonstrated. 'Taking a selfie. Like this. Everyone does it.' I showed him my phone. 'See, there's a camera this way too. Teenage girls are famous for taking selfies. Everyone thinks we're *very* shallow.' I pouted and held the phone up in front of us. We were both on the screen, but when I took the photo it was just me.

'Oh my God,' he said. 'I'm not there. Look at that. I'm not even there.' He turned and touched the wall behind him, which had appeared in the photo instead.

'I bet that if you could take a photo I wouldn't be in it.'

We stared at each other, eyes wide.

'I can't be in your photo because I don't exist in your world,' he said.

'And I don't exist in yours.'

'I know it's not the weirdest thing,' he said, 'but it is fucking freaky. I'll bring a camera and we can try it. But!' He shook himself. 'Gus.'

'Yes! OK. I pretended to be taking a picture of myself, but it was just so I could get a photo of Gus for you. I tried to make it look like I was using the camera that faced me, but really I was using the one that faced him. Right?' Joe nodded. 'Do you want to see it?'

He nodded again, and I knew that part of him really, really didn't. I held the phone out.

'Here,' I said. 'Here he is, on his Sunday-morning run.'

I saw a middle-aged man in loose running shorts, huffing his way across a field. Joe saw something completely different. He gasped and tried to touch it with his finger.

'My brother,' he said. 'Gus. It's really him. But he's . . .' His voice trailed off. I carried on talking, knowing we had limited time.

'Joe,' I said. 'Do you remember I told you that Gus has kids? And a partner called Abby Fielding?' He nodded. 'And that I thought I could try to get babysitting work with them? It probably won't lead to anything, but I put a note through their door just in case. Did you have a red-and-yellow plastic car when you were a kid?'

He looked utterly dejected. 'Yeah,' he said. 'I think so. You moved it around with your feet. I thought I was the coolest guy, driving my own car.'

'It was in their garden. It looked really old.'

He didn't reply to that, so I just carried on talking. 'Do you want me to do this, Joe, or is it too much? Not just the babysitting, but all of it. I've been thinking about what else I could do. If you like I could try to work out what happened to you. It might help. Do a bit of, you know, detective work, if that doesn't sound too stupid. At least we might know then. And your family would know too.'

'Yes,' he said after a long pause. 'Yes. Please. The babysitting and the detecting. If you don't mind. I think it would be good for them all to know. And I'd probably feel a bit better if I knew. Otherwise you just . . . imagine.'

'They probably won't need a babysitter.'

He screwed up his eyes. 'Did you tell me what Gus's kids are called? Are there any photos?'

'I didn't tell you their names,' I said, 'because I didn't know them then. I do now. They're called Zara and Coco. They're about – I'm not sure. From the photos, I'd say maybe five and sevenish? Something like that. Abby's on Facebook, and she has loose privacy settings.'

I caught his expression. 'Yeah, I'll explain another time. Do you want to see photos?'

I looked him in the eye. I could see how confusing and awful this was, but he gave a small nod, so I opened my photos and flicked through the screenshots I'd taken during my comprehensive stalking operation.

'Here you go. This is your sister-in-law. And these are your nieces. She doesn't show their faces on Insta, but she does on Facebook. Fuck. I'm sorry, Joe.'

I scrolled through Abby's Facebook photos and let him look at the girls for as long as he could. It turned out that all Joe wanted to do was gaze at these pictures. He didn't care what Facebook was, or privacy settings. He only wanted to see his brother, grown up, and his unknown sister-in-law, Abby, the woman he'd never met, the woman who must have known him only as someone who was lost. Most of all, though, he wanted to see the girls. He was desperate to look at them. He would have gazed at their little faces forever.

'Ariel . . .' he said, just as we knew our time was coming to an end. 'This sounds weird, but can you print these pictures? Could we keep them in here? Can I look at them? I know I can't see the girls in real life, but if I could just . . . if I could just . . .'

He stopped, overwhelmed.

'Sure,' I said. 'I can sort that out. I'll do it at school. I think I've got some more print credits.'

I was saying anything just to keep talking. Actually I realized at once that I wouldn't print out photos of children and stick them up here because it would be incredibly strange and inappropriate, and also Joe probably wouldn't be able to see them. 'And tomorrow tell me absolutely everything that might be useful. Can you make notes about everyone you see at school?'

I watched him draw in a deep breath and look at the door. Then he was gone.

18

It's the weirdest thing to wake up half knowing something that is impossible. There's a piece of paper beside the bed with a message about the cupboard at Beachview and a girl from the future called Ariel, but I already know it. It stayed in my head.

It stayed in my head! That is new. I'm sure it's new. I know that I'll go there after school, and I know that I have lived this day thousands of times, and I will do it again today and again tomorrow, if there is really any concept of a tomorrow.

I know that I must be dead. It's a fucker of a thing to find out about yourself. I stagger into the bathroom and look at myself in the mirror. I think of Ariel and fill my head with the blue of the sky.

There it is. I'm glowing bright blue. She was right.

Dad shouts up to me. I manage to half fall down the stairs and say goodbye. I know that this is going to be the last time he sees me for a very long time. Who am I kidding? He's never going to see me again. I know that. He doesn't.

'I love you, Dad,' I say, and I hug him. 'Always remember.'

He steps back and smiles at me.

'You know, Jojo,' he says, 'I can see you're feeling anxious.' He looks stricken. I remember how I used to be, and try to step back into that Joe. I smile, attempt a swagger.

'Nah,' I say. 'Not really. I was just trying to get in touch with my empathetic side. Mrs Dupont told us to do that.'

What the hell am I even saying? Still, it seems to work. His face relaxes a bit.

'Sure? Mrs Dupont is a wise woman. Are you missing Mum? I can see how much you wish she was here right now, to wave you off to France. Sorry she's not, mate.'

'Yes,' I say, and he's right. Mum is not here, on this day, and that means I haven't seen her for twenty years. I wish with all my heart that she could have still been at home on 11 March. I work hard to stay in my persona as old-Joe, even as I realize that I can hardly remember my mother. She has long hair and dark eyes. She wears floaty clothes. I haven't seen her for twenty years. I will never see her again. The day she went away was the last day of my life when I had a mother.

She's in India (I think? I can't remember much of the past any more) and now I'll never see her again.

If she was here maybe this wouldn't happen.

I shake my head. There's no way I can blame the one person who has nothing to do with this. She's miles away: this isn't her fault.

'She'll be back,' Dad says. 'You know that. But before then: the French exchange! You'll have a blast.' I see him

125

searching around for an appropriate phrase in French, but not finding one. '*Comme çi, comme ça,*' he says instead. '*Voilà! L'addition, s'il vous plaît!*'

I give him a blast of the most sincere smile I can manage, and do a little dance for some reason. A kind of jig on the spot that looks stupid, but this is Dad and it's the sort of thing he likes.

'*Vraiment bien,*' I say. I'm not at all scared about the French exchange because I'm not going. 'It'll be fine,' I say. 'Interesting. I mean, it's going to be weird, right? But also I'm staying with my friend Enzo in France and that'll be cool.'

'That's the spirit. Good. So I'll see you before you go, and then you'll be home before we know it.'

Gus comes down the stairs noisily.

'You still here?' he says to Dad, who looks at his watch and says, 'Bums!'

'Bums?' I say.

Dad shrugs.

'If I said *bums* in front of a kid at work it wouldn't be the end of the world. It's arguably their favourite word. So I can allow myself that from time to time.'

'Allow yourself a bum from time to time. Quite right,' says Gus, and I want to cry. I'm going to miss them so much.

I meet Troy on the corner and we talk bravely about how much better our new life in France is going to be, about how we'll have baguettes and croissants and snails.

126

'I probably won't come back,' he says, and he spins a fantasy about living in a Parisian attic with a beautiful woman and discovering his talent as an artist. I'm sure I've heard it before, but I go along with it, asking questions, stretching it out all the way to school.

We pick up other people as we go, and I look at all of them, knowing that they will be adults and I won't, that they'll tell new people, 'When I was at school one of my friends disappeared.'

I'm going to see them tomorrow too. And again and again and again. Every single day until the end of time.

I look at Jemima and she grins back at me. I know she's really pretty and that I used to have the most massive crush on her, but I don't feel anything. I remember an intense friendship with Marco that went somewhere unexpected, but I don't really remember that either. I realize I have no idea whether I like girls or boys, or a bit of both, because the only person I have any feelings for is Ariel, and it's not so much that I fancy her. I did, when I thought we were both real, and of course I still do, but it's been complicated by the facts.

I remember that I'm supposed to be gathering information for her, and let Lucas walk with me, so I can work out how much he hates me. We don't really get on, but it's quite a leap to think of him killing me later today.

Lucas is just a bit of an oddball, I think. He's huge and seems much older than the rest of us (though I'm thirty-five, so I beat everyone). He makes me feel uncomfortable, which I guess makes him a suspect.

'Hey,' I say.

'All right, Joseph?' he says. He gives a stupid grin. '*Comment ça va?*'

I ignore the French.

'Lucas?' I say. 'Would you murder me if you could definitely get away with it?'

He gives me a weird look. 'Why would I want to murder you?'

'Is that a no?'

He frowns and walks off.

As soon as I get into the tutor room I start recording our conversation in my notebook.

'What are you writing?' says Troy, trying to look at the page. I hide it with my hand, like when you don't want anyone to copy your spellings in primary school. All I've written is Lucas didn't say no when.

I hope Troy didn't see. He'd assume this was going the way of my friendship with Marco, which I can barely remember, though Troy will, very clearly indeed.

Marco isn't in our tutor group. I'm sure I never see him beyond the occasional glimpse of the back of his head today, and that must be why I can hardly even picture him now. I wish I could. He made me have feelings.

Throughout the rest of the day I ask people if they'd murder me if they could get away with it, and a surprising number of people don't say no. A few say yes, but I think they're just trying to be funny. I write it all down.

*

I'm in maths when I remember the other thing. Ariel did find something: Gus has a girlfriend and two children. Gus! He's thirty-seven. Ariel saw him out for a run and took a photo. It all comes into my head at once, as if I'd opened a door and found them all on the other side of it. Coco and Zara. My nieces. A woman called Abby Fielding.

I have no idea how I'd forgotten that, or why I've remembered it now. I know that I can't just sit here, trying to solve simultaneous equations. I have a bit of power, even if it's tiny.

I stand up. Mr Patel looks at me. When I say, 'Gonna be sick,' he gestures to the door.

'Go with him, Troy,' he says. I shake my head.

'I'll be fine,' I say, and I dash out of the room, and, to make it convincing, into the boys' loos.

Troy follows anyway: I'd have done the same. I run into a stall and lock it, and think about making vomit noises, but what's the point? I flush, then come out and give him a shaky smile.

'You all right?' He pulls himself up on to the window sill, but his feet still nearly reach the floor. The room is echoey, clattery and smelly. The window is frosted and smeared with grime. All the stalls are open.

I nod and say, 'No'.

He says, 'I knew it. Go on then.'

Troy and I have been best mates since we were four. We're the classic old friends who met when we were cuter than we realized in reception class, and just never fell out. He's taller than everyone, and very lanky, with bright red hair and olive skin. I only know that he gets stopped by scouts from modelling agencies because it's happened when I've been with him. 'You have such a strong look,' they say. 'So distinctive.'

Anyway. I realize I have nothing to lose.

'Troy,' I say. 'You'll think I'm batshit, but listen. Something terrible is going to happen to me today. I'm going to . . .' I stop. I can't do it. The words won't come out.

I watch him trying to work out where I'm heading with this.

'OK,' he says in a guarded voice. 'What are you going to do? Mate, you're not thinking of doing anything stupid, are you?'

'No! But. Oh God. It'll sound mad.'

'I can handle mad.'

I force the words out. 'I've been living through this same day for twenty years. Every day after school, I meet a girl at Beachview. Except for when it's Sunday for her. It's never Sunday for me. She's from 2019. The Y2K bug never happened, but some planes fly into the World Trade Center in 2001, and global warming . . . Anyway, I know I'm going to disappear tonight and twenty years from now no one will have any idea what happened to me, but Gus has a girlfriend and two daughters. Zara and Coco.'

I frown at the floor as I speak. When I do look up, I have to stop because I can see that he is mentally flipping through emergency procedures.

This might be the best thing that will ever happen to me. If he gets me taken away it could change the course of my life. I'll stay alive, and meet my nieces and live my life. If that happens I will find Ariel in the future and do everything I can to make her life brilliant.

For a moment I'm elated.

'Mate,' Troy says, and I see him looking at me hard. 'Shit. OK. I think we should go and talk to someone. I'll call your dad.'

'OK,' I want to say, but it turns out I can't speak any more, and then I fall apart quite dramatically, and when I come back to the surface I'm sitting in the head's office and they're calling my dad to come and get me.

I can't speak. I can't do anything apart from cry, and I can't even do that properly. I am going to die. I am going to disappear. This is the last day of my life, and every time I say it they think I'm madder than the time before because no one, *no one* believes me. Only one person understands, and she won't be born until 2002.

Dad arrives and he is so worried that it makes me worse.

'I'll get a message to Mum,' he says, and I shake my head. There's no point: she won't get here in time. I suppose she's going to have to come back anyway. He'll have to call her in a few hours when I go missing. I change my head-shake to a nod.

'Yeah,' I say. 'Call Mum. Tell her I need her.'

I can feel them exchanging glances above my head, and I let myself become passive, which everyone knows is not the Joe Simpson way. They can do whatever they want. I'm not going to Beachview, and that means I won't die. If I keep my bum on this chair I'll stay alive.

131

Dad says he'll take me home. Mrs Dupont comes in and they talk quietly about withdrawing me from the French exchange. The deputy head, Mr Marks, is the first-aider, but this is too big a job for his tub of plasters and TCP, so he calls the GP and then says I need to go to the walk-in centre at half four and get referred for emergency assessment. I let it happen: inside I'm starting to glow. I can do this. I can get myself checked into some secure hospital-type place, somewhere where they lock the doors, and then I won't be at Beachview at quarter past five, and that means – surely it means – that I'll stay alive. I can take control by doing absolutely nothing. I've changed the course of the day.

The car is stuffy and has a definite smell of fast food.

'You been having McDonald's in here?' I ask Dad, picking up the tiny end of a straw wrapper. Dad is always lecturing us about healthy eating.

He looks so pleased that I've spoken that he confesses at once.

'I have,' he says. 'Guilty as charged. I had such a yen the other night. I just thought of it, and it took me right back to when McDonald's first arrived in this country. How excited we were to go down there. We pretended to be American. So I had the feeling that it might still be the best thing in the world, even though I know it's actually not. I went to the drive-through, and then I sat by myself in a car park to savour it.'

'And?'

'Yuck. I ate the chips. Threw the burger away. Enjoyed

132

the milkshake.' He nods to the scrap of paper in my hand. 'Which was my undoing.'

'The great detective has uncovered your secret,' I say, waving the end of the straw wrapper at him, though my heart isn't in it.

'We can get you a milkshake now if it'd cheer you up,' he says carefully. 'Or a happy meal. A Fish McGuffin or whatever.'

'Egg McMuffin.'

'Sure!'

'No. I mean it's Egg McMuffin or Fillet-o-Fish. Not Fish McGuffin. I don't want anything. Thanks, though.'

'OK. Do you . . . I don't know. Do you need some water? Want me to sing a song? Or should I shut up? What can I do to help you the most?' He puts his hand on mine and the car swerves, so he takes it away and shouts, 'Sorry, mate!' out of the window.

I love my dad. There's no one like him. He must have had a terrible time when Mum left, but I'm pretty sure he never showed so much as a glum face to me and Gus.

I think about Mum. I wish I had a phone like Ariel's so I could look at photos of her. That would be cool, to be able to look at any picture I want any time. To swipe through them in that casual way.

I don't remember Mum leaving. I just know that I haven't seen her for ages.

When I realize where this clinic is, all my optimism is flushed down the toilet like the shit it is. Where else could it possibly be but round the back of Beachview? And what else could Dad possibly say but, 'We've got half an hour or so. Shall we go in?' And of course he goes off to the loo, leaving me to buy us both a Coke, and of course I walk into some angry man and then go in. I don't want to, but I do it anyway. My legs take me there. Of course, of course, of course.

I can't even get myself sectioned out of this.

19

On Thursday I got a text before school.

Hi Ariel! My name's Abby – I got your flyer about babysitting.
Wondering if you could do this Fri? As in tomorrow?! Our
babysitter's ill and we're a bit stuck. Two girls, 6 & 8. If you're free
maybe you could come over and meet us all, see how you gel?
Always seems better if you already know each other. Thanks so
much & hope to meet you! Fingers crossed!! Abby

I forced myself to wait until morning break. Then I spent
ages making sure my message had the correct breezy tone.

Hi Abby! Yes, I can totally do tomorrow actually. I could come over
this afternoon if that suits? I have a club so can't do straight from
school – would 5.30 be OK? Or is that too late? Also what's the
address? Thanks! Ariel

I hadn't expected it to work. But it had, straight away, and
this made me feel weird. I hoped Joe would be all right with it.
It was one thing to approve my babysitting plan in theory, but

135

here it was, under way, and that was something different. If he felt it was too much I'd cancel tonight's meeting after I'd seen him.

I knew that if he didn't turn up one day it might mean he'd managed to change things and not die. If he repeatedly didn't turn up then I was going to go and look for him in real life, as a thirty-five-year-old. We had agreed that. It was the outcome I most wanted. I felt that, together, Joe and I could do anything. We ought to be able to change the course of history. It was impossible, and we were impossible, and so it should have worked.

I had something I needed to ask him to do before that happened.

Abby replied five minutes later, saying, **OMG lifesaver! See you at 5.30! X** and giving me the address I already knew. I was smiling so hard at my phone that I almost walked into Ms Duke.

'Ariel,' she said, steadying me with a hand on my shoulder. 'I was hoping to catch you. Have you got a second?'

I felt instinctively guilty and tried to think what I'd done. The answer was: nothing. I'd been doing better since I met Joe because nothing puts one's own problems into perspective like meeting a boy who has been stuck between life and death for twenty years. Also, I was never in trouble with Ms D, and she looked out for me. It was her job to check that I was all right.

'Yes,' I said. 'Sure.'

She smiled. 'Don't worry. Nothing bad. We just haven't caught up for a while, have we? A few of your teachers have said that you seem to be in a better place lately. I know you're good at masking, so I wanted to see how things really are.'

She walked companionably beside me, and I worked hard to pretend there wasn't a girl with a high ponytail and platform trainers walking on the other side of her. I pulled my hair back and tied it into a ponytail too, with the elastic I had on my wrist, because I liked the way the ghost girl's hair swung around. I looked at her out of the corner of my eye and walked in step with her, swinging my hair in time with hers.

I was on my way to French, so Ms Duke and I would walk all the way there together and I'd arrive with her. Quite the teacher's pet.

'I am actually doing better,' I said, and I looked her in the eye and smiled to prove I meant it. The high-ponytail girl went into an English classroom as we passed. I carried on swishing my hair around. 'I guess . . . Well, I suppose a lot of it's Sasha's baby. Just having a new human being on his way is the most brilliant thing. And also it . . .' My voice started to falter.

Shit. So much for being all sorted. Five seconds of agreeing that I'm fine and I fall apart. I pressed on. 'It's beginning to feel like this is just how it is now. Mum can't come back, and if Dad tried we wouldn't let him in. I can see now that Dad always bullied Sasha, and she protected me from him every single day. She's so much happier without him. I'm kind of seeing that in some ways we're lucky.' I was thinking about Joe's family. 'Lots of people have a worse time than we do. I'm going to work hard and do as well as I can in my exams this summer, to keep my options open. I mean it's shit. Sorry! I mean rubbish –'

She interrupted me with a smile. 'It's OK, Ariel. I have heard the word *shit* before. I may even have uttered it myself.'

'You just did!'

'Exactly.'

'Yeah. So it's shit, but it's bearable shit, and I know that our baby's whole world is going to be Sasha and me and Jai. So I can't be moping around, missing someone the baby will never even know, because I'm not going to create a world that involves our baby being sad. No way. So.'

I noticed that we were approaching the classroom and wondered why the fucking fuck I'd said all that while walking to a French lesson. I hadn't intended to. 'Yeah. That, I suppose.'

'How wonderful to hear you sounding positive,' said Ms D. 'I'm so pleased. When's Sasha's due date?'

'July the second.'

'Wonderful. Ariel, if I give you my card could you let me know when he's born? You'll have left school by then, and I'd like to drop round a little present.'

I grinned. 'Of course! I promise.'

She handed me a business card, which wasn't actually a real one but a rectangle of paper on which she'd handwritten her name, number and email address. Florence Duke. It was a cool name. It sounded like someone from the Renaissance.

'Thanks,' I said, but she'd already opened the classroom door and turned back into the teacher.

'Ariel?' Izzy had cornered me. 'You're doing something secret. What is it? Tell me it's not that boy who ghosted you?'

Izzy was way too sharp.

'No,' I said. I tried to add some more reassuring words, but I couldn't think of them. I hadn't been expecting an ambush. 'No, it's not.'

'No?' She was looking at me, expectant. I was silent, scrabbling around for something to say. 'Because you do something after school. You go into town on your own every day and you never tell me why. I just thought it might be that boy Joe?'

I shook my head. 'I never saw or heard from him again,' I said. 'You win some, you lose some, I guess.'

Izzy's face changed a bit, and she touched my arm. 'What is it then? Are you OK?'

I sighed. 'Yes,' I said. 'I promise. I know I'm a bit distracted. Sorry. Let's do something at the weekend.'

She nodded. 'I was thinking we could totally do a day trip to London sometime. Head into Exeter and then it's just a couple of hours on the train? That's nothing. How cool would that be? Would Sasha be OK with it?'

I forced a smile. 'I could convince her. Yeah. It would be amazing.'

Joe looked terrible, but once he heard about Abby's texts he cheered up.

'Seriously?' His eyes filled with tears. 'You're going to Gus's house? Right now? Oh my God, Ariel. If I could come with you . . . Will you get photos for me?'

'Only if I can do it when no one's around. I guess that'll be on Friday, not today.'

'Pictures of the girls?'

139

I thought about it. 'I don't know,' I said. 'It would be super inappropriate. But I'll do it if I can. I'll tell you everything. Absolutely every minute of my time there. OK?'

He smiled the saddest smile I'd ever seen. 'You're the best.'

I walked through the little front garden with the plastic car in it, and up to the blue front door. I stood on the doorstep and took a deep breath before I pressed the bell. I was only here, I reminded myself, to meet the girls. It was only going to take maybe fifteen minutes max. It was nice that Abby wanted her daughters to meet their potential babysitter before leaving us alone together. I thought that she must be a cool mother.

I tried to put the sadness away and fixed a smile on my face as I heard footsteps approaching.

'Ariel? Hi!' Abby looked exactly like she did in her social-media photos. She was shorter than I'd expected, with bobbed brown hair and a nose sprinkled in freckles. She was wearing a flowery dress. 'Thank you so much for coming over. Cup of tea? Or a cold drink?' She held out a hand for me to shake. It was bony, delicate.

'Tea would be lovely,' I said, stepping into the house with a thrill. I'd done it. I was inside.

'Come through to the kitchen. The girls are looking forward to meeting you. Well, Coco is. Zara's very shy, but it's nothing personal. She'll be fine as soon as she's got to know you. That's why I needed to invite you over first really.'

I followed her into the house, which was a more stylish version of ours. The ground floor had been knocked together so there was a huge, bright yellow kitchen/sitting room/ dining room with a pan of tomato sauce bubbling away, and a packet of spaghetti waiting on the side. A dark-haired girl ran straight up to me, curtseyed and said, 'Hello. My name is Coco.'

I crouched down. 'Hey, Coco. I'm Ariel.'

Abby laughed. 'The curtsey is because she's just started ballet. She's very taken with it. We're all supposed to curtsey to one other now.'

I stood up so I could curtsey to Coco, who laughed and flung her arms round my legs. This was going to be easy.

'Are you a mermaid?' she said into my leg. The very part of me, you'd have thought, that answered her question.

'Only when I'm in water.' I looked around for the other girl.

Zara was sitting in the corner of the sofa, wrapped in a blanket that she was using to hide her face. I turned to Abby, who went over to her.

'Hey,' she said, tapping her head. 'Knock, knock! Zara. This is Ariel, remember? She's going to look after you girls tomorrow when Daddy and I have to go to the work thing. We'll be back home when you wake up in the morning. Just say hello.'

I walked over. 'Hello, Zara,' I said. 'Hey, how old are you?' She didn't answer, so I said, 'I'm sixteen. I bet you're nearly sixteen too, aren't you?'

The blanket moved. 'Of course not,' said a withering little voice. 'Then I wouldn't need to have a babysitter. I'm eight.' Abby pulled the cover off her face, and I gasped.

She was Joe. Zara was exactly like her lost uncle, in a way

141

that hadn't come through in the Facebook photos. It was in the essence of her, the way she held her head, the way she smiled and looked down. He was right there, in her. Even her hair was like his, darker at the roots and light at the ends.

My relationship with Joe had become real. Here he was, a piece of him, in the physical world, a spark of Joe inside a girl he could never know. He had crossed over to my world. He was alive in 2019 in Zara.

The feelings were too much. It broke inside me, a tidal wave of loss. Zara had lost someone before she was even born, just as Sasha's baby had. I missed Mum. I missed Joe, for Zara, for Coco, for Gus. I wanted to stick all the pieces of everyone back together. I blinked hard, and when I saw Abby looking at me I knew I needed to cover it up so I did the only thing I could think of in the moment and faked a sneeze.

'I bless you!' said Coco, from behind me. I looked round: she was extending a hand like the Pope.

'I thank you,' I said, and turned back to Zara, wrestling myself under control. Focus on the girls.

'You're eight,' I said, making myself smile like an idiot as I blinked the tears away, 'and that's half sixteen. But when you're sixteen I'll be twenty-four, and when you're twenty-four I'll be thirty-two and that's hardly any difference at all.'

'My mum's thirty-nine,' she said, and Abby rolled her eyes.

'Yeah,' she said. 'Cheers.'

'Daddy's thirty-seven.'

'That sounds old!' I said.

'Anyway!' Abby was brisk. 'I can see straight off that you

and the girls will be just fine. Coco, even though it's nearly dinner time, do you want to fetch us all a biscuit?'

Coco scampered off and I sat beside Zara. *Nearly dinner time*. Did that mean Gus would be home?

'So,' I said. 'What time should I come tomorrow?'

'About quarter to seven?' Abby said. 'Gus and I should head off at seven. We'll walk to town. His work thing is at the Italian place. You know, just up from the harbour. Venezia something? They've hired out the whole restaurant and we've got a set menu. Somehow we're meant to eat, like, pizza at the same time as listening to speeches and clapping people getting awards and all that. Not the most fun way to spend an evening, but I guess it'll be OK.'

'My sister worked there when she was in sixth form,' I said. 'It's nice. I mean, they have good standards in the kitchen and they don't spit in the food.'

'Good to know! I'll tell Gus.'

She grinned at me. Abby, I thought, was genuinely lovely. I couldn't wait to report all this to Joe.

Coco handed me a Bourbon biscuit with sticky fingers, and I ate it all, the top layer first and then the edges of the bottom layer, and then the creamy middle. I drank the tea that Abby gave me and found that people don't tend to tell you about their lost brother-in-law the first time they meet you, in front of their small children.

I left at six. Gus wasn't back, but I was definitely going to meet him tomorrow.

20

I wake up, knowing everything. I write it down and make a plan.

Action.

'I feel sick!' I run past Dad, into the bathroom, and lock the door. I push my fingers down my throat to make myself vomit, but it doesn't work. How do people do that? It makes me shudder. I push my fingers as far back as I possibly can, but I don't seem to have a gag reflex. There's just nothing.

I fill the jug that lives on the side of the bath (a hangover, I think, from when Mum used it for some complicated bath-hair manoeuvre) and tip it into the loo. It sounds close enough, and I yell, 'Oh yuck!' loudly, just to make sure. Then I start brushing my teeth and open the bathroom door with the toothbrush in my hand and a foamy mouth.

Dad looks so worried. He's been totally taken in.

'Joe!' he says. 'Oh, you poor boy. Were you ill in the night?'

I open my mouth to say no, but change my mind at the last second.

'Yeah.' I give a brave nod. 'I tried to keep it quiet. I didn't want to wake anyone.'

'Bullshit.' That's Gus.

'Language!' says Dad.

'Sorry,' says Gus. 'I mean: *bums to all that*. You love waking people. I bet you tried really hard to get us up so we could all fuss over you. Precious little Jojo not feeling very well.'

I shrug. I can see that Gus knows I'm faking, but I also know he won't come out and say it. Dad makes me go back to bed, and puts a hand on my forehead, and fetches a glass of water, which I sip bravely.

'I'll call school. You stay here.' He slaps his forehead like Homer Simpson. 'D'oh! The French exchange. You can't go with a vomiting bug. Enzo can come here when it's his turn. I'll sort it out. You just rest. Leave it to your old dad. I'll give Mrs Dupont a call.'

'I *bet* you will,' says Gus from the doorway. I snigger, although I hate the idea of Dad fancying Mrs Dupont. It's all wrong. I wonder, sometimes, whether Mum has a boyfriend in India. The idea makes me feel sick, so I guess my faking gets a lot better.

'Shall I stay home with you?' Poor Dad. My strategy is just to stay where I am and see what happens at four. We've agreed that if I don't turn up for two days in a row Ariel will go and look for me in 2019. Imagine if she found me.

Just imagine that. Imagine if I was out there after all, living. Being thirty-five.

I look at Gus, who is acting cocky, letting me know he

knows what I'm up to while he tells Dad he should definitely go to work. *You're going to have a partner called Abby*, I tell my brother, in my head. *And two daughters called Zara and Coco. Cool names.*

If I stay in bed today and don't even try to go to Beachview, then I will – surely, surely, surely – change the course of my life. I'll stay alive. I'll meet Gus's girls and be a regular uncle.

I climb back into bed, and allow Dad to gather up my clothes and books and pile them on the chair. He picks up my maths book and looks at its cover.

'Don't read that!' I yell, throwing myself out of bed and rugby-tackling him. He sits down suddenly as I pull his legs out from under him, and looks confused as he rubs his bum.

'Ouch!' he says. The book is still in his hand. I rip off its cover and tear it into pieces and eat them. It's easy to swallow. It shouldn't be, but it is. Eating the cover of a maths book actually feels exactly the same as eating a school dinner or a piece of toast or a Crunchie or a bag of chips.

Nothing tastes of anything.

'What was that?' Dad says. 'Joseph! You didn't just eat a piece of paper. Did you?'

'No,' I say. 'It was a magic trick. Sleight of hand.'

He looks unconvinced. Unfortunately he knows about magic tricks and sleight of hand, and he clearly knows that wasn't anything of the sort.

'What was it?' he says. 'Creative writing? I really didn't mean to pry.'

In fact, it said:

ARIEL IS GOING TO BABYSIT GUS'S DAUGHTERS TONIGHT.
1. Give Troy back his trophy. 2. FAKE ILLNESS. Try to stay off
school all day b/c if I don't leave the house I can't die.

I really needed Dad not to read that.

'Yeah. Creative writing. It was personal. Sorry to throw
you on the ground.'

I get back into bed and try to look sickly and weak. It
feels less convincing this time.

'That's OK,' says Dad, rubbing his bum again. 'I
wouldn't have looked if I'd realized.' He pauses and it's full
of meaning. 'You don't really think you're going to die if
you leave the house, do you?'

'Creative writing!'

'I'm starting to worry, Joe.'

'I'm fine.'

He fetches another glass of water, even though I haven't
drunk the first one. I get comfy in bed, ready to wait it out.
If I don't get up I can't die. I will not go anywhere or answer
the door to anyone. I'll just stay exactly where I am and
when I wake up tomorrow it might be a new day.

Every time I go to school, no matter what I do, I end up
at Beachview. If I don't leave the house, then I won't. It
feels like a logical, achievable thing.

'You can go to work,' I tell Dad imperiously from my
fake sickbed.

I hear Gus bundling him out of the door, even though

147

he's saying things like, 'But if there's norovirus in the house . . . and I need to look after Joe . . .'

I know there isn't norovirus in the house, and Gus does too, and Dad does as well really. I hear the door slam, in the end, and then Gus's footsteps on the stairs.

'Why are you faking it?' he says, standing in the doorway of my room.

'I'm not faking.'

'Joseph.'

'I don't feel well. So I don't want to go on the trip. Imagine being seasick and real sick at the same time.'

'Bullshit. Actual reason?'

I sigh. I can't think of a single thing that will work. I need to avoid saying anything that might get me taken to the emergency doctor at Beachview.

'I just feel a bit depressed,' I tell him, which is true enough. 'I want a day lying in bed. Or on the sofa. I just want to watch telly all day. I . . .' I hesitate. Could this work? 'I miss Mum. Do you think she'd have made me go to school?'

'Yeah. You wouldn't have fooled her for a second. You fooled Dad because he never lies to anyone, and the kids he looks after are too little to be good at being sneaky, so that kind of thing isn't on his radar. He's an innocent. Seriously, though – you're staying home because *you miss Mum*? What are you, three?'

I nod to both questions. Yes, I miss Mum. Yes, I'm three. If today doesn't work I could grab my passport and go and find her. India would be far enough from Beachview, surely?

All I'll need is hundreds of pounds for the plane ticket, and enough money to get to the airport, and probably a visa (none of which I have). My mind is leaping all over the place. Should I bolt and catch a train? Could I get myself far enough away to be out of danger at four o'clock? I don't care what happens after five fifteen.

I'll try that if this doesn't work.

'I'll stay with you,' says Gus, and I drag my duvet downstairs, and we sit side by side and watch daytime TV and eat all the food, even though I'd clearly be just as happy eating a notebook. When Gus is upstairs, I smash my plate against the wall and swallow a shard of it. It goes down fine and tastes exactly as good as the toast did. I eat the whole thing to avoid having to explain it to Gus.

Is this real? What is this version of Gus? The Gus in Ariel's world wouldn't remember today. Would he?

We talk about nothing in particular, and I hang on to the fact that this might work, because if I don't believe that I'll fall apart. I'm fifteen. This is not the last day of my life.

Gus rustles up some toasted sandwiches for lunch at two and I make an effort to eat the sandwich and not the plate. Channel Four are showing *The Producers*. It's funny: if I see Ariel again I'll ask if she's ever watched it. Three o'clock comes. At three fifteen Gus says he's going to the shop. Dad will be home at twenty past five and at that point I'll have done it. The rest of my life will unfurl in front of me.

At ten to four there's a knock at the door. I ignore it, but it carries on. In the end I go and look through the peephole.

It's Troy.

I guess school ended twenty minutes ago. I have not given Troy a thought since early this morning, but now I can give him his trophy and cross that off my to-do list at last.

'Hey,' he says. 'So you're sick? Not coming to France?'

I try to look really, really, really ill.

'Yeah,' I say. 'Better keep away from me. I've been throwing up all day. Seriously.'

He's already in the living room. 'This,' he says, 'is a lot of chocolate wrappers for someone who's been sick all day.'

'Gus stayed home,' I say. 'He ate all the snacks in the house so now he's gone to the shops. He skipped his classes.'

I pick our wrappers and empties up and take them to the kitchen. Troy follows. With my back to him, I eat a Club biscuit wrapper. It's almost nice. I pour him a glass of juice and get myself water, for authenticity.

'I do feel a bit better now,' I say, sipping the water and trying to look tragic and brave. It occurs to me that I could bite into the glass too, but that would give me a one-way ticket to Beachview, so I don't. 'But not enough to go on the trip. I mean, my dad'll never let me, not when I've been throwing up.'

'Oh, man! What am I meant to do without you?'

That hits me right in the chest. What *is* Troy meant to do without me? 'I know,' I say. 'Sorry, man.'

He's going to have to live without me forever.

'Have you seen my football trophy?' he says. 'I can't have lost it. The moment I win something . . .'

'Yes,' I say, and then the phone rings. I let the answerphone get it, and Gus's voice blasts into the room.

'Joe! Joe, I know you're there. Pick up! Pick up right now!'

I do it because of his tone of voice.

'Hey,' he says. 'I need you. Come and meet me. Emergency.'

'What kind of emergency?' I'm already hopping, pulling on one shoe, hoping that my pyjama bottoms will look like crap trousers. 'And where?'

'I got hit by a car,' he says. 'I'm fine. I mean, I'm alive clearly. But I need you to come and help. They brought me in here, but now they won't let me leave unless someone picks me up and Dad's phone's off.'

'Where are you?'

I know, though. Of course I do.

'Beachview.'

The walls close in. The ceiling comes down. Whatever I do, I'm going to end up there. I can't escape. I have no agency at all. Every road leads to the same place.

At four I'm back at Beachview. I try to go to the emergency doctor's to pick Gus up to take him home in a taxi, but my legs walk me into an angry man, and then into the cupboard where Ariel is waiting.

21

Joe turned up as usual. I looked at him with sympathy.

'What did you try today?'

He sighed. 'Stayed home. I wasn't going to leave, no matter what.'

'And?'

'Gus went to the shop and got hit by a car. I had to go and pick him up from the doctor just over there. I never made it because my legs brought me here instead.'

'Was Gus OK?'

'Yeah. He sounded it. And it wasn't real Gus.'

'Did you see the angry guy?'

'He's always there.' Joe looked worried. 'I hope Gus didn't really get hit by a car.'

'I'll see if I can ask him.'

'Oh my God,' he said. 'You could ask him in twenty years!'

We stared at each other and then Joe shook himself.

'Anyways. Tomorrow I'm going to try the train to London. But now you're off to look after my nieces!'

'I sure am,' I said. 'So. We've got the list of everyone you usually talk to. I'm working my way through it, but there's nothing that jumps out at the moment apart from Lucas. Have you thought of anyone else?' I took out my notebook and pen, and looked at him. Joe nodded at the change of tone.

He started counting people off on his fingers. 'Are these people all on your list? Dad and Gus, of course. Troy Henry. The neighbour, Mr Armstrong. Jemima. I think I see the back of Marco's head some days. There's Alicia, Lucy. Lucas Ingleby.'

I nodded. We'd been over these names several times now. All his old schoolfriends were living regular lives in Devon or London, apart from Troy who seemed to have vanished altogether.

I wrote down Joe's teachers' names: as far as we could work out only the benign Mr Patel taught us both. The most significant one on Joe's last day was Mrs Dupont because of the upcoming trip, but neither of us thought she was about to burst into this room and murder him.

'Dad fancies Mrs Dupont,' he said, and told me a story about his dad flirting with her at a meeting. It was rare for him to remember things from twenty years ago so clearly, so it must have made an impression.

I had to work very, very, very hard to play it cool when Gus opened the door because he was Joe's brother and I wanted to tell him everything straight away.

'Hi,' I said. 'I'm Ariel, the babysitter.'

'Ariel!' He grinned and gestured for me to come in. His face was lined in a gentle way because he was thirty-seven and he'd lost his brother. 'Thanks so much for coming. I've been hearing about you from the girls. You made an impression. Good to meet you.'

I followed him inside. Gus was taller than I'd expected, and he looked, of course, exactly as he had when I'd spied on him the other day. I wished so much that Joe could have come here with me.

'Your girls are lovely,' I said, nerves making me talk fast. 'It was so nice to meet them. I think we'll have a good time together. I'm going to be an aunt in July, so it's nice to spend time with children. You know. Get used to not being the youngest any more. I've always been the youngest in my family.'

I was babbling, trying to seem friendly. I wanted to be someone they could talk to, to tell Gus things so that he might tell me things back.

'A little niece or nephew!' Gus looked mildly interested. 'That's nice. First one?'

'Yes,' I said. I took my phone out of my pocket, looked at it and pantomimed relief. This was shit, but it was the only plan I had. 'Oh phew. Sorry. My friend got hit by a car yesterday, just really mildly, but she had to go for a check-up today. And it's all fine.'

The girls were watching TV, and Abby was rushing around in a fog of perfume, wearing a wrap dress and sparkly earrings.

'Oh no!' she said. 'Is she really OK? Hit by a car doesn't sound good.'

'I think she managed to jump out of the way just as it hit her. She's actually fine. The doctor told her it happens more often than you'd think. Has anything like that ever happened to you?'

'Happily not,' said Abby.

'Me neither,' said Gus when I looked at him.

I filed that away. We already knew that it wasn't the real Gus in Joe's day, and this proved it.

'Do you know what the baby's going to be?' said Abby, kissing me on each cheek. 'Thanks for coming, Ariel. You're a lifesaver.'

'It's a boy,' I said. 'It'll be weird having a boy in the house. Did you find out with the girls?'

God, it was so easy. No wonder adults never seemed to run out of things to say. You lobbed them questions about their babies and children and it went on forever. Even if you didn't know the person, you could just ask about their children and be instant friends.

'We did,' said Abby. 'I couldn't bear to know that the technology existed and not use it. A little nephew! How lovely. Right. Coco goes to bed at eight, Zara at eight thirty. They'll try to get you to read them stories, but don't let them bully you. Watch TV if you want. There's biscuits in the tin up there and ice cream in the freezer. Help yourself to anything at all. Tea's here. Coffee's here. There's squash over there, if you prefer. We won't be later than eleven. I can't tell you what a relief it is to be able to say, "Got to go – babysitter!" '

And, just like that, they were gone.

We played a few games of hide-and-seek, then I asked the girls to get changed. It was easy. Sasha, I thought, would be a great mother because looking after kids was fun. Coco agreed to go to sleep after five stories, but Zara wanted to talk.

We sat on her bed in her tiny room and I wished with all my heart that I could take her to meet Joe. He would be so happy to see her. Meanwhile being with her was the closest thing I could manage to being with Joe in the real world. I felt a bit psychotic when I admitted to myself that I had leveraged myself into this little girl's life to try to solve a twenty-year-old mystery, and not because I'd actually wanted to look after her. I'd never had any desire to babysit, had never been remotely interested in children.

That was changing, though. I was enjoying myself.

Zara was still a bit shy, but I chatted away about how my sister was going to have a baby, and asked questions about when Coco was tiny, and she slowly opened up.

'She was so annoying,' she confided. 'She still is, but when she was little she was actually mad. She just threw things on the floor. One time I spent ages doing a picture, and she just came along and ripped it up. I was so sad. Mum made her draw me a new one, but it was rubbish, so I ripped *that* up. I wanted to make her cry, but she laughed.'

'I'm the little sister in my family, so I must have been annoying like that to Sasha.'

'Sasha is a nice name. But Ariel's better.' She looked at me with big eyes. 'Is it nice to have the name of a mermaid?'

'Usually, yes. Sometimes it's annoying.'

'My mummy's called Abby. What's your mummy's name?' she said.

I hadn't even thought this might come up, and it was a stab in the chest, just for a few seconds. I took a deep breath.

'My mummy died,' I told her. 'Last year. Her name was Anna. She was really nice. It's just me and Sasha in our family now because our dad doesn't live with us.'

Zara's eyes were wide. 'Oh no,' she said. 'Oh, poor you, Ariel.' She patted my arm tentatively several times.

I blinked hard. 'Thank you. It's OK, sweetie. She got ill and in the end she couldn't get better. We miss her every day. It's funny to think that Sasha's baby will only know her from photos.'

Mum would have been furious at Sasha getting pregnant, but I knew she'd have quickly come round. By this point in the pregnancy she would have been wildly excited about becoming a grandmother. I couldn't bear to imagine it because she would have been so wonderful. She'd have known how to do all the things that baffled us.

I decided, again, to ask Joe to go and look for her in his world. I kept nearly doing it and then being scared. I knew that if he couldn't find her – if she hadn't been in town on 11 March 1999 – I would be utterly crushed. It felt better to think that she might be there than to know that she wasn't.

'You're the baby's auntie,' Zara said, and I nodded. Her brow was furrowed. 'I have an uncle I don't know. He died before I was born. He was my daddy's brother. My uncle Joe. That was so sad for Daddy and for my granddad and grandma, wasn't it?'

I made myself look surprised. My heart was pounding.

'It really was,' I said. 'Your poor daddy. Did your mum know him too?'

157

She shook her head. 'No. He disappeared when he was still at school. They never found him, but they think he must have died.'

I realized that she was a small child and that she was supposed to be going to bed. This was terrible babysitting.

'Maybe your uncle Joe and my mum are in heaven together,' I said, and she gave me a sceptical look. 'Perhaps they're watching us now, talking about us because we're talking about them.'

Zara nodded. 'Yeah. They might be ghosts. They might be here right now. Sitting on the bed next to you. I hope so.'

I felt warm inside because she was closer to being right than she could possibly know.

'I hope so too,' I said.

When I tucked her in, I couldn't help kissing her on the forehead like Mum used to do.

'Night, Ariel,' she said. 'Night to your mummy Anna. Night to my uncle Joe.'

As soon as the girls were asleep, I set to work, digging deeper in my search for Troy Henry and Claire Simpson. Most of Joe's friends and family had been easy to find: after everything Joe said about Lucas Ingleby I'd half expected him to be in prison, but he was, in fact, an accountant. Jasper Simpson's name cropped up from time to time online and he had a private Facebook account. Claire and Troy had absolutely nothing.

I stopped when Izzy phoned.

'Just checking in on you,' she said. 'There's something different about you, Ariel. You know, you really can talk to me about anything any time.' She paused, and it suddenly felt awkward between us. That never happened.

'I'm OK,' I said.

I imagined myself saying the next words, but it would hardly *stop* her worrying about me, so I didn't add, *I've got another best friend. You remember that boy who ghosted me? Well . . .*

We had a strangely stilted conversation instead, and I ended it by pretending one of the girls had woken up.

I arrived home by taxi at half past eleven. Sasha was already in bed, and I popped my head into her room to wave at her, but my mind was spinning and I couldn't sleep. I got out three big sheets of paper from my art folder and cleared a space in all the clutter on the table. I started to get down everything I knew so far.

PEOPLE FROM THE LAST DAY, I wrote on one, and I listed everyone we had discussed:

Joe's dad, JASPER SIMPSON: Still alive, has a very small online presence. He seems to be in Devon, but impossible to find his address so far.

GUS SIMPSON: Contact established.

MR ARMSTRONG: a man called Thomas Armstrong died locally in 2004, aged 90 – possibly him.

TROY HENRY: Vanished without trace.

LUCAS INGLEBY: Accountant in London.

MARCO MANCINI: Music-vid/advert director, sometimes based in London, sometimes Italy, sometimes LA.

JEMIMA SAUNDERS: Mother of three still lives in town, sells crafts online.

ALICIA KAMINSKY: I think she married, changed her name and moved to Australia, though not 100% sure it's the right person.

LUCY JONES: Married and changed name, lives in Brighton, 12k Instagram followers.

Teachers: MRS DUPONT no longer at the school and probably retired by now.

MR PATEL: Teaches us both, doesn't seem the murdering kind.

The angry guy at Beachview: ??

CLAIRE SIMPSON: Joe doesn't see her on the last day, and she's not a suspect, but also impossible to track down.

On one of the other pieces I sketched a really terrible map of the area, from Joe's old house to the school, to Beachview. The whole thing had happened on streets I walked every day. I was in the right place, but at entirely the wrong time.

22

I'm at the train station at seven in the morning. I got up early and left a note for Dad, though I'm almost sure that even if he's worried it doesn't matter because this isn't real Dad. I hope Ariel managed to ask Gus about the car thing, so we know for sure, but I think these people are kind of avatars of themselves.

I hoist my bag on to my back. It's just my schoolbag, but I've packed a few things from home in it. They're nonsense things: I don't need food, but I put in a multipack of Club biscuits because there was something poignant in the fact that they're always in the cupboard today. I have my Discman, which only ever has *Different Class* in it, and I have a book with me, by Margaret Atwood, recommended by Ariel. The one she wanted me to read (*Oryx and Crake*) hasn't been written yet, so I bought *The Handmaid's Tale* instead. I'd never have chosen it myself, but I like it.

The morning is cold and the platform's busy. I look at a man standing near me. He's wearing a work suit and carrying a work bag. I guess he's about thirty-five. *Me too*, I want to say. *I'm thirty-five like you.* The man is frowning

161

and staring across the train track at nothing in particular. I see his breath huffing out around him in the cold air. I look for my own breath.

My breath isn't huffing.

The nearly empty train comes along and everyone starts doing polite shoving to be sure of getting a seat, because it only has two carriages and there are loads of people waiting.

I pause at the back of the little huddle around the door. Am I doing this? Catching a commuter train on a school day?

I don't have a ticket and I have very little money, but I don't really care because what's the worst that can happen? They take me to prison? Brilliant. More realistically, they give me a penalty fare and I don't have to pay it because I'm dead.

I find a seat by the window and stare out, listening to 'Common People'. I can see the grey line of the sea horizon in the distance, beyond the roofs of the houses. The man with the huffing breath sits next to me, and gives me a little nod, but I can tell that he doesn't want to speak. He gets out a book, and that reminds me, so I get mine out too. He's reading *Bridget Jones's Diary*: he laughs from time to time and tries to pretend he's not.

Twenty minutes later we're in Exeter, and everyone disperses. I join the crowd that masses over to platform four, to wait for the London train. If I see a ticket inspector I'll go and hide in the loo. If it comes to it I probably have enough money to buy a ticket from wherever the last station was.

I don't know why I'm worrying.

Actually why am I? I've never worried about not buying a ticket before, and I've talked my way out of a penalty fare loads of times. You just make them laugh and they let you off. The trouble is, I can't imagine being able to do that any more. I used to be funny and now I'm not.

I find an aisle seat at the end of a carriage, within easy reach of the loo in case I have to hide. I'm next to a woman who's knitting a pale pink thing. She looks maybe about fifty, and has a nice face, a white fluffy jumper and expensive-looking hair. When I sit down, she gives me a little smile, but mainly we ignore each other, like you do.

The train starts moving and just like that I'm on my way to London, with no plan except to be as far from home as I can get by four o'clock, and specifically to be nowhere near Beachview at quarter past five. We pass through Tiverton Parkway and more people get on, but quite a lot of them have to stand. I look at them, ready to give up my seat if there's anyone who particularly needs it, but everyone I can see is a young-enough man in a suit, and I can't be arsed to get up for them.

In a minute we'll be out of Devon.

Soon after we leave Tiverton the woman beside me says, 'Excuse me a moment, darling,' and I get up to let her out. I'm not looking, but I see what happens next out of the corner of my eye. There's a flurry in a clear part of the aisle and when I look properly I see that she's doing a cartwheel there. Just turning a perfect cartwheel in the aisle of the train, her feet briefly stretching up to the ceiling, her toes pointed, the standing commuters edging out of range of her socked feet. I look down. There are her boots, on the floor of the train.

Of course. Of course I end up next to the nutter.

I look at her knitting on the flap-down table. It's so soft. I wonder if it's going to be something for a baby, and that makes me think of Ariel, and of Gus's girls. Then I turn back to her. She's walking towards me, laughing.

There's something odd about this woman. A look in her eyes.

A few people are saying, 'Well!' and 'Did you see *that*?' but the overwhelming majority are ignoring her because they're train commuters and I guess that's what they do.

I stand up again to let her back to her window seat.

'Different, huh?' she says, and I nod. 'I do it every morning. They never tell me not to because they're so uptight and British. It's fun. Sometimes I stand on a table and recite poems, to mix it up. You should do something.'

'I can do this,' I say, and I pull the shoelace out of my trainer and eat it. She nods, unsurprised.

'I'm Lara,' she says.

I take her hand. We look at each other.

I see it in her face.

It's the same thing I see in the mirror. It's a weariness, a simulacrum of life. A resignation. You can run down a train carriage, turning cartwheels all you like, but if you know that you're going to die, that you've already died, that every day will go blank at the same point, and you'll have to wake up and do it all over again forever, then a

164

train cartwheel doesn't count for anything. Neither does eating a shoelace.

I fill my head with the blue of the sky and look at Lara again. There it is. The blue is pouring out of her.

'Do you and I have something in common, darling?' she says quietly.

'I think maybe we do.' I look again at her knitting. I wonder why she does it. I can't imagine that any baby is ever going to wear that jumper.

'Where did you spring from? It's a delight to meet you. I haven't seen a new ghost for . . . well, for a long time. It's hard to keep track, isn't it? It took me ages to work out what was going on.'

My brain is trying to catch up. For a second I'm surprised at her casual use of the word *ghost*, but I can hardly argue with it. So I got on a train and sat beside another . . . ghost. It doesn't seem possible, but neither does anything.

'I don't think I'd ever have worked it out,' I say.

'But you did. March the eleventh 1999, right?'

I stare at her. 'You die today too?'

She sighs. 'I do indeed, my dear. I stay on this train to London, get off it at Paddington, and walk up that ramp where everyone smokes, and then it all goes blank, but I'm pretty sure I get knocked down by a taxi or maybe a bus. Not sure. I liked my job in London, but I never get to do it any more.'

'Right,' I say. 'Oh my fucking God, I have so many questions.'

She leans back and nods. She's grinning. 'Good. Fire away. Tell me your story.'

I start talking. When I get to Ariel, I see her face change.

'Back up,' she says when I move on to Gus. 'Back to Ariel. Holy shit. You're saying that your friend Ariel is a live girl, living in the future, but that you can *speak to her*?' She shifts forward in her seat and leans right in towards me. 'You speak to a real girl? Are you actually saying that?'

'Yep.' I see from her reaction that this isn't normal for ghosts. 'We meet in the room where I guess I'm going to die. She was upset because . . . well, she has family stuff. We see each other there every day. Almost every day. She can't come when it's Sunday for her because the shopping centre's closed.'

'Right,' says Lara, almost to herself. 'Holy, holy, holy shit. So we can talk to real people. You lucky bastard. And she's in 2019!' She leans back in her seat. She turns her face to the window and stares out at the fields outside, and then turns back to me, and so many of my feelings are on her face that I want to stay at her side forever. 'Oh my God – 2019. We've been doing this for twenty years? Fuck, fuck, fuck, fuck. What's it like in the future?'

I tell her. Millennium bug, World Trade Center, climate change, the internet, Brexit, Trump. I see her confidence in me beginning to waver. Her expression becomes a bit horrified, a bit sceptical.

'Anyway,' I say, wanting to move on, 'can we only meet other ghosts with the same death day as us?'

'Yes, I believe so,' Lara says. 'I've done some work on this

166

over the years. About fifty million people in the world die every day. Only about fifty of them will be within range of Exeter and, of those, only a few will be unresolved, and this seems to be the key thing. We're here because our deaths are left hanging in some way. Other people die and don't get stuck here. As far as I can tell – and I'm not the expert, but I've spoken to him a few times – you "glitch" if there's something that's not known about how you died. God knows what that is with me: I've been working on it for twenty years apparently, but I still have no idea. And, with you, it does sound like you might be about to be murdered, honey. Sorry.'

'If I can make it to London, though,' I say, 'it might be different.'

'Yeah,' she says in a flat voice. 'Sounds good, but it won't work. Trust me. There's nothing you can do to stop it. I pushed that to its limit and jumped in front of a train. It took me ages to overcome the bullshit instincts. You know: *But I might die!* Yeah, that ship has sailed. So anyway in the end I did it.'

I mean, I already knew this really. I did. But all the same I feel as if Lara's picked up my last piece of hope and flung it into the flames. It burns brightly and is gone. I'm a shell, a husk, a pile of burnt twigs. I'm a glitch.

'And?' I manage to say.

'I woke up, and it was morning, and I just got up and went to work.'

I don't want to cry, but it's too late. I'm crying. If I can't hold on to the hope that I'll be able to change the course of my day I don't know what I'm going to do.

Lara's tone changes. She starts to jolly me along like Mum used to. 'Hey, you've got a detective on the outside! Can you get her to look me up? I love the idea of a ghost detective.' She puts an arm round my shoulders. I lean into her. Weirdly, she's the most solid person I've met in twenty years.

'Of course!'

'That would be magical. I'm Lara Billingham. I live in Exeter and work in London. I'm fifty-two and my son Josh is about to become a dad. Hence the eternal knitting. It's for my grandbaby.'

'Oh. I'm so sorry.'

'Can you see if you can find out about the baby? Maybe if I give you Josh's old address?'

'Josh Billingham?' She nods. 'Does he live in Exeter too?' She nods again. 'That should do it. Ariel does it on her phone. It's like magic. You just put in someone's name and it brings up everything about them. Their favourite photos and everything. It's weird.'

'I'm glad you got on my train, sweetie.'

'Me too.'

'I wonder how they'll get you back to your shopping mall in time. The universe, or whoever it is that does it. Something will happen.'

As she says that the ticket inspector appears. I look at Lara.

'One adult and one child to London, please,' she says.

'How old is he?' says the ticket guy. Oldish, grumpy.

'Fifteen,' I say.

'Any ID?' he says.

168

'Nope.'

'Convenient for you to be the oldest possible child age,' he says.

'You got me,' I say. 'I'm thirty-five.'

He rolls his eyes, huffs and gives me a child ticket. Lara pays for them both. We look at each other.

'What if I do make it, though?' I say. 'What then?'

At some point around Reading I look at my mobile phone. There are a million calls from Dad, and school, and Troy and Gus. I don't listen to the answerphone messages. I switch the phone off and put it away. They can't get me like that. I talk to Lara. She tells me about how she came to realize that she was reliving the same day.

'God knows how many times I did it before I worked it out,' she says. 'Though I could hazard a guess now that you say it's 2019 out there. It started as a sense of déjà vu, and then I realized that it wasn't that I *felt like* it had happened before: it was because it completely had happened before. Everything came gradually into focus, and then, when you piece it all together, it's devastating, isn't it? So we don't have long before we get to London. Listen to this bit: there's a guy in Cornwall. Leo. I decided to get up earlier and catch a train in the wrong direction once. I was so sure it would work, and it did for a bit, but the train broke down at Bodmin Parkway and I ended up on the fast train to Paddington. Anyway, there was a lovely old-fashioned station cafe at Bodmin, and I got a cup of tea just for the comfort of something warm to hold. There was a guy in there dancing around and being weird, and after a while we realized we were the same.'

'How did you know?'

'The same way I did about you. You did about me. The blue thing that you only see when you start looking for it. The blue light that shines out of someone.' She looks at me, questioning. 'At least that's what I see.'

'Yeah. Me too. Ariel does as well.'

'It's always there, but it's never the first thing you see. So Leo thinks he dies on the train, or maybe falls in front of it, and he tends just to wait at Bodmin station or in the woods round there, if you ever want to find him. He's the one who calls it a *glitch*. His theory is that if your death is unsolved you can't rest. Or go on to whatever else is out there, or anything.' She gives me a big grin. 'And that's something, isn't it? I take a huge amount of comfort from it: the fact that there's life after death. I was brought up Catholic, then I was an atheist for years and years, but we are actual walking, talking proof of an afterlife, right?'

'Right,' I said. 'And you think we'll go on to something else, when we sort this out?'

'God only knows what. I doubt it's going to be a glittering heaven or a flaming hell. I guess the whole point is that we can't imagine it. So, according to the Bodmin guy, you glitch if the official story of your death and the thing that really happened don't match up. You can't move on without an ending: it's about your life making sense.' She grimaced a bit. 'He also reckons we're all in a simulation, that we're not so much at the mercy of God as some kind of technology programmer in the future, but you know. Whatever. Maybe they'll fix their computer? Or God will notice us. Or perhaps those are the same thing.'

I try to take it all in. I know I'll be coming to visit Lara on this train a lot. I feel warm inside, better and less alone than I have for ages.

'But what happens if they don't?' I say. 'Can we move on?'

I notice how quickly I've abandoned any kind of hope that I might be alive and thirty-five. I think I knew, really, that I've been dead for many years.

'I'm guessing here,' she says. 'There's not exactly a textbook on the subject. But there was a woman I used to see at Paddington. We spoke a couple of times. She was definitely glitching. We compared notes, and then she stopped being there. I haven't seen her for years. My theory – well, Leo's really – is that if the "mystery" gets "solved",' she adds, making air quotes with her fingers, 'then you can go on to . . . whatever's next.'

'So I really, really need Ariel,' I say. 'If I want to stop all this.'

'You do,' Lara says. 'And I need an Ariel of my own. Shit. You know, I never thought to try to find someone from the future to help. It's weird, yes? Because we're living outside of time. Your Ariel is in 2019. Which must mean that in some way it's 2019 now, but we can only live in 1999?' She stares down at her knitting. 'Is this baby nearly twenty? Fuck. I'm going to need a bigger jumper. Or is time different? Is it no year at all? And have you two just collided for whatever reason?' She looks at me with narrowed eyes. 'Do you fancy each other? Is it that? A love story outside of space and time?'

171

I laugh. 'Lara,' I say, 'of course I fancy her.'

I stop and listen to what I've just said. It sounds so straightforward and I know that it's true. I haven't properly admitted it until now.

'She's beautiful, and funny, and alive, and until I met you I thought she was my only friend in the universe.'

'Can you . . .? OK, pretend this doesn't sound creepy. Can you touch her?'

'No!' I laugh because finally someone understands. I laugh because otherwise I'd cry. 'That's how we found out. I was pissing her off and she was standing in the doorway and I wanted to leave so I tried to push past. She said it felt really strange for her, when my hand went right through her. Kind of fizzy and cold. I didn't feel anything, but I don't quite like to tell her that.'

'Mmm. That would be annoying for a girl to hear. You make me feel . . . nothing.'

'Can I be your boyfriend?' I say in a stupid voice. 'I'm dead, and if I was alive I'd be inappropriately old for you, and also when I touch you I feel absolutely nothing.'

We laugh and laugh. I'm annoyed when the train slows down and I realize we're coming into Paddington. I don't want to be there, not yet. I'm not ready for Lara to die. I'm not ready to be carted back to Devon, but I know those things are both about to happen.

The police are standing at the ticket barriers.

'Joseph Simpson?' says one.

'No,' says Lara, stepping in front of me. 'That's not his

name. This is my son, Kevin.' I snigger a bit at being called Kevin, then stop because what if this works? What if it actually works? 'So please leave him alone.'

She's using a kind of teacher voice now, and she sounds scary. I'd leave me alone if I was them, but that's maybe why I would never have been in the police.

'I'm sorry, madam,' says a woman, who's very small but hard as nails. 'We can clear this up quickly. I just need to see his ID.'

I wonder whether this glitch could possibly allow me to pause time, write some 'Kevin' ID and then start it again, but of course it doesn't.

I pretend to fumble through my bag. I take out the Club biscuits, the book I haven't read, my Discman, my switched-off phone.

'This will do.' The woman takes the phone out of my hand before I can stop her.

She switches it on, with Lara saying, 'You can't do that!' and looks at the screen. Then she turns back to me with a half-smile.

'If you're not Joe Simpson,' she says, 'then why do you have his phone? And why do you look like him?'

I sigh. 'Do I have to go home?' I say.

'Your parents are extremely worried,' she says. 'We're going to drive you to Devon.'

'How about me?' says Lara. 'I kidnapped him. You should arrest me. Put me in the cells!'

'Yes.' I realize what she's doing. 'She did. She kidnapped me on the way to school and made me pretend to be Kevin.

173

She's mad and dangerous. You should definitely lock her up until . . . at least lunchtime.'

'Or even just half past eleven,' says Lara.

They don't bother to reply.

Paddington station is clattery. Its roof is glass, and very high up, and there are lots and lots of people. There are, in fact, many more people than I ever see during my regular day in Devon, and they're different people, more interesting ones. These are not the thousand mainly white Devon teens who populate my usual day.

I follow the police across the station concourse, looking around at everything, dragging my feet and going as slowly as I can. I listen to the sounds of the trains, the clanking, the hum of voices, the beeping of the buggies that carry people and luggage around. I love every bit of it. I'm aware of Lara walking behind us, and when I turn to look at her she grins at me. She points to her eyes with two fingers of her right hand and then to herself.

I realize what she means: she wants me to see what happens to her.

The police car is at the bottom of the sloping bit that leads up to the main road outside, which I realize is the place Lara mentioned, the last place she goes. Soon she stops being able to remember what happens and that means she's about to die. People are standing around, smoking, and further up there's a row of taxis. I take a long time getting into the car, fussing with my bag, stopping to tie my remaining shoelace, and Lara walks past. She gives me a look. I make her eyes gesture back at her. When I have to get into the car, I shift across so I'm on the right side, and watch as we drive slowly up towards the road.

I see her walking, but we overtake, and I turn round to stare out of the back windscreen. She isn't looking at me. We are pulling out to turn right when I see her standing on the pavement. We've gone before the next thing, whatever it is, can happen. I am so frustrated I could scream.

They drive me to Devon. It's boring. We get there at three, and Dad is waiting. They take me to the emergency doctor for a psychiatric referral. We have a little bit of time to wait at Beachview. Dad gives me the money for a can of Coke. I turn and crash into a man who swears at me, and then I walk into the little room exactly, exactly, exactly as I always do.

23

Joe was different. He was glowing, buzzing.

'Oh my God, Ariel.' He was practically dancing. 'I went to London! And on the way I met another ghost! I met her on the train. She dies on the same day as me!'

I pushed down my stab of jealousy because it was so stupid and selfish.

'Tell me everything.' I forced a smile, imagining Joe and this girl ghost reliving their joint last day eternally, and being happy and in love together forever.

When he said she was fifty-two, I was ashamed at how relieved I felt. I looked her up at once. There were a few memorials to her on the internet. Lara Billingham had been travelling to work in London and was knocked down by a car that didn't stop, just outside Paddington station. The driver had never been found. There was a suggestion that she'd been pushed.

I shivered all over when I saw the date: it had happened on 11 March 1999, just as Joe said. No one knew who had done this to her or why, and that, I supposed, was how she had come to be destined to commute to work every single day.

'She was knitting a jumper for her grandchild on the train,' he said. 'The baby was due a couple of months later. The knitting was pink, so I guess it was going to be a girl? I didn't think to ask. Her son's called Josh Billingham.'

It didn't take me long to find the answer to that too. Mabel Billingham had been born on 7 June 1999, and so was nearly twenty. I showed Joe her photo. She had long straightened hair and wore lipgloss, and she was a student in Leeds, studying engineering.

'Oh fucking hell,' he said. 'I wish I could show this to Lara. I'll go back and tell her.'

'Do,' I said. 'I'm glad you met someone else.' I thought that Lara could be a kind of replacement mother for him, but I didn't say that. 'Are you going to go and see the guy in Bodmin?' I asked instead.

'Yeah. Now that I know he's there I have to.'

'We're going to do this,' I said. 'It's so bizarre that what's unusual isn't your glitch, but us. The two of us.'

I liked that. I liked the way it sounded. Us. We were the thing that was unique in the universe. I looked at Joe and I knew it was true. Also, he said that Lara had called me a ghost detective, and I liked that too. It was my secret identity. Who wouldn't want to be a ghost detective?

'So I need to be your detective,' I said, 'and try harder to sort everything out. I've written it all up on a big chart and made a map. I'll see if I can get anywhere with Lara as well, if you want, but I'm going to focus on you, right?'

'Right,' he said.

We had a lot of work to do if I was actually going to solve

this, but there wasn't enough time to talk it through. Instead, remembering the stab of jealousy that the idea of a female ghost had given me, I said, 'When you were alive, did you have a girlfriend? Apart from your crush on Jemima, I mean?'

Joe smiled and I could see that meeting Lara had given him such a boost that this question didn't even upset him.

'No,' he said. 'But I had lots of offers.' He gave me such a sleazy look that we both burst out laughing. 'Actually I was picky,' he said. 'If I'd known how little time I had I'd have loosened up. I fancied girls and boys, but only a few of them, and not the people you'd think. I mean . . .' He stopped and looked a bit embarrassed. 'I'm probably allowed to show off a bit right now?'

'Be my guest.'

'I was quite fit. I got . . . interest. I had friends and I was sporty. Gus was jealous because I could get on with people and he couldn't.'

'Yeah,' I said. 'I was a bit like that too. Before Mum. Like you, I mean. Not Gus.'

'You are! I can totally see it. We're alike. Maybe that's why we can meet. I don't know. So I had a mad crush on Jemima when I was thirteen. You know that. She turned me down, but in a really kind way. She was fourteen. No way was she going out with some kid.'

'And now she has children and an Etsy shop.'

There was a pause during which I watched him deciding not to ask what an Etsy shop was.

'I mean, obviously Jemima didn't kill me, but I'd like to know what she's like now. Not just the facts about her kids and that. But how she actually is. I hope she's happy. She deserves to be. The other big one was Marco. That was weird, probably because I was second-guessing my feelings all the time. It was like: am I gay? Am I straight? Am I both? Help!'

I hadn't expected this. 'Marco Mancini. He's a director.'

'Yeah. I was totally not expecting to have those feelings for a boy. We had an intense friendship. Then we kissed twice, and I got scared, and I was so confused because I didn't know if I was straight or gay.'

I started to speak, but Joe waved his hand. 'I know. I know it's not that clear-cut, but I wanted it to be. I mean, you fall in love twice in your short life, and it's one boy and one girl?'

I saw his eyes fill with tears and realized mine were doing the same.

'I don't know what I would be like now,' he says. 'If I was thirty-five. You can look people up and find out what's happened, but no one can look me up because I'm still fifteen. Marco's a director. Jemima has kids and an *Esty shop*. What am I? It's not fair.'

'Not fair at all,' I managed to say.

'Your turn,' he said, wiping his eyes with his sleeve and turning his huge eyes on me. I wanted to kiss him so much. I wanted us to hold each other and look after each other.

This is different from the shallow *fancying him* that I did when we first met, before we realized. This is deeper and, under the circumstances, absolutely terrifying.

'I had a boyfriend for a bit,' I said. 'Jack. Jack Lockett. He's completely gorgeous, but we broke up when Mum got ill. It was fun, but not intense. It was more that we had a laugh and

179

he was a brilliant friend. Jack's a skateboarder. He's cool. I know he'd go out with me again tomorrow if I was up for it. But when Mum got sick I couldn't do anything like that any more, so it really was a case of "it's not you, it's me". But, Joe? I'm glad you've had those experiences. And another thing: honestly you can be whoever you want and no one's going to judge you. If they do, then fuck 'em. Seriously, here in 2019 you really can be whatever you like. Your life. Your rules.'

'I just wish I could get there,' he said.

It was nearly time to go and I knew that it was time to ask.

'Just one more thing,' I said carefully. 'I've been wanting to ask this for ages, but I was a bit scared. OK – I was massively scared.'

He looked up, alarmed. 'What?'

'Oh, it's nothing bad. It's just . . . if you wouldn't mind – one day would you look for my mum?' My voice shook, but I carried on. 'I have no idea whether she's in town today, and that's the thing that's stopped me asking you. What if she went shopping in Exeter and came back at five? You'd never be able to see her and that would be so crushing. But she might be here. I know I'm not born yet, but Sasha's about six months old and that means Mum will be on maternity leave. I know it won't be the real her. It'll be an avatar, but still. You could maybe just have a little look? She's Anna Brown, and they live at twelve Sheringham Road.' I swallowed. That had taken everything I had.

'Oh shit,' said Joe. 'Of course. I'll do it tomorrow. I can't believe I didn't think of that. Sorry. I haven't got a phone that takes photos, but I'll steal Gus's camera. I promise that by the time I see you tomorrow I'll have found your mum and your sister. It'll be my first priority.'

We were smiling at each other when Joe vanished.

24

Twelve Sheringham Road is a nice normal house, with lots of plants growing in the front garden. It has a blue front door and about a thousand daffodils, which makes it look like a house from a story.

I've done my fake vomiting again, shooed Gus off to college this time and here I am, skipping school so I can stalk Ariel's mum and baby big sister.

I look at the front of the house. I can't knock on the door because I don't know what I'd say. I could just explain to Anna Brown, but I don't want to upset her.

Then again it's not the real her. I can do anything.

I psyche myself up for it by smashing a brick on the pavement and eating it. That proves that I'm not a human being: I'm a glitch and the rules don't apply to me. My world really does feel like a computer simulation. I climb on to someone's garden wall, take a few deep fake breaths and dive into their greenhouse as if I was diving into a swimming pool (a skill, I suddenly remember, that I used to have). My fingertips smash through the glass, but it doesn't hurt. I land on my head on a wooden shelf of tomato plants, which all fall to the ground, covering it in leaves and soil and splinters of wood and shards of glass, but it doesn't matter because they're not real tomato plants, and it wasn't a real greenhouse, and the glass is all fake glass. I stand up, note that I am completely unscathed, and jump back over the wall before some angry person comes running out to shout at me and make me pay for the damage.

Then, ready at last, I knock on the door of number twelve. The woman who answers has a baby on her hip and looks so much like Ariel that I think our time slip has done something weird and brought future Ariel into my timeline with her nephew. If time isn't the static thing we thought it was, then anything's possible.

No, though. This woman is in her twenties.

'Hi,' she says. 'Can I help you?'

'Oh my God,' I say. 'Yes, you can. You're Anna Brown and this is Sasha, right?'

She takes a step back and her face closes.

'I'm sorry,' she says. 'Should I know you?'

'No, you shouldn't. Sorry to turn up like this. I'm just so, so pleased I found you. My name's Joe and I'm a ghost. This is a long and weird story, but I can prove it. I'm a friend of your other daughter, Ariel.'

She gives a half-smile, but takes another step away from me.

'You're a ghost,' she says. 'Right.'

'Yes. I know a lot of things about you. I'm really sorry to do this. Hey, Sasha!'

Ariel's mum turns to shield the baby from me. I realize that, even though this isn't the real her, I can't tell her that she's going to die on 14 March 2018. I can't tell her what I know about her husband.

'Sorry, but you need to go,' she says. I realize that I'm scaring her. I try to take a step back while keeping one foot inside the door, but she's faster than me, and she pushes the door closed and shoves my foot right out. That would probably have really hurt if I had been able to feel it.

I hear her locking the door from the inside. I hear her putting a chain on and murmuring to the baby in a soft voice. I hear her footsteps walking away from the door, and then the curtains in the window beside me are pulled closed.

That went well.

I contemplate breaking the window and just pushing the curtains aside and stepping into her living room. I imagine myself kidnapping baby Sasha and taking her to Beachview to wait for Ariel. I decide that, on balance, I'd be better off coming back tomorrow and trying a subtler approach. I could do anything here now. Anything. But I need to control myself.

I don't smash the window and snatch the baby. I walk away from the house and down to the end of the road. Because the house is on a hill, there's a very steep path down to a bit of brown beach below, and I start to walk towards it. What's the point, though? I sit on my bum and slide down like a kid who's forgotten his sledge and decides to go for it anyway. I scream as I go, unexpectedly exhilarated, bumping up into the air, but always pulled down, down, down, still, in some way, at the mercy of gravity. I throw my arms in the air and yell. The not-quite-rainy air slaps me in the face. This feels like the best thing I've ever done.

Then I'm lying on the damp sand, laughing my head off. I'm going to do that again. Again, again, again. I don't care if people are looking at me. I can do anything. Maybe this is a simulation. That means I can find the edges and push them. I'm the plumber guy in *Donkey Kong*, but I don't have to jump over the barrels. I'm the only one who knows that none of this is real, and I'm the king of my own world.

I've done the first part at least. I've discovered that Anna and Sasha are in town today. I slide down the cliff path three more times and my trousers don't even get dirty. I walk through the water, round the headland, to the town's main beach and I don't even feel wet. I am immune to the way people look at me. I can do anything.

And, since I'm stuck here, I will.

25

I set off from home in my uniform, called the school's absence office and left a serious message, pretending to be Sasha, and then went to Beachview and changed into normal clothes in the loos.

Izzy messaged: **Are you really sick? Are you OK?**

I don't feel great, I replied, and that was true enough. I would never have done a thing like this before. I'd never once considered it: even when schoolwork was boring, I had to get on with it because it paved the way to more interesting things.

Can we talk later? She was persistent. **I'm worried about you. If there was something going on you'd tell me, right?**

I wrote: **I'm fine. I promise.** I set my phone to silent and put it away.

I walked over to Smith's. *Could* I tell Izzy about Joe? I hated having secrets after everything she'd done for me. I hit the same barrier every time I tried to imagine it: she wouldn't believe me.

How amazing, though, to be doing this detective work with Izzy at my side. Maybe there was a way.

I set off round Beachview, looking for security staff. I was going to be the busiest I could possibly be, to stop me from obsessing over what Joe might be doing, at a time that was both right now and twenty years ago. He had promised he'd try to find Mum, and if I did all this for him then he'd be more likely to be doing that one thing for me. The idea of my Joe and my mum occupying the same space made me feel very strange. It fuelled me to do every single thing I could for him today.

'Excuse me?' This security guard couldn't have been working here when Joe went missing. He was young, with acne-scarred skin, and seemed friendly enough.

'You OK?' he said.

'Yeah.' I took a deep breath. 'This is going to sound weird, OK? I know it is, but I'm looking into something. My cousin went missing around here in 1999, and I'm just hoping to talk to anyone who might have been around then. I'm not trying to be a, like, girl detective or anything.'

I cringed at myself for having said the words. I hated that the word 'girl' made the concept of 'detective' sound like a joke. I was a *ghost* detective, which was much cooler, but I couldn't exactly introduce myself that way.

'I just promised I'd help my aunt out,' I said quickly. 'She's not well and she really wants me to talk to anyone who might have been around on that day. I mean, obviously *you* weren't.'

He laughed. 'Yeah, as weren't you.'

I tried a bright smile. 'Right? I was a few years off being born.'

'I'd have been three years old. Joe Simpson, right? I'm aware of him. Everyone is. Shit happens here all the time, but

187

nothing on that scale since I've been here, thank God. I know there are a couple of the guys who are still around from those days. You'd be surprised at how much people don't move on. You could try having a word with Pete – he's on duty today. You'll find him round the outside of Boots, in plain clothes. Older guy. Been here forever. Tell him I sent you over. I'm Dan. He's a grumpy sod.'

'Thanks, Dan,' I said. 'How will I know it's him?'

'Old. Lanky. Scowly. Don't tell him I said that. Knackered, poor guy.' Dan pointed. 'Look. Over there. Jeans and blue fleece. He thinks dressing like that means he doesn't stand out.'

Pete was nowhere near as nice as Dan. *Scowly* had been an understatement, and he was a bit too tall for comfort. He loomed over me and I took half a step back, then wished I hadn't.

'Your cousin?' he said. 'So you'd be who?'

Joe had told me what to say if this came up, though I hadn't expected it so soon.

'I actually would have been his second cousin. I'm Alice. My mum is his dad's cousin. I never met him. I do know Gus and Abby and the girls. I babysit for them. Do you know the family?'

'Bit,' he said. 'Enough. I just wanted to check you weren't a journo. You couldn't be, though, could you? Unless you're working for *Newsround*. Or the *Beano*.'

He chuckled in a dismissive way and I was suddenly furious. How dare he be so patronizing and horrible?

188

'Dan said you were working when Joe disappeared.' I glared at him as if he was a suspect, and, for all I knew, maybe he was. He was the only person I'd met who had been in the same place as Joe that afternoon.

'Might have been,' he said. 'What's it to you? Like I told everyone at the time, I have nothing to say because nothing happened. I was working, yeah. Uniformed, which means you're just standing around as a deterrent. Here, in plain clothes, I see them shoplifting, but in uniform you're just a warning. I didn't see Joe Simpson, or if I did I didn't notice him. Why would I? By the time he was reported missing I was off shift. I know he turned up on CCTV, but it was patchy back then and they didn't see anything that meant anything. As you very well know. If you think I'm going to tell you something the Devon and Cornwall police didn't manage to get out of me back in the day then you have a bit of a jumped-up sense of your own skill, Little Miss Marple.'

He glared back at me. I took another step away, then stepped forward again, twice. I was so close now that I could smell his breath. Coffee and mints, with an underlying tang of meat.

'OK,' I said. 'What do you think did happen?'

Pete started to say something, then stopped and shrugged. 'It's hard work being a young man, isn't it? I've a son. He hasn't had it easy. None of them do. Happens all the time. Bullying? What is it they have – mental health issues? Family problems? You'd know about them, of course, if you're his cousin. Topped himself. That's what I'd say, and no sleuthing you do is going to change that.'

189

'Yeah,' I said. This was bleak. 'Well, thanks for –'

I was about to ask his surname for my records (knowing that it would be easier to ask Dan) when he ran off, grabbed a woman who'd just gone into Boots, and was immediately involved in a shouting match with her, which centred on the fact that she was barred and everyone knew it. I watched him looming over her, intimidating her with his size. I watched her yelling in his face until she turned and gave up.

I sighed. He was wrong about Joe. Wasn't he?

The words he had used were odd, though. *Something the Devon and Cornwall police didn't manage to get out of me.* That was an odd way of putting it, wasn't it?

I moved to a bench, opened my notebook and started to write:

Pete. Security guard, 65ish? Mean. Was on duty, but says he didn't see/notice Joe. Thinks he killed himself. Didn't want to talk. Is he telling the truth? Probably. Will he talk to me again? Not if he can help it.

'If you think I'm going to tell you something the Devon and Cornwall police didn't manage to get out of me back in the day then you're very wrong.' Suspicious thing to say? But people say strange things.

NB: Cousin thing held up because I could talk about Gus and the girls. For some reason I told him I was called Alice??? Panicked. Better than Ariel, I guess, as less memorable.

It was my first piece of evidence and it was thin. I put on my bravest face and decided to stake out Joe's old house.

This was a difficult move because I was going to need to find out who lived there without looking weird. If Joe's dad was still in this house Gus or Abby or the girls might be visiting, and it would be difficult to explain why the new babysitter was knocking on the door with some kind of spurious question. It was daytime, though, and I was banking on everyone being at work or school.

I thought I'd just watch the house and see what happened, though I knew that I'd probably spend hours staring at absolutely nothing. Maybe that was how stake-outs worked. I could see why the police did this with a car and some doughnuts, on TV shows at least.

It was a nice terraced house with a grassy front garden, and it was up on the hill where you could see the sea. We lived halfway down this hill on the other side, in a bigger semi-detached house, because a year ago we were a normal family with two parents who each earned a good salary. It would take about ten minutes to walk from Joe's house to mine. Twenty years and ten minutes.

I took photos of the front of the house. The curtains were all open and there were no lights on. The parking up here was on the street so I couldn't tell if there was a car belonging to the house. No one moved. A cat walked across the garden and jumped on to the fence, but that didn't mean anything because cats thought they owned everything.

I stayed for half an hour, but it was no good. I was almost completely certain no one was there, and even though I didn't think anyone was watching me I felt I was starting to look super conspicuous. It was only when I'd definitely decided to leave that I felt confident enough to ring the doorbell, just so I could tell Joe I'd tried. I looked at the things inside the front window. There were the backs of some birthday cards. I took a quick photo and then, to my horror, I heard footsteps approaching from inside the house. I shoved my phone back into my pocket and tried to calm my thudding heart as the door opened, and someone was standing in front of me, looking surprised.

This made no sense at all.

'Ariel?' she said.

'Oh,' I said. I tried to think of something to say, but I had nothing. 'Sorry. Wrong house.'

'Wrong house?' said my French teacher, and she raised an elegant eyebrow.

Ms Duke lived in Joe's old house. I filed this away to think about later because right now I was skipping school and had literally knocked on the door of a teacher. Who, come to think of it, seemed to be skipping school herself.

I made up a story on the spot, trying to piece it together as I went, hoping that my mouth would come out with some plausible explanation under pressure.

'Sorry,' I said. 'I didn't know you lived here or I wouldn't have knocked. I was . . .' I paused. 'I hadn't planned on seeing a teacher, so I'm going to have to fess up.'

Think of something, Ariel. Say something good.

'I didn't go to school because I was feeling so bad.' I remembered that I was allowed to say *shit* to her.

'So shit,' I said. 'Don't tell Sasha, but I called the absence office and pretended to be her. But please don't grass me up. It's the first time I've done it. And then I was just walking around and, I mean, I think I was having a bit of a panic attack, and I bought a huge bottle of Coke to give me some energy and then I needed the loo and I was pretty sure this is the house where Izzy's aunt lives and she doesn't work at the moment as she's got little kids, so I was just hoping I had the right place and that she'd let me use her toilet.'

I attempted a smile. *Seriously, Ariel? Best story?* 'But not only is it clearly the wrong house, but it's your house. Sorry. I guess that means I'm busted.'

I ventured a look at her at this point. She was laughing.

'Oh, Ariel,' she said. 'I have no idea what you're really up to, but that was the least convincing story I've ever heard. Come in.'

I tried not to smile. 'Sorry.'

I stepped over the threshold. I was in Joe's old house.

This was the house in which he started every day. For the past twenty years he had woken up here and lived 11 March. He'd woken up here today, in his world. And now I was here, twenty years later, in mine. What about Ms Duke, though?

'I should be at school too,' she said. 'I can see you thinking it. I don't actually have classes on Monday afternoon, so I came home to catch up on marking and wait for a delivery. I thought you were someone bringing my . . . well, my order.'

'Sorry! I don't even have a parcel for you. I'll go. I'm sorry.'

The hallway had wooden floorboards and pale green walls.

There was a huge mirror on the wall and I saw myself in it. I shouldn't have been here, but there I was, reflected.

'What are you really doing here, Ariel? Actually don't tell me if you don't want to. I'm bemused, but you can tell me in your own time. Do you want to talk? It's nice to have a break from marking, actually.'

She walked down the hallway and into a kitchen. It was nice. A bit messy, with paperwork piled up on the side and cookery books on top of each other on a shelf. She flicked the kettle on.

'Cup of tea?' she said.

'Are you sure?'

'Yes, I'm sure. I don't know what the rules are, but since you've turned up on my doorstep I'm quite sure there's something wrong, and we're going to have a cup of tea and you can tell me what's up, if you want to.'

I didn't know how to answer that, so after trying to think of something I just said, 'You're so nice.'

'Do you really need to use the loo?'

'Yes, please.'

'You do look like someone who's drunk too much Coca-Cola. In the sense that you've got the caffeine jitters. Have you?'

I just nodded. She pointed me to the downstairs loo, tucked away under the stairs. I remembered that Joe sometimes used this very room to do some of his fake illness, and that blew my mind. It was smaller than I'd imagined from his stories. I did a wee, flushed, washed my hands and took photos of every bit of the tiny room. The soap was liquid, lily-of-the-valley scented.

The hand towel was pale green. I documented it all on my phone and wondered what Ms D would think if she could see me doing this. I felt pretty shabby.

She pushed some papers aside so we could sit at the kitchen table. I didn't know what to say, but I did manage not to ask her how come she lived in Joe Simpson's house. I could see that she thought I'd sought her out as some kind of cry for help, so I went along with it, and we talked about my dad.

'He hasn't even *tried* to get in touch,' I said. 'I'd never tell Sasha this, but I sent him an email a while ago, on Mum's anniversary. He ignored it. He knows his grandchild is due in less than three months. He tried to take me out of school to move to Scotland with him, but he hasn't even written back. I don't care because we're better off without him, but still. He knows we lost our mum. He doesn't give a shit, does he?'

I found that I was crying, but they were tears of anger, of frustration.

'Oh, I'm so sorry.' Ms Duke passed me three chocolate digestive biscuits on a plate. 'He doesn't deserve you girls. That's a huge understatement. I suppose people respond to loss differently, but everything he's done is a textbook "how not to". You and Sasha are doing great, Ariel.'

'Thank you,' I said. I meant it more than I could say. Ms D was brilliant. I had no idea how to ask when she'd moved here, and where the previous owner had gone, so I said, 'This is a nice house. Have you lived here long?'

'Twelve years or so,' she said. 'It doesn't feel long to me, but for you, of course, that's most of your life.'

195

I stood up as soon as I finished my tea and a fourth biscuit. There was a pile of exercise books next to me and I knew she needed to get back to work, that I had massively overstepped by showing up here.

As I was saying thanks there was the sound of a key in the front door. I looked round.

'That'll be my husband,' Ms Duke said. 'Don't worry. He's tame.' She called out. 'Darling! I have a visitor.'

It had never really occurred to me that Ms Duke might have had a husband, in spite of the rumours about her many marriages. I checked her hand. She did wear a wedding ring. I'd never looked. I felt super, super awkward.

'Hello!' called a man's voice. 'A visitor, hey?'

Then he was in the kitchen with us, kissing Ms Duke on the lips, and turning to me with a smile, his arm round her waist, and my blood was pounding and my legs were wobbling, and I had to focus so intently on trying to look normal that I didn't hear what he said at first.

He was shorter than I would have expected.

'This is Ariel,' said Ms Duke.

'Hi there, Ariel,' said her husband. 'I'm Jasper.'

He held out a hand, and I concentrated very hard on shaking it while faking the best version of normal I could manage. My mind started racing. She had called him her husband. He *was* her husband, obviously. They both wore wedding rings. He'd just kissed her on the lips. The evidence was in.

He was definitely her husband.

And he was definitely Joe's dad.

My French teacher lived in Joe's house with his dad. She was married to Jasper Simpson.

Joe had said his dad fancied his French teacher, Mrs Dupont. But Ms Duke couldn't be Mrs Dupont as well as Mrs Simpson. Could she? Wouldn't that be too many names for one person?

I stammered apologies and goodbyes, and got the hell out of there as quickly as I could.

'OK,' I said to Joe. 'This is mind-blowing. I don't understand it myself, so I'm just going to say it. I met your dad.'

'What?'

'He was really nice. I went to your house. I was right in the house. I did a wee in the downstairs loo.'

'And he was there?'

'Not in the loo.' We both smiled. 'OK. You know your French teacher? Mrs Dupont?' Joe nodded. I had a screenshot from the school website on my phone ready to show him. 'Is this her, twenty years on, would you say?'

My hand trembled as I held the phone out.

Joe looked at it and nodded again.

'Yeah, definitely. What are you . . .?' I could see him trying to make sense of this.

'So. I went to your house,' I said, taking it back to the beginning.

I sat close to him, put my hand through his leg, shivering, but hoping it brought him some comfort. I wondered what it would be like to touch his leg but I knew I would never know.

'At first I thought no one was there.' I told him the story,

197

ending with Ms Duke's husband coming home. 'So my Ms Duke is your Mrs Dupont. She's lived in that house for twelve years.'

'Why's she got so many names?'

'I know! I've been thinking about that. At school they say she's been divorced five times, but I never believed it. All the same my guess is that she divorced Monsieur Dupont at some point, and went back to her maiden name, which could be Duke – she isn't actually French after all – and then she didn't change it when she married your dad. Loads of people don't. Particularly when you're a teacher, I guess, and you have to get everyone to call you something different and they all gossip about it.'

Joe thought about that. 'Yeah. That would make sense.'

I looked into his eyes. I wanted to see what effect this had on him. I hoped he was OK with it.

'Your French teacher is my French teacher,' I said. 'My personal tutor is your stepmum. Oh, and I took some photos.' I showed him twelve pictures of the downstairs loo, plus six of the outside of the house, and a very blurry one through the front window, the one I took just before Ms D opened the door.

He stared at them. He put his finger through them. He got me to enlarge the one of the front window and hovered his finger above the screen.

'Oh God,' he said. 'See this? In the living-room window. That's the back of an award Dad won for being best clown in, like, 1983 or something. I can't believe it's still there. That's exactly where it always was. I saw it there this morning.'

All I could see was a vague shape in the window. It had a curved edge and was facing into the room. In my head an award for being best clown would be in the shape of a miniature clown with a red nose and a scary smile. I wasn't one of those people who were terrified of clowns, but it did sound unnerving.

'Was your dad an actual clown?' I said. 'I mean, he didn't look like one today.'

Joe laughed. 'Not in the way you're thinking. He wasn't . . . Ronald McDonald. If that's still a thing?'

I nodded. 'Yep.'

'And not a creepy one from a horror movie. If you ever want to get him talking ask him about the subtle art of clowning. He can talk about it for hours. It's an art form. It's misunderstood. The thing most people think of as clowning is a travesty. It's related to mime artistry.' His eyes filled with tears. 'Yeah. Ask him that stuff.'

'I will,' I said. 'I'd love to. I'd love to do that, Joe. And I've been in the house now. I've had a cup of tea. I've met him. His wife is my personal tutor because she's a trained counsellor.'

Both of us realized that she must have used those skills a lot with Jasper over the years. 'She's probably exactly who your dad's needed. We're getting closer.'

'What happened to my mum then?' said Joe.

I saw him take a deep breath and realize that, although we didn't know the answer, we were going to find out.

'So today's a big day for us,' he said, 'because you saw my dad. And Ariel? I saw your mum. I didn't handle it very well, but tomorrow I will. She's here. She's in town. She lives in my world. I met her.' I watched him force a smile. 'I guess we've met the parents.'

26

'I saw your mum,' I say. I am so pleased that, for once, I have something to give to Ariel after everything she's done for me. 'I didn't handle it very well, but tomorrow I will. She's here, Ariel. She's in town. She lives in my world. I met her. I guess we've met the parents.'

'Did you take a photo?'

'Not today, but tomorrow I will, I promise. I know what to do now. I talked to her, Ariel. She was carrying Sasha, so now I've met Sasha too! Cute baby. Tomorrow I'll say the right things.'

My dad is married to Mrs Dupont. It sounds like they're happy. Good, I guess.

'Tell me everything,' Ariel whispers, and I do, although there isn't much more to say. I knocked on the door, knew her mum's name and her baby's name, and told her I was a ghost. She pushed me out, locked the door and closed the curtains. I sledged down a cliff a few times and walked through the sea.

'She looked like you,' I say when I've finished. 'Completely like you. So much that I thought it was you with Sasha's baby and that I'd gone further into the future. You can't be at all like your dad. How old is your mum?'

'Twenty-six,' she says, so quickly that I know she calculated it long ago. 'Sasha's six months old. Mum was twenty-six when she had Sasha and thirty when she had me. She had two miscarriages in between.' She frowns a little in thought. 'Ask if you can tidy the garden or something, for charity. Something that doesn't involve you going into the house. Then chat about the baby and tell her your mum left you to move to India. She'll feel sorry for you.'

I say, 'I guess your dad would be around in my time then?'

She shrugs. 'Maybe. He can go fuck himself.'

'I was just wondering if I could go and find him and tell him that. Just because it would feel good.'

Ariel grins. 'Yeah. You can.'

'Have you not heard from him at all?'

'No. Can you believe that? I sent him an email that one time. I didn't tell Sasha. And he ignored it.'

Ariel stops abruptly and takes some deep breaths. 'I guess I should be charitable and look on it as him having a mental breakdown, but I can't. I feel stupid for trying to contact him. He's as dead to me as Mum is now. More so.'

'Was he bad before? Before your mum got ill, I mean?'

She looks into my eyes. 'Yes. Sasha could never do anything right as far as he was concerned. He was always making sure she knew he was disappointed, whatever she did. And he was mean to Mum. He always shouted at her

201

that we needed to move out of this dead-end town, that she'd forced him to live a small life in a crap place.'

She reads my unspoken question and answers it. 'He was never violent. Not exactly. He would punch the walls, or smash things, right next to Sasha or Mum, but he didn't hit them.'

'Still sounds violent.'

'He did the same thing to me, just before he left. I said I wasn't going, and he punched the bed and then the wall. I'm almost glad, you know? I felt bad when he was treating me differently. It was uncomfortable. He'd take me to the arcade, but if Sasha wanted to come he'd say things like, "No, this one's just me and Ariel." He'd often come home with little presents for me, but not for her. I was never in trouble, but she'd be pulled up on every little thing. I was his golden child and I hated it. I knew it wasn't because he liked me. I was just a way for him to get at Sasha.'

'That must have been weird.'

She shrugs. 'I guess it came to a head when he tried to get me to creep out of the house with him to go to Scotland, and when I said no he turned against me too. It's a relief, in a way, but a bigger relief for Sasha. I thought it might be awkward as we'd always been treated so differently, but she's full of Mum's kindness. If it was me who'd told him I was pregnant, and planning to have the baby, he might have got on board with it. Because it was Sasha, he ignored her for a bit and then ran away. It was when she found out she was having a boy. Maybe that made it more real to him?'

'Bastard.'

'Right?' Ariel sighs. 'I wish I could step into your time.' She looks at the door. 'The idea that Mum is there is such a headfuck.'

'Do you still see the 1999 people at school?'

'Yeah, they're still around, but they don't bother me any more. They're a part of you, in a way. I like to think of the colour blue and watch a room light up. I look for you, you know. I'll keep looking. They used to terrify me. Now I'm just pleased to know that I'm seeing your friends.' She stops and frowns. 'I'm going to try to talk to them again actually. You never know. That might really help.'

'I haven't been to school much lately. I might go, though. Maybe we could see each other.'

Ariel grins. It lifts my heart. 'Let's try it! Why don't you go tomorrow, and I will too, and we'll see if we can meet? Let's go in early. You know the geography corridor? Second floor?'

'My tutor room's up there.'

'Perfect. Meet there at eight twenty? It might work.'

'Yes,' I say. 'Let's try it. It's a date.'

We grin at each other. The word *date* sparkles in the air between is. I can almost see it there, hanging in the stillness as we both hold our breath. D-A-T-E.

I have a date with Ariel, outside this cupboard. It may be taking place on the geography corridor, but it's a date nonetheless, and I'm grinning stupidly when the door opens and everything goes blank.

27

I got up at half past six, had a shower, ate a big breakfast and left a note for Sasha:

Gone to school early. Coursework project. Remembered at midnight x

She'd be pleased with that: it was exactly the kind of thing that she wanted me to do. I used to be conscientious about my work and always do it as well as I could, right on time. Now I was more distracted than ever. I didn't care what grades I got this summer as long as it was enough to get me into sixth form, and even then I couldn't bring myself to be that worried about it because I was pretty sure the college would take me anyway, and Joe was more important. If it was a choice between getting the best possible grades and saving someone I cared for, with every atom of my being, from being trapped in an abyss outside of time and space I knew what I had to do.

I texted Izzy and told her I was going in early to do some work. She replied **k**, which meant she was annoyed, but I'd make it up to her at school.

We always walked there together. She had listened to me for the past few years and, now that I was coming through the grief, I was hearing more about her own stuff too. I loved it when she talked about her home, which was happy and normal, and made me feel warm inside.

Now I knew she felt I was shutting her out and she was hurt. I was going to have to give her something, but I couldn't tell her the truth. I hit the same barrier every time I thought about confiding in someone. I couldn't tell Izzy, I couldn't tell Sasha, and I couldn't tell Gus or Abby, or Ms Duke or Jasper, because none of them would believe me, and all of them would think I was crazy, and the people in Joe's family would be horribly hurt.

An empty school is an eerie place. My shoes squeaked along the corridors and up the stairs, and then I was outside the geography rooms, where there were posters of volcanoes and oxbow lakes, and right at the end of the corridor . . . there he was. There was Joe. He had that blue thing around him right away because I'd looked at a picture of a river just before I saw him.

I ran to him, my arms outstretched. I ran through him, just for fun, and shivered at the sensation. 'Oh my God!' I said, laughing.

'Well, hello, you,' he said. 'It worked.'

'Look at us!'

We couldn't stop smiling at each other. I didn't think I'd ever been so pleased to see anyone.

'What does this mean?' I was trying to work it out. My phone pinged. I ignored it.

'It means we're amazing!' said Joe. 'That's what it means.'

'Right?' I did a little dance. No one in 2019 was watching after all. Joe joined in. He grinned and attempted a cartwheel. It was shit, but that didn't stop him doing another three. I could see him beginning to embrace his world.

'And it might –' He stopped abruptly, then started again. 'It might mean that if we can be in the same place at the same time of day, and if it's a place that exists in both our worlds, we can meet up and do things. Or it might not,' he added quickly. 'I have no idea.'

'Let's work out a time and place. See if we can do it. It would be the most . . .' I had to stop speaking. It was too much. I checked my phone instead, then grinned and held it out.

'Hey! Look!'

Ariel. Sorry for short notice AGAIN, but could you babysit for a couple of hours tomorrow, 4 to 6ish? My mum's going into hospital and I really want to be with her. It would involve picking up the girls from after-school club, because I know you have school yourself so can't be there at 3.20, and taking them home, just hanging out, and then Gus will be back at 6. I understand short notice & that you're prob busy. Could've asked other babysitter, but girls insist on you!! Abby xxx

I closed my eyes for a second and did my breathing exercises. In for a count of five, hold for five, out for five. Cloud tops of Venus. It was the idea of someone's mother being ill.

I calmed myself down.

'Do it,' Joe said. I wasn't sure whether he'd noticed me

panicking. 'I mean, if you want to. I can manage without seeing you tomorrow. Plus, I'm seeing you twice today.'

I nodded and gathered myself to reply to Abby. **Sorry to hear about your mum**, I wrote. **Hope she's OK? Yes, that's no prob.**

You are amazing!! she replied. **Mum's fine. It's a scan, nothing immediately worrying. So it's Manor Park Primary and the after-school club is in the hall. The girls will be deeeeee-lighted! xxx**

I turned back to Joe, aware that people would start to arrive soon, and I had an idea. Of course it was fine to be holding one side of a conversation in a deserted corridor. I could be as animated as I wanted, as long as I changed one thing.

I fished my earphones out of a pocket, plugged them into my phone and put one into my ear. 'Now I can say what I want without looking mad,' I told him, pleased with myself.

He nodded. 'Don't you feel stupid, though? Talking on a mobile phone? I do when I use mine.'

'Not at all. Everyone does it.'

He looked around. 'I can't believe we can meet somewhere else. This kind of opens things up?'

'I saw a boy once,' I said, remembering. 'He was writing "help me" on the wall out in the playground. It wasn't you. I don't know why it wasn't you. It should have been, don't you think?'

'What did he –' Joe started, but then a boy came into focus. He walked up to Joe. I thought of blue and he was blue.

'Talking to yourself?' he said.

Joe sighed and pulled a face I hadn't seen before – irritated, mean even. 'Lucas,' he said with a bit of a swagger

– maybe this was what his human self had actually been like. 'No, you twat. I was practising for the play.'

'What play?'

'It's not a school thing. It's for a drama course I got into. National Youth Theatre.'

I laughed at that. What a random lie, and how easily he'd told it.

Lucas laughed too, not believing him any more than I did. 'Yeah,' he said. 'Right. Sure it is. Shouldn't you be *parlaying en fransay* today?'

'If I knew how to say fuck off in French, mate, then believe me I would.'

Joe walked away, looking cocky and completely unlike the Joe I knew.

I walked with him.

'Hey there, Mr Attitude,' I said. I looked back at Lucas, who was clearly hurt. 'National Youth Theatre? Congratulations. I hear that's an incredibly difficult audition to pass.' Joe gave me a side-eye and a half-smile. 'So that's Lucas,' I said, still pretending I was talking into my phone. 'I could totally see and hear him. You were pretty harsh.'

I remembered that I was going to try again to talk to Joe's people, and spun round. 'Lucas!' I called. I waved my arms. 'Hey, Lucas Ingleby? You OK?'

He couldn't hear me. I turned back to Joe, who whispered, 'How did he feel to you?' I could see his anxiety. He was the Joe I knew again now. 'My mind always comes back to him, and that must mean something. Maybe he . . .'

I interrupted. 'You were much worse to him than he was

to you. You f-bombed him. He was just mildly taking the piss.'

He looked surprised. 'D'you think?'

We both jumped as a bell rang. It meant we had to go to registration. I was standing outside a geography room that was a tutor room in my time too, so lots of people were suddenly pushing past.

'See you later,' I said, and I reached out so my hand could float through his, and then set off down the corridor, alone, between the crowds of Joe's people and mine, shivering as I went.

I tried to concentrate all day, but I'd stopped caring. I cared about Joe, who was dead, but no one knew why. Joe, who was going to visit Mum and Sasha again today. I cared about my nephew and my sister, and Zara and Coco, and Izzy. I had no space left for quadratic equations after all that. I was going to get some GCSEs, but, more importantly, I was going to work out what had happened to Joe Simpson and free him from this glitch. I was hoping quite hard that I had it in me to do both those things at once.

Izzy, though, was pissed off all day. She barely spoke to me.

'Sorry,' I whispered when we were in tutor.

'What for?' she said tightly. 'You haven't done anything.'

'Exactly. What's up?'

She shook her head. 'Doesn't matter. There was something I was going to talk to you about this morning, but you weren't there. And you always run off after school. Are we even friends any more?'

'Oh, Izzy!' I felt terrible. 'Of course we are! I love you. Let's do something at the weekend.' An idea was forming in my mind. 'In fact, why don't we go to London, like you said?'

She raised her eyebrows. 'Really?'

'Really.'

Later I found Sasha watching Netflix from under a duvet, with a McDonald's milkshake next to her. She looked exhausted, and I felt bad for being out after school every single day. Sasha never questioned it because she thought I was studying.

'Hey.' I climbed under the duvet with her, and she took my hand and placed it on the baby.

'You OK?' she said.

'Yep.'

'How's revision?'

I sighed. 'Boring.' Boring *and* sketchy. 'You know what it's like. I'll just have to hope I'm doing enough.'

'You are. I have faith.' She sighed. 'Do you think we should move house? I've been wondering.'

I looked at the telly. Sure enough, she was watching *Selling Sunset*. People were looking round a huge mansion with a pool, in the Hollywood Hills.

'We can't move to *that* house,' I said.

'Yeah. But you know. *A* house. Smaller. One that's not Dad's.'

'We can't,' I said. This was Mum's home, and since I'd been seeing Joe I wondered whether she could still be here, walking round us every day, watching us, checking on us. She might be. She might be waiting for the baby, like Lara on the train.

'Yeah,' said Sasha. 'It's still Mum's house.'

I nodded. We were silent for what felt like a long time.

'I'm babysitting tomorrow,' I said, remembering. 'After school, up to six.'

'Ariel,' Sasha said, leaning back and frowning. 'That's when you study. Can't you just do evenings? If you have to do it at all.'

'I know,' I said. 'Sorry. But it's only two hours. How about this: I won't take any more daytime ones.'

'OK. Do tomorrow, then stop. We just need to get through this summer. You pass your exams –'

'And you have a baby.'

She stroked her bump and I noticed again how tired she looked. I wondered, all of a sudden, where her friends were. Sasha had always had a crowd of people around her. Now she was always on her own, at work at the cafe, or collapsed at home.

I knew where they were really: they were at university, almost all of them, and the ones who weren't had still moved away to do apprenticeships and things. Sasha was the only one of her noisy, laughing gang who was still around.

'You look exhausted,' I said. 'Let me run you a bath. And while you're in it I'll cook a chilli, and nip out for chocolate.'

Sasha nodded. 'Now you mention it,' she said, 'those would be the best things in the world.'

28

I knock on the door of number twelve. Anna Brown answers with baby Sasha on her hip and looks at me with the same polite expression as she did the first time.

Today, though, I have a different script. Today's lines have been written by the child who hasn't been born yet.

'Hi!' I say. 'My name's Joe. I'm doing a charity thing. Sorry to disturb you, but do you need any help with the garden? We're collecting for the children's hospice.'

She looks surprised, then smiles.

'Of course!' she says. 'What a lovely thing to do. I've been neglecting the garden a bit since this little one arrived. If you don't mind, could you just pull out the weeds around the daffs? Pile them up in the little garden bin in the corner. That would be perfect. Thank you so much!'

'No problem at all,' I say, and I don't put my foot inside the door, which, on reflection, was a pretty aggressive move last time. I kneel in the garden instead and start pulling out the weeds. I feel a bit shabby about the children's hospice part of this, but I know that if I did make a donation to them it would be imaginary.

It's almost raining, as ever, but I don't care. There are a few snowdrops and crocuses in the flower beds too, which I leave. I yank up everything else by the roots and hope that I'm not pulling out anything precious and rare. I dump it all in the compost bin in the corner.

After about an hour Anna comes out, carrying a tray, which she puts down on the doorstep.

'Here you go,' she says. 'The baby's asleep. I brought you a glass of squash and a biscuit. That's not patronizing, is it? I hated tea when I was your age.'

I grin. 'I'll drink anything,' I say truthfully. I'd drink a gallon of petrol and be fine. I could drink the Atlantic Ocean and not even need a wee.

She goes back in and fetches her cup of tea, then sits on the doorstep.

'Is this a school thing?' she says. 'Because it's a school day, isn't it?'

'Duke of Edinburgh's,' I say, and she nods. 'I need this kind of distraction because my home life is kind of weird.' I flash her my best version of an old-style Joe Simpson smile.

'You poor thing,' she says at once.

'It's OK,' I say in my brave voice. 'I mean, nothing dreadful. My mum moved away to India and I miss her. That's all.'

'Oh, that must be terribly difficult,' she says. She is, as Ariel says, lovely. And she's exactly like Ariel. This is what Ariel will be like when she's twenty-six. We talk for a while and I manage not to say anything stupid. She drains her tea and goes back indoors. I finish the weeding and am pleased with my work. My hands are filthy, but I just lick the soil off them.

'That's wonderful,' she says when I ring the bell to say that I'm done. 'Thank you so much.' She hands me five pounds, and I decide to ask Ariel to give five pounds to the children's hospice, or maybe a bit more because of inflation.

I take Gus's camera out of my bag. 'Do say no to this, but could I take a photo of you in your garden for our records. Happy customer? The furthest it'll go is a display board at school.'

She laughs. 'Sure, if you like!' She stands in the garden and smiles, with Sasha sitting on her hip. I take eleven pictures in quick succession.

I did it. I'm so pleased with myself that I head into school. Instead of going to any of my lessons, however, I skulk around in corners, looking for Ariel. Today is Friday for her, and I can't remember her timetable, but eventually I find her walking down a corridor just before afternoon lessons begin.

'Hey, guess what!' I walk in step beside her. She jumps and then smiles at me. I see her wanting to talk to me, but she's clearly with other people. It's not fair that she can see my friends, but I can't see hers. I just see Ariel. I only have eyes for her. 'You don't have to talk back to me, but I did everything we said and it worked! Ariel, your mum is so lovely! We had such a nice conversation. I weeded her garden. And got eleven photos of her and Sasha!'

Ariel is beaming. She stops and bends down to sort out her shoelace.

'I'll catch up in a sec!' she calls. I crouch next to her.

'Did you?' she says in a whisper. 'Oh my God, Joe. That's amazing. Thank you so, so much! Can I see the pictures now? Shit, I have to go to history. Can you come in and show them to me? I won't be able to say anything, but I'll be so incredibly happy to see her. I can't wait until tomorrow. Oh my God.'

She stands up and stumbles off. I follow her into a history classroom, which, luckily for me, is empty in my world. I kneel down next to her desk. I have no idea what else is going on, but I get out Gus's camera. The quality is nothing like what she's used to on her phone, but the camera does have a little window on the back that shows the pictures I've taken, and all eleven of them are of her mother and sister. I switch it on and show it to her. She gasps and motions to me to hold it closer.

'No, I'm fine,' she whispers to whoever is next to her. 'Period pains.'

I hold it up to her face and click through the photos. They're kind of all the same, but when you look at them in quick succession you get a sense of the way Anna moves, the way Sasha waves her arm around and smiles. I go through them all twice, and then forward and back and forward and back until Ariel smiles and nods to say that's enough.

'Shall I go?' I say, and Ariel nods. Then I realize I have a better idea. What's better than leaving? Making Ariel laugh is better than leaving.

I walk to the front of the room and stand on the teacher's desk. 'O Captain! My Captain!' I bellow, hoping she's seen the film. I look across and see her stifling a laugh. I jump on to the nearest table, and then leap from desk to desk across the room. I climb up the shelves to the ceiling and fling myself on to the floor. I start singing. I sing 'Common People', giving it my best Jarvis impression. I do my crap cartwheels round the room, channelling Lara.

I look at Ariel from time to time. I see her watching me, eyes wide. I see her cover her mouth with a hand. Biting her lip. Rolling her eyes. Then she sits up and says, 'No, sorry. I'm fine, thanks,' in a voice that means she's being pulled up by a teacher.

I am lying on my back on the floor, singing 'Tinky Winky, Dipsy, Laa-Laa, Po!' at the top of my voice when I hear someone clearing their throat in the doorway, and Mrs Dupont says, 'Joe? Joe Simpson? Is that you?'

Fuck it. I don't care any more, so I jump to my feet and say, 'Why yes, it is. You're going to marry my dad, Mrs Dupont. I hope you'll be very happy together.'

Things start to follow the usual route: they want to call Dad and I know how it goes from there. I decide to let it happen. I want to see him, and I'll end up at Beachview no matter what.

I sit in the car and watch him drive. I don't bother to pick up the piece of McDonald's wrapper that's next to my foot this time. Dad has put on a jumper over his work polo shirt: I think he's going for a Cornish fisherman look, but the effect is actually more Christmas Day. He's so perfect. I hate to imagine what he's been going through for the past twenty years.

'What's up with you, Jojo?' he says as he drives. 'Care to talk about it? You don't have to go on the French trip, you know. Your well-being is the only thing that matters. Shall I get Mum to come home?'

We've been through this one before. 'Yes, please,' I say. 'Though I wish she could get here now. I'd really love it if I could see her today, but I know I can't.'

He looks surprised. 'She can get here today! Why wouldn't she? Of course. She'll head straight home. You know she will.'

I look out of the window, my heart pounding. My fake heart fake pounding.

'Where is she?' I say in a mousy little voice.

'Joe? You remember?'

I shake my head, but I want to answer him, so I say, 'She's doing a . . . yoga course?'

'That's right! See? You do know where she is.'

'Where's her course again?'

It can't be India. It can't be because he just said she could get back today. But if it's not India . . .

'In Reading,' he says. 'The last bit of her yoga teacher training. You knew that, mate. She was just away Monday to Friday. We none of us had any idea you'd struggle with it, Jojo. I suppose you do need your mother to wave you off when you're leaving the country alone for the first time, but you don't have to go. You really don't.'

I cannot believe this. I try to breathe (though who cares? It makes no difference. I'm not a human: I'm a copy of a human).

'I thought she'd gone forever,' I whisper. 'I forgot.'

Poor Mum! She goes away for five days and loses her son.

I went through Reading on the train the other day. A plan crystallizes. I can see Lara on the train and then get off at Reading and go and find Mum.

I can find Mum. Tomorrow.

A new feeling sweeps through me. I can see my mum before I die. I haven't seen her for twenty years and now I know where she is.

We get to Beachview a bit early for my appointment. Dad goes off to the loo. I buy a drink that I don't want and walk into an angry man and go into the little room quite happily, even though I know Ariel's not coming today.

I'm going to see Mum. Tomorrow.

29

'Where are you going?' Izzy was standing in front of me, blocking my path on what was, in fact, the one day I wasn't going to Beachview. So I had a good answer.

'I'm going to pick some kids up from primary school and babysit them.'

She gave me a sceptical look. 'You? Seriously?'

'Seriously. The girls I looked after the other night. Come with me. You'll see.'

She didn't look convinced, but started walking with me anyway.

'Look, Ariel,' she said. 'OK, I wasn't expecting you to be looking after kids, and I know you said we can go to London on Saturday, but none of that stops me worrying about you. I've been wanting to chat outside school for ages. You always run away. We never hang out any more. And you won't tell me where you go. You just manage not to answer every single day. Don't hate me, but I texted Sasha. Because I'm worried about what you're doing.'

Izzy was looking at me with her big brown eyes, nervous but resolute. Her hair was blowing across her face in the wind.

I froze.

'What?'

'Don't hate me.'

'What?' All my words had gone. This was a total ambush.

She turned away. 'I know. I'm sorry. I knew you'd be like this, but I have to do it. It's only because I know you're vulnerable. And I'm sure you're meeting someone. You're acting weirdly. And in the past, no matter what was going on, you've always talked to me about it. What's so bad that you can't tell me? It must be something really serious.'

I put a hand on her arm. 'Izzy, stop! You texted Sasha? When? What did you say?'

'What do you think, Ariel?' She was almost shouting. Izzy never raised her voice. 'Actually we haven't spoken yet but we're arranging to. I'm going to say that you run off into town every single day after school, and that I know that you pretend to her that you're working in the library, but you're not. I'm going to tell her that I'm absolutely sure you're meeting someone. Some guy. And keeping it secret. I know you better than you think, and something's up. What's happening? What have you got yourself into?'

'Please don't tell Sasha,' I said. 'Have you already said that?'

Izzy pulled away. 'No. Like I said, I texted. I asked if we could talk because I was worried about you. She said she's working until six and she'll call me then. I'm actually going to be busy, but I'll take some time out to talk to her and you can't stop me. I'm doing this for you, Ariel, even if you can't see it.'

I screwed my eyes up and pictured this from Izzy's point of view. I knew she was looking out for me. It wasn't her fault. This had spiralled because I hadn't been able to tell her I was hanging out with a ghost. That he'd been arsing around in the history room and making me laugh, right in front of her. That he had done some gardening for my mum and taken eleven photos. It was so mad.

'Can you come with me to pick up the girls?' I said. 'Now?'

'Not really. I do actually have other things to do, like I said.'

'What are you doing?'

'Meeting someone.'

'Who?'

She looked down. 'I've been trying to tell you for ages, but you're never there. Don't worry. We can do that another time.' She looked at her phone. 'My thing's at five. So I guess I could walk with you for a bit.'

'What's your thing?'

Izzy sighed. 'Look, my stuff is much less consequential. I don't mean that in a passive-aggressive way. Your life went to shit over the past few years. Mine's fine. Seriously, don't worry. And *do* let me worry about you. I actually think you're being groomed by some older man and that, after everything you've been through, you're incredibly vulnerable to that kind of thing. I remember how quickly you fell for that boy who gave you the wrong number. Are you honestly telling me it's nothing like that?'

'Nothing like that at all. Tell me about you.'

'Tomorrow.'

I gave her a hard look. 'You're right,' I said. 'It's rubbish

221

being shut out. OK. Can you come to Manor Park School? Izzy, I'm sorry. Let me tell you because it's really not what you think.'

'Really tell me?' she said. 'Now? The truth?'

'Right now.'

'Go on then.'

I took off my blazer, stuffed it into my bag and put a hoodie on instead.

'OK,' I said. 'Promise you won't think I'm mad. I mean, think what you like, but promise you won't *hate* me for being mad.'

I wasn't looking at her but I knew she was smiling.

'I promise I won't hate you,' she said, taking my hand, and I risked a glance at her and then stopped for a hug. Her hugs were small, but surprisingly powerful.

'Right,' I said. 'I'm not meeting anyone. Seriously. Not anyone real. I go to that little room at Beachview on my own. I've been going there after school for ages and just sitting and talking to Mum in my head. It's really calming. Almost like meditating.'

She took my hand again and squeezed it. 'Oh, sweetie,' she said. 'But what about –'

I nodded. 'And then I discovered that something happened in there once. In that very room. There was a boy of about our age. Joe Simpson. A different Joe from the one who ghosted me,' I added quickly. 'Obviously. He was last seen there twenty years ago. And then he vanished. No one ever saw him again. I've become . . . well, I guess I've become obsessed. I'm desperate to work out what happened to him. I have to.

I hate it that it's an unsolved mystery. I work on it every afternoon.'

'Right.' Izzy took a deep breath. 'Have I got this right? The boy you go to meet every day is the memory of a missing boy from twenty years ago?' She smiled a bit. 'Can we just clarify – not an older man who's getting you to send him nudes.' She paused. 'Not someone who's saying he's the real Joe Simpson, all these years later, for example?'

'Oh God, Izzy! Definitely not that. Nothing like that at all. I have to find out what happened to Joe Simpson. I just have to. It's because of Mum. There's no mystery about what happened to her. She got sick and she died, and I was there through it all. It was no one's fault. Not that part. With Mum, it's straightforward. She died and we scattered her ashes. And that makes me feel so terrible for Joe's family because twenty years later they don't know what happened. Whether he ran away or committed suicide, but I don't think he did either of those things.'

We were getting close to Manor Park Primary. I slowed my pace.

'You don't know,' she said. 'You really don't, Ariel. Mental-health issues in boys are complicated, and back then there'd have been less awareness.'

'I know,' I said as we approached the gates. 'But I don't think that's what it was. Look, I'll tell you more later. I need to get the girls. I guess you have to leave now?'

She checked the time again. 'Four ten? I've got a bit longer. Where do they live?'

'By the cricket pitch.'

'Perfect. That's on my way. I'll walk with you and them, if that's OK. And I'll tell you my stuff on Saturday, if we're still going for our day trip?'

She looked at me, expectant.

'Of course we are!' I said. 'But if you're going to meet them you probably need to know one more thing. This is kind of what got me into this babysitting business in the first place.'

She looked at me, a question on her face.

'Ms Duke is married to Joe Simpson's dad. And these two girls are Joe's brother's children. They'd be his nieces.'

I walked fast up to the school so she couldn't say anything.

The girls were happy to see me, and Zara wasn't shy any more. She warmed slowly to Izzy, while Coco danced around her and talked her through her school day in meticulous detail.

'And then we went outside,' she said. 'And there was a game of It, but I didn't want to play, so we got a football and we played football instead, but . . .' It went on and on.

'I'm happy that you're here,' said Zara as we dropped behind Coco and Izzy. 'We told Mummy we wanted you.'

I grinned at her. 'Thank you!'

We talked about school and about the differences between her school and mine. Zara's best part of school was reading and writing, and I told her that I liked that too, but that history was my favourite, and we talked about how nice it was to be allowed to give up subjects you didn't enjoy and then, before we knew it, we were at their house, and Izzy was leaving for her mysterious appointment. She gave me a look. I gave her one right back.

'Come in, Izzy!' shouted Coco. She stamped her foot. 'Come *in*!'

'Literally can't,' she said, holding up her hands. 'Your parents only asked Ariel. I can't come into your house as a stranger when they don't know me and you kids are here. Basic safeguarding, Coco. Tell you what, get them to invite me next time and I'll totally come in then, OK? Also, I have to be somewhere at five so I need to dash.'

She left, half running, and I went into the house and settled down to watch TV with the girls because after a long day of school that was all any of us wanted. I made a jug of squash, thinking of the squash Mum had given Joe today, and handed out biscuits, and found that I quite liked being in charge. I'd always been the youngest and I still often felt as if I was about Zara's age.

I watched Zara watching telly and laughing, and overlaid her with Joe. I knew that, right now, he was at Beachview on his own and I hoped he was all right, though I knew that, in spite of the joyous pissing around he'd done today, nobody could be less all right than Joe. I sometimes had a bleak vision of him, two hundred years into the future, sitting there every day. Forget the flames: waiting for eternity in a Devon shopping centre, long after everyone you knew was dead, was surely hell.

When the episode finished, we had a game of hide-and-seek, which was raucously entertaining for about half an hour before it ended scarily when we really couldn't find

Coco. For ten horrible minutes I hyperventilated at the idea that I was going to have to tell Joe's family that another child had gone missing. She turned up, curled in a ball, in a laundry basket under a towel.

'I won! I won!' She laughed as she jumped up. 'You lost and I won!'

I was so relieved I was almost crying.

'That was next-level hiding, Coco,' I said. 'Are you always this good?'

'It's easy for her,' Zara said. 'She's small. She can squeeze in anywhere.'

'Yes, I AM always so good,' said Coco, and I looked at the clock. It was quarter to six. Joe would be gone now, and, in this world, Gus was about to come home.

'We need to calm down a bit,' I said, and I managed not to be persuaded to have one more game. 'Does anyone need to do anything for school? Any reading?'

'You read *me* a book!' shouted Coco, pointing at me.

Zara turned her liquid eyes on me and she was entirely Joe. 'I could read to you from my reading book?'

'Yes, please,' I said. 'How about we do that, and then, Coco, I'll read a story to you, if you find one you'd like?'

I felt like the number-one top babysitter in the entire world. I was brilliant at this. I was going to be an awesome aunt. I realized that nothing had made me feel confident for a long time.

Zara and I sat on the sofa and she read me a chapter of a fairy-tale book, but we diverted into talking about why a princess might need rescuing, which led us to the patriarchy. Then Coco arrived with a picture book about a mum turning into a monster when the children were crap at tidying up, and that gave me a vivid flash of grief, just when I wasn't expecting it.

I was blinking back tears, and hoping the girls wouldn't notice, when Gus walked in. He was wearing a suit and looking flustered, but I saw him making an effort to be polite and friendly to me. He didn't look very much like Joe today; he was sandy-haired where Joe was darker, and his face was different. All those genes had gone right through him to his eldest daughter.

'Ariel,' he said. 'Thank you so much. You've been a lifesaver. And I know you've got exams coming up, so thank you even more for making time for this.'

'It's a pleasure,' I said. 'Really. The girls have been great.'

'Ariel is going to be our babysitter now,' said Coco. 'She's nicer than Jane. Me and Zara think so. We want Ariel all the time.'

Gus laughed. 'Luckily you're the queens of the world, so you get to make all the decisions. Ariel's a bit busy, darling.'

I remembered what I'd promised Sasha. 'I've got exams soon, so I *will* be a bit busy, but I can always do evening babysitting and bring my schoolwork with me.'

'See,' said Gus. 'Ariel's sensible and she gets on with her homework.'

'Not always, but I do need to concentrate now. My exams finish in the middle of June. And after that I'll be totally up for hanging out with you two. Though my sister's baby's due at the start of July, so I might be a bit tied up around then.'

I saw a look cross Gus's face and recognized the feeling that had hit me when I read the book about the mum. Sibling things must be complicated for him. I felt it stabbing me through the stomach. Gus's brother had gone out as normal and never came back. I imagined Sasha doing that.

'I can't wait to meet your sister's baby,' said Zara, and I was so happy I wanted to hug her.

'That would be great, wouldn't it?' I said. 'I'd love that too. You can come to our house, if you like.'

'I do like.'

Gus went upstairs to change out of his suit and came back down in a T-shirt and the sort of shorts people's dads wear. As he walked over to us, Coco scrambled to lie on the sofa and pretended to be asleep, pulling a blanket over herself.

'Wake up!' Gus said. 'Wake up, Coco.' He did a theatrical walk towards her. This was obviously something they did.

'Can't,' she said out of the corner of her mouth. 'I'm a zombie.'

'I am a zombie,' said Gus in a monotone. 'I will eat your brains.'

'You used a robot voice to be a zombie!' said Zara. 'You're silly!'

Coco leaped up and put her arms out like a zombie. 'You are silly,' she said in a robot voice. 'I will eat your silly brain.'

Gus looked at me. 'Sorry,' he said. 'It's a game called robot zombies. It goes years back.'

*

I was standing on the doorstep, saying goodbye, before I got a chance to blurt something out to Gus.

'Zara told me about your brother,' I said, and I saw the jolt of surprise. I thought of Joe singing the *Teletubbies* theme song in my history class today, then pushed the memory away. 'I'm really sorry. My mum died last year and I know how . . .' I couldn't say any more because a tide of sobs was trying to come up instead of words. I was supposed to be talking about Joe, not my own feelings. But it wasn't something you could compartmentalize.

Gus reached out, but his hand hovered above my shoulder before he retracted it.

'Yes,' he said. 'I don't know what Zara said, but she's become . . . interested in Joe lately. My brother. I suppose it's a fascinating thing: the uncle you never met, who you'll never get to meet. That whole robot zombies game back there? That's based on the last conversation I can remember having with him. Zara asked me and I told her, and she absolutely seized on it. Why not, you know? It's nice to see him in her.' He sighed. 'But yeah, I've had to come to terms with the fact that he probably died years ago, but we've never had any certainty over it. It's hellish. I'm so sorry to hear about your mother too. These things are awful.'

I wanted so much to tell him everything, but I couldn't.

'Same,' I said. 'I'm really sorry about Joe, I mean. I can't even imagine. He just vanished?'

Gus nodded. 'I can only think that either he had some kind of accident without witnesses, or he was in the wrong place at the wrong time and was killed and his body hidden. Both of them are unthinkably awful and we've never had the first clue about any of it, though I used to think one of his friends knew something he wasn't saying.'

This brought me up short. I bit back the word *Lucas* just before I said it. He had to mean him, though.

'Seriously?' I said instead. 'How come? Who?'

Gus ignored that. 'But then you end up suspecting everyone. And, in turn, people automatically, and forever, suspect the family, which is grim as hell.' He sighed. 'Sorry, Ariel. You've lost your mum. I'm not trying to trump that. It's just interesting that Zara spoke to you about Joe. She usually takes longer to warm to people, but she's really taken to you.'

'I hope that one day you find out what happened to him.'

'Thanks. Me too. Abby wants to get married, but I just can't have a wedding without my brother. Other family weddings have had this gaping hole in them, where he should have been. My parents aren't in the best of health and it would be nice if they knew what happened to him before they died, but we know that it's unlikely now.' He looked bleak.

'Do your parents live locally?' I regretted that at once, since I'd met Jasper. I was juggling a bit too much here.

'Yeah,' said Gus, and he looked back over his shoulder at a shriek from Coco. I could see that the conversation was coming to a close. 'My dad and stepmum are just up the hill. They're great. My actual mum's here for a few months of the year generally, and in India the rest of the time. She only comes over to spend time with the girls. After Joe she just couldn't bear it, you know?'

'I can imagine,' I said. 'Well, I can't.'

'Right. Better go and see what's happening,' said Gus. 'But thanks so much, Ariel. And sorry to talk about my brother like that. I don't usually, least of all on the doorstep. You're a wonderful find. Not sure how Abby discovered you, but we're all glad she did.'

'I put notes through doors offering babysitting work,' I said. *While you were out jogging on the field just over there*, I didn't say. 'I tried to target houses that had kids, so it was that car that got you one.' I nodded at the battered red-and-yellow pedal car that was on the gravelly front garden.

'Oh, that old thing!' Gus laughed. 'I should get rid of it. Look at it! It was Joe's and mine when we were little. We loved it so much that Dad kept it for imaginary future grandchildren, and now even they're too old for it. Time marches on, I guess.'

I pictured a toddler Joe playing in it, scooting himself along with his feet, feeling like the coolest guy with his own car, and smiled.

'It does,' I said.

On the way home I got my phone out to read Izzy's messages. Or at least I would have done, if she'd sent any. I had been so certain she would have fired me loads of things about Joe, and the girls, but she hadn't sent anything.

Her life wasn't all about me.

I had no idea where Izzy was or what she was doing. She hadn't told me who she was meeting at five. I sent a quick one saying **Thanks for listening, can't wait to hear your news**, but she didn't reply to that either.

When I got home, Sasha said, 'What's up with you? Izzy

was worrying about you. I called her back after work, but she said that actually everything was OK. All a bit mysterious. Is everything all right?'

'Yes. It really is. She was concerned about me, but we talked and it was just a misunderstanding.'

Sasha nodded. 'OK. How was babysitting? What's for dinner?'

I looked at the fifteen pounds I'd just earned and said, 'A takeaway.' While we waited for a curry delivery I sent another message to Izzy:

Sorry I've been such a shit friend, and thanks for picking up the girls with me. Whatever your thing is tonight I hope it's been good and can't wait to hear about it. Are you still OK for Saturday? We can talk about everything then. I have a mission in London, if you're up for it.

I looked at the little grey dots of her typing and stopping, typing and stopping, but when her reply came it just said, **Let's do your mission. I had an amazing evening. Loads to tell xxx**

30

I creep out of the house before six, leaving a note:

Had to finish homework. Went to school early. See you later.

It's lame and they won't believe it, but it doesn't matter.

I walk to the beach first and stand on the sand, in the early-morning light, fake breathing the sea air that doesn't smell of anything at all. I do my best to hang on to the feeling of being alive, even though I'm not. I run across the sand and look back at my footprints, pleased to see that they're there. I take my shoes and socks off, hitch up my trousers and wade into the sea. I try to walk on top of the water, but it doesn't work. Instead I paddle round the headland to the other beach, and sledge down the cliff a few times. I practise my cartwheels, wondering how long I'll have to do that before I can backflip across the beach and look cool. I decide to learn a language and take up an instrument, though we don't have a piano at home, so it will have to be an instrument I can easily find every morning.

The dog walkers look at me. I don't care. It turns out

that if you don't care what people are saying about you, you can pretty much do whatever you like.

I run as fast as I can and I don't get out of breath. I stand on my head. I am, weirdly, having fun.

Today is my death day, and I am as certain as I could possibly be that I'm not suicidal, despite what everyone thinks. That means I either had an accident or someone else was involved.

Someone killed me.

If it was an accident they would have found my body.

It's probably near Beachview because there's no trail. In fact, I'm likely to be looking at it: my twenty-years-ago bones are probably somewhere in the Atlantic Ocean where they will never be found. You can see the roof of the mall from the main beach. It's no distance at all.

I think back to the things Ariel writes in her notes. We haven't got anywhere. I know a lot about the people who have moved on, but nothing about what happened to me.

I start walking towards the station, still wet but perfectly comfortable.

My thoughts always go back to Lucas.

I examine my feelings about him. There's something different there. Something new. I'm almost at the station by the time I admit to myself that the word for it is almost certainly *guilt*. But it's not *his* guilt.

Every time I see Lucas, I say something mean to him. Ariel has seen me do it. I remember the look on her face when I said *fuck off* to him. She was surprised and disappointed.

234

Was I awful to him?

Was I a bully?

I put on my headphones. I only have *Different Class* on me, but that's fine. I know every word of that album.

Lara is knitting a blue thing today, and she puts it down and moves her stuff so I can sit next to her.

'Joe!' she says. 'I thought I'd scared you off. Oh my God, I'm glad you came back.'

'Sorry I didn't come before,' I say. 'I needed to think. Guess what, Lara? I found out that my mum's not in India! She's in Reading.'

She laughs. 'Easy mistake.'

'I know. I feel such an idiot. I just filled in the blanks and got it wrong.'

'Oh, darling.'

'I knew I didn't see Mum today, and I think over the years it all stretched to make me feel I hadn't seen her for ages and I developed a story for that. I took the fact that she wasn't there, and that she was retraining as a yoga teacher, and made up a scenario where she was doing yoga in India. And in fact –'

'In fact, she's doing yoga in Reading?'

'Yeah. She's only away Monday to Friday, and only this week. Sucks that it's always Thursday.'

'Doesn't it? Are you getting off this train at Reading then?'

'Yep.'

She smiles broadly and pats my arm. 'You're going to

find your mum!' She looks genuinely delighted. I beam back.

'I got the address of where she is. Some place called the Yoga Dojo.'

'Yoga Dojo? Someone's a bit confused.'

'I'm glad it has a silly name because it's easy to remember when you reset. So we have two and a bit hours until we get there, don't we? Right. Ariel looked you up. Most importantly, if you're going for traditional colours you had it right last time.' I nod at her knitting and wait for her to realize what I'm saying.

'I should be knitting in pink? The baby's a girl?'

'Mabel Lara Billingham. She's going to be born on Monday, June the seventh.'

'Her due date! How perfect. And they gave her my name.'

I can see Lara's emotion, and I understand it in a way that I don't really understand anything else. 'She goes to university in Leeds, doing engineering. She has long hair, very straight, and wears lipgloss. She's doing really well, Lara. So you don't need to worry about her anyway. She's OK. I've seen her social media, and she really does seem happy.' I look at her face. 'Social media is the writing and photos on the internet. It's how Ariel finds out about people. I wish I could show you.'

We talk about Mabel for ages, and I think about the amount of love that goes into Lara's daily knitting, for an unborn baby who's grown up and gone to university. Knitting is the only way she can demonstrate how much she loves her granddaughter. It's the only thing she can do for her and it's completely pointless.

'Thank you, Joe,' she says in the end, visibly making an effort to calm herself. 'This is incredible. They did say they liked Mabel as a name. I said it was a bit old-ladyish, but I guess by the time she was born it didn't matter what I thought.'

I checked the time.

'Next thing,' I said. 'I didn't see what happened to you last time. We'd driven off by then. Want me to try again sometime?'

'Would you?'

'Course. I'll come back in a couple of days. I'm sure I can cover my tracks so the police aren't there to meet me. I'll at least buy enough time to walk up that slope with you. If you want me to.'

'Thank you,' she says. She takes my hand and it's the most real contact I've had in twenty years. I never want to let go.

There are no police waiting at Reading. I get into a taxi and ask for the Yoga Dojo, and the guy knows where it is and starts driving. I watch the meter, wishing I'd taken more money from home. I have £8.25, but of course it doesn't matter if I run away without paying for the cab. Also, it's taking me to my mum. She'll pay because she's my mum.

In the end, though, it's close to the station and I have £4.50 left over. There's a shop selling flowers just down the road, and £4.50 gets me a bunch of pink and white carnations, and I steal a box of chocolates on my way out too, because Mum probably still likes chocolates. Everyone does.

The dojo is on the first floor of an office building, and no one stops me when I go in through the main door.

No one stops me going up the stairs.

There's a reception desk with a man sitting behind it. He has a ponytail and is dressed all in black: his air is more *dojo* than *yoga*. The whole place smells of cinnamon, I think, and the floor is polished with rugs on it. I'm glad Mum's been somewhere nice all this time.

'Hey there!' he says with such huge enthusiasm that I wonder whether he's on drugs. 'Can I help you?'

I plaster on my best smile. 'Yeah,' I say. 'I hope so. This might sound a bit weird, but my mum's doing a course here this week. It's her birthday so I've brought her some flowers and chocolates as a surprise from me and my brother.'

'*Ahhh*,' he says. 'Well, aren't you adorable?' He checks the time. 'They're in studio two, and there's a break coming up at half ten. You OK to wait? Who's your mum? Hang on – Claire, right?'

It's ten fifteen. 'Yes!'

'Gus or Joe?'

I am so happy that I want to dance. I do a little jig just because I can.

'I'm Joe,' I say.

'She talks about you two all the time. It's adorable. Have a seat. Want a glass of water?'

I shake my head. It's nice not having to bother with that stuff.

The world's slowest fifteen minutes crawl by, but I surf it on a wave of *Mum talks about me all the time*. Until yesterday I thought she'd forgotten us. Instead she's boring people in Reading by going on about me and Gus. I guess there's going to be a change in mood this evening when one of the boys she keeps banging on about disappears forever.

I look at the man, hoping that he's not bored enough to check my mum's date of birth on some list and realize that it's not her birthday at all. He answers the phone and tells someone that the Saturday classes are usually full, but that they could turn up early and try their luck.

'Not at school?' he says, turning back to me.

'Staff training day.'

After one million hours a door opens somewhere in the building, and the man says, 'Here we go.'

I'm shaking from head to foot.

'Claire!' he yells. 'Claire! You're a dark horse. Thought you could get away without mentioning that it's your birthday? You've got a special visitor.'

I hear the most familiar, perfect voice in the world saying, 'Dan, what the hell are you –' Then she comes round the corner and stops. 'Joe!'

I am on my feet, and I run right into her and hug her. I feel her arms closing round me. I am ten, seven, two, a baby, a foetus. I am just a child who really, really needs his mum.

'Oh, Joe,' she says. 'Joe, what's happened? Are Dad and Gus OK? What's going on?'

'They're fine.' I lower my voice. 'Sorry, you have to pretend it's your birthday.' I thrust out the flowers and chocolates and she takes them.

'Thank you!' she says loudly. 'You didn't need to do this!' She puts it all down on the table. 'What's happening?' she says quietly.

'Can we go somewhere and talk? Just while you're on your break?'

She steps back and disentangles us a bit. 'Of course. Come on. Dan? I'm just going to have to skip out of a bit of the next session, OK? Can you tell Nicki?'

Mum manages not to say anything until we're at the nearest cafe, which is a regular greasy-spoon-type place and very un-Mum. I just keep looking at her, relieved beyond belief to have found her. I'd forgotten what she really looks like. I'd replaced her with a slightly different version, a mother who'd go off to India for twenty years without me. Real Mum has long hair that's going grey. She's wearing leggings and a T-shirt with her coat over the top, and no make-up. Above all, she looks incredibly worried.

'What's happening, Joe?' she says as we sit down. 'How worried do I need to be?'

'Oh, Mum,' I say. 'I just really needed to see you. I'm so scared about something that's going to happen tonight. And I needed to see you one more time before I . . .' I hesitate, edit out the word *die*. 'Go.'

'Oh, Joseph.' She puts her hand over mine. 'Look, you

240

don't have to go on the French trip if it's going to bother you this much. Honestly – it doesn't matter in the scheme of things. Not at all. It's not worth getting worked up about it. Does Dad know you're not at school?' I shake my head. I bought myself time today by making a phone call to school. 'Then I'd better call him. Let's get you home. My course finishes tomorrow, but I can come home with you today. I'll skip the rest of today's session and do a day trip back here tomorrow. I'm sure they'll let me have the certificate anyway. I'll finish my Sanskrit this evening.'

She stares into my eyes with such intensity that for a moment I think she knows everything. I'm warm inside. Happy. She didn't leave us. She's still with Dad. I know that they'll split up later, that Dad will remarry, but right now, today, they're happy with each other.

'Can we go home now?'

'Give me a few minutes to sort it out with Dan and Nicki. And then we'll need to walk down to the hotel to get my stuff and the car.'

'Thank you, Mum. I'm sorry. This is probably the first time you've been able to do something like this for years. I'm sorry for spoiling it.'

She laughs, then reaches over and ruffles my hair. 'Don't be silly. If you were messing around I'd have sent you home. But a mother knows, and I know that this is serious. You can tell when you have to prioritize your kid's well-being above all else, and this is one of those times. Maybe we can talk properly in the car? That's often a good way of doing it.'

I nod. 'It's going to sound mental,' I warn her.

'I can do mental,' she says. 'I, of all people, know how to do that.'

She looks at the road and drives and listens, and I find myself telling her every single bit of it. I tell her I've been living the same day for more than twenty years. I tell her about meeting Ariel. I tell her about all the future things, and about Lara, and about Gus and Abby and the girls. I tell her that in 2019 she lives mainly in India, just coming back to visit her granddaughters, and that Dad's married to my French teacher. I tell her that no one has any idea what happened to me.

She listens without saying anything except, 'Mmm,' and other sounds along those lines. She looks straight ahead at the road, apart from the odd quick glance when she imagines I'm not looking. I know she thinks I'm having a breakdown, but I don't care. It's just lovely to say it all, from beginning to end, to someone who's in a position where she has to sit and listen. She doesn't try to shut me off, or stop me. She just hears me out.

When I've said every bit of it, I wait for a reply. I know what it's going to be, and I'm right. She gently tells me that I shouldn't go to France, and that they're going to get me help. 'We'll start off by getting an emergency doctor's appointment, and take it from there.'

I don't care. I knew I was going to end up at Beachview, but this time I get to go almost all the way to Ariel with my mum.

31

Joe was happier than I'd seen him for ages. He'd found his mum. I could tell that he didn't really want to talk about it. He just said that he'd tracked her down and got her to bring him back to Devon. He'd said goodbye to her forever just outside Beachview, and he was plainly still in shock, mostly at the fact that for years and years he'd assumed that she'd walked away because she didn't love him enough, but that he'd been completely wrong about all of it.

'You sit down,' I said, 'and just let me talk at you. You can sit there and ignore me if you want. I wish I could give you a hug.'

'Me too,' he said.

'So.' I took the pieces of paper out of my bag and spread them out on the floor. 'Can you see these?'

'No. Yes. I think I can only see them when you're touching them.'

'Oh, that's weird!'

We experimented and discovered that yes, he could only see them when I was touching them.

I put my hand on the first one. 'So. This one is the timeline.'

I put a finger on the other. 'This one's my typed-up list of everyone interesting, with my research filled in. I've taken off the people who I was sure weren't relevant and focused on these ones.'

I held it out.

LUCAS INGLEBY: Lives in London. Works in accounts. Found his home address on the open register for the electoral roll. His mum Maria Ingleby works at Greentrees Primary School (not Z & C's school).
Gus said someone was hiding something and I think he was talking about Lucas. Joe was pretty dismissive and mean to him. Does that make him the prime suspect? He's the best we've got.
GO AND FIND HIM IN LONDON ON SATURDAY.

MARCO MANCINI: Lives between London, LA and Rome, works in film. Could track him down at his office possibly if he's in London. No home address, social media all private, but cover photos suggest a husband. Added him on FB and Insta, but he hasn't responded.

TROY HENRY: Nothing on the internet after 2010, but posted about moving to France before that. His parents Sheila and Piet still live here.

JEMIMA SAUNDERS: Still lives here, has three kids, sells baby clothes on Etsy, looks happy and lovely. Easiest to track down: I've ordered something from her Etsy store.

GUS & FAMILY: Still here. Contact firmly made.

JASPER SIMPSON/MRS DUPONT (FLORENCE DUKE): Here.
Contact unexpectedly established.

CLAIRE SIMPSON: All we know is that she lives in India and comes
back a couple of times a year to see the girls. Can't find her at all
online as her name is too common, no matter what search terms I try.
She probably lives deliberately offline.

ANGRY GUY AT BEACHVIEW: No idea who he is – Joe to take
a photo?

'It's not much,' I admitted.

'I keep coming back to Lucas too,' Joe said. He looked at the door. 'Not that I think he's going to crash through there and kill me. But you're right – I was horrible to him. More than I realized. We could have got into a fight maybe, and he might have punched me in the head without meaning to kill me. And if Gus thought he was hiding something, then maybe that implies he was acting oddly? Guiltily?'

'Maybe? But where's your body?'

He sighed. 'The eternal mystery. In the ocean. It has to be.'

Poor Joe. I longed with all my heart to be able to comfort him properly.

'I love you, Joe,' I said.

I stopped, shocked at myself. I did love him, but I hadn't intended to say it. Did I love him romantically? Or like a brother? I knew the answer, but I tried very hard to mean it platonically. Way to go, Ariel. Fall in love with a ghost and accidentally tell him.

I wondered what it would have felt like to put my hand on his cheek. I wondered what he would have smelled like.

'I love you too, Ariel,' he said as if it was super straightforward. 'Of course I do. I absolutely adore you. You're everything.'

'I wish . . .' I stopped. None of this was going to make anything better. 'Well, you know. I wish everything. I won't give up on you, Joe.'

He didn't reply. He just looked back at my piece of paper and sighed.

I took my hand off it to stop him reading it, and paced up and down, as far as the tiny room allowed. 'So,' I said. 'Like it says there, I'm going to London tomorrow. Izzy's coming with me. She doesn't know this yet, but we're going to start off by going to Lucas's address. It's Saturday. Hopefully he'll be home. OK? That's a concrete thing, and I'm going to do it. I wish we could get on Lara's train because I'd like to find out whether I can see her, but we can't go that early, and also that train doesn't exist on a Saturday. I did think about it, though.'

Joe smiled, and I could see that it was forced.

'Thank you,' he said.

'Joe, talk to me.'

'Sorry.'

'It's seeing your mum?'

'It changes everything. I haven't seen her for twenty years and now I've found her. Ariel, I think I'm going to go to Bodmin tomorrow, to find that guy Lara told me about. Maybe I'll see you at the station. But after that I might just go to Reading every day. If I can make a day when I see Dad, Gus, Troy,

Mum, Lara and you then I think that's the best day I can possibly have. And I'm going to learn a language and an instrument and how to do backflips.' He gave a sad little smile. 'I've got eternity. Might as well use it.'

'Then do that,' I said. 'But how do you fit Troy into that day? And actually you didn't even see your dad and Gus today, did you?'

'That's true,' he says. 'Maybe I'll just make two days that I live over and over, in rotation. And whenever I see Lucas I'm going to be incredibly nice to him. That might change something. You never know.'

I remembered how horrible Joe had been to Lucas, how much I'd hated it. I nodded.

'You never know,' I said.

I was walking home with my headphones in and *Different Class* playing because it was the sound of Joe's day, when I felt a tap on my shoulder. When I looked round, I was surprised to see Jack Lockett. His hair was falling over his face, and he smiled shyly and tucked it behind his ear.

'Hey,' I said, grinning at him, taking out an earphone.

'Can I walk with you a bit?' He was taller than me, but shorter than Joe, and he was carrying a skateboard. I supposed I hadn't heard him approach on it because my music was so loud.

'Course!' I said. 'How are you?'

'Oh, I'm OK,' he said. 'What about you, though? I feel like I haven't seen you for ages, Ariel. I just. You know.' He looked adorably awkward. 'I guess I hope you're OK.'

'Thanks,' I said. 'Truly, Jack, I am OK. I'm doing much better than I was before. I know I did sort of fall apart.'

'Hey. Who wouldn't?'

Jack was objectively gorgeous. And he was lovely, and he was into me. We had been the perfect couple for a while. I would always be incredibly fond of him.

If my heart hadn't been entirely captured by Joe I would, I realized, be in a place to spend a bit of time with Jack again. He was thinking along the same lines, clearly, because he said, 'Do you fancy hanging out sometime maybe?'

I nodded, then shook my head and said, 'I'm not sure, Jack. Honestly. I really like you and I'd love to hang out as friends, but . . .'

His face closed and he took a step back.

'Sure. Sorry. See you then,' he said, and set off again on his skateboard.

I went home and told Sasha that I was going to Exeter with Izzy on Saturday, and she nodded without really listening. She was texting Jai, judging by the annoyance on her face. I started chopping vegetables for a stir-fry and waited until Sasha threw the phone down (carefully, on to a sofa cushion) and said, 'Bastard!'

'What?' I said as mildly as I could.

'He wants to be in the baby's life. But not. And then he does. And then he doesn't. He'll support us financially, but not if we're already OK for cash. I've never asked him for anything because it's my decision to go through with this, but if he could stop changing his fucking mind that would be just GREAT.'

'He's an idiot.' I shook a load of salt into the rice pan. I was still a bit exhilarated. I had turned down Jack because I loved Joe. If you squinted and made everything so blurry that you couldn't see the inconvenient parts, my relationship with Joe was going incredibly well.

'He's just so annoying,' said Sasha. 'I've been kind of assuming that when he meets an actual baby that's half made of him he'll want to be a dad because that's quite a thing.'

She sighed. 'But then again he's nineteen. I do know we were just messing around and we didn't plan anything. This baby is my lifeline, not his. I don't want him to marry me! I don't even want him to be my boyfriend. I just want him to step up the tiniest bit for the baby's sake. But he hasn't told his parents. Can you imagine, Mermaid? I'm nearly six months' pregnant, my mum's dead, my dad's left and I live with my little sister who cooks every night because she's an angel, and we are fucking *managing*. And then there's poor little Jai, who has both parents and several siblings, and none of them know that he's going to be a dad. Given that all the money he earns comes from a summer holiday job selling ice cream, I don't know how he's planning to support us if he is, and I don't care! I just want him to be there emotionally. I hate it that I have to be the one comforting him.'

She burst into noisy tears, and I turned the gas down and hugged her. I said soothing things without knowing if they were true or not. I told her that he certainly would come round, that it was one thing to freak out at an idea. 'But you can't freak out at an actual human,' I said. 'You're right. When he sees his son, everything will change.'

'We're actual humans,' she said. 'We were babies once. And Dad freaked out at us. At me.'

'Jai is better than Dad,' I said, and at last she laughed.

'The faintest praise,' she said. 'But you're right.'

'I wonder why Mum married him. And why he stuck around all that time.'

Sasha sighed. 'I don't think it does us much good to dwell on it. But I reckon he depended on her so much. Maybe in his way he loved her too much to be able to manage without her. He always wanted to move away, didn't he? But Mum wouldn't, and he never went on his own until she was gone.'

I shuddered.

'He was horrible to Mum. Remember how he'd punch the wall next to her? That's a toxic way of loving someone too much. I think he's just a wanker.'

'Yeah. Whatever else happens, we've always got that. A central truth.'

We smiled at each other. Everything felt a bit better. We ate the stir-fry, which was nice enough, and then finished all the chocolate we could find.

'An actual baby, though,' I said.

'I know.'

'Can we go shopping yet?'

Sasha had been superstitious about not buying anything until it was nearly time for the birth, but now that she was pretty much six months pregnant I thought we might be able to start stocking up.

'Soon.' She grinned. 'I think we could start with a Moses basket, and some tiny clothes. Take it from there. I mean, tiny clothes! This is real.'

'Pram?'

'Maybe just a sling to start with. We don't need a car seat or anything like that. Since we don't have a car.'

'What about taxis?'

'Ariel! How often do we get a taxi? Never.'

'How about getting him home from the hospital?'

'I don't know.'

We didn't really know anything, but it didn't matter. We would work it out.

32

Bodmin station is in the middle of some trees, with nothing but a car park anywhere near it. It's a nice place because nothing seems to happen here apart from trains.

I arrive at half past nine and spot the ghost quickly among the cluster of annoyed passengers. At least I assume the man sitting cross-legged at the end of the platform with his eyes closed is the ghost.

I picture the blue of the sky. There it is: a glow all around him. I'd expected someone who looked a bit crusty from the way Lara described him. In my head he was a Swampy type. This man, however, is wearing a suit. He's about thirty-five, of Asian appearance, and supremely calm, and he has the glow of the undead. I don't like to approach him in case I scare him, so I just sit down cross-legged at a distance and wait for him to notice me. I can hear him humming.

'Hi,' I say, after waiting a few minutes. I don't have all day after all.

His eyes snap open. 'Hey,' he says.

'I'm Joe.' Did Lara tell me his name? I can't remember.

He jumps up. 'Oh, what a treat. A new one. How did you find me?' He holds out a hand and pulls me up.

'Lara,' I say. 'I met her on the train to London.'

He puts out his hand. 'Pleasure to meet you, Joe. I'm Bodmin Leo.'

'Bodmin Leo?'

'That's how I style myself, so everyone can remember where to find me. It's not always easy to hold things in our heads, is it? I wait around this station every day because I like to be the hub for the Devon and Cornwall chapter. They can come and see me any time they like. I've been doing this for . . . well, time loses significance, doesn't it?'

'Yeah.' I think about what he said. 'The Devon and Cornwall chapter? How many of us are there? And are we all from March the eleventh 1999?'

'We are, Joe, and that means there are very few of us, I'm afraid. Though one more today! Joy. So our chapter is, as you said, people who are glitching on the same day. I wish we could be more expansive than that, but sadly we can't. There are three of us I've met in Cornwall, and a further four, now that you're here, have visited from Devon, including the lovely Lara. They don't come to see me as often as I'd like. Tell me your story.'

He jumps up. 'Let's walk into the woods. I don't want you being picked up and taken back to, I'm guessing, school?'

I follow him out of the station, through a car park and on to a stony path.

'There's a stately home this way,' he says, pointing.

'Lanhydrock House. Victorian. I worked there and I still go to the cafe from time to time. Just for the heck of it. Not today. Today, I think, we'll go to the den.'

This gives me a little pang of worry. Should I really be following a (very) strange and dead man into his den? On the day I know I get murdered? Is there any way that Leo could be the one who kills me? He surely can't be because we were both dead long before we met. However, everything is crazy and nothing makes sense.

I overcome it all and follow him along the path.

His den is a tree house accessed by a hidden muddy track. He swings up into it and so I follow. I calculate that I could push him out if he started attacking me. He perches on a flat branch and indicates for me to sit opposite him.

'So we're *glitching*?' I say straight away.

'We are,' he says. 'Straight to business! I like it. Yes. I call it glitching. My theory is that it's because time and space are entirely different from everything they tell you at school, and nothing is real. I think the world is computer-generated, or someone's plaything. Whatever it is, there's something wrong with the program and one day it'll be fixed. Or it might be to do with the upcoming millennium. The numbers changing. Everything going wrong before that happens. Though the numbers are artificial, aren't they? Just a form of order that humans have attempted to impose on time. Which lends credibility to the simulation theory. So, what's with you, Joe?'

I tell him my story as briefly as I can, but when I get to Ariel he nearly falls out of the tree.

'Say that again,' he says, pointing at me.

'I meet a girl from 2019 every day. She's trying to solve what happens to me. She's met my family in her world. My brother and his family. My dad.'

'Is this true, Joe?' he says, looking at me in a condescending way. 'Or do you think you've concocted it to comfort yourself?'

'It's true!' I'm annoyed by that. 'I can tell you what 2019 is like.'

'Yeah, but you could say anything because I can't check.' Leo looks at me suspiciously. 'I've never known anyone meet someone from the future. If this is real could you bring her here? *If.*'

'Dunno. If she wants to we could try. It would have to be a Saturday because she has school. It's Saturday for her tomorrow, but she's going to London to look up the guy who we think might have killed me.'

We stay in the tree for a while, but I soon realize that just because someone is a ghost like you, you don't have to become instant friends. Leo is spiky and seems put out by the fact that I have more to tell him than he has to tell me. I don't bond with him like I did with Lara. His glitch theory is just that: a very thin theory. We swap last-day stories: he assumes that he's going to die on a train or be pushed under one, but his day fades out just before he reaches the station.

'Want me to get Ariel to look you up?' I say because it seems only polite. 'She did it for Lara and found her granddaughter.'

'Yes! Thank you! Leo Chatterjee. I live in Par and I

worked in conservation up at Lanhydrock. I always took the train here and walked up – it's about half an hour and beautiful. I never bother to go to work any more, since I figured this out. I just wait around the station or walk in the woods. I call in sick first thing. But when I used to live the day normally I'd come here on the train and go to work, and then I'd be heading back to catch the train home, and then, no matter what I've been doing, at five forty it all stops. And I wake up again back in my bed at home. Get her to look me up and come back and tell me! Promise?'

I find I like him more. We have to take our allies where we find them.

Leo's eyes are wild. I wonder what happened to him. It seems unlikely to me that someone pushed him under a train. It would be hard to do that at a station, where the trains move really slowly. A level crossing would be better. A bridge.

I shake myself. That's not a good way to think.

We mess around in the forest for a bit. I find myself building a fort out of branches, and then sitting inside it. Leo's nervous energy is infectious. By the time I catch the train back to Exeter I'm feeling quite different. I kind of like him. I like what he does.

'I'll come back soon,' I tell him.

'Please do.' For a moment he looks desperate, and I see that everything else he does is to hold that at bay. 'Please. Don't give me hope and then never come back. Please don't. Get her to look me up. If she's real. Leo Chatterjee. Double "e" on the end.'

33

We found two seats facing forward as Izzy got travel-sick otherwise, and settled in. I'd brought a sensible packed lunch at Sasha's insistence, even though she thought we were just going to Exeter for the day. Izzy, on the other hand, had a tote bag filled with crisps, sweets and cans of drink. She got it all out on the flip-down table in front of her, even though it was nine in the morning, opened a Twix and handed me one finger.

'Go on then,' I said through a mouthful of chocolate. 'Tell.'

I was relieved to see that it was going to be something good. She was glowing. She turned towards me, bit off some biscuit from the bottom of the Twix and grinned. She was wearing a pink cardigan over a white T-shirt. She looked adorable.

'I met someone,' she said.

'Seriously? Who?'

Izzy had never had a boyfriend. We'd talked about boys, and plenty of them had asked her out over the years, but she'd always said no. She told me that her standards were too high, and I knew that my dramas had distracted me from asking more.

She was so happy that I wanted to bottle it and make it into a perfume, to be used any time you needed to have a brilliant day. There was something else too, though. Underneath it all she was nervous.

'OK,' she said. 'You ready for this?'

For a wild moment I thought that she, too, might have fallen for a ghost.

'Yep! Tell me!'

'It's someone I met online. We chatted for ages and I've met them in real life now too and I'm really happy. I'm so happy, Ariel. I know it's really early days and I'm trying so, so hard to play it cool, but I've never felt like this. Finally . . .'

'Finally you've met someone who meets your high standards?'

'Exactly. Finally I have.'

I began to realize.

'Why are you saying *they*?' I said.

She shrugged. 'Because I was a little bit too shy to say *she*,' she said through a mouthful of Twix. She looked away and then her eyes darted back to me. I hugged her.

Izzy's new love interest was called Tally, and we talked about her for ages. She was seventeen and had lovely thick black hair. They'd met online and clicked straight away. While I'd been looking after Zara and Coco they'd been on their first date. They went for tea and cake and then a movie, and Izzy was buzzing and wild with joy.

'It's not just her,' she said as the train left Devon. 'Although it is her. It's very much her. And it's everything. It's having the confidence to be myself at last. I tried so hard to like boys because I thought it would be easier, you know?'

I realized that I wasn't surprised, that it made perfect sense. I was so happy for her.

I was also a bit sad for myself. I hadn't had any of this, with Joe, and I never would. I couldn't psyche myself up to tell anyone about him because he'd been dead for twenty years. No one would ever be pleased to hear about this relationship. It could never make sense to anyone but us.

And I didn't want anyone else. I could have rekindled things with Jack, but I loved Joe. Only Joe. It could only ever be Joe.

We were supposed to be revising the Power and Conflict poems for English lit, but we didn't even take a book out of a bag. We ate all our food and talked about Izzy and Tally, and then we talked about our mission in London.

'This is nice,' Izzy said. 'Isn't it? A day trip to London. You know what? You're mad, but I want to find out what happened to your boy too. Those little girls were so adorable. Their poor dad!' She shivered. 'If we can help that family then bring it on. I mean, I can't have you going to track down a suspect alone, can I?'

Before we knew it we were passing through Reading and I did a namaste hand thing in what I thought might be the direction of the long-defunct Yoga Dojo. Half an hour after that we were in London.

It was warmer than it had been at home, and there were trees with pink cherry blossom at the top of Lucas Ingleby's road in Haggerston. The sun warmed my cheeks as we walked slowly up to the door of his block of flats. I looked at Izzy, who was clearly regretting the trip now we were actually about to doorstep a strange older man. I could practically see the thought bubble above her head saying, *I could be with my girlfriend*. I was getting psyched up to find the right buzzer when the front door opened.

He went to walk past without even looking at us, but I stepped into his path.

'Hi,' I said, trying to equate this muscular man with the Lucas Joe had told me about, the boy I'd seen in the corridor. His hair was flecked with grey, and that was a jolt, because even though Gus was old too he was Joe's big brother, while this man was in Joe's year at school. They were pretty much exactly the same age. If Joe had lived he might have been going grey too. Instead he was younger than me.

Also, I'd seen this man as a boy very recently, and that was enough to freak me right out. I had heard him talk, watched his hurt face when Joe was unthinkingly cutting.

He stopped. 'Hi?' he said, neither friendly nor unfriendly. He was just a man who was walking down his own street on a Saturday afternoon. On his way to the gym, judging by his clothes and bag.

'Lucas?' I said. 'This sounds weird, but could we talk to you for a minute? We're from your old school and we're writing a thing about Joe Simpson for the school magazine. Because it's twenty years since he disappeared. His brother, Gus, said you used to be friends with him. Do you have a couple of minutes to talk?'

After working through thousands of more sophisticated ideas than this one we had settled on something as close to the truth as possible. It was important that he shouldn't think we were interested in him in a sexual way (gross), and this was the best we could manage. Invoking the authority of the school, implying that some teacher was overseeing this, felt like a safety net.

'Maybe we *will* even write an article about him,' Izzy had said.

'If there was a school magazine,' I'd added, 'then they might even have printed it.'

'So it's practically true.'

Now I watched Lucas, who was, for lack of any other ideas, our main suspect, to see if anything flickered over his face. All I saw was surprise. He hadn't expected to be accosted in the street and asked about someone from twenty years ago, which was fair. There didn't seem to be any panic or guilt, but that didn't mean anything. If you could kill someone and hide it for twenty years you'd have a good poker face.

Then his expression changed again. He smiled. All of a sudden, he looked nice.

'Joe Simpson!' he said. 'God. Blast from the past. Poor Joe. Have they found out what happened?'

'No,' I said. 'We're just doing this story because we, the school, want to mark the twenty-year anniversary. I mean, I know it's technically past, but close enough. I think his family are keen that he shouldn't be forgotten.'

Lucas nodded. 'And you've spoken to Gus? How's he doing?'

'He's OK. He's got a lovely partner and two daughters.'

We seemed to be walking down the road with him. I couldn't help noticing that Lucas hadn't agreed to an interview, but at the same time he hadn't told us to go away either, so it was probably best to keep talking.

'How did you find me?' he said. 'This doorstepping thing. It makes me feel quite famous and all, but . . . couldn't we have done this over email?'

I didn't know what to say.

'We could have emailed,' said Izzy, 'but we were in London anyway, on a day out, and when we looked you up and your address was right there we thought we'd try popping over to see you. Haggerston's cool and we wanted to come here anyway, to walk the canal path.'

I hadn't even known there was a canal path. This new confident Izzy was amazing.

'You looked me up how?'

'Electoral roll,' I said, and he laughed.

'I knew I should have ticked the box that keeps it secret,' he said. 'Look, I don't want to be a buzzkill, but what are you, fifteen? Sixteen? You might not want to go turning up at strange men's houses miles from home on a Saturday afternoon. Email is safer.'

'Yeah,' I said. 'But we're here now. Could we go for a coffee or something? We'll pay.'

Lucas sighed. He had one of those strange body shapes that I thought meant he went to the gym every day. He was very tall and very broad, but the muscles on his upper body were so developed that he looked as if he was going to tip over, while his legs were quite small. His hair was cut very short, but although all those things added up to quite a scary figure I didn't feel that he was dangerous, particularly not if we were going for a coffee in a public place.

'OK, girls,' he said. 'For Joe – of course. I'm off to the gym and I'm all psyched for it now, so I don't want to bail. I'll meet you in in an hour, OK? Since you want to see the canal, let's meet at the cafe down there. Turn right here and then left on to the path and you'll see it in front of you. Hour and twenty maybe?'

'I don't think it was him.'

Izzy nodded her agreement. We were waiting at the cafe, at a table in a corner, watching people cycling and running and walking their dogs and children down the path. We were meant to be revising, but really we were people-watching and talking about Lucas.

'Yeah,' she said. 'He didn't look guilty, did he? He didn't have an air of . . .' She made swirly patterns in the air with her fingers. 'Oh no! My past has finally caught up!'

'He was pleased to talk about Joe, if anything.'

I looked at our list of questions. We were prepared for this. Lucas would probably be ages at the gym. We had exams coming up. I pushed the list aside reluctantly and picked up the revision guide.

'So,' I said. 'Themes of power and guilt, right?'

An hour and a half later he joined us at our table, holding some kind of herbal tea in a china cup, and we pulled our attention away from 'Ozymandias'.

263

'Right,' he said. 'Joe Simpson. Here's what I've been thinking while I pumped iron: why me? I only knew him for, what, a year and a half? Devon must be full of people who hung out with him from when they were babies. And we weren't even very close. Why doorstep me, girls? Or are you going after everyone?'

'Weren't you close really?' I said. I tried to look innocent. 'Gus said you were one of his friends. He thought Joe spoke to you on the day he disappeared?'

'Seriously? I guess he's right about that, but we weren't best mates. You need Troy for that. Have you contacted him?'

'Trying to,' I said. 'He lives in France, I think? He's not on social media at all as far as I can see. It's really hard to find him.'

'I could message him for you. Pretty sure I've got him on something. Yes! I have. He's on LinkedIn.'

Izzy laughed. 'We obviously didn't think of LinkedIn.'

'Yes, please!' I said to Lucas. 'That would be amazing. So. Do you mind if we record this?' He shook his head, looking amused, and Izzy carefully switched on the voice recorder on her phone. 'Lucas Ingleby, thanks for talking to us. Can you tell us your memories of Joe Simpson first of all? What was he like?'

Lucas leaned back in his chair. 'OK. This was a formative time in my life. I was new to the school in Year Nine. It wasn't easy arriving when everyone already had friends. I was an outsider. To be honest I never fitted in, and there weren't exactly many mixed-race guys in Devon, so I always felt like a bit of a target. I was at that school for three years, and Joe's disappearance came halfway through it. Everything is divided

264

into before and after Joe. I really liked him. I'm not just saying that because of what happened. I remember noticing him straight away because he was one of those, you know, cool kids. He had everything and he didn't even know it. He was good at the school stuff, and he was sporty too, but he had that extra something. The sparkle. The energy. The magic. He would've gone on to do something amazing. I'm sure of it. The moment I saw him I wanted to be friends, and I guess that was my downfall. I liked him, but he didn't like me, and he could be pretty harsh. I guess I tried too hard and pissed him off. Plus, he was mates with Troy and they didn't want anyone else because they were fine just as they were. I was jealous. I was big for my age – not like I am now, but tall and a bit clumsy, and . . . What are you, Year Ten?'

'Eleven,' I said.

'Yeah. You two are obviously fine, but you know the kids in your lessons who can't quite pull it together? The ones who don't have best friends and who kick about on their own? It's shit being a teenager. At least it was for me. I wanted a mate, and I wanted it to be Joe, and he thought I was an embarrassment and a twat, but I kept trying and he kept telling me why I was shit. Bit pathetic really. When he disappeared, it had a huge effect on me. Altered my life forever. I don't want to make it all about me because it's not. It's about Joe and his family, but I still had to find a way to live with it. You know what I mean? We all did. They can give you a counsellor to talk to and whatever, but as far as I was concerned it didn't scratch the surface. I fell apart. I don't think you'd have known it to look at me, but I did.

'I was gutted. I mean, more than gutted. Gutted is when they give you the wrong syrup in your frappuccino. I was devastated. My life stopped, but I still had to carry on.'

He looked at us over the top of his drink. I waited for him to say more, but he didn't.

'Sometimes the people who look like they're holding things together actually aren't,' I said. 'I mean, you said we look like we have no problems, but my mum died last year, and my dad ran away, and I live with my sister who's pregnant.'

'Oh! Sorry,' he said, looking a bit thrown. 'I just meant –'

'And I literally just came out to Ariel on the train this morning,' said Izzy unexpectedly.

I took her hand and squeezed it. We grinned at each other.

'Oh God. Sorry again. I didn't mean to be flippant.'

'But what about Joe?' I said. 'He had Troy and his dad and Gus. And his mum. Though his parents have divorced since then. Do you think he was struggling in secret?'

'Did he "do something stupid", you mean?' Lucas made air quotes with his fingers. 'No, I don't think he did, though of course you can never know. But here's why I think he didn't: he would have left a note. He was close to his family. No way would he have done it without leaving one. And also what about his body?'

Lucas was saying all the right things. We'd ambushed him and he seemed interested and helpful, rather than guilty or nervous. Also, I had seen Joe being horrible to him with my own eyes. I didn't want to make him go into that, but it must have meant his feelings were complicated.

Izzy leaned forward and asked the most important question of all.

'What do you think did happen then?'

Lucas looked at both of us in turn. I could see him trying to decide whether to say it or not.

'Can we turn this thing off?' he said, nodding to Izzy's phone, and she stopped the recording. 'I hate to say it, but I've always thought someone killed him. Or kidnapped him. It's the old Sherlock Holmes thing. Eliminate the impossible, and whatever remains must be the truth. My feeling is that he was abducted because of the way he vanished without trace. That doesn't happen by accident. I did try my own detective work in the early days, but I didn't get anywhere. I mean, I had no idea where to start. Who would kill Joe Simpson? The only person he didn't like was me, and I didn't do it. I was pretty sure no one in his family had done it. And people just don't plot to murder normal teenage kids. He's not, like, an heir to a fortune, or whatever might draw the attention of proper bad guys.'

He looked up at the ceiling. 'God, it's weird going back over this. So, if you rule out suicide, which I tentatively do because of the note thing, and if you rule out someone plotting to murder him because there's no one, really, who would have done it – that kind of thing doesn't happen in downtown Devon – then you're left with a few things. Either he died by accident in a way that meant his body was never found, so probably involving the sea, or he was kidnapped. Or else someone killed him by accident, or on purpose, and did an excellent job of getting rid of . . .'

He blinked. 'Sorry. You've taken me right back. I was obsessed with this. I became paranoid about attackers. That's why I decided to get fit. I was ahead of the curve with the gym stuff.' He rolled his eyes. 'Don't put any of this in your article. None of it, yeah?'

'No,' I said at once. 'The article will be short. I'm actually getting really interested in this too, in its own right. I know I didn't know Joe.'

Sorry, Joe, I added in my head. *I do know you. I love you.*

'But I feel like I did, and I can't believe this whole thing is just hanging there. It's so strange.'

'Isn't it? I didn't sleep for years just thinking about it. There wasn't a robbery at Beachview. No obvious bad guy skulking about. There's just nothing. I have no idea. Where would you dispose of a body?'

'The sea,' said Izzy.

'Yeah. It always comes back to that. But even then it would most likely wash back up. I did a lot of calculations on this, and I think I ended up deciding that the river would have been a possibility because it's deep in places, and if you weighed the body down it could stay there forever. But they dredged it. Of course they did, and there was no trace of anything. That's why I come back to abduction. His body's gone, so it must be somewhere else. They could have taken him anywhere in the country.' Lucas looked at us again and smiled. 'Sorry. Again, don't put this in your magazine.'

'We won't,' I said. 'But, talking of the article, can you give us a bit of background on the day he went missing? Can you remember the last conversation you and Joe had?'

Lucas was silent for a long time. When he spoke, his voice was far away and sad.

'Funny thing,' he said. 'You go over something enough times and it stops being real. Like now – am I remembering my last conversation with Joe, or am I remembering myself thinking about it endlessly for years? I'm not sure I can keep the real thing and my memories of it apart from each other. So he was supposed to be going on the French trip that night. They never went, of course. You can't set off on a coach when one of the party has vanished. But I do remember seeing him at school that day. I used to hang around on the way to school, on the road that I knew he and Troy took, and try to walk with them. I sound like I had a crush or something. I didn't. I just wanted a friend, and somehow the more Joe told me to fuck off – he could be direct – the more I hung around like a puppy. Though it would have been quite a puppy: six foot tall and built like a shithouse.

'Anyway. That day I caught up with them just before we got to school. I was mad jealous that they were going to France. That trip cost two hundred pounds, and I remember how impossible that was for my family. I quite liked French, and I would have loved to go – not for the bit where you have to stay with people you don't know for a week, but for the bus ride, the ferry, the friendship, the in-jokes you have when you get back, all that – but I had no chance. I was eaten up with jealousy. I think I tried to talk French to him. *Ça va bien*, that kind of thing, as a way of saying, "Hey, you're going to France today!" and he told me to fuck off. I don't know. I wasn't good at that stuff. I had no social skills. Didn't get any for years and years. If ever arguably.'

269

'You have social skills now,' said Izzy politely. Lucas nodded his thanks.

'I don't think we had any lessons together that day, though as I said it was a long time ago and I don't know what I'm remembering or what I'm filling in. After school I definitely watched Joe walking into town, telling Troy he was going to get a present for the family in France. I wanted to go with him, but of course I couldn't. I wish, though, that I had. I wish I'd followed him. Kept him safe. And we know that Joe went to Beachview and then he was never seen again.'

Izzy said, 'When did you find out that he was missing?'

I was a bit surprised by that. I was surprised by the fact that it hadn't occurred to me to ask. For some reason I'd been incapable of thinking past the moment when Joe's eternal day cut out.

Lucas sighed. 'That night. Everyone did. You can't imagine what it was like, you kids now, but we didn't have social media or any of that. Some folks had mobile phones, but I didn't. People were calling round on landlines, asking if anyone had seen him. Mum knocked on my bedroom door and asked if I had any idea where he was. I think a bit of her thought she'd find him in there, talking to me. If only. We joined in the search they'd started. Small town – you know how it is. *Everyone* was out. We walked all the way round the streets and shouted his name, asked everybody, stuck his photo on lamp posts like people do for cats. I kept thinking we were definitely about to find him. Just round the next corner. Maybe the next.'

He stopped talking, and I realized that, in a way, this was where the story ended.

'But no one ever did,' I said.

'I don't think any of us slept that night because it's really impossible to say, yeah, actually I can't find him, so I'm just going to go home and have a nice kip instead. I didn't sleep for weeks, not more than an hour here and there.' He rubbed his eyes. 'For years. Jeez. Listen to me. Twenty years ago, but it doesn't get easier. I guess there comes a time when you realize that he's almost sure to be dead. Again – not easier. And there's no single moment when you give up hope. You never give it up, not completely.'

'Sorry for coming along and stirring it all up,' said Izzy. I was glad she did: he looked terrible. I wasn't exactly Miss Marple, but I felt as certain as I could that Lucas hadn't been the one who hurt Joe. I could see (and it was uncomfortable) that Joe had repeatedly hurt Lucas, but I was pretty sure Lucas hadn't retaliated with an unlucky fatal punch.

Izzy was saying all the right things. I was barely holding it together, so she had taken the reins. She was brilliant.

'Hey,' Lucas said. 'Sorry for landing all that on you. All you wanted was some quotes for your magazine. It's just good to talk about him. I'm glad you're writing his story. It's important that he's not forgotten. But, seriously, an old guy like me offloading on a couple of teenage girls: that's really not appropriate. Apologies.'

He looked around, as if the other people here might be disapproving, though they were all busy with their own things.

'Don't worry,' I said. 'And thank you for talking to us. It's really nice of you. I promise we'll only take a couple of your quotes for our article.'

'Oh,' said Lucas. 'Print what you like from that recording. I don't care. Will you send me a copy when it's done? I think it's fantastic that you're interested.' He blinked. 'Makes me quite emotional actually. Hey – do you have photos for your piece? I have a couple on my phone. Call me tragic, but I have a Joe Simpson folder right here.'

He found them quickly and handed his phone over. I scrolled through a bunch of pictures of old photos. I could see the creases on them, and the colours were faded and changed.

It took my breath away.

This boy was my Joe, but different. Now, for the first time, I understood why Lucas had been so jealous, why Joe had been a golden boy. There was a life force about him that my Joe didn't have. I adored my Joe, but I saw now that he was a shadow of his living self. In one of the photos he was grinning into the camera, squinting into the sun, and everything about his hair and his skin and his smile was so young. So alive. I blinked hard, and then decided it was OK to cry.

This Joe had been golden, but he hadn't been kind to Lucas. I thought that I liked my Joe better, which was a headfuck.

Another was a class picture. I saw Joe straight away, in the middle of the front row, sitting next to a boy who had to be Troy because he was very tall with bright red hair.

And then I realized I'd seen Troy before.

Troy was looking at Joe, and Joe was giving the camera a cheesy grin and a thumbs up. I looked for Lucas and found him in the back row, frowning.

Troy had been the boy in the playground. He had written HELP ME on the wall with a stone.

'Wow,' I said.

Izzy was peering over my shoulder. 'Joe is *gorgeous*,' she said. 'He kind of looks like Robert Pattinson.'

I ignored that.

'There must be something we can do.' We looked at each other, and Izzy's unconditional support made me cry properly. I didn't care if I looked stupid.

'Right?' said Lucas, and he was blinking hard too. 'Look, give me your email and I'll send these over. You're welcome to use them. And, again, I'm glad you're doing this. It means a lot, to know that the next generation remembers. It's the only thing we can do now. Give my best to Gus and the family. Is it true that his dad married Mrs Dupont?'

'It is! And she's still at the school. She's our French teacher. Ms Duke. It took me a while to piece that together, but we think she changed her name back to Duke when she got divorced from Dupont, and then just kept it when she married Jasper Simpson.'

'No way!' He looked delighted. 'That's so surreal. I know the school changed its name and all that, but it's good to know that some things are the same. She was one of the good ones.'

I wrote down my email for Lucas, aware, as I did it, that it was odd for a teenage girl to start an email correspondence with an older man. I could see that he felt it too.

He hesitated. 'I'll drop a message to Troy, but I wouldn't hold your breath. We were never friends, and after Joe he moved schools. As you're aware he's in France now, and I see him doing corporate stuff in French on LinkedIn from time to time. I just added him because he came up as a connection, but I don't really know much about him. Oh, one thing, though! I think he got married to a Frenchwoman and took her name, the weirdo. His LinkedIn name changed a few years ago.'

'That's so cool!' said Izzy. 'I love that. Smash the patriarchy.'

'What's his new surname?' I said.

Lucas frowned, then knocked back the rest of his tea. 'Can't remember,' he said. 'Something French. I'll find out.'

'Thanks!'

'And promise you'll send me a copy of your magazine?'

'Sure,' I said, wondering whether we could mock one up just for him, or maybe start a brand-new magazine.

Izzy asked if she could take some photos for the article and he posed in a self-conscious way.

My emotions were all over the place as we walked away. I was pleased that we'd tracked Lucas down and spoken to him, but the reality was Joe should have been old like that.

Then I looked over at Izzy and saw that she was, in fact, crying, so I let myself do that too. We took each other's hands and kept walking. By the time we got to the overground train we were smiling at each other. I dried my eyes with my sleeve and we set off into the centre of London to do a few tourist things before we had to go home.

34

I stick with Troy all day. I pretend we're going on the French exchange this evening and work so hard on it that I find I almost believe it myself. I chat to Mrs Dupont, trying not to think about the fact that she is definitely going to have sex with my dad. Fuck's sake.

At the end of school I pull Troy across the playground to a point where no one (not even Lucas, who's lurking nearby) can spy on us.

'Hey,' I say. The words stick in my throat. Why is it so hard to do this? 'I'm really sorry.' *I took your trophy.* Those words won't come. My mouth won't say them. It's the strangest feeling: I want to say it, but there's an invisible cushion in my throat that lets me breathe but doesn't let me speak. I open my bag and hold it out to show him, but when I try to pick the trophy up it doesn't move. When he tries, it still doesn't move.

Troy doesn't say anything. He just glares at me and storms off, clearly believing that I've superglued it into my bag. I wish I could run after him and hug him goodbye, but I can't because he hates me.

*

At Beachview I buy a can of Lilt, walk into the angry man and there I am, in the cupboard at two minutes past four. A minute after that Ariel arrives. I spring up, desperate to hear about her trip to London, but she flashes me a meaningful look and shakes her head slightly, and I step back.

She's talking to someone and it's not me. She's not on her phone. She's with a real person.

Whoever it is, I can't see or hear them, and they clearly can't see me either.

Gus? Dad? The girls?

'*Voilà*,' she's saying. 'The last place Joe Simpson visited before he vanished.'

Ariel glances at me, then looks around. I can see her trying to work out if I can see the other person, or if they can see me. A big no, I think, on both fronts. I shrug and shake my head. Then I realize it's OK for me to speak.

'Who is it?' I say. 'I can't see anyone.'

I'm thinking of the people I would most love to be here, but I realize it can't be any of them because she just last-named me.

There's a pause, and then she flashes me another look and says, 'Izzy. You're my best friend and that's why I've brought you here. This was the last place he was seen.'

I can't hear anything of Izzy's reply. I work it out, approximately, when Ariel says, 'Yeah . . . But just before he came in there was a man in the mall. Joe bought a drink and walked into him, and the man told him to fuck off or something. We need to find him. I don't know how to get the CCTV. I mean, they won't still have it from then, will they?' She pauses while Izzy says something, then replies: 'I don't know. The security guard said.'

I tell her, 'I wish I could see Izzy. How come you can see kids at school but I can't see her?'

'No idea,' Ariel says, to me, and then she turns to her right. 'I mean, yeah. No idea why, but I think that man might have something to do with it. He's part of Joe coming here. There aren't many clues, and that's a lead, I guess. Anyway! You don't have to stick around in here. I just wanted to show you. I'm fine. I'll hang out here for a bit.'

I remember the pieces of paper that appeared in her hand and disappeared when she let go of them. 'If you touch her I might be able to see her!' I shout.

Then a girl appears. She's much shorter than Ariel, and very pretty with dimples and wild hair. I grin at her and she looks right through me. Ariel has her arm round her shoulders. They're walking towards the door.

'Oh my God,' I say. 'I can see her! I can see Izzy!'

Ariel grins. 'Izzy, I'm so glad you don't think I'm mad.'

'Of course I don't think you're mad,' says Izzy, and as they stand in the doorway Ariel grins at me over her shoulder. Izzy disappears and Ariel dashes straight over to give me the closest thing we can manage to a hug.

'Sorry,' she says. 'I would have warned you if I'd planned it. Izzy just asked if she could see the room because she's meeting her girlfriend over the road at half four. She's invested in you now. We're sure it wasn't Lucas and now she's desperate to solve this too. When she goes for something she really goes for it.'

'I can't believe I could see her,' I say. 'That's amazing. But you don't think it was Lucas? Why?'

I almost feel disappointed about this. I wish it was him because then we'd have an answer. I shake myself. We need the truth, not just the easiest thing.

'Because he didn't do it, Joe. I'm as certain as I can possibly be about that.'

I'm writhing inside with jealousy. Izzy is Ariel's friend and they both get a bit older every day. I'm jealous of the real-world friendship I just saw. I've never seen Ariel with anyone else before. It is unsettling. I miss Troy. I wish I could go home with Ariel, walk around with her, become a part of her life. I almost hate the gorgeous, perfect Izzy who came into my space.

There's an uncomfortable silence between us. It's the first time I've ever felt awkward with Ariel. I know I'm being mean: I want Ariel to be happy and have friends. And yet, petulantly, I don't want her to have anyone but me.

'Tell me about him then,' I say. 'You really don't think it was him? Are you sure? He was the only . . .'

'It wasn't,' she says, and I deflate. Of course I don't want Lucas to have killed me, but it would have been the beginning of the end. She sits next to me and I look into her eyes, searching for the tiniest sliver of doubt, but there's nothing. 'It wasn't,' she says again. 'He was nice. He had a lot to say, though he was really nervous of us being young and him looking inappropriate. He's still really cut up about you. He has a folder of photos of you on his phone. Look. He sent them to me.'

I stare at the pictures as she scrolls through them. I look exactly like that now, except that I don't. These pictures show a different boy. I see now that I haven't been that version of myself for a long, long time. He's a stranger. The gulf between me and myself is far bigger than I'd ever realized. I know Ariel sees it too.

'And this is Lucas now.' She flicks through the pictures on her phone. 'Izzy took them. She told him it was for the article. I didn't even think of that.'

Lucas is a thirty-five-year-old guy, broad and muscular, with greying hair. He's smiling at the camera, in a cafe, with people sitting at tables around him. He looks comfortable in the world in a way he never used to be.

I stopped him being comfortable, and now I'm not there.

The room fades around me. This is what my classmates are like. They have moved on. I'm stuck.

I imagine the scene. A cafe in London, the three of them sitting at a table with their cups of tea, existing in the same space and time. I want to break things. I want to charge into that cafe and throw everyone's drink on the ground. I want to smash the windows, turn the tables upside down, destroy every bit of it, to stop people having fun without me.

I decide to give up. Just for a moment. I need a break.

'Ariel,' I say. 'Can we have a day? Can we have just one

lovely day when we forget all this? Another date, but not at school? Shall we do something different?'

She looks at me and I see her face change. She smiles slightly.

'What do you have in mind?'

As soon as I wake up I take the books out of my schoolbag and replace them with a pair of jeans, a sweatshirt, a T-shirt and my favourite trainers. Then, even though I don't need to eat or drink, I add that packet of Club biscuits from the cupboard and a litre of orange juice from the fridge, just because I like feeling normal. I say goodbye to Dad and Gus for the last time, as usual, and leave a little bit early.

Troy is waiting on the corner. He's early too: I'd hoped to get past there before he arrived. He sees me coming and lifts a hand. I walk over, wishing I'd left sooner.

'Hey,' I say. 'Sorry. I'm going to skip school today. I'll see you later, for the trip.'

'Seriously? Where are you going?'

'Just going back to bed once Gus has left. I can't face it today. I need a duvet day.'

'*Duvet day?*'

'Yeah.'

'You OK?'

'Yeah.'

There's a moment. I know he wants to ask more, but he doesn't know how to. I want to give him back his football thing, but I know I can't do it. I guess I died while still in possession of it because any time I try to hand it back I can't. Everything hangs between us, unspoken. I think about how shit it will feel for him when he never sees me again, knowing that everything was left like this. But there's nothing I can do about it, and anyway this isn't the real Troy. He wouldn't remember this as our last conversation. He'd remember the first one, when we said goodbye after school and it was fine.

'See you at school then,' he says. 'Tonight, I mean. For the French exchange. You're going to be OK for that?'

'Yeah,' I say. 'Can't wait.'

I walk the long way to the beach. I pass kids in all the different uniforms. I pass parents (mainly mothers) dragging children to primary schools and nurseries, pushing pushchairs. Even though I'm walking in the wrong direction, no one looks twice at me. I go along Sheringham Road and, on impulse, I stop and ring the doorbell of number twelve. It'll be nice to tell Ariel a new story about her mum and Sasha.

Anna Brown answers at once and I grin at her. I can't help it; I feel that we're old friends.

She's holding the baby on her hip, like before. Little Sasha has blonde ringlets and is pink and adorable.

'Hello?' says Anna, and although she's unsure what I'm doing here she's perfectly friendly. I remind myself not to tell her I'm a ghost. I can't spend the morning weeding her garden either.

'Hi,' I say. 'Sorry to bother you. Do you . . . do you know a girl called Ariel? Sorry, I think I might have the wrong house.'

'No,' she says, and she smiles. 'Ariel. What a lovely name. Like *The Tempest*.'

'She more often gets people telling her it's like *The Little Mermaid*,' I say. 'She'd prefer *The Tempest*.'

'And *Footloose*. Have you seen *Footloose*? That's one of my favourite films.'

'I haven't,' I admit. 'And I do apologise – clearly this is the wrong house. I'm really sorry to have bothered you. Thank you. Hey there, Sasha,' I add as the baby is smiling at me. I just can't help myself.

Ariel's mum stares. 'How did you know her name?' she says, but with a smile. She's one of those lovely people who is always sunny, always positive, no matter what. No matter, in her case, that she's married to a wanker.

All the same, I need to answer. I cast my eyes around and am saved by a splodgy painting on the wall that consists of a load of red and blue handprints and the name SASHA written in the corner by a grown-up. 'It says it there,' I say, pointing. 'I'm guessing it's her artwork.' I smile at the baby. 'It's very good.'

'How observant. Say thank you to the nice boy, Sasha.'

I reach out and touch Sasha's curly hair. It is unbearably soft under my fingers. Sasha is real to me in a way that Ariel can never be. I say goodbye and wave to them both.

As I walk away, I take out my phone. I press the button that will call my mum. Her course begins at nine, and now it's eight forty-five. She has a mobile phone, but she keeps it switched off unless she's using it, so when it goes to voicemail I say: 'Hi, Mum! It's Joe. I'm just calling to say . . . I love you. That's all.' Then I ring her hotel, and ask to be put through to room 237, but she doesn't answer. She must have already left.

I walk faster and faster, down on to the beach and then along it, away from town, to the stony bit at the very far end where no one goes. And there is Ariel, sitting on a rock like a mermaid.

'Hey!' she says. 'There you are. We did it!'

'We did,' I say, and I sit on the rock beside her and we both look out at the sea.

35

That day was, oddly, one of the best of my life. We didn't talk about who killed Joe and how and why and what I was going to do next about it. We didn't talk about Troy cracking up and leaving the country. We didn't talk about the man at the mall, even though I really wanted Joe to take a photo of him. Instead we sat on a rock at the end of the beach and gave names to the seagulls in each of our realities, and threw stones into the sea. We didn't talk about the past or the future, or compare notes or technologies or music, or anything. Joe didn't do mad things just because he could. We talked. That was all.

'Can you see that dog?' he said. I looked, but there wasn't one.

'Nope,' I said. 'What's it like?'

'Black Labrador.'

'Cute!'

'It's running up and down the beach. It looks so happy. It's like . . .' He adopted a gruff doggy voice. 'Hello, beach! I'm looking for sausages. Do you have any sausages, please, beach?'

I joined in, mimicking his dog voice. 'If I dig I might find some sausages. A big hoard of them buried by pirates.'

'Pirate sausages are the bestest sausages.'

We basically just talked nonsense for about an hour, and then I stood up.

'I'm a bit cold,' I said. 'I guess you're not.'

'Nope. I don't feel anything.'

I reached out to touch his arm. It didn't work. I still forgot.

'Let's go for a walk,' I said. 'I came prepared.'

I plugged my earbuds in and put my phone back into my pocket, noticing a text from Jack. **Sorry if I came on too strong the other day,** he said. **Yeah, I'd like to be friends. We could go for a coffee sometime.**

Jack was lovely, but I tapped out a quick **Sure, I'll let you know when I'm free** and muted the phone. I was with Joe. The technology side of things was boring for him now. After the first flash of amazement at the changing role of the phone, there was really no need for him to be astounded by the fact that technology had developed over twenty years. It wasn't remarkable, or even interesting.

'Yeah, and I'll just walk around looking like I'm talking to myself,' he said. 'Who cares? It doesn't matter. These aren't real people anyway. None of this has actually happened and no one will remember it.' He shook his head. 'Bodmin Leo was more eloquent about that. It's a headfuck, but it's a headfuck that brought me to you.'

'It is.' I took a deep breath and just walked with him, enjoying the magic that had brought us together.

*

We walked back across the beach and along a few streets, and then right to the edge of town and out into the country-side. We didn't talk much. It was nice just to be side by side, in the same place at different times. The town was smaller than I'd always thought: it took us less than half an hour to reach the open fields, and then we looked at each other, grinned and ran up a hill.

The sun was shining. Birds were singing. The air smelled like springtime. I felt warmth on my face, felt my blood pumping as I ran. I realized that I hadn't exercised for ages. It was a good feeling.

'This is lovely,' I said, but when I looked at Joe his hair was wet.

'In a weird way,' he said with a little laugh, 'yeah. I guess it is.'

'Is it raining?'

'Is it *not*?'

We sat on the top of the hill, and Joe pulled his hood up while I took my sweatshirt off. It was wonderful up here. The sea glittered green and pale blue below us. The sun shone across it, making a golden path to the horizon. The town was hidden in the valley, and the sky was huge and blue, the grass bright, bright green. It was like being in a child's picture, a drawing made by Coco. Green grass, blue sky, greeny-blue sea. And Joe, and me. A boy, and a girl, side by side.

'What does it look like?' I said.

'It's drizzling,' he said, 'and the sky's grey. The sea's grey. The grass is muddy.'

We laughed at that. Then we just lay back and talked. I told him that Jack Lockett had asked me out again. 'I said no, of course,' I said. 'I mean, politely. I said I'd like to be friends, and he knew what I meant. I only want you, Joe Simpson.'

He smiled at me for a long time when I said that. We talked about the seagulls that were soaring over both of us. We talked about the boats I could see, the walkers who passed him and gave him a worried look as he lay alone on a cliff in the rain. We talked about our childhoods, what we could remember of them.

He called his mum, and this time she answered her phone, and I listened to his side of the conversation, while putting my hand through his.

'Mum,' he said. 'Yeah. No, I'm fine. I just wanted to hear your voice today. I miss you, Mum. I love you. And Dad, and Gus. I love all of you. And the kids Gus will have. The girls. Don't worry, Mum. You need to be happy, no matter what. I'm glad you're doing your yoga course. You should go to India.'

When he put his phone in his pocket, though, he was smiling. He lay back and grinned up at the sky. 'OK,' he said. 'Now I'm ready. As ready as I can be. So, do you want to go to the moon one day?'

'No,' I said. 'It would take too much fossil fuel, and I don't think there's much of a mood for that. There are so many other things to focus on.'

'We all thought that in the twenty-first century there'd be a lot more going to the moon.'

'What do you think it'd be like up there?'

He closed his eyes.

'Grey,' he said. 'Or maybe not? Is that just because we

see black-and-white photos? No, probably greyish. Darkish. Amazing. I mean, standing there and looking down at Earth? That would be an incredible thing, wouldn't it? And the bouncing around. I think it would be brilliant. I'm imagining us living in some kind of lunar module, with enough supplies and water to last us as long as we wanted. Not that I'd need them, I guess. It wouldn't matter, up there, if we were a few Earth years apart.'

'Yeah,' I said, and I wished I could just lean over and kiss him. The feeling swept over me. It was the thing I wanted. The only thing.

'I wish I could kiss you,' he said, opening his eyes, reading my mind.

I sighed. 'Oh God. It's all I want.'

We looked at one another. I leaned towards him, and he leaned into me. It was the most pointless thing, and the most romantic thing, that had ever happened. I opened my mouth a little. He did too. I shivered as our lips went through each other. We couldn't touch, but the thrill went up and down my body.

It was the most frustrating, most wonderful, most impossible thing. We stayed like that for ages, and I never wanted it to end.

It was Joe who pulled away. We didn't speak for a long time. Then I found myself talking, just to break the sudden awkwardness.

'Do you know where else would be a good place? If we're going off-planet? Because there's another one and it's the one I'd like to move to.'

'Mars?'

'Better than Mars. Mars is the god of war. This is peaceful. We should go to the cloud tops of Venus. Mum used to talk about it, and I checked and it's real. No one could come close to stepping on the surface of Venus because it has runaway warming and all that – though you'd probably be OK, to be fair – but above the clouds it's perfect for humans. I think we'd have to live in a Zeppelin or something.'

Joe's ghost fingers stroked my face and I shuddered. 'I could get on board with that.'

'My mum would be there.'

'Cool. I love your mum.'

We mapped out a life above the clouds of Venus. We would live in our Zeppelin, and breathe the air (as this was imaginary it was filled with air that we could both easily breathe; in fact, it filled our lungs and made us sparkle). We would grow our own food.

'Cloud-strawberries,' I said. 'And cloud-ice cream.'

'Cloud-chocolate,' he said. 'Can we have some cloud-burgers? All the things I used to love. Chips from the chip shop, with lots of vinegar. A massive burger with all the trimmings from the fancy burger place.'

'You can have that,' I said. 'Yes. And you'll be able to taste it and swallow it. And we'll just float around in the clouds, and it won't matter who's alive or what year it is because those things will be nothing.'

He lay back and stretched his arms up. I could see that it had stopped raining, for him.

'The thing is, Ariel,' he said, with his eyes closed, 'that's just as likely as this. And so, if we really want it to, it might as well happen. We might as well live there.'

'Yes,' I said. 'So let's do it.'

In the absence of cloud-food I ate my sandwich and crisps and drank my Diet Coke, and Joe had his biscuits and juice, not because he wanted or needed them, but to keep me company. We talked all afternoon. He told me that he'd visited Mum on the way and talked to her and Sasha. I was properly happy for the first time in years.

And then, at the end of it, Joe said he didn't want me to visit him any more.

36

Everything I've been doing is wrong. It takes a kiss that can never be a kiss to make me see it. I had the best day of my death: I knew I could get through this as long as I had Ariel. We talked wonderful nonsense about living above Venus, and at some point along the way I realized.

I'm pulling her into my grave. I've dragged her into my half-dead existence, away from her real, breathing, messy life. I can't live, so I'm stopping her from living too.

Her old boyfriend asked her out and she turned him down. 'I said no, of course.' She'd said it so casually. I know she likes Jack. They only broke up because her mum got ill and she couldn't handle anything. Jack would have been good for her if I wasn't around. Going out with him would be a real step back to normality for her. She likes him, but she didn't even consider it. That's the bit that haunts me. She said no, *of course*. Because of me.

I am toxic. She has to live, but I pull her towards death.

If no one found out what happened to me back then, no one will now. I've been selfish, as I always was. I was horrible to Lucas and, in a different way, I'm being awful to Ariel too. I resent her friends, and as long as we're trying to touch each other and trying, hopelessly, to kiss she will turn down approaches from living boys.

And she has important exams, but here I am, greedily grabbing her attention whenever I can. I can't see her every day when I'm just fucking up her reality.

She was upset when I told her to stop coming, and in the end she stormed off and said *FINE*, that she'd never visit me again. It was awful, but I know it's right. Now I feel a peace I don't think I've known since I was a tiny child.

I'm not going to fight this any more. Ariel can live, and I will find a way to inhabit my existence. I am going to craft a collection of perfect days, and then I just have to get my head round the idea of embracing them forever. I think of the other ghosts I know: Leo has found a purpose by developing his glitch theory, and by positioning himself as a hub for his paltry collection of Devon and Cornwall ghosts. Lara knits for Mabel and dances round the train. I'm the only one driving myself insane by trying to solve my own murder and I haven't got the energy. I'm not going to do it any more. I don't have the agency to fix anything.

First thing in the morning I sit up in bed and write a plan for the rest of my existence. I can make a week's worth of days (not that I need to, but I might as well keep the seven-day structure since it seems to have served humanity well so far) and set it out on the back of my maths book:

Monday:	Train to Reading, chat to Lara, visit Mum and get her to bring me home.
Tuesday:	Stay at home with Dad and have a big breakfast and watch telly.
Wednesday:	Go to school, keep my mind busy and see my friends. Be nice to Lucas.
Thursday:	Call in on Anna and Sasha, then go to Bodmin and visit Leo.
Friday:	Go all the way to London with Lara.
Saturday:	Spend the day with Dad and Gus.
Sunday:	Go to school and hang out with friends.
Throughout:	Learn an instrument and a new language. Practise backflips.

I feel a strange sense of relief. I might be able to do this.

'I love you, Dad,' I say before he leaves for work. He doubles back and hugs me, in his goofy way.

'Why, thank you, Jojo,' he says. 'I love you too! Always know that.'

'I love you, Gus,' I say when Dad has gone. He laughs and puts a hand on my forehead in mock concern, checking for a fever.

'You twat,' he says, but affectionately.

'You're going to have a happy future with a woman called Abby and two daughters called Zara and Coco,' I say, talking fast. I tell him this often. He walks off, shaking his head and making a 'you're crazy' twirly finger gesture. Then he turns back.

'OK, Mystic Meg,' he says. 'What about you? What does your future hold?'

I shrug. 'Ideally, I'd live in the cloud tops of Venus with a girl from the future.'

Gus laughs and pats me on the shoulder. 'You do that, mate.'

I set off to school. I wish I could get Troy's football trophy out of my bag. I stole it twenty years ago, and yesterday. Whatever I do it stays where it is.

I get through the day being relentlessly lovely to everyone. I don't bother to eat bricks or plates any more because that was novelty stuff and I'm bored of it. I chat to Lucas, and find that, as Ariel said, he just wants to be my friend. I can see that I haven't been quite as cool as I thought I had.

'*Ça va, Joseph?*' he says in what I'd always taken to be a mocking tone. I think of the adult Lucas sitting by the canal with Ariel and Izzy, and know it's more complex than that.

Instead of telling him to fuck off, or mimicking his French accent, I say, '*Oui, ça va.* Sorry you're not coming on the trip, mate.'

'Me too!' he says. 'You'll have a great time.'

'We should hang out when I'm back,' I say.

It's easy to be magnanimous under the circumstances, and I want to test whether it's true that he wanted to be friends.

His face lights up. 'I'd love that,' he says. 'Yeah. That'd be great. Cheers.'

I hang behind after registration to chat to Mrs Dupont, since she's my stepmum. I do like her. Quite apart from her joining my family, I know that twenty years from now she'll still be in this classroom, but she'll be talking to Ariel, making sure she and Sasha are all right. She's a link between us, a person who was already in both our worlds, and she will specifically look out for the girl I love. That makes me want to say something profound, but all I can manage is: 'Thanks for being a great teacher.' I look quickly around to make sure no one else is in the room. Luckily, we're alone.

She grins. 'Well, thank you for being a great student, Joe,' she says, and she gathers up her books and bag. 'You're going to go on to do wonderful things with that charm of yours.'

I sit with Troy in the canteen. He eats a plate of school-dinner curry that I can't smell, though everyone keeps saying it stinks and holding their nose. I eat a sandwich, just to look normal, and drink some water. I wonder where it goes? I guess it's no more real than I am, so there's nothing to go anywhere.

'How are you doing?' I say.

'OK. Not bad. I lost my trophy.' He frowns at his plate.

'Oh, Troy!'

It's worth another try. Surely it's always worth trying. One day it might work. 'I'm so sorry.'

The words stick in my throat again. I fail to say, *I took it out of your bag because I thought it was a funny thing to do. Obviously it's not a funny thing to do at all. I feel like it was someone else who did it. I've been meaning to give it back for, like, twenty years.* Though I shout it in my head, the words won't come.

He looks at me. I've seen this look a lot of times.

I reach into my bag to take the trophy out. I close my fingers round it, but it doesn't move. I try to pull, but my hand flies away as I lose my grip. I show the bag to Troy.

'It's here,' I say, 'but I can't get it out.'

He reaches in too, and the same thing happens to him. We can both see it glinting in there, the stylized boot kicking the football, and yet neither of us can move it.

'Have you superglued it?'

'No!'

'Fuck's sake, Joe,' he says. 'You just can't help yourself.'

Troy tips his chair over as he storms off. I know it doesn't matter, that this glitch is only affecting me, but it's horrible and creepy that I can't sort this out; that one stupid thing I did twenty years ago is still fucking everything up between me and my friend.

Later I sit in the cupboard, hoping that Ariel will come, even though I told her loads of times not to. I stare at the door. Four o'clock comes. Four ten. Four thirty. Four forty-five.

She doesn't come. I told her not to. She's doing exactly what I asked.

37

The more I stayed away from Joe, the easier it became. At first it was almost impossible, and I only followed his wishes because I felt bad that I had all the power. He had to be at Beachview at four. I didn't so I made sure that I was busy after school, every single day.

The hallucinations at school faded almost to nothing. First I stopped feeling the blast of cold when I walked through them. Then I couldn't see them clearly, and eventually they were just smudges of blue at the edge of my vision. I missed seeing them around. I often wondered whether one of the blurry shapes was my Joe, but I never let myself look for him.

I missed him with all my heart. I longed for him. But he'd told me he didn't want to see me any more, and so I stayed away. I concentrated at school, only mildly distracted by the hints of ghosts. I did my work and joined lunchtime revision sessions. My mind cleared a bit and I could see the exams coming up, and felt that I hadn't left it too late. If I revised really hard I could do it.

I applied to sixth-form college, for A levels in history, English and French. I didn't think I'd have gone for French if it hadn't been for Joe and Ms Duke, but I was working extra hard at it now because Ms D was the link between my life and Joe's, and because Joe had never been to France, and because Troy lived there and I'd never managed to get in touch with him. Every strand led to France, so learning the language properly seemed like the least I could do, even if I had stopped trying to solve the mystery of Joe's death.

I had never felt alone like this. I didn't have Mum. Izzy was ecstatically loved up with Tally. When I went looking for Jack one day after school, I found him kissing a girl from the year below and backed away.

And I didn't have Joe. I only went into his room when I knew he wasn't there. A few times, between four and five, I stood outside clutching the door handle, but I didn't go in. The more I didn't do it, the easier it became. I supposed he was living by a schedule he had crafted for himself, making sure he saw all the important people in his world, apart from me. I went to an open evening at college, and I knew that he'd been right, that I was growing away from him, that one day I'd be just another adult, and he would still be fifteen.

At the end of April I was dutifully eating a nutritious breakfast (muesli with chopped banana, raisins and yogurt) while reading over my chemistry notes, and also keeping an eye on my phone, when Sasha laughed.

'Look at this!' she said. 'New trick!'

She'd put her glass of juice on her bump as if it was a little table. She took her hand away and it wobbled, but stayed there.

'Wow,' I said, distracted for a moment from the email that I'd just seen in my inbox. 'That's amazing. A built-in shelf!'

'Portable coffee table.' She sighed. 'I'd love a coffee so much. But since I decided to give it up, right back at the start when everything was making me sick, I can't really go back to it now. I can manage nine more weeks without coffee.'

'Nine weeks! Are you serious?'

'Yep,' she said. 'Do the maths. Baby due on July the second. It's the first of May in two days' time.'

I thought about that. 'If it's about to be May, and my exams start on May the eleventh, I should step up my revision.'

Sasha reached across and pushed the fruit bowl towards me. 'Eat another banana,' she said. 'Brain food.'

We called it the 'fruit bowl', but it only contained four blackening bananas.

'I aready had one,' I said. 'I'm not hungry.'

'OK, but we need to get rid of these before they start to smell.'

'I'll make a banana cake.'

'Yes! Can you make it so we can toast it and put extra butter on?' She paused. 'For the baby.'

'Sure thing!'

A part of me was panicking about my exams, even though I knew I was doing everything I should be doing. Until recently I'd thought it would be OK to wing it, and I'd be just about all right, but now I wanted to do extra well. I didn't need to get nines in everything, but I wanted to. Then I'd go and tell Joe, and he'd be pleased for me. That was my aim. If I had a piece of news like that then it would be all right to go back and see him. Wouldn't it?

I walked slowly down the road, opening the email as I went. I stopped altogether to read it and let other people walk past.

> Hi there, Ariel and Izzy. Hope you're both doing well. It was nice to talk about Joe with you the other week. Hope you've got everything you need for your article. I was thinking, it's really going above and beyond to do this sort of research for a school mag rather than just rehashing the old stuff. I think you have great futures in front of you.
>
> Sorry this has taken a while. I reached out to Troy like I promised, but I'm afraid when he finally did reply it wasn't the most friendly. Copied and pasted here. After he sent it he disappeared from my LinkedIn, so I'm thinking he really doesn't want to talk. Anyway, I tried. Sorry not to have something better to report.
>
> Cheers, Lucas

Then, in a different font, it said:

> No, of course I'm not interested in talking about Joe, least of all to some kids. Journos are all the same whoever they're writing for and I have nothing to say to any of them except fuck off. Surprised at you tbh. T

That stung. I'd thought that Troy and I, as Joe's best friends, should have had some sort of affinity.

I needed to find Troy myself.

Then I remembered I wasn't doing this any more. I didn't need to find Troy: I needed to take my exams. This was no longer my thing.

I started to feel angry. I squashed it down.

I didn't think anyone had directly told me to *fuck off* before.

I was never going to live in the cloud tops of Venus.

We had kind of kissed and then I'd been dumped by a ghost.

Dumped by a fucking ghost!

It made me boil with rage.

I didn't care about Troy. He was just some grumpy old man. Of course he didn't want to talk about it. I tried to imagine, nineteen years from now, if someone who wasn't even born yet contacted me because they were writing a stupid little article about the anniversary of Mum's death and wanted some quotes from me. I wouldn't want to talk to them either. I'd definitely want to tell them to fuck off too.

'I know we've dropped the Joe thing,' I told Izzy when we met on the corner, 'but look at this.' I forwarded her the message. She looked at it and winced.

'Whoa,' she said. 'He sounds nice.'

'Right? Anyway, fuck him.'

She tucked her arm through mine. 'Yeah. He makes himself sound guilty.'

'He wouldn't kill his best friend, though. Would he?' That hung there for a while and then I shook myself. 'So. Did your mum book the holiday?'

'Not yet, but I think we're going to Spain. Tally might come too. Do you think you and Sasha will go away? Oh, of course not. The baby!'

'I don't think we would have anyway. It would be weird, me and Sasha going on holiday.' I thought a few years ahead and perked up. 'It'll be lovely, though, to take the baby away, in a year or two. We could go to . . .' I tried to remember where people went on holiday with small kids. 'Mallorca or something. I don't know. Not a city break, but somewhere with nice safe beaches.'

Plans like this made me happy. They were the future.

38

It's a Monday in 2019, so I'm sitting on the train with Lara. Today she's knitting a little jumper with the beginning of the letter M on it.

'Knowing that she's Mabel,' she says, 'has changed everything, even though it changes nothing. You finding that out for me is the most exciting thing that's happened since I died. My great regret was always that I wouldn't ever know, and now I do. And I know that the birth goes well, considering that she's healthy twenty years later. I do think sometimes that you might be making it up, but mainly I believe you. I believe in Mabel.'

'You should believe in her,' I say. 'I'm not making it up. Why would I?'

'Out of kindness,' she says. She looks into my face with that unnerving expression parents have. I turn away.

'Joe?' she says. 'You're different. You're a bit different every time I see you. What's happening?'

I stare at the roof of the train, which has a stain on it. How do you stain a train ceiling? It's brown and splattery. A shaken-up can of Coke maybe?

'I miss Ariel,' I say to the ceiling. 'But I'm making my peace with this. I think it's working. I mean, I'm coming to terms with the fact that I'm in love with someone who hadn't even been born when I died, but who's already overtaken me. Who I can't see any more, or I'll waste her life as well as mine. But every day I hope she'll visit me, and she never does.'

'Oh, darling.'

'She's studying for exams I never took. It's a two-year course and she's almost at the end of it. I only got to do the first six months. It's a headfuck.'

'A fucking headfuck.' Lara squeezes my hand.

'I'm not waiting any more. I know I'm not going to disappear into some heavenly afterlife. We're stuck here. For literally eternity. I'm getting my head round it. I'm feeling OK, considering. Settling in. I'm learning Italian. *Va bene.*'

'Are you keeping track of what day it is?' she asks. 'In 2019, I mean.'

'Yeah. Only by living my seven-day cycle. That way I always kind of know what Ariel's doing too, somewhere out there.'

'You do love her.'

'I mean, she needs to meet someone with prospects.' If I had tears, I'd be close to crying right now.

'Oh, Joe!'

'Pathetic, right?'

Lara hugs me, and I take a lot of comfort from the fact that we have a shared eternity. I don't want to talk about myself any more, so I ask about Josh, and sit back and let her talk all the way to Reading.

I crash Mum's dojo. She drives me home for emergency medical care. I take comfort from her too. I can do this. I have to. My eternity is, at least, going to be populated by the best people.

When we're about halfway home, I say, 'I met a girl, Mum. It's a bit complicated, but I really love her.'

She lights up. She looks so happy that it really is as if someone switched a light on inside her body.

'Joe! That's wonderful. Where does she live? Does she go to your school?'

I tell her all about Ariel, escaping into a fantasy in which everything is straightforward. Yes, she goes to my school and she's in the year above. I tell Mum where she lives. That she has an older sister who's having a baby. That her mother died and her father left. Mum says all the right things and instructs me to invite her over for dinner as soon as I'm feeling better, and I disappear into my imaginary world in which things are this clear cut. By the time we pull up outside Beachview I'm positively glowing.

Mum sends me into the mall to wait while she parks the car. I wish I wasn't compelled to go and buy a drink that I don't ever want. I decide to try to talk to the angry man today, to mix it up a bit.

I buy a can of Cherry Coke. I turn and bump into him. He says, 'Fuck's sake!'

I say, 'Sorry.' He tuts and strides away, so I follow.

He's maybe about thirty, with curly dark hair like pubes, and he looks furious. He's wearing a blue shirt and the kind of trousers people wear to work, and there's some kind of ID on him that I can't read. I run a bit to catch up.

'Sorry I walked into you,' I say, and he throws me an angry look.

'I should've expected it,' he says, 'coming to a place like this. No class.'

'Fuck *you*,' I say.

'You want to watch what you're saying.'

He stops. We stare at each other. This is a seriously unpleasant man. I hate the way his eyes bore into mine. I turn and walk away. Everything about this feels very bad. I don't think he would kill me for walking into him, but someone's about to do it and he seems to hate me the most.

My heart is still pounding as I sit and wait to die. Ariel hasn't been to see me once since I told her to stop, and I regret everything so much. I told her not to see me any more because I love her. I pushed her away because I love her. Even though I know it was the right thing to do, I often wish I could go back and unsay all of it.

I work so hard to be calm, and that man has messed with it. I mustn't fall into a spiral of despair because if I let that happen I'll wake up in it tomorrow, and everything will go to shit.

I take a piece of paper and a pen from my schoolbag. I have to distract myself from whatever that was, in his eyes.

He is most definitely the only person I've met on any of my todays who looks like he'd happily turn round and kill me.

Does that mean he's the main suspect?

I push him out of my head. He can do nothing but damage in there. I start writing without planning what I'm going to put down. I kind of think I'll expand on my thoughts about the angry man, but when I look at the page this is what I've written:

Why I love Ariel
Kind and beautiful.
Clever.
She's determined: I told her not to come any more, and she hated me saying it, but she hasn't come back once, even though she knows where to find me and I wouldn't be able to stop her.
I trust her.
She's sad too – we understand each other.
She's my friend.
The person I trust.
The one.

I met the person I'd want to spend the rest of my life with, twenty years after my death, and then I dumped her.

The worst thing in my universe isn't the fact that I'm about to be murdered.

It's the fact that I told the love of my life, the love of my afterlife, that I never wanted to see her again and she believed me.

Way to go, Joe.

I draw squiggles and little pictures round the edge, and savour the fact that, no matter what, I managed to fall in love.

39

I got up early, knowing that I was too old to be scared on my first day at big school, but feeling absolutely fucking terrified. I had packed up everything I thought I was going to need (A4 paper, folders, lots and lots of different pens) and planned an outfit in what I was trialling as my new sixth-form style (long skirt, vintage trench coat, clumpy boots). I was meeting Izzy at nine because we were due at an orientation session at ten. Yet here I was, sitting downstairs, drinking coffee, at half past six. The baby hadn't woken me: I'd done it myself.

Starting sixth-form college was another big step away from Joe. I wasn't at his school any more and I was nearly two years older than him now. It was that thought that had woken me up and kept me awake.

I hadn't seen him at all for nearly five months, ever since the day he told me not to visit, but I was wondering whether, perhaps, it would be OK if I went today. We hadn't really ended things, and my anger and confusion had faded. I really wanted to see how he was. Whether he was even still there.

When exams finished, I found myself reintegrated with old and new friends. I spent the days with Izzy (who had broken up with Tally solely because she wanted to try dating), but also with Alice, Priya, Jack – who had settled into being a solid friend – and a whole group of new people, friends of friends, people from other schools, or who I'd just never spoken to before. I spent a lot of time just hanging around, sitting on the beach, drinking cider, savouring the feeling that I was kind of normal again. I'd even met a boy called Finn, a friend of friends. Nothing had happened between us, but I thought there was potential, if I wanted it. Finn wasn't Joe, but he was real. He had curly hair and a surfy kind of aesthetic, and I liked him.

It had been almost impossible to make myself turn away from Joe and towards this real boy. That was why I hadn't visited Joe all summer, not even when I'd been in Beachview with Zara and Coco. Not even to tell him about the baby. It was too hard to move on from him and I knew that if I saw him I'd be right back where I started.

I felt a constant low-level guilt, but it was tempered by the fact that this was his plan too. He'd been right all along: my life had come back into focus in the real world and I needed to live it. I was never going to solve the mystery of his disappearance after all this time, when even the police had failed. The last thing that had happened, in that respect, was that email from Lucas with the message from Troy, and I'd just sent a short reply thanking him for trying, and left it at that.

In July the most magical thing of all had happened: twelve days later than planned, on July the fourteenth, Rafael Joseph had burst into our lives, and now nothing was ever going be the same.

Sasha hadn't been sure about the middle name at first because she knew I'd been interested in Joe Simpson and thought the name might bring bad luck. But I persuaded her, in the end, that it was silly to be superstitious, and since I'd been part-time looking after Zara and Coco all summer, and they'd spent many afternoons hanging out at our house, talking about the baby, she came round quickly. Raffy Joe was the best thing that had ever happened to us. I'd considered taking him to meet my Joe, but I hadn't done it. I hadn't gone to visit two weeks ago when I got my exam results either.

I knew that if I went back I'd never leave.

I put two pieces of bread into the toaster and checked the peanut-butter jar. There was just enough, and I went to the list stuck on the fridge and wrote PB on it. I'd been doing most of the shopping and general admin while Sasha was busy with Raffy, and that had been fine. Now that I had college I was going to have to be a bit more organized about it all, but it was definitely easier than being the one in charge of the baby.

I heard footsteps on the stairs, and turned to see Sasha in the kitchen doorway looking sleepy. I rushed over and took Raffy from her arms.

'Hello, Raff,' I said, and he looked at me with his serious face. Raffy had been born perfectly himself. He had thick black hair and huge dark-brown eyes, and when he smiled (a recent development) it was a wide cartoony smile that took up his whole face. It was Mum's smile. He carried her inside him.

He stared at me for a few seconds, then bestowed his huge grin upon me.

'Thanks,' said Sasha, stumbling towards the kettle, yawning.

'How was he last night?'

'Shit. One day he'll be a teenager and he'll be sleeping all morning and I won't be able to get him out of bed. Imagine.'

'You will,' I said to Raffy. 'You'll sleep all morning and Mum will be saying, "*You treat this place like a hotel*," and all those things.'

'Oh Christ, Arry!' said Sasha, looking at my bag. 'It's your first day! Good luck. Have you got everything you need?'

'Everything. And lots of things I don't. And loads of time before I have to go.'

'You show them. I mean, I know you will. You showed the world what Ariel Brown can do with your exam results, so of course you'll show them now.' She paused. 'I'm not sure who *they* are, but anyway. The whole of the world outside this house, I guess.'

'I'll do my best to show them,' I said. Sasha was right: although I hadn't quite got all nines as I'd hoped, my results were close enough, and I was extremely proud of them. It had all come together at the last minute solely thanks to Joe knowing what was good for me better than I knew myself.

Maybe I *would* go and visit him later.

Raffy went purple in the face and started huffing dramatically. I laughed at him.

'Are you doing a poo?' I said as an unmistakable smell filled the room. 'Don't worry, Sash. I'll change him.'

'You are an angel. Coffee?'

'Got one, thanks.'

'Can I have a piece of your toast?'

'Have both. Just put another one on for me, yeah?'

'Sure.'

We still hadn't heard from Dad. We'd made no effort to tell him about the baby, so he probably didn't know that he was a grandfather, though he could have worked it out easily enough from the dates. When I occasionally thought about him, I pictured him in a new relationship up in Scotland, probably with a younger woman who'd put up with his moods.

I hated him, but he had no hold over me any more. He was a stranger and I sincerely expected never to see him again. I had tried once, when I sent him that email in March, but he'd never even replied.

I took Raffy into the bathroom and changed his nappy, expert at this now. I changed his onesie too as he definitely needed a fresh one. I put him into a bright green outfit that Ms D, or *Florence* as I was now supposed to call her, had given him.

'There you go,' I said. 'All fragrant again. Fragrant and gorgeous and really quite neon.'

Sasha had made me some toast, and put another coffee next to my plate.

'There you go,' she said. 'I got you a coffee because I couldn't remember if you wanted one or not.

'Thanks,' I said. I'd drink it anyway.

She took the baby and sat on the sofa to breastfeed. Our house had been entirely baby orientated since the middle of July. It was hard for me to remember a time before Raffy. I sat and talked to my sister about nothing in particular, and then it was time to go to college. I laced up my boots and tried to prepare myself for this new world.

'Good luck!' said Sasha. 'You look good. Studenty.'

At four o'clock I stood outside the Beachview room. I knew he was in there. I put my hand on the door, knowing it would take a second to push it open and see him.

If I saw him would I be able to leave? Would I mess up whatever equilibrium he had? Would it be a massive step back for both of us?

It was too much to risk. I walked away.

40

I wake early, leave a note and go to Bodmin. Leo isn't there.

I walk up and down both platforms. He's always right here. He knows which day I visit. I come once a week, every 2019 Thursday, just after calling in on Anna and Sasha, and he's always waiting on the platform. It's rude of him not to be here today.

I pause and force myself to get some perspective.

It's not rude. I don't own Leo. He's allowed to go to the woods, or to his office at the stately home, or, of course, anywhere he wants. It's not easy for us to keep track of the days, and for him to count up to when it's been seven must be tricky. My novelty has worn off. I'll just wander around, practising my Italian, until I find him.

Maybe another ghost has turned up.

That thought stops me in my tracks. A new ghost would be magical. It's totally possible that someone from further down the line could have caught a train up here. A new person in my life would be incredible. Wild. Maybe it would be a girl.

It wouldn't be the right girl.

I follow the path Leo takes into the woods and check each of his dens. They are all places he's discovered over the years that were basically already there because whatever modifications he makes are gone by the morning. All the same, he spends some days building a magnificent tree house, like Lara with her knitting, knowing it'll be gone the next day, but not caring.

I tramp through the woods, not feeling the cold, not noticing the mud. I start with his main den, the one he took me to the first time I came. He's not up there. I go to the one in a hollow tree, the one at the top of a slope that he calls the Lookout, the one that's almost in a hole in the ground down by the river. He's nowhere.

I check the time. That took over an hour and I'm not sure what to do next. I visit the platform again, look in the cafe, under the seats in the ticket office.

It's quite a long walk up to Lanhydrock House, and I take it slowly, wishing I could smell the air around me. It's slightly warmer here than it is at home today, and I'm sure it would have that spring smell. There are things starting to unfurl all around me in these woods. Shoots are poking up through the earth. The leaves on the trees are mainly buds. I cross a little road and set off up a driveway that is so long that I can't see the house at the end of it. The land around it is grassy and hilly. Everything is so beautiful.

I miss life. I wish I could see this spring turning into summer.

*

I walk round all the parts of the garden that are free to get into, but he's not there. I pay a surprising number of pounds to get in, and ignore all the Victorian things, all the information about a family with ten children and a big fire, in my search for Leo. In the end I stop a woman wearing a National Trust uniform, and say, 'Excuse me? I'm looking for Leo Chatterjee.'

'Leo, you say,' she says. She looks at me, interested. 'He's up in the nursery. Is he expecting you?'

Up in the nursery? What the heck? Leo never goes to work. That's his thing. He hasn't been for twenty years. What's he doing in the nursery? I don't even know if she means babies or plants.

'Yes,' I say. I try to remember what his job actually is. 'I'm doing a project on conservation,' I say, 'and he's going to help me.'

'Then you'll find him up the stairs.' She gives me a set of instructions and I follow them, and end up in a perfect Victorian children's nursery, with a row of little beds and a bookcase of old books, and Leo kneeling in the corner, wearing a dark blue National Trust shirt, checking something.

'Leo!' I say.

He looks up. 'Hi there,' he says. 'Can I help?'

'It's me,' I say. 'Joe.' He still looks confused. He is holding an old book and is clearly in the middle of packing it away. 'I see you every week.'

His face is blank. I step closer and look at him, trying to work out if he's messing with me, but he's not.

Leo doesn't know me.

'Did you have a question about the house?' he tries.

'No,' I say. 'I have a question about why you don't recognize me.'

'I see,' he says, and I can see that he's wary. He stands up. 'I'm sorry. I should clearly remember you but I'm afraid I don't. Were you younger when we met? How can I help?'

I wait for the smallest flicker, but there's nothing. I realize that he doesn't even look the same. He's more polished. Not only is he wearing his work uniform, but his hair is styled in a way it never normally is.

'You really don't know me,' I say. I look at a doll sitting in a little chair. This place feels a bit creepy.

'I do apologize,' he says.

The man who has eleven different dens in the woods, who meditates on the train platform, who has filled his eternity by learning to walk on his hands and speak conversational Spanish is apologizing to me. He doesn't know me at all.

This freaks me right out.

'Never mind,' I say. 'It doesn't matter.'

I try to think of something else to add, but I can't think of anything, and so I run out of the nursery, against the flow of the visitors, and outside. I have three pounds eighty left, so I buy a pot of tea in the cafe, just for the comfort of it, and wait, but nothing happens. After an hour or so I walk down to the station and catch the train back to Exeter and then home.

Leo has changed. The man who came up with the concept of glitching is no longer glitching.

He's gone.

On Friday I break with my routine. I don't catch Lara's train. I leave the house early, with a reassuring note for Dad, and go to the sixth-form college, where I sit on a bench by the main entrance. I'm there at seven, and at first I read my book, but when people start arriving I put on *Different Class* and stare at them. The line 'you didn't notice me at all' comes on and is incredibly appropriate. No one pays the slightest bit of attention to me, even though I am actually not a ghost here, just a boy who should be at school. I feel that I stick out a mile for being a couple of years too young, but in fact I'm just another teenager in a place filled with teens. While they stream past I do my best to check out every single one of them. I can't see them all, however. They come in huge waves, spilling off the buses that bring people in from the villages.

There's a surge just before nine, then another at nine thirty, and then again at ten. From time to time I see someone I recognize from the years above me at school, and a few of them give me a little nod. I know Gus is going to turn up for his maths class at half ten, and when I see him in the distance I hold my book up like a spy in a movie. He doesn't even glance my way.

He is, I see, walking with a girl. Holding her hand.

For God's sake! I've lived this day for more than twenty years and I've only just discovered that my brother has a secret girlfriend. I peek at her from behind my book, just for long enough to see that she's not Abby Fielding. If she was then I'd throw the book down and run over to meet her. This girl is taller than Gus, and she has white-blonde hair. I wonder who she is.

I don't wonder for long, however, because about ten seconds after they've gone into the building, just as 'Something Changed' starts to play for the second time around, Ariel arrives.

As far as I can tell she's on her own, but I guess she's probably not. I can only see her. I've only ever had eyes for her.

She looks older, and I know she's nearly seventeen now. She looks happy and glowing and perfect. She's wearing a long skirt and a white shirt and a cool coat, and her hair is longer than it was before. She walks with a confidence she didn't have when I was colonizing her life.

Can I do this? Can I step back into her world? No, I can't. I turn away, but it's too late. She's seen me. And the smile that breaks out across her face is the sun, the moon, the ocean, the planets. It's my everything. She is my everything.

She's at my side in seconds. I press stop after Jarvis says, 'Life could have been very different,' and take the headphones off.

'Is it you?' she says. 'Joe? Is it actually you?'

I can't stop smiling either. Why haven't we been doing this every day?

'Yes, it is,' I say. 'Sorry.'

'You idiot!' she says. 'I've stood outside that door in Beachview so many times. But I always thought you told me not to come and so I didn't go in. Look, I really have to go to class, but shall I come and see you this afternoon?'

'Yes! Yes, yes, yes, please. Did the baby arrive OK?'

'Yes! He's perfect.'

We grin at each other. I try to kiss her. She shifts over so she's right in me. Then she jumps up and runs off into the building, turning back to wave.

Hours later she runs into the cupboard and does her very best to hug me. I do my best to hug her back. The universe slots into place. This is how things should be. My world is infinitely better.

'So,' she says. 'What's up?'

'Tell me about the baby!'

She does, and the fact that he's Raffy Joe makes me want to cry. She laughs. 'Joe, what other middle name was I going to pick?' She tells me about Zara and Coco, how much they're in her life now. I love to think about the real-world connections that have come out of Ariel and me. I tell her that I say hello to her mum every week and her eyes fill with tears.

'Right,' she says. 'You came to find me for a reason. What is it?'

'It's Leo,' I say. I tell her about my trip to Bodmin. 'He didn't know me. It was like he wasn't a ghost any more. He'd changed into one of the people who are just the avatars of themselves in my day. I think . . . well, I think something's changed with him and his death. I'm so sorry to charge in and find you like this. I'm feeling a bit . . . wobbly. I only know two other people like me, and one of them has gone. Can you look him up?'

'Leo Chatterjee,' she says. 'With a double "e", isn't it? I've done this before, remember, and –.' She stops talking. 'Oh,' she says. 'Right. Oh my God, Joe. I'd forgotten what it's like in your world. Oh wow.'

'What?' I know roughly what she's going to say, and she does.

'It's a news report from four days ago. *Bodmin Parkway tragedy uncovered twenty years on.*' She holds out her phone so I can read the story. There's a photo of Leo. Underneath it says:

A twenty-year-old mystery was solved yesterday when building contractors uncovered the body of a man who went missing in Bodmin in 1999. Leo Chatterjee, 33, was last seen on 11 March 1999 when he left his job at Lanhydrock House. He never arrived at his home in Par, and it was assumed he had left the area. However, building works near the station uncovered a body yesterday. It is thought that Chatterjee, who was unmarried with no close family, suffered a freak fall in the woods and was buried by the earth that fell with him. The search for him centred on Plymouth and further afield as sightings were reported on the train.

'I knew it. His death has been explained now and he's moved on. Shit! Shit!'

Ariel takes a deep breath. 'That proves it, doesn't it? What you always thought. We could –' She stops herself.

'That really was just an avatar Leo who I saw today,' I say. 'It was just a version of him furnishing my imaginary day, packing up an old book. I'm never going to see my Leo again.' I feel as if I've lost a limb but worse because if I lost a limb right now it wouldn't even hurt.

'Joe,' she says, 'I know things have changed. But if you want we could revisit it. At least give it another go. We know now that it can happen. Let's give it one more try. Let me have one more crack at tracking down Troy and you can –' I see her casting around for anything I could do, and finding something – 'take a photo of the angry man. Remember? You never did, did you? We'll make this work. We'll rescue you. It's worth giving it one more shot, right?'

I look at the door. 'Did you really stand out there and not come in?' She nods. 'How many times?'

'Well,' she says, smiling, 'I'd say *several*.'

'Several?' I raise my eyebrows. 'That many?'

I look into her eyes for a long time. This is the antidote to when I did the same thing to Leo earlier because this time I see total understanding.

'I'm scared,' I manage to say. This all feels so real. 'Because if we do it, and if it works, then . . . what if it's nothing? What if Leo's nowhere? What if you go on to . . . oblivion?'

41

There was a spring in my step as I diverted my route home to take in the house where Joe said Troy used to live. On the way I stopped on top of a hill and let the salty air hit me in the face.

Joe had come to find me. That made me completely, uncomplicatedly happy. I had missed him so much. His face in my world made me feel I could do anything, and now I was going to do this.

I thought about Leo Chatterjee and wondered where he was now. Maybe it was nothing, like Joe had said. Perhaps he'd vanished into nothingness forever.

I had to believe that he hadn't. Joe wouldn't have a consciousness now if we were switched off at death. I had to believe there was something else, a place where Joe would, one day, meet my mother, and where, sometime in the deep future, I'd join them.

Plus, Joe was scared that there was oblivion ahead. So what? So was everyone. That fear was a part of being human. It meant he was still real.

*

I rang the doorbell three times and stood there longer than you usually would, but nothing happened. I walked down the road to a little park with a bench in it and wrote a note on a piece of paper torn from a notebook.

It was strange how easy it was to slip back into this.

Hi, I wrote. *Mr and Mrs Henry. Sorry to disturb you, but I'm wondering if you could help with something for an article about Joe Simpson. My name's Ariel Brown. We're doing a feature about Joe and we're trying to talk to as many people as possible who knew him. I know it was very difficult for Troy, and that he lives abroad now, but I'd love to talk to either of you if possible.*

I added my email and phone number, though I knew that, even if they did still live here, they wouldn't call or message. Then I went back to put it through the letterbox, and as I was reaching out to do so the door opened and a man came out.

He was a man I'd met before. This was Pete, the security guard I'd spoken to at Beachview. Joe had said Troy was a quarter Dutch, and I knew that his dad was called Piet. I hadn't connected Pete from Beachview and Troy's dad Piet at all.

I took half a step back. He was tall, with a straight back and a soldier's bearing, and he gave off an aura of hostility, exactly as he had when I spoke to him in the spring.

'Been ringing the bell?' he said.

'Sorry to disturb you.' I screwed the note up and put it in my pocket. I'd told this man I was Joe's cousin, so I couldn't switch stories at this point.

325

'I thought you were someone else. 'S why I didn't answer. What did you want?' He looked me up and down.

'I don't even know if you're the right person,' I said. 'I'm looking for Piet Henry. Troy's dad?'

'Who's asking? Hang on – "Joe Simpson's cousin".' He said it with extreme scepticism. I wanted to run away, but I'd come here to do this, so I had to get on with it.

'Yes,' I said. 'I'm still trying to find out what happened. I didn't realize when I spoke to you before that you were Troy's dad.'

He looked shocked for a fraction of a second, then turned away, and when he looked back at me he seemed to hate me even more than before. He shrugged.

'Nothing to say,' he said. 'Water under the bridge. And you're not Joe's cousin.'

'Do you think Troy might ta–'

He didn't even let me finish. 'No, and you know that very well because you got Luke to ask him months ago. I don't know what you're up to, but you have to stop.'

'But we just –'

'Leave it. If you know what's good for you, you'll drop it. Leave it in the past.'

I tried to think of something else to say, but he went back into the house and slammed the door in my face.

After we'd had dinner (I was still rotating the same meal plan and it worked smoothly enough) I told Sasha I had some reading to do, snuggled Raffy and shut myself in my room, where I created a LinkedIn account and searched for all the variations I could think of on Troy's name.

I trawled through a surprising number of people called Troy, and alighted on Troy H-Laffitte, who had the right-coloured hair in his corporate profile pic. I clicked on the profile. I was pretty sure that he'd know I'd looked at it, that this was how LinkedIn worked (for some reason), but I didn't care. This was the most boring social media in the world and I didn't get it, but I knew how to stalk a profile at least.

His hair looked more like a kind of strawberry blond than actual ginger, and he was suntanned. In his profile picture he was doing a half-smile at the camera, wearing a suit, against a plain white background.

It was definitely him. This was the ghost boy I'd seen writing on the wall with a stone. He had written HELP ME. He'd needed help because his best friend had gone missing. Later he had run away to France. I wondered whether he'd gone to France because Joe had never managed to get there, or whether that was a cringingly trite way of framing things.

Most of his profile was in French. I wished Florence was here to help, but on the other hand I was still studying it, and so I focused and found that I could actually understand it perfectly well. It didn't say anything remotely interesting, though. In fact, it was the most boring thing I'd ever read in any language.

Right at the bottom, however, there was a link to another site. I clicked and it took me to a personal website.

While he had his office job in Marseilles, Troy also worked as an artist, and the blog I was looking at now was his art-selling page.

This was miles better. Some of the site was in English and,

327

best of all, there were lots of photographs. I pored over them. Troy's art was nice: it wasn't earth-shattering or avant-garde, but it was pretty. There were seascapes, landscapes, pictures of vases of flowers and portraits, including one of a baby and another that I was pretty sure was a semi-abstract painting of Joe.

I looked hard into the backgrounds of all the pictures. I inspected every single thing I could in this slice of Troy's life.

And then I saw it.

42

It's Saturday for Ariel, and all I can think of, all day, is how much I long to see her. She didn't specifically say that she'd be back today. I don't really know her life any more, but she has loads of new friends and a nephew, so she might be too busy.

I wake up, thinking that I'll go and see Lara and tell her about Leo, but when it comes to it I don't have the energy for anything, so I follow my usual routine and stay home. I am so good at persuading Dad not to go to work that the part where I either fake vomit or have a breakdown is just a piece of admin now, but today is different. Leo's story has blown my shaky edifice to pieces. He had a freak accident in the woods, fell down and died, and was covered by earth and never found. And then, as soon as his body was discovered, he disappeared.

I never said goodbye. The sense of loss is overwhelming. I need to tell Lara. Tomorrow.

I have a breakdown to make Dad stay home, and for the first time in ages it isn't a fake one. I need every moment of it, every single hug I can get him to give me while we watch movies and he takes me to Beachview to see the emergency doctor and I go to the cupboard and wait to die.

I hope and hope and hope, and then the door opens and she's there. She has something new to tell me. I can see it.

'Joe,' she says, and she kisses me in the only way she can. Our faces disappear into each other a bit. I used to feel nothing when this happened, but today it makes me do a kind of shiver. I missed her with every atom of my non-being, and she's back. I want to hang on to this non-kiss forever, with everything I have.

'What?'

'I found Troy. But it's not just that. I found something else. There's something I really, really need you to look at.'

I walk round the tiny space while she opens up her phone. I'm too tense. There's nowhere to go because the other end of the room is just three steps away, but I do it anyway. Step, step, step one way. Step, step, step back again. Step, step, step. Step, step . . .

'Here. Sit down.'

At first I don't register what she's showing me.

'Oh God,' I say. 'Is that Troy grown up? Is he a . . . painter?'

'Yeah, but it's not that. Look. Down here.'

I'm still staring at Troy. His hair has faded as if he's started to wash the colour out, but he's exactly the same Troy. I see him every day, and now here he is again, smiling awkwardly at a camera, with wrinkles.

I tear my eyes away and focus on the thing Ariel's trying to show me instead. Even this takes a while because my head is so full of the sight of Troy painting in France in his thirties.

He did it. He did the thing he keeps telling me he's going to do. Moved to France, met a girl, became an artist.

Then at last I see it.

Behind Troy in his cluttered studio is a shelf of objects. There are books, jars of brushes, a box, a piece of material. A football trophy shaped like a foot kicking a ball.

I open my bag and take it out. This time it comes out easily. I hold it up next to the screen.

I look at Ariel and see, now, what it was in her eyes.

'I try to give it back to him,' I say. 'All the time. I've been trying to give it back for twenty years.'

'But you never can.'

'I can't get it out of my bag. It's one of the things that's fixed. So how can Troy have it?'

'Joe,' she says, 'I've been thinking about this every moment since I saw it. There's no way this could have happened unless Troy knows a whole lot more than he ever said.'

'He must have seen me just before I died. Or after.'

'Or,' she says, 'during.'

We spend the rest of our time composing the message Ariel sends through his website. There's no point in being half-hearted: we need to write something that will stop him in his tracks. It takes a long time, but in the end she fills in the contact name as Joe Simpson, with a new email address that she's set up in my name. The message says:

Mate. You hate your name because it's an anagram of Tory. In primary school we found a frog on the playing field and took it to the playground to try to scare girls, but they thought it was cute and made it a little hat from a leaf and called it Froggykins. Modelling agency scouts say you have a strong look. You hate it.

You always said you'd meet a French girl and become an artist, and now you've done it.

I took your trophy. I think I was jealous. God knows, but I'm sorry. I was in a little room behind Boots at Beachview. I don't know what happened after that, but I'm here now. In that same room at Beachview. I met Ariel here. She's helping, but I need your help too, mate. Please. I need to know what happened. I'm guessing we had a fight and you threw an unlucky punch. I don't mind any of that. I just need to know. Please help. Just come back to that room, any afternoon except Sunday, between four and five. Please.

Joe

It sounds off-the-wall batshit, but it should get his attention. Ariel couldn't possibly have known about Froggykins.

Knowing what I do of Troy, he'll try to tell himself it's madness for a day or so, but then he'll crack and reply because it'll play on his mind too much.

'Wait,' I say.

If Ariel sends this, then it will make things happen. I don't know if I want things to happen.

She looks at me. She understands.

'I don't have to press send.'

My mind is full of clutter. I don't know what I want.

This thing has momentum, though. I don't think we can stop it now. I can't live for eternity, wondering what would have happened if we'd done this.

'Do it,' I say, and she does.

We sit and look at each other in absolute silence until the door opens and someone – is it Troy? – walks in. Everything goes blank.

43

By the time I woke up on Sunday morning there was a reply in the new Joe Simpson inbox, but it just said this:

> Ariel, I presume. This is a disgusting thing that you're doing. Stop this or I'll contact the authorities. Never get in touch with me again. TL

I also had a WhatsApp message from Finn. Finn, who I'd met over the summer, was in my English class now. We had a lot of eye contact.

> Hey, Ariel! I don't have anything after English tomorrow – do you fancy grabbing a coffee?

I smiled at the phone. I wanted Joe, but Finn was real and I knew what I had to do. I couldn't spend my life being in love with a boy who had been dead for twenty years. My summer had shown me that I needed to live my life, and Raffy wouldn't want an aunt who was hopelessly in love with a ghost. I couldn't turn my back on all the progress I'd made.

Sounds good, I wrote. Then, when I'd sent it, I worried that it was a stupid reply. I should have answered by emoji. *Sounds good.* That's what an old person would have said. I should have sent a flame.

Nonetheless, the upshot was that I had agreed to go for coffee with Finn.

I turned my attention back to Troy.

Joe had predicted that he would shut me down at first, but that later he'd change his approach, so I did nothing. I tried to put it all from my mind and hung out all day with Sasha and Raff. On Monday I went to college and wished I'd spent a bit less time playing with the baby while dwelling on trophy-return scenarios, and a bit more time learning French vocabulary.

Troy wouldn't have killed Joe on purpose. We both knew that. But he might have done it by mistake.

After English Finn and I walked to a cafe that was far enough from college to get us away from any gossip. It was a nice place, with dark varnished floorboards and comfy battered chairs.

'So,' said Finn, after we'd got past the awkward negotiations about who was buying the coffees. 'How are you doing, Ariel?'

'Fine, thanks!'

Troy had come to take his trophy back. He and Joe had got into an argument that had developed into a physical fight. I could imagine Joe being incredibly annoying. Troy had punched him, in the heat of the moment, in the small room. It had been an unlucky punch and Joe died. Troy's dad had been working right there in Beachview. He'd helped him with the body. That had to be it. It explained why Piet was so hostile to me when I asked questions.

I looked at Finn and forced myself to focus. 'How about you?'

'Um, yeah, all good,' he said.

I knew I wasn't doing my bit conversationally, so I started to talk. *Just say anything*, I thought, *and it'll get things flowing*. 'My sister's baby's really cute,' I said. 'I'll show you some pictures.'

'Oh yeah,' he said. 'Cool.'

Ten minutes later I was talking about Raffy's nappies, and Finn was zoning out. I stopped myself.

'How about college?' I said. 'How are you finding it?'

'It's cool,' he said. 'I mean, better than school, right?'

'Right,' I said.

It was the most lacklustre date there'd ever been. In spite of all my best intentions, I could only think about Joe.

44

Lara is knitting in purple.

'Joe!' she says. 'What a treat. What's up?'

I take a deep breath and tell her about Leo. She feels the same as I do. It's shattering.

'Let's not talk about it for the rest of the journey,' I say.

We are all each other has now, and I'm torn between wanting to help her out of here and doing everything in my power to keep her exactly where I can find her.

Also, what if there's nothing after this? It might be the only form of life I can have. A part of me wants to cling to it.

'We think Troy killed me,' I say, determined to move the conversation on in the short time we have.

Lara frowns. 'Your friend?'

'Yes. By mistake.'

I tell her everything. I take the trophy out of my bag and pass it to her. It comes out easily for her. It only sticks when I try to give it back to Troy.

'Strange thing to die for,' she says, handing it back.

I tell her that it's in the background of one of Troy's photos, and I tell her that he moved schools after I died and then went away to France for university and never came back. That his dad was a security guard at Beachview and was horrible to Ariel twice.

'It does seem to add up,' Lara says, and her face wobbles. 'Oh, Joe. You're about to work this out, aren't you? What am I going to do without you?'

'I'll get Ariel to do her detective work for you too,' I say. This feels urgent all of a sudden. 'She might be able to solve your death as well. Maybe we can go together.'

Lara sighs and leans her head back. 'Honestly, darling?' She's looking at the ceiling of the train as she speaks, at that old Coke stain. 'Don't. I've been thinking about this for a long time. I don't mind riding this train, reading my books, knitting for Mabel. I don't mind it at all. I'm feeling that I can take this rather than risk oblivion. Or hell, or whatever. I used to think this was hell, just being stuck in the same morning over and over again. I mean, it's a train operated by First Great Western. It's hardly *not* hell. But I'm used to it. I can do this. At least I'm me, you know? I'm here in a way.'

'I know exactly what you mean,' I say. 'I was thinking that too. What if there's nothing? I feel like I'm going to die, but I already have.'

'I know.'

We spend the rest of the journey trying to think of cities beginning with every letter of the alphabet. Just before we get to Reading I say, 'So. Lara, just in case. Do you want me to get Ariel to try to solve your death or not? Shall we just leave you alone?'

The train stops. I stand up. I really want to see Mum today. I'm beginning to walk away when Lara says, 'Don't do it. I'm staying here. Love you, Joe. Good luck.'

'I'll be back in a couple of days,' I say to her, but as our eyes meet I have the strangest feeling that perhaps I won't.

45

I woke very early on Friday morning with a weird feeling. I looked at my phone and there it was in the Joe inbox – a message from Troy Laffitte:

Beachview at 4.

That was all it said, but there was no way I was going back to sleep after that. I wished and wished and wished that there was a way for me to pick up the phone and call Joe and tell him. Instead I had to have the conversation in my head.

Is this what you want, Joe? I asked and asked, but he didn't answer.

The man who must have killed him, the only suspect we had, was coming to see us. It should have been terrifying, and it was a bit. The only person I wanted to talk to about it was the person who'd been dead for twenty years.

I heard Raffy waking and mewling, and the soothing tones of Sasha's voice as she picked him up. I adored those two and I loved my place in their world: I was an intricate part of it, but my life was a separate thing too. It felt just right. I hoped I'd be able to live with Sasha and Raffy forever. I never wanted to leave home now, and yet I knew that, in fact, one day I probably would.

I lay awake until six and then I couldn't bear it any more. I could hear Sasha downstairs, and I wanted a cuddle with my nephew and a coffee.

'Why don't you go back to bed,' I said to my sister when Raffy was fed and sorted. 'Let me take him for a walk.'

I stood on the beach in the light rain with the baby strapped to my front. He was all snuggly in his snowsuit, wearing the little red hat I'd bought from Jemima's online shop months ago, and I was in my trench coat, a knitted beret and a huge scarf. The autumn morning was cold and the air snapped at my face and made me feel sharper.

This was it. Troy was coming to Beachview tonight. I wished I had a way of telling Joe sooner. It would be quite the surprise for him, to have the two of us turning up at the same time, and then . . . Joe and I might never be alone together again. That was a fact.

I stood on the dark sand and stared out at the choppy waves. 'Look, Raffy,' I said. 'The sea. There's a boat.' He didn't care. He was half asleep. 'Look, Raffy,' I whispered. 'There's Joe. Somewhere out there is almost definitely something of Joe. There are bits of Joe atoms in every wave.'

I knew that, since we all agreed that his bones were likely to be in the sea, Joe's remains might never be found. It wasn't like it was with Leo, where the whole thing had been solved with the discovery of his body. If Joe's body had been dumped in the water it hadn't washed up anywhere and we weren't going to find it.

We would need a confession instead.

'What have I done?' I whispered to the non-judgemental baby. 'I stayed away from him all that time when I didn't need to, and now he's going to go forever.'

Raffy looked up with huge eyes and said he trusted me to do the right thing.

I messaged Izzy. She said she'd woken up early too, and came down to meet us. We walked along the sand and, in the end, I told her.

'Troy's coming over,' I said, and I watched her face to see it sink in. It took her a while, and then she had it.

'Joe Simpson!' she said. 'Oh, Ariel! Didn't that Troy guy say we should fuck off? I thought we dropped it ages ago?'

'We did,' I said. 'But I got interested again.' I wanted to tell her why, but I couldn't.

'OK.' She was frowning. Izzy and I were still best friends, but since we were doing different subjects (hers were sciences) we didn't see each other as much day to day. She had a new girlfriend, Betsy, and I was pretty sure Betsy didn't like me. I was forced to admit, though, that their relationship was good. Izzy was healthier and happier. 'That doesn't completely make sense to me.'

'Me neither,' I said. She reached over and patted Raffy on the head. He still had the thick black hair he'd been born with. 'It seems so weird to me that you look after an actual baby.'

'Yeah. I can't remember what it was like without him. And,

yeah, the Joe thing doesn't completely make sense, but I've been in touch with Troy directly and he's coming over and I'm meeting him this afternoon.'

'That's the worst idea I ever heard.' She was laughing now.

'It'll be fine. I mean, his parents still live here, so he was coming anyway. He just changed his mind about talking to me and I thought why not?'

Izzy was about to say something more when her phone rang. She looked at it, grinned and answered it, saying: 'Hey, babe! I'm on the beach with an actual baby!'

She walked down to the shore. I waved and walked home, the wind in my face. I'd wondered whether she might offer to come and meet Troy with me, but her life was full of other things now.

Since I finished college at two on a Friday I was at Beachview at three, sitting on one of the benches by a scraggly sort of indoor tree. People passed by. I didn't get my phone out of my pocket or my book out of my bag. I just stared at the people and tried to get my head round the fact that soon one of them was going to be the adult Troy, and then we might find out the truth.

This was not a sensible thing to be doing. If it worked, I would never see Joe again after today.

I wasn't ready for him to go. I couldn't bear it. We'd only just come back to each other. The panic rose up and I wished I could go to the little room now and talk to him.

'You're here!'

I jumped as someone sat next to me.

It wasn't Troy.

I turned to look, not quite wanting to believe it, but it was. It was Joe.

'What are you . . .'

'What are *you*?' he said.

He had bunked off school to come here early and found me doing the same thing. We'd turned up in the same place at the same time by chance.

'Amazing!' I said. A woman walking past flashed me a glance, and I took my phone out and stuck an earphone in so I could talk without drawing attention. 'I'm so glad you did this. Joe, I heard from Troy. He'll be here at four. He's come over. We're going to find out what happened.'

We stared at each other. We had an hour to say everything we would ever need to say, and the pressure was too much. People walked by in both our worlds. We talked about Venus and the people around us and time and space, but I could feel the universe pulling us apart. Every second that passed took me away from him, as I grew up and he didn't. It was a succession of tiny moments that already added up to something huge.

He would always be my best friend. If he stayed, though, we'd stop being contemporaries and, although I'd always love him, I'd become his older sister, his aunt, his mum, his grandmother, while he stayed the same. Raffy would catch up and overtake him in no time at all.

I wanted to say all that, but there was no point. We already knew it.

'Lara wants to stay,' he said. 'I asked if she wanted you to try to work out what happened to her, but she said no. She'll take her train journey every day because it might be the best it ever gets. A while ago I would have thought she was mad, but I see it now. I do see it. Where's Leo? What if he's nowhere?'

We looked at each other. I could sense the shift in him. He'd been scared of living this day again and again and again for the rest of time. Now he was scared of not doing it.

When Joe stood up, I realized what he had to do.

'What are you getting today?' I said.

He shrugged. 'A cup of sick would be good. Probably a Coke.'

'Get me one?'

He smiled. 'I'll try.'

I watched him go to the little room with the drink in his hand. I waited, and then Troy was there. I recognized him; he, of course, didn't know me. He was much taller than I'd expected, even though I'd known he was going to be tall.

'Troy,' I said. He looked down.

'Ariel?' he said. He took half a step back.

'Yeah.' In spite of everything, I'd half expected him to be like Joe, to be fifteen. 'Thanks for coming,' I added lamely.

'I've got no idea what's happening,' he said. 'But yeah. You freaked me out enough to get me over here because that was Joe writing and . . .' He looked around, took a deep breath. 'I mean, Joe's alive?' he said quietly. 'You've met him. You must have done. You couldn't have written that message otherwise. Where is he? Where has he been all this time?'

My conviction that Troy had accidentally killed him and thrown his body into the sea began to waver.

'Come with me,' I said, and I led him to the little room. I opened the door.

I don't know how, but Joe saw Troy and Troy saw Joe.

I didn't even have to have a hand on Troy's arm. They saw each other.

46

The door opens and Ariel comes in as usual. Then she ushers in someone else.

And I can see him.

'Troy.' It comes out as a whisper. Ariel and I wait. We look at Troy, and he looks right back at me. I watch him taking it in. I'm the Joe he used to know. I am not what he was expecting.

'Who are you?' he says. He looks at Ariel, and then back to me, and then to her again. I can see his panic rising. 'Does Joe have a child? Because you look so much like . . .' He can't finish his sentence, and I don't blame him.

'No,' I say. 'I'm not Joe's child. Joe didn't grow up. It's me.'

We both look at Ariel.

'OK,' she says. 'Troy? Rewind a moment. You can see him? You can see Joe?'

'No. Of course not. I can see a boy who looks like Joe. Joe's son? What happened? How did this . . .?'

'You can see him. Oh my God.' Ariel and I look at each other. It's magical. I have Troy, twice. I have my Troy in my world and future Troy in Ariel's.

'So,' she says with a smile at me. Her manner becomes almost formal as she introduces us. 'Troy. Yeah, this is Joe. It's always been just me who can see him. Until now.' I nod. 'As you can see Joe doesn't live in the same reality as us.' She demonstrates by putting a hand right through my chest. I hear Troy gasp. 'But he's real. See – there's a kind of blue thing about him. Think of the colour blue and look at him.'

Troy walks slowly up to me and reaches out to put his hand on my shoulder. He pulls it back quickly and steps away. He goes as far away as he can get, right to the other side of the tiny room, and presses himself against the wall.

'Blue,' he says. 'Yes. Is this a –' I can see that he's desperate for something rational – 'a hologram?'

'I'm a ghost,' I tell him. The words sound quite cool. I don't think I've ever said it quite so baldly before. 'I'm Joe's ghost.'

The room is quiet for a long time. In the end Troy says, 'So you died?' His voice is shaky.

'Yes,' I say. I go to stand next to him and he doesn't run away. Ariel stands on his other side. Troy is much taller than me. He's a bit taller than he was at fifteen and much bulkier.

'I was sure you were alive,' he says. 'At first I ignored your message. I thought it was just kids messing around again. But I couldn't shake it off and in the end I knew I had to come. The frog. The Tory thing. You said things no one else could have known and, even though I tried to ignore it, when it came down to it I knew it was you. As soon as I faced up to that, I caught the first flight to London, and the train here. I was trying to imagine what could possibly have happened. I thought you must have been kidnapped and held hostage somewhere. You hear of it happening, don't you? About people escaping from a basement or whatever twenty years later. I thought that was why you were contacting me in the way you did.'

I look at Ariel. She stares back at me. We were so sure it was Troy, but he's not faking this. Our sole suspect doesn't seem to have done it.

'Sorry, mate,' I say, and I sense Ariel trembling. 'I wish it was that. No, I don't. I don't know what I wish.'

'Tell me what happened.'

We sit on the bench, the three of us in a row with Troy in the middle, and Ariel and I tell him everything. He mainly listens in silence until he enters the story, when Ariel describes sitting in a cafe by a London canal with Lucas.

'I freaked when I got that message,' Troy says. 'I was just a bit, *how dare you rake up what happened for an entertaining little article?* It never gets better, you know? And the idea that some kids were trying to investigate for a magazine, thinking they might be able to solve it after all these years, like it was a game? It made me angry and I wrote back to Lucas without stopping to think. Honestly. I could picture him lapping up the attention from a couple of teenagers and it riled me right up.'

'That's OK,' I say.

I can feel Troy's energy. He has grown up and I never will. Everything's different. I sense the chasm; I feel everything I've lost in a way I never have before. I know who Jemima and Lucas and Troy became, but not me. I didn't grow up into anyone.

Ariel knows what I'm feeling. She knows me. She knows she needs to move things on quickly before I collapse.

'Troy,' she says, 'how come your football trophy is in the background of one of your pictures?'

It hangs in the air. This is the key. It's everything.

'Oh,' he says. He looks at us both in turn. 'The trophy. You took it from me, didn't you? You never admitted it, but I knew you'd done it, and I felt so shit because I was grumpy with you about it and who gives a crap? I fell to pieces when you disappeared, and part of it was because I was mad at you, and then I never saw you again.'

'I'm so sorry,' I say. 'I've been through the day again and again and again, and I've tried to say sorry and give it back so many times. It never works. Me having the trophy is one of the unmovable things.'

'Maybe it was to get me here now,' he says. 'I'm sorry I gave a shit about something so meaningless.'

'No,' I say. 'I'm sorry I was such a tosser. I'm pretty sure I was going to present it to you on the coach, in front of everyone. I thought it'd be funny. No idea what I was thinking.'

'I was always in your shadow,' Troy says, looking at me with the most intensity I think I've ever seen. 'Always. I was your funny friend, the ginger one, the tall one who looked odd. Girls would try to set their best friends up with me so they could get their hands on you. And then I won that stupid thing and it felt like the first time I'd actually been better at something.'

He stops. 'None of that matters. It doesn't matter at all. That wasn't even your question, Ariel.' He turns to her. 'OK. Why do I have that trophy? It took me a long, long time to get past the fact that my best mate and I had parted on bad terms, and to accept that it was going to be forever. I had a lot of therapy. A lot. I moved schools, and when I could I emigrated. France felt right because it was such a part of your last weeks, Joe. I met Amélie there and everything fell into place. When we had a boy, he had to be Joseph.'

He says it again in the French way, 'Joseph. I've been a French citizen for years. But I couldn't have done any of that without finding just enough peace to get me through.

'It was a counsellor who suggested I should find a re-placement trophy, years and years ago. Maybe when I was about twenty? Mum helped me track one down that was exactly the same. I gave it to myself, from you, and it put that side of things to bed for me. It worked. I had it again and I knew that you would have given it back to me. It let me move on. It sounds like shite, but it did actually work.'

'It doesn't sound like shite,' says Ariel, through tears. I can't speak so I just nod in agreement.

The door opens and, even though this is the last thing in the world I want to happen, everything goes blank.

47

Joe had gone and I was in the secret room with Troy. It felt weird, just the two of us. The dynamic was different and unsettling. I edged away. Troy didn't notice.

'Where is he?'

'He always goes at this time. The time of his death, we think. You can see him again tomorrow.' I explained the way it worked and he seemed to calm down a bit. He closed his eyes and, when he opened them, looked around as if he thought Joe might have come back.

'This is . . . well, I'm glad I came. Did that really happen?'

'Whatever "really" means. Yeah. I can't believe someone else can see him. It's always been just me. He could see my friend when I brought her in here, but only if I was touching her, and she couldn't see him. I guess . . . I don't know. I always thought I could see him because my mum died, and I needed something too. I needed him and he needed me.'

'I've always needed him,' said Troy. 'And maybe he needs me. Maybe he needs me like he needs you. I suppose it depends on what we do now. I feel like we're almost there.'

'Let's go out into the mall.' I walked out of the room

because I didn't think it was great to be in such a small space, alone, with a strange, freaked-out man. Even though I found that I trusted him. He'd gone from killer to sidekick in a couple of minutes.

We walked back out into Beachview, and I led him back to the bench. Lots of people were around. It was good out here. Noisy, ordinary.

'This is difficult to say,' I said, watching a woman pushing a pushchair and thinking of my mum in Joe's version of this place.

'Everything's difficut,' he said. 'Go on.'

'OK. When we saw the trophy in your picture, we thought it meant you'd killed Joe. That you'd come here to get it back from him, and then you'd argued and you'd punched him in one of those freak ways, and he died. We didn't think you'd done it on purpose. Your dad works here, doesn't he? So we thought he'd helped you cover it up and that was why you moved to France.'

Troy didn't look shocked.

'I guess that would make sense,' he said. 'But it didn't happen. Thank God. I would never have been able to keep quiet about it. I'd have confessed straight off. I mean, my conscience has messed me up for years as it is, and I didn't even do anything.'

'Yeah. I know that now.'

I realized that we'd been so sure of our theory about Troy, and now we were back to square one. I'd been gearing up to say goodbye to Joe forever and he was staying.

'So what did happen?' said Troy.

I told him about the angry guy from the mall. In the absence of anything else at all it was the only lead we had left.

'Have you got a picture of him?' Troy said.

'No. Joe was going to take one with Gus's digital camera, but then we got all caught up with you. Sorry. I feel really shabby about suspecting you now.'

He waved that away. 'I'd have thought the same. Forget it. Joe should take a photo.'

'Yeah.'

'God, this is frustrating! If he's stuck in that room every afternoon it's likely to have happened there. At least that's all we've got to go on.'

'Yes.'

'Let's dig deep into this. As deep as we can. When you thought Dad had helped me with the body, how would that have worked? Because it wasn't Dad, but I guess someone did it.'

'He'd have got it out.' I thought about it. 'He'd have got it out without anyone noticing. So probably not through the mall.'

'Yeah. Wrapped in a carpet like in the movies would have attracted attention, particularly once the whole town was looking for a missing kid. Is there another way out?'

'I don't know. Is the wall hollow? Maybe you could get something out that way? Air-conditioning ducts, also like the movies?'

'I know someone who could tell us about that. Ariel, I realize it's Saturday tomorrow, but if you're free would you be able to meet back here? Before we see Joe, I mean?'

We exchanged numbers and I went home. I didn't know what to do with my feelings, so I took Raffy out to look at the sea again and, again, I imagined Joe's bones somewhere out there, smuggled out of Beachview through the walls and washed by seawater over the years. It made me cry and cry, but then I cuddled the baby tight, and smelled his baby hair, and felt his baby warmth, and turned round to go home.

The fact was we were alive and Joe wasn't, and it was time we sorted everything out.

48

I get up at five because I'm too full of everything to sleep. I don't know what to do with myself.

I have seen Troy.

And he could see me too.

And he didn't kill me.

I want to dance round the house, like Lara dances round the train. I'd never realized what a weight it was, trying to accept the fact that my best friend had accidentally killed me over a football trophy. Whatever the truth might be, it won't be as bad as that. I find that I'd rather be murdered by a stranger, a proper bad guy, than by the person who'd been my best friend for almost all my life.

Now, like Lara, I want to stay. There might be nothing out there. Here there is something. And I would rather live the same day until the end of time than be nothing. I know that with all my dead, unbeating heart.

All the same, I take Gus's camera and decide that I'll break with my routine and spend the whole day at the mall, just in case Ariel and Troy go there too. I should have arranged that with them, but I didn't think of it before the door opened, so this is my only way of clawing it back. It's their Saturday. Maybe Ariel will bring the baby. If she was holding him I'd be able to see him. I love her face when she talks about him and I adore the fact that she gave him my name.

I get ready for school as normal. Mr Armstrong offers me his old francs. Troy comes along and I grin at him, so happy to see young Troy when I have old Troy in my head too.

At that point I change my mind and decide to spend the day with young Troy. I love the fact that I know that, in spite of what's about to happen, his life will basically be good. He's happily married to a Frenchwoman. He has a child and he called him Joe.

'Wish we were going to Paris,' he says. 'Now, if it was Paris I would seriously just stay there. Eiffel Tower. Mona Lisa. The city of love.'

'Would you find a French girlfriend?'

'Easily. We'd live in an attic overlooking the river, and I'd probably discover I was an amazing artist and so I'd become the new Picasso or something.'

'Yeah,' I say. 'Shame we're not going to Paris then. We go past it on the bus, so you could jump out.'

He nods. 'Might do. Tell the driver to stop because I'm sick and then run off to my new life . . .'

'Troy, mate,' I say. 'You'll end up living in France. You'll get married to a Frenchwoman and change your surname to hers because you want a completely fresh start. You'll have at least one kid. A boy called Joe. And you'll be an artist. You'll sell your paintings on the internet.'

Troy laughs. 'OK. Sure. I'll take that. Selling on the internet? That's very futuristic of me.'

'That's because it'll be the future.'

I don't mention the trophy because we've dealt with that now. There's no point in my trying to give it back. It's nice not to dwell on that for once.

At the end of school I say goodbye to Troy, and then head to the mall to meet Future Troy. Past Troy thinks we'll be back at school in a few hours to go on the French exchange, and I keep things as light as I can, then run to Beachview and sit on a bench, waiting for the angry man. I've been meaning to take his photograph for ages. I might as well do it today. You never know: Troy might recognize him.

I sit by a drooping plant, camera on my lap. At ten to four I see him charge in, frowning, and go into Boots. I take a picture as he passes, but it won't be a good one. I stand up and decide to get a chocolate milkshake this time so I can annoy him to the max by throwing it all over him and then taking a photo of his reaction. I'll put the camera right in his face.

The choreography works as it always does. I turn and bump into him. This time I take the lid off the cup and throw it on to his shirt. For a few seconds we stare into each other's eyes.

He pulls himself together and snarls, swears even more than usual, and while he's doing it I drop my cup so the drink splatters all over our shoes and take his photo. He tries to grab the camera. I duck away. He runs after me, shouting. I run round the corner and into the cupboard.

Ariel and Troy are there. They have a box with them and they're doing something to the wall. I'm startled, again, by Troy as an adult, and I wonder what they're doing, but then I realize that I'm not the only 1999 person in this room.

I didn't think the man would follow me here, but he has. I turn, full of adrenaline, and laugh at him.

'What the fuck,' he says, 'do you think you're doing? Did you attack me with some baby drink and take my photo? You owe me new shoes. Give me your camera.'

'No.'

'What's going on?' says Ariel. 'Who's here? Make them go away. We've found something, Joe. It's urgent. Make that person go away.'

'What the . . .?' says Troy.

'You know you're a wanker,' I tell the angry guy, over the sound of Ariel and Troy. 'I see you every day. You're a bastard. I hate you. I bet everyone hates you. You should try being nicer.'

'You should try fucking off,' he says.

'I said *nicer*,' I say. 'Not more of a wanker. Yes, I did spill my drink on you on purpose because you deserved it, and I don't care about your shoes.'

I only said that so Ariel would know who it was that I was talking to from 1999, but of course it enrages the man more than anything. He squares up to punch me. I am ready. He wants to kill me: I can see it in his face. Have I solved it? Is this my killer?

He huffs and takes a step back.

'You're not worth it,' he says. He walks out, slamming the door behind him. I wait. He doesn't come back.

I sit on the bench, gasping for breath, even though I don't need to breathe. I'm trembling all over.

Ariel is beside me. Troy sits on my other side.

'I thought he was going to kill me,' I say. 'He wanted to hurt me so much. He was going to. Then he walked away. It feels so weird. I was geared up for it to happen.'

Ariel puts her hand on mine so we're overlapping. Troy doesn't say anything.

'The angry man,' she says.

'Yes.' I stand up, pace around and sit down again. 'I chucked my drink all over him and then took his photo because I thought Troy might have recognized him from twenty years ago. It was a long shot, but you never know.' I'm still trying to calm myself. 'What were you two doing in here? Are those screwdrivers?'

'Yeah,' says Ariel. 'Joe. We have things to tell you.'

I register the tone of her voice, so I focus on what they're trying to say.

'I've been in here today with my dad,' says Troy. 'He was working so he couldn't spend much time on it, but he told me which panels were hollow and let me borrow his tools. He thinks I'm mad, but that's OK. He already did. A son of his changing his surname. There's no coming back from that with him.'

'I came over a couple of hours ago,' says Ariel. 'Troy and I arranged it all yesterday.'

I tell myself not to be jealous of them doing things without me. They are alive and I'm not. And they're doing it for me, even though I'm not sure I want them to.

'Troy and I have been talking a lot about this. Since there was never any sighting of anyone taking anything that could have been a body out of this place, we thought maybe –' She has to stop, overcome.

'We thought you might not have gone anywhere,' Troy says. 'It was just an idea, but this is a strange building, and maybe you went out through some kind of heating vent thing, or maybe you're still in it somewhere. Maybe that's why you always come back here, every day, no matter what. This room was never part of the investigation. We know about it, but hardly anyone else does. All they know is that you were seen on CCTV outside Boots. Then they dredged the river and did what they could with the sea, but we're not sure anyone ever looked right here.'

I nod. I don't know what to say.

'You can't see it, can you?' says Ariel. 'We've taken the wood panelling off this wall. Is it there in your world? Is there a panel of wood painted white?'

I look at where she's pointing, at the panel of wood, shiny white with a smiley face drawn on it.

'Yes. It looks quite new.'

'Amazing,' says Troy. 'Because now it looks really old. It doesn't look as if it's been repainted, or replaced in the past twenty years, and it has graffiti and stuff on it.'

'We've unscrewed it,' says Ariel. 'And we've just got the front bit right off. I wrote some of that graffiti – that bit about my dad.' She touches it, and for the first time I see it.

'What's behind it?' I say. I'm afraid. Very afraid. A wave of terror crashes in the place where my stomach would be, if I had one.

'Just before you got here,' says Troy, 'we found – well, we found your schoolbag. And this was on top of it.'

He reaches down and picks something up very gingerly, holding it by the edges. I look down.

'The football trophy,' I say. We all stare at it. There it is at last. The foot kicking the ball. The real one, the one that's in my bag.

'Tell us about the angry man,' says Ariel. 'We don't have much time. He followed you in here?'

I make myself calm down. Forget the trophy. Yes. The angry man.

The trophy, though.

'He did. I was extra rude to him. I took his photo, right in his face. He came after me and said he was going to take the camera and that I had to buy him new shoes. But he didn't take it. He didn't do anything. He just stormed off.'

'It's not time yet,' says Troy.

'That's true,' says Ariel. 'He might come back. Can we see the photo?'

I get out Gus's camera and switch it on. Its small screen is nothing like the tech from the future, but all the same I got some good shots. He's staring right at the lens, face contorted in fury.

I hold it out.

'Here he is,' I say. 'See how lovely he is? Ariel and Troy, meet the angry guy.'

Troy leans in and looks at it. He tries to touch it, to bring it closer, but finds he can't.

'He seems nice,' he says. 'Don't recognize him, though. Sorry.'

Ariel looks.

She leans forward and looks again.

'Oh,' she says.

'What?' I say.

'Ariel?' says Troy.

Ariel doesn't look at either of us. She just carries on staring at the screen. Then she stands up, walks over to a wall and leans her forehead on it. She goes to the part of wall they've taken apart in their world and looks into it. I don't know what's wrong. Troy and I exchange glances. Neither of us has the faintest idea of what is going on with her. She has her arms up round her face and her back is shaking.

'Ariel?' I say it this time. I look at her back. She's kind of leaning right into the wall. It looks extremely weird. It's proper ghost behaviour.

Then she leaps back.

'Oh my God!' she says. 'Oh shit!'

Troy and I both jump up. I try to put an arm round her shoulders, but I can't. Troy can and for a fraction of a second I hate him.

'Ariel?' he says. 'What? Tell us what's happening.'

I watch her force herself back under control.

'There are bones in the wall,' she says, her voice expressionless. 'Bones. Down there. At the bottom. In the wall.' She takes a deep, shuddering breath and speaks fast. 'And that's not all. The angry man. The man in the mall. The one who killed you. That's my dad.'

49

The angry man was Dad.

And Joe's bones were in the wall.

My dad. My dad, who became so furious, so easily, but who had, for all my life at least, been careful never to hit anyone. My dad, who had nevertheless ruled our house by making us all terrified of him.

My dad, who had always been hiding something.

My dad, who had always wanted to move away from this town, but who wasn't strong enough to go without us, for all he pretended to be hard.

My dad, who ran away when Sasha found out her baby was a boy.

My dad, the angry man in the mall. My dad, the killer.

If these bones were Joe's, then he had been right here, in this room, all along. Every time we'd sat in here, we had been beside his body. I'd written the words *I HATE YOU ALEXANDER BROWN* on the panel that hid the evidence, and that panel was leaning on the bench now. I had written that I hated my dad on the very thing that had hidden his crime for twenty years. There was so much unravelling around me that I didn't know what to deal with first.

The body. The body was the thing. I looked at Troy, relieved beyond belief that he was an adult, that he would be able to work out what we needed to do next.

'I'll get Dad,' he said and, much as I had disliked Piet Henry on the two occasions I'd met him, I was glad that he was nearby, that Troy could get the authorities to deal with this.

My dad. That part was impossible. I couldn't think about it properly. Not yet.

I looked at Joe and realized that everything was ending. It was happening fast and it was out of our control. I didn't think it mattered what happened next; I was almost certain that when he left today he was never coming back.

Troy left the room. Joe and I looked at each other.

'No,' he said. 'I don't want to go! I don't want to go. I need to stay. I didn't want this! I want to stay, Ariel! Help me stay!'

'I don't know how,' I said. 'And I don't know what I'm going to do without you. I can't bear it.'

'I love you, Ariel.'

'I love you, Joe. I'm sorry I didn't see you this summer. I wish I'd come every day.'

'Shh. I wanted you to live. I'm glad you did. It makes me so happy.'

'But if I'd known it would end so soon I would have seen you every single day. I'd have broken into the building to see you on Sundays too.'

'I know. I know you would, and knowing is enough. Thank you, Ariel. You're the best person I've ever known.'

'If you go somewhere then . . . wait for me.'

'I will.' He looked into my eyes and I knew he would do it. I loved him with every part of my being. 'I'll wait for you. I promise. Whatever happens next, and whenever you get there, which I hope won't be for a very, very long time, I'll be there for you. This isn't the end. It can't be because we've proved that there's life after death. This won't be it. So you just need to live. Be happy. Do it for me. Live the best life you can. Experience everything. It's not goodbye forever. It's not.'

'Find my mum. Tell her we miss her every moment, but we're OK. Tell her about Raffy.'

'I promise.' I shivered as Joe stepped right into me, so our entire bodies were overlapping.

Then Troy was back in the room, and Piet was behind him, huffing and frowning.

'Oh, what the bloody hell have you done?' he said, looking at the wall. He glared at me. I shifted to the opposite corner of the room, but it was so small that we were all on top of each other. Joe came with me. I felt the tingle he always gave me. I loved this feeling. It used to freak me out, but now I longed to keep it in my life.

Troy gave us a little smile and I thought I should give him and Joe a moment together, that they needed to say good-bye too.

'Taken the whole wall off? What the heck?' said Piet. 'I know this is the kind of thing she'd do.' He nodded at me. 'She's like a dog with a bone. But you're a grown man with a family.' He shook his head. 'Let's have a look.'

It changed fast after that. There were bones in there, and

we all knew they were Joe's. Piet went off to fetch someone. There was a sense of urgency in the air. It was nearly time for Joe to go, and we knew that he was leaving for the last time.

'I'll step outside,' I said. 'I'll let you two have a moment together.'

'Don't go,' Joe said at once, and Troy said, 'There's no need, Ariel.'

'Sure?'

'Stay,' said Joe. 'I've only got a few minutes. I need you.'

'Yeah,' said Troy. 'Stay.'

We sat there together.

'I'm glad it wasn't you,' Joe said to Troy.

'Me too,' said Troy.

'I can't believe you have a kid,' Joe said. 'And that you named him after me.'

'And you know my nephew is Rafael Joseph.' I put my hand through Joe's thigh. 'You see?' I said. 'You might be dead, but you have a legacy. There are two little boys with your name, and two little girls with your genes. That's pretty good going for a fifteen-year-old.'

'Hell, yes,' said Troy. 'Ariel's going to take me to meet Gus and his family tomorrow. It'll be good to see him.'

Joe looked from me to Troy and back to me.

'I hope I'm going somewhere,' he said, talking fast as the seconds evaporated. 'I hope I get to see your mother, Ariel. I have so much to tell her. She'll be so proud. Troy, I'm so happy that I know it wasn't you. I'm . . .' He paused, and I thought he was going to cry, but realized he was smiling instead. 'I'm sorry about the football trophy.' He burst out laughing. 'I do one stupid thing and it haunts me for eternity.'

I smiled at that too, and so did Troy.

'I'd have given it to you,' said Troy, 'if I'd known it would cause this much trouble.'

Troy stood up and took half a step away, and I knew why he was doing it. I edged into Joe and whispered, 'I'll love you for eternity.'

He said: 'And I –'

And then he was gone. I was left with the certain knowledge that he had gone forever with the words 'love you' on his lips, and that was the best way it could possibly have happened.

50

'And I love you and I always will. You're the love of my life, and my afterlife.' That is what I'm trying to say, but the door opens and I'm cut off after the first two words. I think she'll know.

I look up.

It's him. It's the angry man from the mall. He's come back. Her dad. We knew he would.

I look back at Ariel, but she and Troy have gone. I have never lived this bit before, apart, I suppose, from the first time. I know how it ends, but I don't know how we get there from here. I suppose I may as well hurry it along.

'I know your daughter.' I'm taunting him. I just want it to be over.

'You don't.'

'I do. Your wife, Anna, is much nicer than you are. She's hot.'

'What the fuck?'

'Your daughter Sasha is very cool. But it's your other daughter, Ariel, who's the best person I've ever met.'

'Are you on drugs?'

'I wish. Are you?'

'You are a little shit, you know that?'

'Why did you come back?'

'I had a fucking awful day. The worst. I don't want to go home to my family. Half the people in this town come through my clinic and they all know me, so wherever I go someone's watching. I just need to get away. Work out what to do. No one appreciates how hard it is.' He takes out a bottle of water and a bottle of tablets, and shakes three pills into his hand and downs them.

'*You're* on drugs,' I say.

'Medication!'

'So you didn't come back in here to kill me?'

He laughs, but it's a barking, scary kind of laugh. 'Why would I do that? My life is shit enough already, thanks. If I did, you wouldn't even be the first person I killed today. Most people make a mistake at work and nothing happens. Maybe they have to sort out the paperwork a bit later when it gets noticed. I make a mistake at work and someone dies. I killed someone. I killed a patient. She was only young. I panicked and changed the records to make it look as if I hadn't done anything. I made it look as if her heart just gave out. What do you think about that? I made a mistake and, by the time I realized, it was too late. So I covered it up. It's one of those things that happens from time to time, but fucking hell! Fucking hell! You're meant to own up and take everything they throw at you.'

I watch as he punches the wall. I think of Ariel's stories about him doing that.

'You can't tell anyone this.'

So that's what it was. He'd told me what he'd done, and then realized I was going to dob him in. I wish I could tell Ariel, but there's nothing I can do because I'm not going back to 2019 ever again.

'I'm going to call the police,' I say. I probably said it less baldly first time around, but I just need to get through this now. 'I'm going to call them as soon as I get home. You can't get away with killing someone and faking the paperwork or whatever.'

I stand up and walk towards the door, just in case that turns out to be possible, but it isn't. My legs won't take me across the threshold, and my hands won't reach for the handle.

His hand is on my shoulder. He grips it tightly. Here we go.

'Where are you going?'

'To tell someone what you just told me.'

'No one would believe you. I'd deny it.'

I shrug. 'Yeah, I'm sure you'll get away with this. You'll get away with it forever, but you'll never be the same again. You will never be the same person and you'll never forgive yourself. But yes. You'll get away with both of us. I know that.'

I feel his hand on my shoulder.

'You wouldn't know who to tell. You don't even know my name.'

'Alexander Brown.' I wonder how I knew this first time round. Maybe I read it on his badge.

He swings me round. Yes, there's his name in tiny letters on that lanyard. I wish I'd bothered to read it on one of the many thousands of times I've seen him over the past twenty years.

Whatever those pills were that he just took, they've done something, or maybe he's just like this anyway, or it could be adrenaline or God knows what. Whatever it is, there's something inhuman in his eyes. Something insane.

He pushes me up against the back wall. I make an effort and laugh in his face. Because I just want it to end. Then he leans down to the bench and picks something up, and then he's swinging his arm back and I see that, after all that, it's the football trophy.

'You're not telling anyone,' he says.

The murder weapon. That fucking football trophy.

His arm swings forward. The trophy catches me on what I know must be the very worst part of my head.

Everything

goes

blank.

And then everything is new.

51

26 October 2019

I sat in a pew near the back of the chapel, between Sasha and Izzy, and I let myself cry. Sasha had Raffy on her lap, and she was crying too, much to Raffy's confusion. I understood the toxic blend of grief and guilt that was running through her. She hadn't known Joe (well, only a tiny bit, on the days he'd spoken to her when she was a baby, days that didn't happen in her real life). She was crying for Mum, and because she was a mother looking at Jasper and Gus and Claire, and she could probably imagine something of the pain they'd carried for all these years.

The guilt, though. That was the worst thing. Our dad had killed Joe and the horror of that was too big, no matter how much anyone said it wasn't our fault. All those lists I'd made, the lists of suspects. They'd always focused on Lucas and Troy, with 'angry man at the mall' as an afterthought at the bottom of the page.

We had to learn to live with it. We had to add it to the fundamental facts about ourselves.

Jai was on the other side of Sasha, holding her hand. I was

glad, for her sake, that he wanted to be involved with Raffy now, but selfishly I didn't want him to move in with us and change the way everything worked. I was, however, doing my best to be nice. I knew I needed to try to be grown up about it because I was seventeen next month, and life moved fast. I couldn't keep Raffy from his father and, when it came down to it, I didn't want to.

Zara turned and waved at me and Izzy, and we waved back. I knew it was a strange experience for these little girls, to be at the funeral of the uncle they'd never known. I was picking them up from school one day a week now, and I was intensely relieved that Gus hadn't stopped that when it turned out that my father had killed his brother. That was quite a thing. He and Abby had been incredibly kind about it, and kept saying that I'd been the one who'd brought some peace to their family, that as I hadn't even been born I could hardly blame myself for what my dad had done. They were going to get married next summer, now that they had an answer about Joe.

Abby was sitting close to Gus, her hand on his knee, and I hoped that one day I might have someone I'd be that close to. It could never have been Joe, and although Jack and Finn had done a lot to pull me back to the present day, it wasn't either of them either. Finn and I had had a couple more dates after that terrible one, but it had never taken off. He was seeing someone else now and I didn't mind at all.

I imagined Joe right here beside me, holding my hand. Joe, two years younger than I was. I imagined it so hard that I truly believed he was sitting there, at his own funeral. It was, to be fair, exactly the kind of place where he would turn up.

I looked at him. He smiled. I tried to touch him, but my hand met Izzy's thigh, and she reached down and squeezed it. Joe leaned forward and whispered in my ear: 'I love you and I always will. You're the love of my life, and my afterlife.' Then he was gone, and it was just Izzy. She was real.

I shivered all over. I would hold on to Joe and his love for the rest of my life, and I would hold on to my best friend too, for as long as I possibly could. Raffy was dozing in Sasha's arms, and I stroked his little nose with a fingertip.

The service was beautiful. The church was full of people who'd known Joe, as well as people who hadn't. Troy was there, and so were Jemima and some of their other classmates. Lots of teachers came, including, of course, Ms Duke, who was in the front row next to Jasper. He had taken my hand, and looked into my eyes, and said, 'Ariel, I'll never, ever be able to thank you enough for finding my Joe.'

I was taller than he was. I'd shaken my head, rejecting his thanks.

'It was Troy too. We just had a feeling.'

I hadn't really been able to explain what had happened: Troy and I had talked about meeting by accident in the little room, talking about Joe (my reason was because of my babysitting for the girls; Troy's was obvious), and then looking at the wall panel and unscrewing it on impulse. And finding, as well as the bones, which were all that was left of his body, Joe's schoolbag and the football trophy which, it turned out, still had fingerprints and Joe's DNA on it. I'd told the police to check the fingerprints against my father's, inventing a drunk semi-confession he had once made, and, when they did, he'd been arrested at an apartment in Inverness where he lived with a girlfriend who, it transpired, had had no idea that he had two daughters and a grandson.

There were traces of various chemicals down there. The wall cavity had been big enough to fit a fifteen-year-old boy inside it, and (the police surmised) Dad had gone back with the right substances from work and used them to minimize the odour of decomposition. He couldn't have hidden it entirely, of course, but the cavity was ventilated by the air-conditioning system, and Piet, among others, remembered the drains outside being cleared because of a smell a couple of months later. No one had made the connection to the missing boy.

We would never know exactly what had happened between them unless Dad decided to talk, but we knew enough. For some reason my father had killed Joe. Not just because he spilled a drink on him, though, surely? It was the one time Joe hadn't been able to come back and report the details. I was wondering about the old unlucky-punch theory that we'd tried to fit to Lucas, and then Troy. Would that explain why Dad had always been so careful to punch walls instead of people?

Whatever the truth, this was why I couldn't allow Jasper to thank me. I was the daughter of the man who'd killed his son. Jasper seemed able not to hold it against me. So did Gus and Abby, and Ms Duke had been entirely amazing. Joe's mum Claire, however, was avoiding me and I didn't blame her.

It was strange to see her: for so long Joe and I had thought she'd walked out on him and Gus and Jasper, when in fact she'd only been in Reading. I had to remind myself of that every time I looked at her. She'd gone on a course and never seen her son again, and those many, many times that Joe had caught the train to Reading to spend his last hours with her hadn't happened in the version of her life that she remembered. She had long white hair and loose yoga-person clothes, and she drifted around with perfect posture. I looked, now, at her straight back, her lifted chin, and I wished her comfort and peace.

There were lots of other people around them. They were family members who had come from all over the world. Joe had once mentioned that he had cousins, but I couldn't really remember him saying anything about them. Here they were, though: adults with families and jobs and busy lives, all gathered to say goodbye to Joe. There were numerous next-generation cousins too: the ones of my age or thereabouts. One of them had particularly caught my eye because he looked far more like Joe than anyone else in this church apart from Zara. I kept finding myself staring at him, and then looking away.

Enzo was here. The French exchange boy who Joe had been perpetually about to visit had actually come over from St Etienne to say goodbye to the friend he'd never met. He was warm, friendly, chatting to everyone in brilliant English, and I knew that if Joe had been able to go on the trip they'd have become good friends.

Troy was sitting in the second row with his wife Amélie (dark and gorgeous, wearing a lovely floaty dress) and baby

Joe, who was up there with Raffy in the *most adorable baby* stakes. He had squishy rosy cheeks and a beaming smile that lit up his whole face, and he was wearing a Babygro with *escargot* written on it and an embroidered snail.

'Hello, baby Joe,' Sasha had said. 'This is baby Rafael Joe. You're the two Joes. How lovely is that?' She and Amélie had talked about the babies so animatedly that Troy and I were abe to have a conversation without anyone overhearing.

'We did it,' he said. 'Ariel. Thank you. We actually did it.'

'I still can't believe it was my dad.'

'I'm so sorry. Do you miss Joe very much?'

I looked around, but no one was listening. 'Yes,' I said. 'Oh God, Troy. I miss him with all my heart, every single day.'

'Me too.'

Then Jasper came over, and I remembered something Joe had once said.

'Jasper?' I said. 'Someone told me I should ask you about the subtle art of clowning.'

He laughed. 'That can only have been Gus. Yes, clowning has a very unfair reputation. It's not just squirting noses and unicycles. It's not *It*. It's not Ronald McDonald. No, the origins of clowning . . .'

You told me to ask him, I said to Joe in my head. *And I did*.

I heard Joe saying: *Thanks, Ariel. I knew you would*.

After the service we all went to the pub by the beach for the wake, and I drank some lemonade and then some wine. Sasha and Jai took Raffy home, and Izzy drifted off to meet Betsy. Joe's old schoolfriends set off on a pub crawl, and I realized that I was in danger of being the only non-family person left.

I crossed the road, walked out on to the dark sand and stared at the sky. The evening air was harsh on my face. It was a clear, starry night, and the waves were breaking gently in front of me. I took my shoes off and went to stand in the freezing shallow water.

I was pretty sure that the bright star in front of me was Venus.

I stared at it. I looked at the edges of it, where the cloud tops might be.

'Wait for me, Joe,' I said. 'Wait for me, Mum. I'll see you right there.'

I drew in a deep breath of night-time sea air. I held it. The water was icy cold around my feet. The moment was perfect.

'Hi.'

I looked round, and there he was. I smiled at him. Joe had come back one last time.

'Hey there.' I wondered how he'd done it.

'Hey, yourself.' As he said it, he settled into being not-quite-Joe. He was a bit older than him, and his face wasn't exactly the same.

He was the cousin.

I smiled and tried not to be disappointed.

'Oh,' I said. 'You looked like someone else for a moment.'

'Sorry,' he said. 'I'm Max Simpson. Joe's cousin, I guess. You're Ariel, aren't you? You're the girl who found him.'

I walked back towards him with a smile.

'Yes,' I said. 'Yes. I am. The girl who found him.'

'Want a drink?' He was holding a bottle of wine. I took a swig.

'Thanks,' I said.

We sat on a rock together, me and this boy who wasn't my Joe. This boy who was alive. His arm brushed against mine. And something changed.

EPILOGUE

19 November 2019

I was walking to college early on the morning before my seventeenth birthday when I realized someone I didn't know was walking next to me. She was a woman in her twenties, with very long, tangled hair, and I thought she was wearing a hospital gown under her coat. She looked like a mermaid, but with legs and odd clothes.

''Scuse me,' she said.

I smiled because she reminded me of a mermaid, and I was Ariel. I was in a good mood. Max was coming down this afternoon and it was my birthday tomorrow.

'Yep?'

'Sorry. You don't know me. You're Ariel, right?'

I nodded and stopped walking. I looked at her face. I definitely didn't recognize her.

'My name's Mia,' she said. 'I've come from the hospital. I only went in for a knee operation, but . . . well, I need to ask for your help. I've heard you might be able to give me a hand with this little tiny, massive, huge problem I've got.'

This was freaky. I waited for her to say more, but she didn't.

'How would I be able to help? I mean, I guess I will if I can, but I really doubt that I'd . . .'

She interrupted with a huge smile.

'Yay! You will if you can! That's wonderful. Thank you so, so much! I know you can do it. It's hard for me to get out of hospital. I can only do it early in the morning because I have to be back by ten. But the other day I managed to get on a train at seven and I met a woman called Lara. She said if I seriously wanted to escape from this, then I had to find Ariel.'

'Really?' I had a bad feeling about this. *Lara*.

I started to realize what this meant.

'She said you're a ghost detective,' said Mia. 'But it's not urgent. I mean, it can wait until you have time.'

She reached out to touch my arm.

As I had known it would, her hand went right through me.

Acknowledgements

Ghosted has been a long time coming: it was well underway before Covid hit, and I was grateful that it was already set in 2019 as I hated the idea of Joe waiting in a closed shopping mall for months on end while Ariel dealt with lockdowns.

Ruth Knowles, my wonderful editor, has been there every step of the way, with suggestions and edits that are always right. I feel incredibly lucky to work with someone so astute and talented, and even more lucky to be able to call her a friend. I'd like to thank everyone involved in the production of the book: the amazing Wendy Shakespeare, Bella Haigh, Jane Tait, Anthony Hippisley and Niamh O'Carroll. Thanks as ever to my super-agents Steph Thwaites and Isobel Gahan for everything they do.

Charlotte Gapper made an incredibly generous donation to FareShare to help feed hungry people, in exchange for Jack Lockett's name appearing in the book. Jack, I hope you like your alter ego. Your mum is brilliant.

Bess Revell, thank you for the advice on yoga teaching, and huge thanks to you and Silvia Salib for those Friday evening solidarity sessions.

Lanhydrock House appears briefly in this book: it was written before I worked there in summer 2021, but I was able to change details during copy-edits to reflect my experience. Thanks to all my fabulous Lanhydrock colleagues (Gabrielle, Donna, Richard, Laurence and the whole team) for an incredible three months and for giving me an insight into what it's like working somewhere so inspiring.

Finally, eternal thank-yous to everyone at home: to Craig for everything from early-morning coffee to reading each draft and reassuring me at every stage; to Gabe, Seb, Lottie, Charlie and Alfie for reminding me that there's a world beyond the page in front of me; and to all my friends and family, for everything.

Read on for an extract from . . .

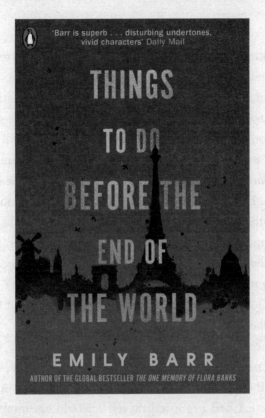

'Barr is superb . . . disturbing undertones,
vivid characters' Daily Mail

THINGS
TO DO
BEFORE THE
END OF
THE WORLD

E M I L Y   B A R R

AUTHOR OF THE GLOBAL BESTSELLER *THE ONE MEMORY OF FLORA BANKS*

The air is running out. We think there's less than
a year of it. We are the last humans.

What do we do?

Make a list.
Heal rifts.
Do the things that scare us.

12 December

You know when you worry about everything all the time? Sometimes it turns out that it's the thing you haven't bothered to think about – the thing that's too outlandish, even for you – that turns out to be the one that's going to get you. That was what happened that day.

It was a cold afternoon, a Thursday. There was a Christmas party going on at college and everyone else was there. I never went to parties, so I had slipped out of the building and melted away (knowing no one would notice), and now I was walking round the park to kill time. Mum worked at home, and I didn't want to see the pity and frustration on her face when she realized I hadn't gone to the Christmas thing. I was planning to wait it out for a bit and then pretend I'd had a lovely time.

The grass was still crunchy underfoot in the shade. I crisscrossed the park to stomp on the crispest leaves, telling myself that I would need to be braver than this in future, because I had promised myself I would audition for the play, and a girl who couldn't walk into a dining hall to eat a handful of Quality Street and listen to the student choir singing 'Jingle Bells' wasn't going to be very good at standing on a stage and declaiming Shakespeare.

Whenever my stomping took me close to the children's playground I looked at the toddlers running and climbing and tried to remember if I had ever felt so carefree and un-self-conscious.

I wished afterwards that I could go back and recapture that ordinary boredom and mild self-loathing, but it turned out that nothing feels the same when all your assumptions about what might happen next have been ripped away, and you've discovered you don't have a future at all.

It changed slowly, and then fast. A man was staring at his phone. Then half the adults in the park were doing the same. Someone cried out. The atmosphere changed (appropriately), and I took my phone out of my pocket to see what had happened.

A newsflash had been delivered to my lock screen, even though I had settings that definitely didn't allow them.

The United Nations, in conjunction with a coalition of the world's governments, has confirmed that an accelerated atmospheric shift is underway and that it will have 'profound consequences' for the Earth and its population. Click for more details.

I clicked, but there were no more details because the network had crashed. I didn't need to see those details anyway, because I'd seen the rumours over the past few months, and had happily ignored them while worrying instead that I couldn't speak to the girl I liked, and that I wasn't sure if I was brave enough to audition for Juliet. That proves that even if you try to keep yourself safe by dwelling on all the bad things you can think of, something huge will always manage to slip through. I knew what the story was: the thawing of the permafrost had unleashed such an unexpectedly massive load of carbon dioxide, laced with various toxins, that it was fast becoming impossible for humans to live here. We didn't have time to evolve to thrive in our new atmosphere. That at least was what the rumours had said.

Later, when I did get to read the detail, I discovered that it was all true, and a date had been calculated for the definitive change of the air: September the seventeenth. Less than a year away.

Anyone with existing breathing difficulties would probably die before that. So would the birds, and some of the animals. We had done this to ourselves, and to the creatures, and there was very little we could do about it. It was the catastrophic breakdown of everything.

In the park everyone was just staring, like I was. Even the children, who couldn't possibly have understood, seemed to be frozen, mid-jump, mid-climb, mid-shout.

If the robins in the trees had had phones, they would have been looking at them too (and tweeting: 'The birds die first?'). The squirrels in the branches ('And the small animals?'). The dogs on the leads. The cats. The rats. The ants and the mice. The newsflash beamed across the world in a moment, invisible until it landed, and then everywhere.

The world paused. I watched the other people. Everyone had taken something out of a pocket. Everyone was staring. There was a hiatus, because it was not a thing you could understand at first.

Then things continued. A discarded burger wrapper was the first to move. The wind blew, the children jumped, the birds flew, and everyone apart from me started to talk. A man started crying. I watched people trying to make phone calls. The rumours had been around for months and it shouldn't have been a surprise – and yet it was.

I walked to the nearest bench and sat down. There was a woman already there, who was old enough to have been my grandmother and I wished she was (my grandmother had died last year), and we looked at each other, then quickly away.

'Well,' she said. 'How about that?'

I couldn't answer.

'OK for me really. I've lived my life and I'll take all my pills before this happens. This isn't the way I'm going to go, thank you very much. It's you young people . . . I mean, look at them, the kiddies. And you. A pretty girl like you. So much ahead.'

I wished she would stop talking. I followed her gaze to the children in the play park, and thought of Sofie and Hans-Erik. I pulled my hair round my hand and nodded. I wrote a text to my mum that just had a couple of words in it (*Oh, Mum*) but it didn't go through. I wanted to see Zoe, and I wondered what the scene was like at the Christmas party. I pictured it: happy, noisy, and then frozen, as everyone realized that there wouldn't be a next Christmas. I sat still for a while and just stared at the park. The grass was scrappy at this time of year, and I wondered whether the worms were going to be all right.

I didn't realize I was running, but when I looked down I saw that my feet were slapping over cold grass, and I was heading for the street. I bolted down the pavement, ignoring everyone, swerving on to the road when I needed to. We lived two blocks from the park, and as soon as I was running downhill towards home, the door swung open and there was my mother, on the threshold, waiting. I ran straight into her, and she grabbed me and held me, and even though I was taller and chunkier than she was, I wanted to be her baby again.

When I stopped trembling we sat on the sofa. Mum made us both sweet tea, handing me the mug with a hand that wasn't quite steady. She had somehow gathered together all the chocolate in the house and laid it out on the coffee table.

'Right,' she said, when she'd settled down beside me. She handed me a Twix. I opened it. 'OK. So it seems I was wrong.'

My parents (all four of them, but particularly Mum) had insisted that the stories were rubbish, and I'd happily believed them. Teachers said it was scaremongering, and that we were being hysterical by believing it. Mr Baxter, my drama teacher, had given us a whole month of lessons themed around doomsday cults and mass hysteria, to give us what he called 'much-needed perspective'. Everyone had come together to push the view that these rumours were what happened when you allowed anyone to say anything they wanted on the internet anonymously.

My mum – the person I looked to for reassurance above everyone else – had insisted so hard that there was no truth in it that I had been a tiny bit suspicious of what she really thought. She'd called it 'laughable' and 'stupid'. She said science didn't work like that. She did big laughs out loud to show how ridiculous it was. She agreed that there were lots of things to worry about, but insisted that we weren't all heading for a mass extinction in the immediate future at least, that if there was something like that on its way, scientists would have sorted it out by now.

She said we should take it as a wake-up call and clean up our act.

Now, of course, she was struggling, but, still, she was trying to be brave. I had chosen to believe her, and Mr Baxter, and everyone else, because it seemed too outlandish even for me to spend too much time worrying about this. It had barely made my top-eleven worries until now. I knew that I would have to scribble over the other ten because this was now the only thing.

I pictured the permafrost. I imagined it thawing out, and a green cloud coming from it and spreading across the planet. There was a reason that that stuff had been locked away, and we had undone it.

I dropped the Twix and grabbed Mum's hand and gasped for breath. Thinking about it made me panic and fill my lungs with all the air I could, as fast as I could, while it was still there.

She held me and muttered into my hair. 'Oh, Libby,' she said, and then she whispered something about violence, but I didn't stop to ask what she meant. I supposed there would be violence, but I had no capacity to think about that. Not yet.

There was, of course, a caveat, and when Mum found it in the small print she seized upon it. 'Look!' she said. 'It might be all right. They might be able to sort it out.'

I didn't understand how, but there was a chance that things might be OK. There was an operation underway to minimize the effects, to recapture the carbon and neutralize the other stuff. Meanwhile, finally, we *were* cleaning up our act, for all the good that would do. All fossil-fuel plants had been closed, all flights had been stopped, and forests were being intensively planted in an attempt to try to push the genie back into the bottle. I didn't read the science: I just looked at the numbers. Seventy per cent, they think. Seventy per cent we all die. Thirty per cent, somehow, life continues, though it might be through gas masks.

Seventy per cent was a lot. If I got that in a test at college I would be quite pleased.

One minute you're walking in the park, pretending to be at a party. Then you discover that the next nine months will probably be your last. Everyone's last: a reverse gestation. You realize that you happen to be alive at the time when your species becomes extinct, and you wonder whether any part of you could come to find that quite interesting.

You have to decide whether to go with it meekly like you usually do, or to do something brave, to live your last months with all the energy and bravery you can muster, to rage against the dying of the light.